ALIBI ON
ICE

Ben F. Small

Printed in U. S. A.

For information address:
Durban House Publishing Company, Inc.
7502 Greenville Avenue, Suite 500
Dallas, Texas 75231
214.890.4050

Library of Congress Cataloging-in-Publication Data
Ben F. Small, 1946-

Alibi on Ice / by Ben F. Small

Library of Congress Catalog Card Number: 2004115667

p. cm.

ISBN: 1-930754-72-8

First Edition

10 9 8 7 6 5 4 3 2

Visit our Web site at
http://www.durbanhouse.com

Book design by Jennifer Adkins
Cover design by Eric Lindsey

Acknowledgements

Mount Rainier has captivated me since the first time I saw it, as I crested a hill on a bright afternoon after a rainy week in federal court. I first thought Rainier was a cloud formation, then when realization sank in, had to pull over my vehicle and stare. That ten minutes of gaping early in 1980 gave root to what became an obsession for me: I had to climb that sucker.

Over the course of the next few years, I spent many weeks at what became my mountain. I met the guides and climbed as much as possible, finally summiting in 1983. Still not sated, having dreamed of writing, I began working on this story when back surgery took the pack off my shoulders.

Numerous people helped me bring this story about. First and foremost is my wife, Rebecca Maxwell, who's never complained about reading my stuff and whose comments I value most. A lawyer too, Rebecca knows the importance of being direct and succinct. She's my secret weapon.

Next is Robert Middlemiss, my editor. It's a wonderful thing when an author and an editor bond in a synergistic collaboration. Bob, my friend, thank you. Your lessons will linger, just wait and see.

My son, Derrick B. Small, is an avid reader. He spurred me on, challenging me. Granted, he may be biased, but his encouragement kept me going.

When I thought I had a good first draft, I asked my brother-in-law, The Honorable James Zagel, a noted author, and my friends, Rick and Nancy Kosakowski, and Nancy's mother, Carol D'Haene, to critique it. Their comments were invaluable.

Others deserve credit too, for their support, suggestions and encouragement. People like Chris Mattingly; Jackie Baxter; Pam

Curtis Smith; Rick and Sue Smith; fellow authors Tom Miller and Greg Ellis; Peggy Zagel, my wife's twin sister; Jeff Smulyan; Richard Hunt; Greg Long, the best trial lawyer in California; Max Brittain, the best labor lawyer anywhere, who lent me his name despite my giving his character a skin affliction; and my oldest son, Ben F. Small IV (poor fellow, who'd like to be a IV?). Thanks also to Lyn Topinka of the USGS for the great cover picture, to Eric Lindsey for the graphic arts and Jennifer Adkins for copy editing and typesetting.

Special thanks to John Lewis of Durban House. Thanks, John. I hope to make you proud.

Mount Rainier is a full-blown character in this book. It lives and breathes just like humans do. I've tried to get it right, but if there are errors, they are mine, not the mountain's, nor attributable to anybody who lives or works there. This is a work of fiction. Nobody's real in this book, except the mountain; and if I got that wrong, I hope it doesn't kill me in vengence.

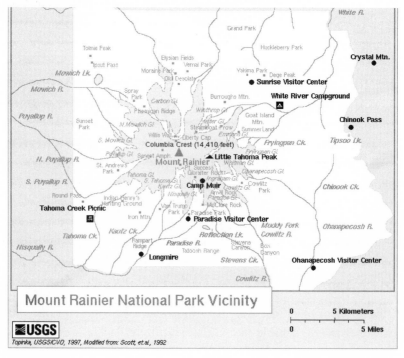

PROLOGUE

Summer, 1994

High on Rainier's south flank, Aimsley Castle couldn't sleep. His ears were assaulted by the all-too-familiar creaking of nearby beds and the snores of occupants. He looked at his Timex Triathlon watch and illuminated its digital readout: 9:45. In just over four hours he'd be awakened to start the torture all over again. "Christ!" he muttered. "How did that sonofabitch talk me into this?"

His thoughts drove sleep away. He had been threatened, a squirrelly, ugly feeling. And he didn't know about those damn private brokerage accounts or the margin calls. How the hell could he have known? Sure, he could have questioned those sales and profit projections... But they wouldn't give him the underlying information. And now he had been threatened... How dare he threaten him?

Rolling over, he groaned from aching muscles and joint pain. His worn mattress did little to cushion the bite of the rusty chain link beneath it. But it wasn't the crude bedding in the stone hut that was keeping him awake. It was the threats, and he wasn't going to take them any more. Tomorrow, he'd just leave. And when he got back to Seattle he'd call a board meeting, reveal what he'd learned and resign. He'd let the management team try to cover their asses with the shareholders, the outside directors and the SEC. He'd be ruined, but he'd have some self-respect.

"Maybe I'll write a book about the whole thing," he whispered into the snoring dark. "I'll bury that bastard."

He rolled over again, grimacing. His face made contact with the grungy mattress, and he sat up. "Shit!"

The boot camp warrior from Fort Lewis in the bunk next to him rolled over and opened his eyes. "You okay, fella?"

"Yeah. These mattresses are for shit. How do the guides expect anybody to sleep?"

The warrior sniffed, "This ain't the Four Seasons," and turned away.

Castle was quiet a moment. "I'm going outside. Maybe get some pictures in the moonlight, salvage something out of this night."

"Be careful, man. Glaciers all 'round. Swallow you whole."

 Outside, the night was still. Moonlit snow was fluorescent except where the hut and out-buildings cast long shadows. A light breeze made the quiet all the more profound.

Castle trudged to the north, the crunching of his boots breaking the eerie silence. The hut for the general public was over to the right, about fifty yards away. Scattered around it were tents of hopeful, unguided climbers expecting a big day tomorrow. But for now, he was the only person moving.

The Guide Shack and Ranger Station were dark also, and his anger rose again as he imagined that threatening bastard sleeping peacefully in the Guide Shack.

He pulled his camera and some 1000 ASA film out of his

camera bag. After loading the film, he captured some of the marvelous sights around him, the process easing his anger. The mountain was tranquil. Some of his stress was lifting, as if blown away on soft winds. Heading out onto the Cowlitz Glacier, he decided not to turn on his headlamp; the mountain was bathed in light. Off to his right, he could see depressions, which he knew from yesterday's training were probably hidden crevasses. Danger areas. But if he followed the rocks, stayed close to them, he should be safe all the way to the trail over the Cathedral Rocks, three quarters of a mile away. The tracks of yesterday's climbers were visible. Castle decided to follow them, maybe catch some shots of Little Tahoma, the small peak shaped like a tail, shooting off the east side of the mountain.

After several hundred feet of easy walking on the hard-packed snow, he stopped to shoot the massive Gibraltar Rock behind him. He remembered reading in Dee Molenar's book, *The Challenge of Rainier,* that the summit route back in the 1930s had been a trail right up the side of that monolith, but one day in 1936, shortly after a group had passed over it, the trail just broke away.

Some thirty minutes later, he'd crested the Cathedral Rocks ridge. "Sure enough," he muttered aloud, seeing Little Tahoma gleaming off to the right. "Jesus! It's magnificent!" He swung his camera up and began taking shots. Then, sighting through his lens, he turned slowly to the left—toward Rainier's summit. Ought to be able to get a good one. But instead of the brightly lit summit in his viewfinder, he saw an eerie cloud cap swirling like cream in stirred coffee. "What the hell is that?"

The cap was mesmerizing, almost spiritual. He clicked off exposures until he ran out of film. He lowered the camera and fumbled through his camera bag until he found another roll. He hurried to reload. The light wasn't as bright as before; he was on dark rock now instead of snow. Frustrated, he sat down and turned on his headlamp.

When his loading was done, he shut off his headlamp, stood up and waited as his eyes adjusted to the ambient light. He felt a breeze, colder, steadier and stronger than before. Was the wind picking up?

The cloud cap had rotated down and picked up more density, as if it was being poured from above and stirred. For a while longer he watched, transfixed by the swirling, growing and ever-darkening cloud mass. The wind started to gust. The air was charged with static electricity, and his hair stood up.

Castle began retracing his steps. He switched his headlamp on.

The wind was roaring by the time he reached the bottom of the ridge. It bit at him, stung his face with icy needles. Fight the panic. Fight the panic...

He was running now; not fast—the winds prevented that—but at a brisk jog, following the tracks on the edge of the glacier parallel to the ridge. He looked up. The whirling mass now obscured the top of the Cathedral Rocks, and Gibraltar Rock ahead was invisible. He ran harder, pushing against the ever-increasing winds, breathing labored, progress sluggish.

Now it began to snow, light spits in the beam of his head-lamp; then, as the cloud descended, larger, icy flakes drove down on him. "How much farther?" But his words were lost in the blow. Altitude and conditions were draining him; he was tiring rapidly. Finally, he saw the turn that would take him to Muir.

But the wind now roared about him. It drove icy daggers into his face. He was having difficulty breathing; he needed great gulps of air, but could manage only small gasps. Snow blowing into his mouth caused him to cough. Sucking air through his teeth gave only small amounts of altitude-thinned oxygen to his starving lungs. He stopped and bent over, hoping for some unfettered breaths. He used the moment to pull up his hood. But it wouldn't stay up in the ferocious winds. And Castle feared if he removed his gloves to tie it shut, his hands would freeze. Instead, he sucked in more breaths, straightened up and plowed ahead.

The trail was hard to follow now, but he could occasionally see rocks—or what appeared to be rocks—off to the right.

Snow and winds grew stronger. His hood was snapping him in the face, and he couldn't breathe. There was only one sound, a locomotive, and it was running him down. The camera around his neck banged him in the face. He let go of his hood to secure it. The hood flapped back, exposing his head.

Terrified, Castle turned to the right. Got to find the rocks. But snow was blinding him. And he was off-trail; he knew it because the snow was deeper, each step an ordeal. He stumbled and fell, then groped for something solid. He couldn't feel or see the rocks, but he was sure they were near. They had to be.

He cursed himself for being stupid, for ignoring warnings, for not telling anyone where he was going. But wait! He'd told that soldier! Maybe he'd heard the storm, told someone there was somebody outside. Surely he couldn't be sleeping through this storm!

Fear, doubt and cold gripped him. Shielding his eyes, he willed them to see, and thought he sensed movement.

"Here! I'm here! Help me!"

His shouts were swept away on the howling wind.

He sensed movement again and stumbled toward it. He felt himself being caught, held by strong, confident hands.

Thank God!

Castle felt himself being straightened up and between gasps, tears of relief froze on his face. He brushed his arm across his eyes. A shoulder grip released itself.

The hold on his other shoulder remained tight. *Thank God!* Once more optimism found purchase. He forced his eyes to focus. But as his vision cleared, panic seized him anew, and he opened his mouth to scream.

His scream was blocked by the serrated blade of an ice axe embedding itself in his skull.

The man wielding the axe grabbed the body by the parka hood and walked out onto the glacier, dragging it effortlessly behind him. He stood immune to the howling winds and driving snow.

Some several hundred feet out, he stopped by a slight depression in the snow. He raised the body up, swung it around and gazed with satisfaction at its dead eyes. With a small push, he released it. The depression opened like a hungry mouth, and the body of what had been Aimsley Castle, Vice President and General Counsel of the giant Eastman Aerospace Corporation, disappeared—sucked in through the maw of one of Rainier's hidden glacial crevasses. In a few hours, the crevasse would be entirely covered over again, as if it had never existed.

It had been so easy: no blood, no body, no worry.

Thursday, July 25

Two-faced. Emery Boyd toyed with the words, familiar to him, like worry beads, passing across his mind as beads would slip through his hands. All his life he had honed sharp the public front, the persona for what few friends he had, people like John Whitney—friend and climbing companion since childhood—and the fools he dealt with daily, especially those with threat... like Herman Klein. Something to be done there... Boyd's empty blue eyes focused on the mountain outside his window. Rainier thrust its bulk at the gray sky, its peak lost from view, buried in brooding clouds. Holding its secrets, perhaps, the way he hid his own.

His office in Seattle's Tahoma Bank Building offered the mountain in all its moods, something he found comforting. While an Egyptian cotton shirt, gold ice-axe cufflinks and a handpainted Italian silk tie projected a practiced image of power and respectability, underneath those fancy clothes there was a sinewed body driven by primal instincts, at one with the mountain.

Herman Klein would come by soon. He ran his fingers through his black, silver-streaked hair, took in a cleansing breath and let it drain out, soothing his tense muscles, his agitated mind. Rules of survival: don't contemplate violence when your thoughts are in disarray.

A gentle buzzing of the intercom turned his gaze from the window. He stabbed at the button. "Yes, Jenny, what is it?"

"Mr. Cole is here. You wanted to see him."

"Thank you."

As soon as Cole left, Jenny walked in and shut the door. Boyd watched her, taking in the Dorothy Stratton good looks, always supple and pliant under his strong hands. Mewing sometimes as he routinely found the touchstones of her release.

"Any chance you'll consider staying in town tonight? You know, a quiet dinner, some time alone…"

He gave the combination smile, desire mingled with regret. "Jenny. I have to leave tomorrow." His gold cufflinks caught the overhead light as he pointed out the window. "Mountain climbing requires preparation. Besides, we could both use some sleep— remember?" She remembered all right. Even some of his own tension had drained away last night, leaving him in an oasis removed from Herman Klein.

A pout crept across Jenny's face. "But you'll be gone a week… Can't you prepare tomorrow, so you can go up early Saturday? Besides, I don't like you climbing at night. What if you fall into a crevice?"

"'Crevasse,' Jen." Boyd smiled. "I'm not going beyond Muir tomorrow night. The trip there is glacier free."

"But why can't you go Saturday? Surely, you can still reach the summit in the afternoon…"

If he drove his forefinger into her eye it would go straight through into her brain. "Jenny," he said softly. "If I did that, I'd be up at the higher reaches late in the day. Rainier softens in the afternoon;

snow and ice move and snow bridges give way. I'll be carrying a week's supplies and equipment—a lot of weight. No, I need to reach the higher levels while everything's hard. Besides, John will be waiting for me. He's still mad at me for canceling our last climb. If I piss him off again, he'll throw me off the mountain."

"Screw Whitney. He's a jerk."

Boyd watched her. "Maybe he's a little rough around the edges, but he's the nearest thing I have to a brother, Jen."

She sighed and turned to leave. "Just be careful."

His eyes, empty as windows in an abandoned house, followed her out.

Herman Klein....

In the hallway, Herman Klein was beating a familiar path toward Boyd's office, on his way to the men's room midhall on the east side of the floor. He varied his route each day, so he could pick up the tempo of the various departments, and because he was a snoop. Bent over a stack of CCH tax advance sheets, he looked smaller than five-foot seven and one hundred thirty-five pounds, and older than his forty-three years, the latter perhaps because of a balding head and the carpet-remnant-like suits he wore. The only thing missing from the stereotypical image of a tax lawyer was a green eyeshade. It was on a hook in his office.

But if Herman Klein's appearance was drab and unimposing, no similar charge could be made against his mind. Many in Seattle—even some of his competitors—acknowledged that there was no better tax lawyer. Herman had risen to chair his firm's tax department and had higher achievements in mind.

As he came to Emery Boyd's office, the door opened and a smiling Dan Cole stepped out. Klein stopped. "What's up, Dan? Not often I see someone coming out of that office smiling."

Cole glanced up and down the hallway. "Emery just named

me Assistant Department Chairman."

"He did what?"

"He made me his assistant departmental chairman."

Without another word, Herman hurried back to his office. He strode past his forty-ish, slightly overweight secretary, Marge Simmons, who was in deep concentration over her computer. He slammed his door hard. After a moment, Marge shrugged and went back to work.

In his office, Herman dialed Sam Terry, the firm's managing partner. The phone was answered by a familiar, curt and husky female voice.

"Miss Voss, this is Herman Klein. Is Sam in?"

Helen Voss was the firm's curmudgeon; one of her duties was to put a little acid into everyone's day. The payback was in graffito on restroom walls.

"I'm sorry, Mr. Klein. Mr. Terry is unavailable."

Klein hesitated. "Miss Voss...er...uh...Helen. Can he be reached? It really is very important."

"I'm afraid not, Mr. Klein."

"Are you sure? If you tell me where he is, I'll try him. You needn't bother."

"I'm sorry, but Mr. Terry is cruising Vancouver Island with friends. He left word that Mr. Boyd should be contacted in his absence. Maybe you should see him."

Thursday, July 25

After he hung up, Herman called his wife. As the phone rang, he envisioned the buxom Emily rushing for the receiver before the five-ring switchover to voicemail. Emily hated voicemail—hated the phone really—but especially voicemail.

She answered breathlessly mid-way through the fifth ring. "Hello!"

"I'm glad I caught you."

"Oh, it's you." Silence spiraled down the wire. "I was resting."

Emily rested more than an old dog. "Boyd appointed Dan Cole his assistant department chairman."

"So what? When Sam learns what you know, it won't matter. Boyd will be finished."

"But I don't just want him gone. I want to split up his department. I'm afraid Sam may just appoint more assistant departmental chairmen."

"Oh. Can Boyd do that? I mean, without running it by the management council, or maybe the full partnership?"

"I don't know. The issue's never come up." He paused. "I'm

concerned about how Cole changes the dynamic. I mean, he's an innocent party—well-liked. No one will want to hurt Dan."

"Maybe you should talk to Sam now."

"I tried and can't.... But now, I think that's maybe just as well. Hold on..." Not waiting for a reply, he put the receiver down and walked to the door. He peered out and saw that Marge wasn't at her desk. He returned to his chair and picked up the phone. "Sorry. Just wanted to make sure nobody was listening in."

"You alone now?"

"I'm alone. Look, I have to play this carefully. I don't want Sam telling Boyd—ever."

"I can understand that."

"See, Boyd could say that Sam and I knew all about the blackmail and any fraud, if there was any..."

"I get it, Herman. I'm not a fool..."

"Hell, there must have been fraud..."

"Of course there was. Why else would Boyd have blackmailed a federal judge?"

"That's right, Em. And both Sam and I were heavily involved with EAC before and during that shareholder suit. So what if we didn't know about Boyd's doings? How could we prove that? Nobody would believe us; it would ruin us. No, I need to persuade Sam that we need to keep this between us. We can come up with some other reason for getting rid of Boyd. But I need time—and Boyd out of the office."

"That makes sense."

Herman looked around his office. In the light, he could see dust on his CCH plaque. "Emily, what I'm doing is unethical. Boyd should be prosecuted and run out of the bar. But we can't tell what I know. Sam and I will just expose ourselves, and we're innocent." He drummed his fingers on the desk. "Or at least, we were." Thrummm... "Damn! I wish I'd never heard of Schneider or EAC!"

"Calm down, Herman! Stay focused. You planned to tell Sam

quietly next week. Monday morning, you just retrieve the confession from your safe deposit box and go see Sam."

Still mired in guilt about the ethics of what he was about to do, Herman missed what she'd said. "Uh… I'm sorry. What about a safe deposit box?"

"You have it in a safe deposit box, don't you?"

Shit.

"Don't you?"

He cleared his throat. "Uh…no. It's buried in the probate file."

"What! If that confession disappears, you've got nothing! Sometimes you amaze me, Herman; so smart, yet so blind. My God!"

"Look. I promise. Okay?"

"I should think so!"

Herman said nothing; he knew better.

"As I was saying," Emily continued, as if she'd been interrupted. "Here's what you do: Go talk to Boyd. Wish him a pleasant vacation. Make him feel at ease."

"Talk to him? Why? Won't he think I want him out of the office?"

"No, Herman. He'll know you've learned about his promotion of what's-his-name. It would be strange for you not to react. So you tell Boyd you have some questions. As a member of the management council, you've got to consider the best interests of the firm. Also, you're a department chairman; you need to explore whether the idea might work for you. Wish him a nice vacation."

Herman terminated the call after again promising to put his secret file into a safe deposit box. Now he sat back, his feet propped up on his desk, and enjoyed a deep cleansing breath. His mind tracked back to the beginning of this nightmare…

When U.S. District Court Judge Thomas Schneider's widow asked Herman to handle her husband's estate after his car plunged over a cliff in the Cascades at a treacherous bend of a snow slicked mountain road, he had no idea that going through Schneider's office desk, he would stumble onto a hidden compartment containing an "In the Event of My Death" envelope. Inside the envelope was a signed handwritten confession from Schneider that Emery Boyd had blackmailed him into fixing the giant Eastman Aerospace Corporation stock manipulation class action suit filed by the corporation's shareholders.

That suit had claimed that in the early to mid 1990s, EAC fraudulently overstated the number and value of its purchase orders for new generation aircraft in an effort to maintain the inflated value of its company stock. Damages in excess of a billion dollars had been claimed. Worse still, if it lost at trial, EAC faced government prosecution, the potential loss of billions in government contracts, the suspension of its export licenses, and possible suits from suppliers, who in turn had ramped up their investment and production in reliance upon EAC's forecasts. Several well-known corporate raiders were rumored to be watching EAC's stock price, looking for an easy score. Simply put, the lawsuit, if the class was certified and the suit proceeded, would have laid EAC bare, potentially causing a feeding frenzy upon the hapless giant's carcass.

But Schneider's non-certification decision had ended all that. Without class status, no individual plaintiff wanted the risk and expense of taking on one of the world's largest corporate entities, an organization prepared to fight to the death. The suit was dropped.

Once the threat and its potential for disaster were averted, EAC had then entered the most profitable years of its existence, which continued until the September 11, 2001 terrorist attacks. And Emery Boyd had gained national prominence from his victory, ensuring for Terry, Davis & Sherman a steady flow of new litigation business.

Now Herman knew the suit had been fixed.

Schneider's confession was several pages long and dated January 8, 2002, just two days before his death. It revealed that during Schneider's confirmation process, Emery Boyd had found something in his past and used it to coerce him. Boyd had taken him away to a cabin in the San Juan Islands, where on a laptop they had written the critical decision. What Boyd held over the judge—someone whom Herman had always respected—wasn't revealed. The confession laid out only what Schneider and Boyd had done, and how badly Schneider felt about it. Guilt was killing him, Schneider wrote; he couldn't stand it any more.

"Bastard! Son of a bitch!" Herman's curses had been so loud that Schneider's secretary had hurried in. Struggling with his composure, he'd asked to see the judge's 2001 calendar. It disclosed that the EAC hearing had been on August 7; Schneider's decision was on September 6. In between, from August 16 to August 22, the dates the judge and Boyd were in the San Juan Islands, the calendar said Schneider was attending a Chicago Cubs home stand.

Herman hadn't left Schneider's chambers until late that evening. A serious crime had been committed. What was he to do?

Desperately needing an advisor, he had confided in his wife, Emily; he trusted her judgment and her discretion.

Emily argued that the worst thing Herman could do was hurry his investigation. He needed more information; he needed to learn, if possible, what hold Boyd had on Schneider.

So he and Emily spent time with Sue Schneider and encouraged her to speak about Tom. One night, while she was talking about Tom's depression, Sue said it had begun just before his trip to Chicago. Tearfully, she revealed intense guilt because she hadn't taken his condition more seriously. She'd thought he was just bored or maybe having a mild mid-life crisis.

Tom had called her during his Chicago trip, but he'd seemed guarded and down. She'd asked him who he was with, but he'd replied, "Some old classmates and colleagues," and changed the subject. When she raised the subject again, he told her it was nobody she'd know. After that, he hadn't called again, and it was several more days before he returned.

Afterwards, Tom became reclusive and drank heavily. Then, the publicity of the EAC decision hit like a wave, pulling Tom more into his shell. Sue urged him to seek professional help, but he became belligerent and defensive.

Herman knew from autopsy results that Schneider was drunk the night he died. And he knew from newspaper reports that Schneider had driven over the cliff just after a farewell dinner with a clerk at the Salish Lodge.

He'd called the former clerk, John Carmody, now a litigation associate at Booker & Boggs, and they'd lunched the next day.

Carmody hadn't been reluctant to talk; he knew Herman was handling Schneider's estate. Over a sensible salad, he said that Schneider had been drinking that evening, but hadn't appeared drunk. Schneider's alcohol intake had been increasing for some months, and changes in the judge's behavior had been noticeable and unpleasant. Schneider became impatient, would yell occasionally, and sometimes he'd just stare out the window or at the wall. Something was obviously troubling him.

The night of his death, Schneider had made 6:30 reservations, and they'd driven separately. It was snowing, and Carmody arrived a bit late. He found Schneider having a martini and talking to some lawyers in the north bar. Carmody left at 9:30, but the judge stayed on, saying he wanted to have a nightcap with friends. Carmody hadn't particularly noticed these friends, so he wasn't able to identify them.

While Carmody prodded his salad with a fork, Herman asked when this strange behavior first began. Carmody thought for a moment, then said it was shortly after Schneider's return from a baseball trip to Chicago. Carmody had opined that the EAC class should be certified, and Schneider had erupted, railing at him, yelling that he'd write the decision himself.

Herman asked if there'd been any other hint as to Schneider's leaning on the decision. Carmody laughed, wiped his mouth with a napkin, and said, "You should have seen the hearing! Schneider was all over Emery Boyd—practically accused him of bad faith. He really disliked Boyd."

"Why?"

"I don't know. The judge said, 'There are good lawyers, bad lawyers and Emery Boyd, a special case.' I asked him what he meant, but he wouldn't elaborate."

Herman also contacted the restaurant manager at Salish Lodge, who said he didn't know Schneider. He assured Herman that if the judge had been drunk, he wouldn't have been allowed to drive home. "We have strict rules on that," he insisted, from over his table floor plan. "We have to; we're in the mountains."

The ABA had been next. Herman asked about the investigation files and learned they'd been sealed after Schneider's confirmation. The investigators had been Joe Krieger, David Dawson and Emery Boyd. Krieger was dead, so Herman called Dawson, saying he needed to find Schneider's relatives for probate proceedings. Dawson said he couldn't help: Emery Boyd had conducted the personal background portion of the Schneider investigation. Dawson complained that Boyd took so long he and Krieger had threatened to report without him.

What had Boyd found?

Herman got up and headed back to Emery Boyd's office.

THREE

Thursday, July 25

As Herman looked through Emery Boyd's open door, he saw Boyd on the phone. He took a moment to watch him, catching the inevitable gaze out the window at Rainier—what did he see in that thing?—sitting there all gussied up in his fancy suit, his Egyptian shirts, his gold cufflinks and hand-painted ties, just staring out the window. Even from the hallway, Herman caught the gleam of Boyd's fancy cufflinks, gaudy trophies he so loved to flash. What had Carmody said, Schneider's remark that there were good lawyers, bad lawyers and Emery Boyd? Like the sonofabitch was in a class by himself. An odd discomfort ran down Herman's spine. Well, soon Boyd would be out, with his cufflinks, ties, fancy shoes and those expensive suits, and none too soon. Herman headed for the restroom, conscious of his own well-worn but serviceable suit. A tax lawyer gets shiny pants no matter how much they cost, why not save the money? Hell, Emily couldn't care less how he looked, why should anybody else? Clothes didn't make the man when money was at stake; it was brains that counted.

A few minutes later, Herman found Boyd free. Jenny Larson—leg spreader extraordinaire—gave him an icy stare as he passed her without a word.

"Mind if I come in?" Herman came through the door, not bothering to knock.

Boyd looked up, his eyes catching the light. He watched Herman settle into a chair. "Hello, Herman. You don't usually come calling without an appointment."

Herman wasn't comfortable in the low chair across from Boyd, but he allowed himself to sink back. He stared up at the hulking Emery Boyd.

"I just thought I'd stop by."

"No doubt to wish me a happy vacation, and perhaps, the best of weather? Well, Herm," he used the nickname Herman hated, twisting it like a stiletto. "I'm just winding down."

Jenny Larson had stopped typing. Herman saw she was listening. He got up and closed the door. Back in his low-slung chair, he said, "Well, that's part of why I'm here. Where are you going? Mountain climbing again?"

Boyd picked up a paper clip and unwound it, a cufflink glinting.

"Rainier again?" Herman said into the ugly silence. "My God, I'd think you'd be bored with those same tired trails by now."

The paper clip was malleable in Boyd's big hands, bending around a long, thick finger. "Herm, I'm curious; I don't recall you coming to me before, inquiring about my trips. Would you be planning something while I'm gone? Like maybe for the partnership meeting in two weeks?"

Herman's eyes fixed on the paper clip. Bend, bend, twist… Had Marge said something to Jenny Larson? "Why? Are you worried about the partnership meeting?"

Boyd tossed down the paper clip. "Not at all. You don't think I'd leave if I was concerned, do you? Or is that your purpose here—to try to plant some seed of doubt?" Blue eyes mocked, then turned away. Beyond the window, the mountain offered itself. "If so, forget it. The meeting will be routine, despite that crazy notion you're spreading. You know, that several of the departments you control should merge. You don't really think that silly stunt will succeed, do you?" He leaned back in his chair.

Herman stared at the paper clip, bent and twisted until it had no meaning. "It makes sense, Boyd, especially when you consider the extent to which the tax, corporate and probate departments share similar interests."

"Yeah, but they're all paper lawyers, pretenders—not real lawyers. They're bookkeepers, Herm—just like you."

"So you say, Boyd. But it's the future. Resist all you want, but you gladiators are old school; accounting, taxes and financial planning are the new wave. Why not put all of these features under the same coordinated control? It's practical and it benefits our clients."

Boyd watched him, selecting his words with the same ease he moved across a cliff face. "It benefits you and you only, you conniving worm."

Herman's shirt was slippery with sweat. He could smell it. "I figured you'd say that. But it does benefit our clients: it lessens the number of interdepartmental consultations; the same lawyer fulfills more functions, is involved in more client matters—hence, better relations and more efficient service, with a cost saving. How can the client fail to benefit?" He sat there in his sweat, small in his low chair.

Boyd rubbed a thumb over a cufflink. "Tell me, who would you envision as chair of this beast?"

"I'll let the will of the partnership decide that."

"Well, Herm, that's mighty big of you."

Klein shook his head. "We'll see what the partners say."

"Yes, we will." Blue eyes shaded darker. "But remember, you have the burden of proof. I'll let you make a fool of yourself, let you run out your string. Look for me at the meeting, Herm."

Herman licked his lips, knowing Boyd saw it. "This is not one of your courtroom battles, Boyd. This is a partnership meeting."

"Oh? I disagree. You're the proponent and the partnership is the jury, Herm. A jury which will be made up mostly of litigation lawyers. No, I think there are some very definite parallels here. But if you don't... so be it. As I said, it's your proposition. This law firm's been litigation-based a long time. I doubt many of my litigators will take kindly to a paper lawyer using tricks to change the basic nature of this firm."

Herman leaned forward, his shirt sticking to his back. "I find it ironic, Boyd, that you—of all people—should be so concerned with the immutable structure of this firm after what you've just pulled."

Boyd picked up the paper clip and dropped it with a ding into a wastebasket. "Oh? And just what have I 'pulled' that's so obvious even you picked up on it?"

"You know damn well the charter requires that all management positions be determined by the partnership. You deliberately ignored that requirement."

Silence played out, some malignant echo to Herman's words. "Herm, let there be no mistake about this: I manage the department, no one else." Boyd rocked back, glancing toward his window. The sky, so dark before, was showing a glimmer of new light. For a moment he took in the fast-moving clouds, the changing shapes caressing the base of the mountain. Then he turned back to face Klein. "I asked Dan Cole to assist me in some administrative matters, Herm. But he will do only what I tell him to do and when I tell him to do it." He watched the skepticism drag at Herman's face. He should really just reach out and snap that bony neck. "Are you saying that if I ask Jenny to handle some more administrative functions, I need to take that to the partnership too? I see no difference here."

"Well, I do. The charter clearly provides for a partnership decision in such matters. You didn't even consult the management council."

Seeing that Boyd was about to respond, Klein waved him off, a gathering of nerve as sweat trickled. "Enough! I haven't made up my mind yet. Hell, I just found out about this."

"So is that why you came by today—to whine and find out what I had in mind for Cole?"

"I wanted some clarification, that's all." Herman paused, faked a smile. "But I did want to wish you a good vacation, although I don't understand your fascination for that rock."

"Of course you don't, Herm."

Herman waited in the silence, but Boyd said no more. Then, suddenly and with a grin, "Well, what do you do for relaxation, Herm? Knit?"

"I do have interests. Frankly, I find my greatest peace fishing on Lake Washington, especially early in the morning—even before dawn—when the lake is peaceful and there's little boat traffic."

"Yeah? How often do you do this?" He made it a throwaway line, but inside he coiled in anticipation.

"I'm usually there early Saturday and Sunday mornings. It's my time."

"To each his own, I guess." Boyd fingered a cufflink.

"Really. I like watching the dawn glow move over the water. We're on the west side of the island, you know. The darkness lasts longer in the shadows, and the fish feed later. You can hear the birds awaken, and nature is alive."

Boyd nodded and glanced out his window again. "Why don't you leave now? You've said your piece."

Wordlessly, Herman got up and headed for the door.

"Leave the door open, Herm." Boyd watched him leave, expressionless eyes taking in the dreary suit and shiny pants.

Early Saturday and Sunday mornings…

Good enough.

As he walked back to his office, oblivious to all around him, Herman had one thought: Marge! Had she said something to Jenny Larson about his meeting plans?

Finding Marge schmoozing with another secretary, Herman grabbed her arm and pulled her roughly into his office, shutting the door behind them. "What did you say to her?"

"What?" Marge angrily wrenched her elbow away from his grasp. "Listen, I don't appreciate…"

"Larson. What did you say about my proposals, damn it!"

"Is that what this is about?" Marge said, aghast. "Nothing, Herman! Do you think I have no loyalty?"

"Boyd knows about the merger proposal!"

"Surely, you can't think I said anything." She stared in disbelief. "But how about you? I know you've told others—for instance, some in the corporate and probate departments. You can bet it's been the subject of hallway discussions. So don't look at me. I haven't said anything to anyone. And I resent you saying I did." Her eyes were misting now. She turned away.

She was right. He had mentioned his ideas to some lawyers, as notions to bounce around. And there was an active rumor-mill inside the firm. He apologized. For her part, Marge just stared, wavering between anger and acceptance. Then, shrugging, she said, "It's okay, I guess. You've been tense lately. Why don't you go home, Herman? You need to relax."

"You're right. We've got a full day tomorrow."

Marge opened the door. "Oh, Marge. I need the Judge Schneider file."

"Okay."

"Uh… Marge. Thanks for putting up with me. I am sorry. I don't know what I'd do without you."

She gave him a forced smile as she walked out.

When Jenny left, Emery Boyd walked to his window. It was just 5:00 P.M., but already daylight was wearing out. Clouds around Rainier were dissipating. He anticipated the growing golden glow which would soon shine over his mountain, a deceptive radiance which the early Indians believed promised splendor and an abundance of game.

Like his mountain, he'd been plunged into roiling clouds of his own, his anger seething. And like the mountain, his black depths were masked under a glacial calm. Soon he would throw his blood and sinew at it and survive. Not like others with whom he dealt, the weaklings who fretted and plotted against him. They were no match for his dual world of façade and occasional murder. Take Donnie, for instance…

Donnie had been easy…

And now the mountain was clearing, and it was Herman's turn. Maybe the Indians were right: maybe the rising golden glow did promise splendor and game. Game in a rumpled suit.

The word had come from Helen Voss this afternoon. Herman Klein was urgently trying to reach Sam Terry. He nearly panicked; it had to be the Schneider thing. He'd feared he'd have to take the risks that come without a plan.

He'd found Herman's "secret" Schneider file last weekend. Saturday, he'd run into David Dawson at an early morning workout in the Bellevue Athletic Club. Dawson asked whether Herman Klein had spoken to him yet and described his meeting with Klein.

Boyd had offered his engaging smile, then hurried to the office. Herman knew something; there could be no other reason for the questions he'd asked Dawson. And he must have documents—what was an accountant without documents?

But where were they? What were they? If they were beyond

reach, like in a safe deposit box…

There were too many people around Saturday to chance being caught searching Herman's office. Instead, he'd pulled the Judge Schneider estate file, saying he had to grade an associate up for partnership. He needed to review the work he'd done on life insurance claim defenses. For cover, he asked for several of the associate's other files as well.

The files had been brought, and he'd closed and locked his door before beginning his search. Finding Herman's file was easy; it took only fifteen minutes. For a moment, Boyd had envied Herman his open, guileless life, so different from his own. And less work. He took the damning file materials from their folder, labeled "Miscellaneous." He wiped its binder free of his prints. Then he turned to the other files he'd requested and briefly reviewed them, this time leaving his prints on a number of pages. He made some handwritten notes on the associate's performance, dated them and signed his initials. Then he returned all the files to the file room and left to read and burn what he'd taken.

But the question prowled in him: What to do about Herman? He could deny everything, or say that Sam and Herman had known about it all: both the blackmailing of Judge Schneider, and Boyd's involvement in the EAC stock manipulation which had led to the blackmail. But that was risky. And the fact that the material was still in the Schneider file meant that Herman hadn't told anyone—yet.

No. Herman would have to go the way of Donnie. Too bad it couldn't be something poetic, beating his head in with a calculator, or shoving a 2H pencil under his jaw, driving it through the soft palate into his brain.

His plan, when it crystallized like glacial snow, was more mundane, befitting a rumpled-suit existence. Donnie would have appreciated it.

It was now almost time to leave for home, where his final preparations would begin. But first, one last call: John Whitney, the closest friend he had. He was glad he and Whitney didn't relate in the world at large, where Whitney might sense Boyd's inner beast. Whitney viewed him through colored glasses, his perception bathed in old loyalties, the sort engendered by the shared loss of mothers at an early age and by years of shared mountain adventures. But Whitney didn't know him; he just thought he did. And that was good; it would keep John Whitney alive, for Whitney was the only person Boyd knew who could equal him in brute courage, in determination and stamina, in raw strength and ferocity. But if he ever learned about Donnie…

He dialed John's number.

"Rainier Guide Service, John Whitney speaking. May I help you?"

"Hi, marmot-breath, I hope you're in shape." Boyd watched his reflection, the pleasant face, engaging, almost kindly.

"Shit! Good enough to lead you, Boyd, but then so's my grandmother. I've been taking care of your ass up here ever since we were kids."

"Bullshit. Who got you to Everest, my friend?"

"Yeah, but I had to carry your sorry ass half the way up, just so you could claim the honor of being the youngest to summit. If I'd had half a brain, I'd a' left you behind and claimed that one myself."

"Well, if it hadn't been for my pleading with Jameson to let you come, you wouldn't have been there."

"I'd a' been there if I'd had to pay my own way. You only got to go because Donnie disappeared. He was beating your ass, as I recall."

The two were silent for a moment, John remembering Donnie's tragic disappearance during the race for a slot on Chief Guide Al Jameson's Everest team, Boyd remembering Donnie's expression, the odd cushioned effect of the ice axe going in. Boyd had to win, had to…

Boyd's doodling pencil snapped in two. He tossed both halves into the wastebasket, much like he'd tossed Donnie's body into a crevasse.

"So, when you coming? Or have you figured out a way to duck me again?"

"Not this time, John. I'm gonna teach you some skills. And it's about time: you've been masquerading as a mountaineer long enough. But when I arrive depends on when I can get away from here. Maybe Friday night, more probably Saturday. What are you doing Saturday?"

"I'll be over on the east side supervising the excavation of the ice caves."

"What! They haven't been open for years. You can't tell me that with all the snow we've had this summer, they're exposed. You're bullshitting me."

"No, Emery, they're not exposed. But I'm tired of waiting. We've got almost a hundred Park Service volunteers this summer, and I borrowed some bulldozers from the highway department. Even got a chopper to carry 'em up. But we've got to do it in two days, or I gotta pay rental. So that's tomorrow and Saturday. Wanna help?"

"No. And don't tell me you need me. Supervising my ass! You'll be up there banging the college girls, as usual."

"Might be some of that too, Em. Sure you don't want to supervise?"

Boyd watched his reflection laugh. "That'd be just like old times, buddy, and certainly worth the diversion. But I want to do some serious climbing. You know, work out the kinks from too much time in a chair. And I only have a week. But I think it's great you're going to open up the caves. How far will you have to dig?"

"I figure about sixty feet. 'Course there'll be a lot of diggin', seein' as it's not real easy to tell where the hell the openings are. I think I've got a pretty good idea, but we'll have to move a lot of heavy, wet snow."

"You going to open all of them?"

"Many as we can. They're all in the same general vicinity, as you know."

Boyd picked up another pencil, eyed its sharpened point. "When can you join me?"

"I'd guess sometime late Saturday. Where do you want to meet? Muir?"

"Yeah. Let's not push our luck; let's meet there." He doodled a stone hut, its bricks uneven and irregular.

"Okay. But make sure you stay at the Muir Guide Shack. You don't want tourists puking all over you. I'll let 'em know you might be comin' up there."

"You shouldn't talk about your meal tickets like that, John. I'll check in with the Guide Shack, but if it's nice, I may sleep out under the sky."

"Don't blame you. It's clearing now, but who knows how long that will last—especially this year." Whitney was silent for a moment. "Say, any chance you'll lead a summit group Saturday morning? Be a big thrill for the tourists to have a 'Snowball' lead them."

Anger stirred in Boyd, but his laugh sounded genuine. "Haven't heard that nickname for awhile. But I guess the three of us deserved it. I'm amazed Jameson put up with us that summer. We were so damned young."

"Yeah, that's why he had me supervising you two. Donnie woulda made it, but as usual, we had to carry you along."

"You're so full of bullshit, Whitney, you fart and it'll be heard in Oregon."

Whitney hesitated, trapping a thought. "You still got that stainless steel avalanche beeper Jameson gave us?"

Boyd dropped his pencil, reached into his pants pocket and fingered his key chain. "Yeah, right here. But I never take it on climbs. Wouldn't want to lose it, what with that nice inscription on it. You don't carry yours, do you?"

"Nah. I keep it in a drawer. I'm usually with a bunch of people anyway, so I often don't carry one." Whitney paused. "So what do you say? Will you lead a summit attempt?"

"Look, John, if I make it Friday night, it'll be late. I'd rather sleep in. Who wants to get up at 1:00 or 2:00 A.M. on their vacation to lead a bunch of sheep?"

"I hear that."

They bantered on for a few minutes, then said their good-byes. As Boyd hung up, he reached for his briefcase, then pulled his hand back. No, he thought. Tonight would be a different preparation.

As Whitney hung up, his office door in the Rainier Guide Service Shack opened to admit two senior guides, Jim Carlton and Joe Grogan, to his cramped, paper-strewn quarters. Rising to his full six-foot-five-inch height, mountaineer Whitney stretched a grin across his tanned and chiseled face. "Just the two I wanted," he said. "Welcome back, Jim. How was your vacation? You were gone a long time."

Grogan, the shorter and younger of the two, sniffed. "He met a girl."

Whitney's eyebrows shot up. "So that's why you were gone so long." He took in Carlton's canary yellow parka, a stark contrast to Grogan's standard Guide Service red one, and raised his hand as if shielding his eyes from glare. "Did she help pick out your new duds?"

Carlton blushed and fidgeted. Grogan reached over and unzipped Carlton's parka, revealing a bright red turtleneck underneath.

Whitney poked Grogan with an elbow. "A new and stylish sweater too, Joe. This is starting to look serious."

As Carlton's discomfort grew, Grogan nodded. "Yeah. And he won't say nothin' about her. Won't tell us her name, what she looks like, where she's from… nothin'."

Carlton waved them off. "Knock it off, both of you. You'll meet her soon enough."

"Oh, she's coming here?" Whitney said. "This sounds serious. My goodness, Joe, Jim even seems to be standing a little straighter, don'cha think?"

"He sure is. I tell ya, John, this boy's in luuuvve."

Carlton's face was approaching the color of his sweater. "C'mon, guys. Yeah, she's special…very much so. As soon as you meet her you'll see why, although why I'd ever introduce her to you two, I'll never know."

"Well, when's she comin'? We have to plan on a proper welcome for her."

"I'm not sayin'. The last thing I want is you turkeys makin' a fuss over her. Besides, I gotta figure out a place for us to live. No way am I letting her near the Guide Quarters, with all the lunatics we have around here. She's mine and I wanna keep it that way. So, for now, I'm back and that's all you need to know."

John smiled. "Okay, Jim. All in good time, eh? But still, that fluorescent canary parka's gonna take some getting used to."

Carlton frowned as Grogan clapped him on the back and made a point of feeling the material. He slapped Grogan's hand away. "You said you were looking for us?" he said, hoping to end the teasing.

"Just got off the phone with Emery," John said. "He's coming tomorrow or Saturday. Jim, since you'll be at Muir, would you let the crew know? Tell them he's to stay in the Guide Shack. And keep Diane Edwards away from him. Send her down if you have to. I don't want her draping herself all over him, making him uncomfortable."

The two men laughed. Carlton said, "Sure, John. Will he lead a summit attempt? I'd like to tell the tourists how lucky they are."

"I doubt it. See if you can talk him into it when he gets here. And Joe, I'll need you to replace me over at the caves on

Saturday."

"Sure thing, John. Just let me know when."

"And make sure you keep that Romeo Maselli away. I don't want him sniffin' around the college girls. Got me?"

Both men nodded.

"Now, how do the glaciers look? Still safe after all this rain?"

"There's some movement up there," Grogan said. "Nothing major. I think they're okay."

Worry lined Whitney's face. "I don't like this much rain and snow in summer. Keep your eyes peeled, Jim. Let me know if conditions change."

"Will do. Anything else?"

"Nope." As Grogan and Carlton began filing out, John's "Tweet, tweet" followed them.

FOUR

Thursday, July 25

Boyd pulled his black Mercedes ML430 out of the bank's garage and headed east toward the I-5 entrance ramp. Once southbound on the interstate, he streaked past his normal exit for the Sorrento Hotel, glad that tonight it wouldn't be home. Whenever he could, usually a couple of nights each week, he drove the two hours—less if he pushed it—to his lodge-like home at the base of Mount Rainier.

As he drove south the eighty miles or so, past the airport and beyond, he looked to the southeast, catching whatever glimpses of Rainier were available. He'd read about the eruption and mudflows in the late 1800s that had buried the south Seattle suburbs under fifty feet of sludge. And about the great Osceola mudflow some fifty-eight hundred years ago—half a cubic mile of mud running forty-five miles. Rainier was overdue for a major eruption, it was said. Would the next one be as great as Mount St. Helens, or would St. Helens be a piker in comparison? Would Rainier blow toward Seattle, maybe leveling the city's skyscrapers in a pyroclastic cloud, or would mud flows sweep down and deluge Lake Washington? Was Seattle the next Pompeii? He'd read that Rainier had once been five thousand feet higher. What if the whole mountain blew and left a bottomless hole like Crater Lake?

Thoughts of a cataclysm moved him, something primal, a force of nature, a symbiosis of violence personified in him. Rainier was a living, breathing thing, magma-veined and threatening. Its majesty and horror were drug-like. The mountain stirred his loins, and not for the first time.

He turned off I-5 onto highway 167 and passed south through Puyallup on his way to Eatonville. Here was a fifteen-mile stretch where the mountain loomed large before disappearing into the deep forests along a narrow stretch from Elbe. He would follow the Nisqually River, his thoughts dwelling on Herman Klein. The man would soon be gone; today's meeting had determined the where and when. And John Whitney would be his alibi. Poor John, he really had no idea what had happened to brother Donnie—and he never would.

The Mercedes surged, its engine purring as he blew by a station wagon loaded with children. He ignored their waving hands, their grinning faces.

Donnie Whitney was destined to die young. From their first fight during a high school football game, which led to their expulsion from their respective teams, grudges had formed which for Boyd could only be sated by death. At least, that's how he'd seen it. He and Donnie had called a truce during their Guide Service apprenticeships. But only because Al Jameson, the legendary chief guide, had threatened to throw them off the mountain if he saw any "funny business." "You'll get no breaks or sympathy from me," Jameson had said. And then he had assigned them tasks intended to break their backs and spirits.

Boyd redirected an air vent and dialed down the fan.

And their truce had held, at least outwardly. Not even John Whitney, who was a year older and had already served one season's apprenticeship—to whom Jameson had assigned their daily supervision—suspected that hostilities still simmered. The boys worked well together and excelled at their tasks. And while they worked, John taught them all he knew of the mountain and mountaineering: how to power breathe to maximize lung capacity; how to pause-step to conserve energy; how to glissade steep slopes on a garbage bag; how to perform an ice axe self-arrest to prevent a precipitous fall; how to crampon their boots for glacier travel; how much food to eat to maintain their stamina; and which water they could drink safely.

Eventually, their dedication, hard work and surface amiability even won over the crusty Jameson, so much so that he dubbed them and John "The Snowballs." At the end of their first season, he presented each boy with a joke gift: a stainless-steel avalanche beeper inscribed with both their names and nickname, specially fitted so the batteries couldn't fall out. Jameson had laughed and said the presentations were appropriate; he didn't want to lose his Snowballs.

Thinking back about that first summer as his blinker flashed a turn onto Highway 7 for the short jaunt through Alder to Elbe, Boyd fingered the shiny steel beeper on his key chain. Looking up at the rearview mirror, lifeless eyes gazed back. He felt no guilt about Donnie's murder and never had; his only emotions had been fear—the primal fear of discovery—and power—the exhilarating thrill of the kill.

Donnie died at the end of their second season during a base-to-summit-to-base race Jameson had arranged to fill a vacant slot in an Everest expedition. Emery's fury at falling behind grew the more Donnie outdistanced him, especially after a bad fall required bandaging his knee and the loss of more time. His rage tore loose when he learned that Donnie, with John's assistance, had tricked him by stashing cramponed boots at Camp Muir. So, when Emery saw Donnie descending Disappointment Cleaver, he lay in wait, because it was the right thing to do. He then clubbed Donnie with his ice axe. The killing part had been easy, even gratifying—the timing, the swing, that moment when their eyes locked, Donnie's wide in shock, his own a natural emptiness rarely seen. Hurriedly, he'd removed the beeper's batteries, washed his axe, and dumped Donnie's body in a deep Middle Ingraham glacial crevasse several hundred yards in from the trail. The murder, disposal and cleanup had taken only minutes. Emery had pushed on and won the race, stumbling across the line just ahead of the second-place finisher.

But would he get away with it?

His Mercedes ML430 was now passing the Nisqually overflow lake at Alder on his way to Elbe. He recalled the desperate fright which had gripped him later. He had been scared then, frightened yet exhilarated. But now, cocooned in his wonder of German engineering, a seasoned killer, his heart beat at a normal pace and his brow was dry. He slipped a Megadeth CD into his Bose, cranked up the volume, and for a moment zoned into heavy metal chaos.

Donnie's big lead had been called down from the summit, so when Emery finished first, everyone swarmed around him, shouting, asking where Donnie was.

He'd had the good sense to make a show of surprise, looking around as he was gasping for breath, his wide eyes reflecting exhaustion, confusion and incredulity. Then, as Jameson began to organize a search party, Boyd had risen on his good knee, struggled to his feet, and taken some tentative steps toward the mountain. Before anyone could stop him—and without even a jacket— he was straining back up the mountain.

It had been, he reflected, good theater.

But he'd taken so many chances that day, and so much could have gone wrong. Raw instincts and anger had governed reason. Luckily, there'd been no witnesses. He and Donnie were the only two climbers on that route. But he remembered it all like it had been captured on film. The speed... Donnie's eyes... the spraying blood... Donnie in a heap... the wrenching of the serrated blade from Donnie's skull...deciding where to put the body.

Twice he thought they had him. The first time was when metal detectors were brought up, but he relaxed when he found out their reach was shallow. The second was when the searchers began looking in crevasses further out on the Ingraham. As they moved closer and closer to Donnie's hurried tomb, fear tightened Emery's intestines. But then Jameson stepped in, ordering them back; the footing was too unstable.

Finally, after three days, the search was called off and he could breathe again. No one questioned his story: his look of surprise, his tireless search efforts and his feigned sorrow had carried him through.

Lesson learned: murder requires planning.

Well, he wouldn't have that problem this time...

Now, midway between Alder and Elbe, as guitars clashed and his Mercedes' tires tracked up the drainage of the Nisqually River, he thought of the irony and justice of Donnie's murder. In the spring of his eighteenth year, as Emery Boyd became the youngest person to stand on the summit of Everest, John Whitney, Donnie's co-conspirator, was by his side. For a moment, Emery and John had regarded each other, then John reached into his pack and pulled out Donnie's stopwatch. Emery Boyd watched John bend over and place it on the summit, then rise and raise his arms into the air.

Paybacks are a bitch.

From Highway 706 came the nine-mile stretch from Elbe through Ashford to the park's Nisqually entrance. Here dense rain forest smelling of damp fir and moss offered a few scattered housing developments and the occasional restaurant or motel. He flipped off his Bose as he turned on Skate Creek Road, just south of the park entrance. He was heading east through high fir, hemlock, spruce and cedar trees and the fern-covered blankets beneath them. Five miles on, as the road turned south, he veered off onto a rough gravel trail alongside Horse Creek in the Snoqualmie National Forest. He only drove his Mercedes here during the summer months. At other times, he used his GMC YukonXL for the rugged two-and-a-half-mile passage to his home. The house was situated one-half mile from the south park border at the base of Lookout Mountain, a fifty-four-hundred-foot Rainier foothill.

The house had been built over seventy years ago as a hunting lodge by his grandfather, Derrick Boyd, the founder of Boyd Millworks in Olympia, now Boyd International Corporation, a publicly held company with interests in lumber, paper mills and construction materials. Emery was BIC's largest shareholder but played no active role in the company's management. Ian— Emery's father—had expanded the lodge in the early 1950s to its present fifty-five hundred square feet and had added modern conveniences, running electrical and phone lines in from Longmire at no small expense.

Most of Emery's satisfying memories were of the times he'd spent here, exploring the mountain forests, ignoring the hunting laws and shooting at deer, beaver or marmot. He would shoot to wound, following blood, not leaves and trail. Occasionally, he took pictures and hid them under mountain photos tucked away in album stacks deep inside his closet. The Mercedes revved in traction, air buffeting him. His mother had died during his child-birth, and Ian never remarried—claiming he hadn't the time or the inclination. Ian devoted his life to the business, leaving the rearing of his unwanted son mostly to a succession of nannies. Emery neither loved nor hated his father; he had simply been a presence. And love? What was that? Something beyond reach and interest. He had kept only one family picture. One of his mother, a picture his father had never shown him, one he found only after his father's death. And which he kept by his bedside, along with his 9mm semiauto. It was actually a picture of his father and mother, but Emery had cropped Ian out of it. When Ian died while Emery was in law school, he refused to attend the funeral. He chose instead to take a day off from studies and spend it hunting. Blood, wet leaves, and trail took his full attention.

As a boy, he was a fierce competitor and used to getting his way. He was larger than his contemporaries, powerfully built, and always ready to show who was best. His pursuit of victory was single-minded, relentless and ruthless. He had few friends, none close.

At school, Emery excelled easily academically, although his social skills lagged markedly behind. Emery could project a polished charm when it served his purpose, but he was not well-liked or trusted by his peers; generally, he was regarded as stand-offish and an elitist—a loner.

But Emery hadn't cared; he had his mountain—his spirit twin. And now he was home.

FIVE

Thursday, July 25

As the Mercedes rounded the last bend on the makeshift sawdust driveway, the big cedar lodge, or "home," as Boyd called it, became visible. It rested on a flat spot on the first slope of Lookout Mountain. Two stories tall, the lodge had two roomy bedrooms upstairs and a large master bedroom suite with cathedral ceiling downstairs. The attached garage, like the rest of the lodge, was oversized. It had room for three large vehicles. A stairway along its left wall led to an attic spanning the full expanse of the garage.

Emery pressed his remote control, the left side garage door opened, and he drove the Mercedes inside. He walked to the line of switches on the wall and flipped several. Instantly, the garage and upstairs attic were flooded with light.

He didn't go inside the house. Instead, he removed his suit and grabbed a blue, floor-length, grease-stained mechanic's coverall off a rack. Once changed, he removed three sets of keys from a wall-hung key rack and began testing gasoline tanks, oil levels and starting the vehicles he would need. First was the black

GMC YukonXL next to the Mercedes, followed by the older of two snowmobiles and an all-terrain vehicle. He gassed the ATV and snowmobile, oiled them and made them ready. Next, he inspected the wheel bearings on his trailer and hitched it to the ATV.

Now he walked over to the wall, ten feet in front of the Mercedes, and reached around the back of a beam to lift a long metal key, like an old skeleton key, from its hiding place. He climbed the steps to the attic and inserted the key in the lock of a large, heavy steel door. He pushed the door open.

Inside was a sight Boyd permitted no one to see, his gear room, where he kept all manner of weaponry, excursion clothing and equipment.

A casual observer might have thought Eddie Bauer lived here.

Emery walked over to a large oak desk situated in the middle of the room and opposite some metal lockers. He pulled out a drawer, took out some paper and a pen, sat down on an old wooden desk chair rocker, and began making a list.

So much to do.

Friday, July 26

Emery slept until 8:00 A.M. After working out for a couple of hours, he showered and shaved, then made the long drive back to Seattle. When he arrived at the office, he buried Jenny with dictation, wrote several e-mails, and sent correspondence to expert witnesses, board members of Boyd International Corporation and to opposing counsel on various legal matters.

He then set about returning phone calls and dealing with e-mails, tasks which required about two hours more. After ordering a late lunch, he summoned Dan Cole for an hour of departmental administrative matters.

Herman Klein was suffering through a rotten day.

It had started last night. He knew better than to drink coffee in the evening. But he'd been tired, his feet felt heavy, his eyes burned and his neck was stiff. He recognized the symptoms and knew their cause—stress. But still, duty called: he had to review his client's file before the audit today.

So he'd had coffee at dinner and more later. It spiked his energy level but ensured a sleepless night, made all the worse by Emily's incessant complaints and "I told you so's."

So he'd awakened—assuming he'd slept at all—just as tired as he'd been the night before. And he dragged his exhaustion with him like an anchor. Each blink of the eye reminded him how sleep deprived he was. Ironically, coffee didn't help today; it just raised his stress level. After he'd showered, staring hard into the mirror, Herman had been shocked to see wrinkles and puffiness—a haggard look—which seemed to have appeared overnight. He vowed to avoid mirrors all day, half afraid he'd see the progression of Dorian Gray.

Then came the audit.

Herman had predicted to his clients, the members of a real estate limited partnership, that the audit would take half a day. But the IRS agent opened the meeting claiming he'd uncovered fraud on the part of the general partner. Then a Special Agent had entered the room. The rest of the day slid through mud.

Herman had been there all day. When he'd finally concluded the meeting and arranged for new—and criminal—counsel for the general partner, he headed home, deciding that a stiff drink was preferable to an office side trip to pick up his Judge Schneider materials. He hoped Emily was in a good mood.

If not, there was always alcohol...

It was 6:30 P.M. Emery pulled his ATV and trailer outside. Wrestling the old, unregistered snowmobile around, he started it and drove it up onto the trailer. Once it was situated and tied down, he arranged his equipment around it and began tying it down. There was his big pack, crammed with a week's worth of supplies and weighing about seventy-five pounds; a folding shovel; an ice axe; skis, and ski poles. Next, he changed clothes and by 7:15 was back in the attic re-checking his list and gathering more equipment. He grabbed three parkas: one each red, white and camouflage. Donning the red one, his usual, he stowed the others. A large survival knife, a wool stocking cap, some surgical gloves, another large, empty excursion pack, two large garbage bags, some heavy twine, and a blond wig also went into the Yukon. It only took a moment to burn the list and flush it.

He shut the garage door and placed the remote in a side pocket of his pack. Then he fired up the ATV and revved the engine, listening to its subdued purr. ATVs were illegal in the park, except in emergencies, so a few years ago he'd found a mechanic in Olympia who designed a special muffler for him. The ATV wasn't silent, but it would be hard to detect at distances of more than a hundred yards.

After re-checking his gear on the trailer, Emery hopped aboard the ATV, flipped on its headlights, and took off toward the right side of his property to a hidden utilities trail leading to Longmire, several miles inside the park.

The riskiest part of the trip would be on the road from Longmire to just below Paradise. For that ten-mile trip, he was at risk of being observed by a passing vehicle. Of course, by the time a report was made and responding vehicles dispatched, he'd be long gone, but he feared the report might jeopardize his alibi. To avoid detection, he'd turn off his headlights, and he'd pull off the road if he saw another vehicle.

The trip to Longmire took the better part of an hour, then it was another forty-five minutes to his breakoff point just below Paradise. He arrived just after nine, confident no one had seen him.

Once off the road, he turned on the ATV's headlights and continued on a little-used ice cave trail to the snowline, bypassing Paradise by a wide margin. He reached the snowline in about ten minutes. He continued on for awhile, then pulled off the trail, stopped the ATV behind a cluster of firs, and slid the snowmobile off the trailer before grabbing his shovel, headlamp and pack.

Donning his headlamp, he flipped it on, then began digging a deep trough in the snow. When its depth and proportions satisfied him, he drove the snowmobile into the trough. Ten minutes of shoveling later, the machine was buried. He marked the spot with two crisscrossing branches, then covered his tracks to the snowline.

He was ready for the trip to Muir, and fair weather made the trek uneventful. Emery arrived just after 1:00 A.M. At that hour, the guides were rising, preparing to awaken their tourists for the summit effort. They were in a jovial, expectant mood. Emery's façade slipped comfortably in place, and he was pleased to see several of his old friends, especially Max Brittain and Jim Carlton. Although Brittain and Carlton were only about five years his senior, their weathered, sun-darkened faces made them appear older, and Brittain's face looked cancerous—there were lesions dotting both of his cheeks and his forehead. Emery expressed his concern and asked Brittain if he'd had his face checked. Brittain waved him off, grunting that he'd worry about it when the season was over. A typical response from a career mountaineer.

Emery looked at Carlton, a lean, handsome man of average build with a full head of still-black, close-cropped hair. "Nice parka, Jim." He smiled and covered his eyes. "You auditioning for Big Bird?"

Carlton kicked at the snow and mumbled something under his breath as Emery and Brittain both laughed. "His girlfriend bought it for him," Brittain said, sing-song, batting his eyes.

"Jim has a girl?" Boyd said, astonishment on his face. He clapped him on the back. "Since when? Someone up here? I thought you didn't approve of dating tourists."

Carlton picked up a harness and began tying it into a rope. "She's not from here; never been here," he muttered.

Emery grinned. Carlton was notoriously shy, especially around members of the opposite sex. Women were attracted to his bashfulness and rugged good looks, but as far as Boyd knew, Carlton had never enjoyed a serious relationship. And neither had Boyd, for vastly different and ugly reasons. "Well, where the hell did you meet her? When are we going to meet her? Where's she from?"

Carlton dropped the harness. "C'mon, Emery."

"Bullshit, Jim," Boyd said. "Look, we're not trying to pry. We're just curious about what kind of woman has hooked our good friend. She must be very special."

Carlton shrugged, a hint of smile across his face. "She is...." But the smile disappeared when Brittain began laughing. "Look, I met her on vacation, okay? For now, I'll visit her. Later... well... we'll see. That's all you guys need to know for now."

"Well, what's her name, Jimbo?" Brittain asked. "You gotta tell us that."

"Just leave it alone. You assholes will meet her soon enough."

Emery nodded. "Okay, Jim. But I can't wait to meet her. Just don't introduce her to Whitney. He'll feed her so much shit about you, she won't stop running until Mexico."

"Ain't that the truth," Brittain said. "He's already calling Jim 'Tweetie Bird.' "

Carlton looked away, disgusted. "Say, Emery," Brittain said, "how 'bout leading the summit attempt. It would be great for business."

"Aw, Christ, Max. I just got here, and I'm tired as hell. I

worked all day and want to get some sleep now, maybe out by Gibraltar. How about if I speak to them instead?" He knew that would satisfy his friends. Manipulating people was like moving puzzle pieces, shifting them around until he had the picture he wanted. Sometimes a piece had to be removed from the board.

It took Brittain, Carlton and the other guides a half-hour to get the climbers up, fed and dressed. When the group was ready to rope-up, Brittain, lead guide today, introduced Emery with fanfare. His name and exploits were well known, and the client group, about thirty strong, mostly men but with several hardened women, welcomed him enthusiastically. Boyd raised his hands to quiet them, thanked them, then spent about twenty minutes relating humorous anecdotes, including the Snowball story. There was laughter all around, and when he concluded, he signed a few autographs. As he signed and smiled, he went over his list in his head. He was ready.

Boyd waited until the climbing party was well out on the Cowlitz before he bid goodbye to the remaining hands at Muir and struck out to the northwest toward Gibraltar. He didn't go far: just out of sight from Muir. He dumped his pack after removing his ice axe, skis, shovel and remote control. He removed his red parka, stuffed it inside the bag, then buried the pack next to a large rock outcropping. Satisfied, he slapped on his skis.

The trip down was quick. Strapping the skis and his shovel down inside the trailer, Boyd fired up the ATV and roared off. He arrived home a little after 3:00 A.M., and fifteen minutes later, he was in the Yukon heading toward Mercer Island.

Boyd knew where Herman lived; he had no difficulty finding his house. It was located a half-mile off I-90 Exit 6A, on the west side of the island, and was bordered on the right by the tree-shrouded Procter Landing, a narrow public access pier at the end of the equally narrow Procter Lane.

The house was a large, brown brick Tudor mansion with a sharply sloped cedar shingle roof. It sat at the junction of 60th

Avenue SE and SE 32nd Street, an L-shaped intersection. Procter Lane, a graveled finger leading to a dead-end some 300 feet from the pier, forked off to the right. A gray masonry wall ran the edge of the property line almost to the water. The wall was not of uniform height. It sloped down toward Lake Washington, beginning at about seven feet, then sliding down to four feet near the water. The public pier extended some fifty feet out into the lake. It adjoined Klein's pier, separated only by some five feet of space.

Boyd arrived at Herman's house just before dawn. Shutting off the Yukon, he rolled it backwards down the hill to the end of the gravel finger, careful to hug the wall.

Twenty minutes later, first light was noticeable on the hills across the lake. He turned off the Yukon's interior lights, hit the tailgate button and climbed out to open the rear. He donned his camouflage parka, the blond wig, the stocking cap and surgical gloves. He pulled out his ice axe, survival knife, excursion pack and garbage bags. The pack and garbage bags he laid out behind the vehicle; the knife and axe he tucked into his belt.

He walked down to the pier, his best vantage point, his empty blue eyes watching the house. What he saw would determine what he did next—and to how many. The house seemed quiet—just one light upstairs on the right. As he watched, the light went out. Good. No need to turn it off if Emily was up. He suspected Emily was snoring like Ma Kettle.

Now a light came on downstairs toward the center of the house. The kitchen. Probably Herman making coffee; he wished he had some. Too bad he couldn't just off him in there and enjoy a cup. No smile touched his mouth. Then that light went out.

Boyd crouched low, barely peering over the end of the wall. A few minutes later, he saw Herman's stooped, slight frame leave the shadows of the house and follow the stone path to the lower tiered lakeside terraces. *Where's your baggy suit, Herm?* He was walking slowly, as if balancing a load. The whole world on his fucking shoulders. *Not for long...*

Boyd moved up a hundred feet to the higher wall and its heavier darkness. He noticed that Herman was carrying fishing poles, a tackle box, a jacket of some kind, and a coffee thermos and cup—fishing rites of passage.

Herman moved awkwardly, juggling his load as he walked the still-dark path. At the lower terrace he placed the thermos, tackle box and cup on the second terrace tier and leaned the poles on the far wall next to his live-well. He put on his jacket, selected a pole, unhooked its line and bent over the tank.

Boyd moved down the wall to where it dropped to the four-foot level. Quietly he scaled it. His boots made no noise as he dropped into a crouch on the other side. Overhead, a bird shrieked and took flight, rustling branches. Herman whirled around and stared—*right at him!*

Sure he'd been seen, silhouetted as he must be against the gray wall, Boyd grasped his axe, yanked it out of his belt and started to rise, but then saw Herman turn around and bend over the live-well once more.

It took Boyd a few moments to regain composure. His muscles relaxed, his breathing steadied. He looked once more at the house; it was dark—asleep. He moved forward out of the bushes and the protective darkness, each step carefully placed.

He was thirty feet behind Herman, now twenty, now fifteen. Raising his axe, focusing on the back of Herman's head, Boyd readied himself to strike, only to feel his right foot slip out from under him in the early-morning dew. He went down hard and slid down the embankment onto the upper portion of the stone terrace. His right arm struck stone and his axe fell free, clattering on the stone, shattering the early-dawn peace. *Jesus!*

Herman spun around, mouth hanging open. That's what Boyd would remember. A gaping mouth in the gray of morning, like it was waiting for a fish hook....

Herman had awakened promptly at 5:00 A.M., the unconscious alarm in his head buzzing. Looking over at his still-slumbering wife, he was pleased she'd finally come to her senses last night and decided to sleep in the matrimonial bed; although for the last several years the term "matrimonial" was more a euphemism than anything else. Still, Herman hoped the gesture of her being there meant that some of her anger was spent. He winced, remembering the angry words and yelling that the neighbors *must* have heard.

And all because of that bastard Boyd.

Well, that wasn't entirely true. It was his own big mouth that had gotten him into trouble. He winced again from under the warmth of the comforter as he remembered his mental lapse, his comment that he'd left the file on his desk. Emily had picked up on it immediately, and the rest of the evening had been hell.

Herman slid out from under the big down comforter that kept him Eskimo warm, and rolled his feet onto the floor. He turned on the light. That wasn't a problem: Emily slept with blinders.

He slipped into a pair of khaki slacks, a long-sleeve sweatshirt and loafers, turned off the light, and tiptoed out the door and down the staircase.

Herman made his way into the kitchen and fixed coffee. While he waited, he looked out the window to check the weather. Off to the west, across the lake, he could see dark clouds in the emerging dawn light.

Good! The fish would be biting.

Now it was time to grab his jacket, poles and tackle box. In the basement, Herman selected three poles of different sizes, his largest tackle box and a jacket, then returned for his coffee.

He pulled his maroon Harvard cup out of the cabinet, then reached under the kitchen counter and grabbed his "fishin' " thermos. Coffee was ready. He poured the thermos full and screwed on its top. Then he slid into his jacket and gathered his equipment, somehow juggling it all and turning off the light with his elbow. He shuffled out into the crisp morning air, kicking the door shut behind him.

It was a slow walk down the stone path and across the manicured lawn, managing his awkward load. On the bottom terrace level he placed his thermos, cup and tackle box on the second tier and his poles next to the stone live-well. He grabbed a pole, freed its hook and bent over his live-well, looking for a suitable sacrifice. A large sucker swimming actively. He snatched and hooked it.

Behind him, the tranquility of the early morning was broken by the wild screech of a bird and the rustle of branches.

Herman straightened up, but saw nothing in the deep shadows.

"Damn cats," he muttered, then turned back to retrieve his line. He found it easily and cupped the struggling fish. When he heard the thud and the strike of metal on stone, Herman whirled around. What he saw made him drop his bait. On the terrace, not five feet away, was a huge man dressed in camouflage, with long, flowing blond hair covered by a stocking cap. He was struggling to get up, to reach for something a few feet away.

Herman ran for the steps, but as he reached the top terrace tier he felt his ankle seized and pulled. Falling hard, he opened his mouth to scream, but a huge hand clamped around his throat.

He kicked, punched, grabbed and twisted. But the hands holding him were unrelenting. Steel fingers tightened around his throat. Blood escaped through his ears and nose, and an incredible pressure compressed his eyes. He tried for the eyes of his assailant, but couldn't find them.

Just for an instant, he caught a glimpse of his assailant's face and recognition dawned. He tried to speak. Another huge hand on the back of his head, then a terrible wrenching. He didn't hear the pop of oblivion.

Boyd raised Herman's lifeless body and with a heaving shrug hurled it away from him. It fell against the wall and live-well, scattering the fishing poles and creating a splash.

Boyd fell back exhausted. *Jesus Christ.* Slipping on dewy leaves. *Jesus Christ.* He lay on the terrace. Gradually his breathing eased. But he collected himself a moment longer before rolling onto his stomach and looking around.

All was quiet.

He got up and retrieved his axe. He slipped it through his belt loop and moved over to Herman's body. The head—bent at an odd angle—and the shoulders were in the live-well, the body sprawled along the wall, like a discarded marionette. Baitfish swam excitedly in the tank, fearful, yet curious. A few flopped on the terrace.

Grabbing Herman's belt with his left hand, Boyd pulled the body off the tank and wall. He carried the body like luggage, lugging it up the steps and over to the wall. Then he hefted it over and let drop on the other side. Turning for one last look, he saw the coffee thermos. *Why not?*

Some minutes later, he scaled the wall and carried the body to the back of the Yukon. He bagged his load in plastic, stuffed it inside the excursion pack, and fastened its straps snugly. Then he hoisted the pack into the vehicle's rear compartment, covered it with an army blanket, tossed in his ice axe, then closed the tailgate.

Walking toward the front of the Yukon, he looked around, assuring himself there were no prying eyes. Satisfied, he retraced his steps from the wall, looking for traces of blood, material or footprints. He saw nothing obvious, but in the poor light, he couldn't be sure.

He tossed the thermos onto the passenger seat and climbed

into the Yukon. The survival knife went under the seat as he started the engine. As he headed toward I-90, he removed his surgical gloves and stuffed them in his parka pocket.

Time for some coffee.

He adjusted his wig.

Saturday, July 27

Boyd arrived at the Nisqually entrance at 8:00 A.M. There was a steady stream of traffic into the park at this hour, and Boyd was still wearing the blond wig, so he was not worried that the guard at the gate would recognize him. But he kept his face turned. He paid the entrance fee and followed traffic up to Paradise.

As he drove up the mountain, he was pleased to see the morning grayness and light rain had turned to fog at higher elevations. Paradise was blanketed in a gray soup.

Most of the traffic to Paradise was heading to the Visitor's Center on the west side of the expansive complex, or to the lodge. The outer rows of the parking lot were empty. Boyd parked the Yukon in the furthest spot on the east side.

After fastening his survival knife to his belt, he popped the tailgate, grabbed the thermos and exited the Yukon. He locked the doors as he walked to the back of the vehicle. At the tailgate he left his wig on but shrugged out of his camouflage parka and into the white one. Before pulling the Herman-pack out, he stuffed the thermos and his camouflage parka into its side pockets, then righted it and slipped into its straps, locking the strap clamps tightly across his chest. The load was balanced and manageable. He pulled out a pair of heavy mountain gloves, worked his way into them, then grabbed his ice axe and closed the tailgate door.

Boyd hiked to where he'd left the snowmobile. It required two rest stops and an hour to reach. He dropped his load and axe into the snow and began digging out the sled with gloved hands. When it was mostly uncovered, he grabbed the sled's tail-bar and dragged it out of the hole. The engine fired smoothly. He let it warm as he moved back to his pack and axe.

"Hey, you!" The voice behind Boyd was familiar. He went rigid, adrenaline pumped. He whirled around, not knowing what to expect—except trouble.

Twenty feet below, barely visible through the fog, stood a figure in a bright yellow parka.

What was Jim Carlton doing here?

"Hey, buddy!" Carlton shouted. "What are you doing here with *that?*" He was pointing at the snowmobile. "This is a national park! How'd you get that thing in here? They should have stopped you at the entrance!"

Boyd's immediate reaction was to spring, but he checked himself. He needed to know if Carlton was alone. Pulling up his cap and wig, he grinned and said, "Hi, Jim!"

Carlton's jaw dropped. "Emery? Is that you?"

Boyd smiled, sliding over to his axe some ten feet away.

"Sonofabitch! It is you!" Carlton shook his head, trying to make sense of what was in front of him. "I don't get it…. What are you doing here? And with that? I thought you were up higher. And what's with the wig?" Carlton climbed closer.

Boyd smiled again, one he had often practiced in the mirror while shaving, amiable, a tad embarrassed. He glanced over at his axe. Too far. A move toward it would be too bold. Carlton had an axe too. He needed to take Carlton by surprise. Knife work. "I'm playing a joke on Whitney. He said he'd be over at the caves. Have you seen him?"

"Nah. I was just going there. I took some climbers who couldn't make the summit back to Muir, then Whitney radioed asking me to relieve him. I had to come down to get my stuff."

"Ah. Tough luck getting stuck with the laggards, huh?"

"Nah. The group won't get far in this shit anyway." He waved a gloved hand at the weather. Boyd could clearly see his features now: friendly but cautious. "It's really socking in up there, and moving down. That must be why you came down, huh?"

"Yeah. I saw it coming, so I figured I'd play with Whitney."

"Well, the weather service says it's gonna storm like hell. Maybe blizzard conditions even below Paradise."

"That's quite a storm for this time of year. Anyone in trouble?"

"No, we look okay. Rangers say they got to everybody but you, but I guess they don't need to worry about you now, huh? But... how come you didn't check in?"

"I figured I'd check in with Whitney."

"Yeah. But you shoulda checked in sooner. You know that." He paused, confusion overlaying caution. "Well, no harm done, I guess. We can go over and see John together. He'll love the wig. Say, where'd you get the snowmobile?"

Boyd took a couple of steps down the hill toward Carlton. "Found it. Looks like someone stashed it here, maybe for a little poaching. Figured as long as the key was in it, I might as well give John something to yell about. Want a ride?" He turned to his right slightly and beckoned Carlton forward. As he did, his right hand slid unseen underneath his parka and popped the button on his sheath.

Carlton shook his head and stepped upward, but he stopped suddenly, wearing a worried expression. Fucking guy couldn't keep his face straight. "Yeah. But, Emery... I still don't get it.

Where'd you get the wig and the white parka? And what are you doing here? There's a much more direct route to the caves from Muir…"

Boyd took a step toward him. They were now seven feet apart. Maybe Boyd's movement was too swift, maybe the smile wasn't working, needed more mirror practice, but Carlton stepped back. Boyd leapt at him, pulling out his knife as he closed. The sudden movement startled Carlton, and he fell back and lost his balance. His arms windmilled backward and he landed on his right side, his axe pinned beneath him, his head downhill. His eyes bulged as he saw Boyd's blade, and he let out a primal cry as he tried to roll off his axe and grab at Boyd. His left hand found purchase in Boyd's left parka pocket, and instinct caused him to pull down. Something ripped as Boyd landed heavily on him. Carlton squirmed to free himself, but now the weight of two bodies pinned his axe and arm. With only one free hand and the downward slope, there was little he could do. The serrated blade entered Carlton's neck and ripped through tissue and cartilage as it drove through his voice box and into his spine. Carlton's body jolted, then sagged back, lifeless into the snow. Blood ran. It stained the snow under his neck and the back of his head. Dark rivulets draining deep into the white.

No sooner had Carlton's body gone still than Boyd cleaned his knife, rolled over and up, and began cutting off long strips from Carlton's parka. Draping the strips around Carlton's neck, he tightened them down into an effective tourniquet. Then he pulled the body over to a tree and propped it in a sitting position. Only then did he rest and begin to consider his predicament.

After a few moments, he sheathed his knife, removed his parka, and walked over to examine it in the glow of the snowmobile's headlamps. There was some blood, but not much. Most of it had run downhill. He washed the parka in the snow, knowing that while a forensics lab would find blood traces on it, the waterproof material and high humidity would prevent staining. Then he removed his shirt and held it before the headlamps. No trace of blood at all. While he was shirtless, he moved over a few feet and, ignoring the cold, bathed his head, neck and face in clean snow. He pulled on his shirt, then his parka, and checked his pants. Clean.

Time to deal with the body and the scene.

He had been lucky. The attack had occurred on a downward slope. Most blood flow and spatter had been directed away from him. And there wasn't as much blood as he would have expected, although in the poor light and snow conditions it was difficult to be certain. Maybe he'd missed the carotid and the jugular. There wasn't enough light to determine whether the flow was arterial or venous; it just looked brown.

Boyd removed what was left of Carlton's yellow parka and searched its pockets. He found Carlton's radio, avalanche beeper and wallet. He tossed them over by the snowmobile. Finding some parachute cord in Carlton's pack, he turned the parka inside out and tied it tightly around Carlton's head.

Now he moved to the still-idling snowmobile and wrestled it around so the front was pointing at clear snow. He pulled his excursion pack over, and using more of Carlton's parachute cord, tied the pack to the tail-bar in a horizontal position. Thus fixed, he clamped Carlton's pack to his own and let Carlton's pack drape over the tailbar. Pulling the radio and avalanche beeper apart, he removed their batteries and shoved them, the now-useless radio and beeper, and Carlton's wallet in a pack side pocket.

Moving to Carlton's propped body, Boyd was pleased to see that he'd staunched the blood flow. He grabbed Carlton by the belt, lugged him over to another tree, and propped him up again. He wanted to let Carlton's blood settle and coagulate as much as possible before he moved him again. In the meantime, he'd clean up.

For twenty minutes he scooped up gobs of snow and deposited them over blood stains. Over time the blood would dilute, but with a storm coming, it might freeze in the near term. He wanted to hide the scene long enough for the weather to either bury the area in new snow, erasing all traces, or melt the stained snow. His dilemma was that he'd disturbed the area significantly with the digging out of the snowmobile. Filling in that hole would disturb the area even more, calling more attention to it. And there was no telling how long the fog would last. It would likely disappear with the first snowfall. He used snow from the dig to cover the blood.

Time to go. He looked over the area and could see no blood. But the light was bad. He could run the snowmobile around, flash his lights over the area, but that would just disturb the snow all the more, and he'd already covered the bloody patches. He didn't want to undo that work. No, he'd just take his chances. Hope the coming storm cut him another lucky break. The area was off-trail, and that trail was seldom used. The odds were good. Carlton would just go missing. It happened all the time on this mountain.

He walked over to Carlton's body and inspected his head wrap. No new blood. Satisfied, he lifted Carlton by the belt and turned him over, keeping the head off the snow. Carrying the body with both hands, he climbed up to the snowmobile and lifted the body onto the seat, facing backwards. He used more cord to tie Carlton's head to the packs. No blood from the head area, if it leaked, would stain his back or neck.

Seating himself on the Arctic Cat bench, he scotched back to ensure Carlton was tightly wedged between him and the excursion pack. He slid his axe in a belt loop, then gunned the engine forward to test the sled's maneuverability. It was heavy but surprisingly agile. The added back weight made the tracks bite the snow, while the lightened runners turned freely. And there was more room on the bench than he'd expected. The only problem was side-weight balance. He'd have to be careful to take grades head-on, or the sled might topple. He'd use his feet for stability on small grade traverses, but he'd avoid the steep ones.

Satisfied, he turned the sled uphill and gave it some gas. It surged forward like a sprinter out of the gate. But after the initial run up through the trees, he slowed. The fog required caution; this was no time to be reckless.

Boyd followed a ridge over Edith Creek. He passed Panorama Point a thousand feet to the east, then crossed further east to the lower tip of the Paradise Glacier. He crossed that glacier, using extra caution because of the poor navigational conditions and the possibility of crevasses, then passed a thousand feet over the ice caves—much too far away to be seen or heard—to a point near the Cowlitz Rocks at seventy-four hundred feet. From there, he drove to the middle Cowlitz Glacier, passing a thousand feet below the old fire lookout cabin at Anvil Rock. For an hour or so, a heavy, wet snow had been falling in large flakes and the wind had been building, creating conditions that made navigation and balance dangerous considerations. From time to time, as white-out conditions were encountered, he was forced to turn upgrade, dismount and navigate on foot. While such conditions might prove deadly for the inexperienced, for Boyd, they were an inconvenience. They slowed him down but didn't threaten his progress.

Once on the Cowlitz, he traversed to a level spot where he felt relatively safe from avalanche, then dismounted and moved on foot, looking for a suitable spot. Conditions had worsened. He no longer felt comfortable driving a heavy sled on a surface pocked with deep crevasses. Visibility was almost non-existent in the driving, biting snow. The wind was near hurricane force. Landmarks like Cowlitz Rocks and Anvil Rock were invisible.

He didn't have far to walk. He found what he was looking for. A hundred feet ahead of the sled was a crevasse which looked perfect. Narrow but probably deep, it would soon be covered over in this storm. Back at the sled he mounted and drove slowly toward his spot. He stopped twenty feet in front of the slip and tossed his axe to the side, lest it get caught in his package and drag him into the depths. Standing on the bench seat, his knees bent, he gunned the engine toward the crease and jumped free. Satisfaction blanketed him as he lay in the snow and watched the snowmobile—and its cargo—disappear in a roiling white cloud.

Boyd was at his hiding place an hour and a half later. He retrieved his cache and replaced his white parka with his usual red one, noticing that a pocket of the white one had been torn off. He thought back to the struggle with Carlton and how Carlton had grabbed at him and pulled him down. Cutting the parka into strips, he buried them, then covered and patted down their hiding place.

Boyd stumbled into the Camp Muir Ranger Station at 5:30 P.M. to much jubilation and relief, and promptly collapsed. Taken to the Guide Hut and stripped of his parka by Max Brittain, he was placed in a warm sleeping bag layered over with wool blankets. Brittain brought him a container of hot and hearty beef stew and urged him to eat.

The assembled guides and rangers, he knew, were eager to learn what had happened, where he'd been and how he'd made his way back, but they knew better than to press him now.

In his exhausted state, sleep was creeping up on him, and Boyd didn't trust his mind. He mumbled only, "Kautz Cleaver," before blackness prevailed.

SEVEN

Saturday, July 27

Emily Klein awoke at about half past ten Saturday morning and didn't bother glancing at Herman's side of the bed; she knew he wouldn't be there. For several minutes, she lay there thinking.

Herman.

He'd lied to her, while claiming to need her help. Unforgivable! She looked out the lake-side window, confirmed he'd left for the office. Good, she'd have time to determine what her attitude toward him would be today. She got up and waddled to the bathroom, used the toilet, brushed her teeth and took a long shower. As she hung her towel on the rack, she inadvertently touched Herman's towel, which was dry.

She finished her routine, dressed, and went downstairs to the coffee machine. She could see he'd been there; the spent grounds were still in the filter. But where were his cup and thermos? And where was the newspaper? Herman usually read it at the break-fast table. As she waited for the coffee to perk, she went to look for the morning paper and found it on the front stoop.

An hour later, she'd finished her coffee, read the paper and decided to forgive Herman—gradually. She'd make him work for it, but she wouldn't rant and rave this time. She'd already done that, as the neighbors knew well.

The phone rang. Sue Schneider offered to take her to Nordstrom's. She accepted happily.

John Whitney was tense and irritable. The tall, chiseled mountaineer was charged by a range of emotions: boredom, impatience, worry, anger, helplessness.

Luckily, most people sensed his mood and stayed away from him. The additional snow meant there was that much more white stuff to remove, but that hadn't developed into a problem yet. The real problems were visibility, working conditions, shift changes and manpower. He was glad they'd provisioned well and that the caves were open. The storm had created a little community up here, and they were stuck for now.

Still, there was the problem of getting the bulldozers off the mountain. He'd be charged for a day's rental if he couldn't get them off by tonight, and that would seriously eat at his budget.

Shit.

He'd instructed the helicopter pilot to start picking up the dozers as soon as the storm lifted. But when would that be?

And the volunteers were bugging him. He was tired of these college kids, even the one who'd crawled into his sleeping bag last night—although he'd discovered he could tolerate her for a while. "Miss Knockers" he'd called her, and she'd loved it—and him.

Then there was Emery Boyd. Where was he? Why hadn't he reported in? He knew the procedure. Was Boyd in trouble? Carlton had said Boyd was going over to the west side of Gibraltar. Surely, he'd seen the storm coming from there....

And where the hell was Carlton?

John paced, anger and frustration growing. He glanced at his watch: 1:00 P.M. "Damn!" he muttered and spat into the snow. He pulled the radio out of his pocket and hit the transmit button. "Whitney to Station."

There was static on the line.

"Whitney to Station!" he repeated.

"Go ahead, John, this is Station, Maselli speaking."

John visualized the handsome Italian stud sitting on the counter at the Guide Service Shack, decked out in tight red stretch pants, legs spread, radio in hand, trying to impress some young girl. The vision made him angrier.

"Get me somebody who knows something."

There was silence for a moment, then the voice of Senior Guide Norm Reiter. "Yeah, John, what's up?"

"What the hell you doin' lettin' that pussy-chasin' fool have the radio?"

"Sorry, John, I was over at the ranger station getting the latest weather."

"Anything new on Boyd?"

"Negative. We don't know where he is, and we can't launch a search until the storm lets up. Still seems to be strengthening; no let-up in sight. Muir group and known climbers all secure, 'cept Boyd." He paused. "He shoulda seen that storm coming, boss."

"Yeah," Whitney said, distracted for a moment by a shoving match and angry words between two volunteers. "Okay, Norm. Keep me posted." He watched two husky boys of about nineteen circle each other warily and tried to wave another guide over between them.

"Where the hell's Carlton?" he shouted.

"He should be there, boss. He came down hours ago; said he was on his way to relieve you. Changed packs and gear and took right off again."

"Well, he isn't!" John's anger was cresting again. He watched the two youths collide and tumble to the ground in a cloud of white. "Hold on a minute."

John dropped the radio and trudged over to the two battlers rolling in the snow. Scooping up a handful of snow, he threw it at the guide standing helplessly nearby. "I wanted you to stop this nonsense." Now standing over the writhing figures, John grabbed both their belts and hauled them up and apart. He heaved them face-first into the snow. "I see any more of that crap, I throw you both off my mountain."

He retrieved his radio. "Sorry Norm, I'm back. Now, back to Carlton... Do you suppose he got sidetracked with tourists in trouble? No word from him at all?"

"Nope. And we can't get him on the radio."

"Shit, he knows he's supposed to call in if he gets side-tracked."

"Maybe his batteries are dead. Those new ones aren't worth a shit."

"Yeah. Okay. Listen, keep me posted, will ya? If you don't hear from Carlton or me in an hour, send someone else up here to relieve me. Have him take the trail you think Carlton might have taken."

"Got it, boss."

"And that doesn't mean Maselli! He's the last person I want to see here."

"Gotcha, John."

John replaced the radio on his belt and turned to see "Miss Knockers" coming over.

Oh, what the hell...

Frank Maselli's ears were burning and his face was hot. What did he have to do to please Whitney? Nothing seemed to work. So what if he liked to chase a bit? So did Whitney. What was the difference? Guides were babe-magnets, especially when they looked like he did. Hell, Whitney's prowess was legendary, Emery

Boyd's too. Why shouldn't he knock off a little once in a while too?

"Maselli!" It was Reiter.

"Yes, sir."

"You were here when Carlton took off, weren't you?"

"Yeah."

"Did you hear him say where he was going? I mean which route?"

"I dunno. But I know the route he took two days ago. I went with him."

"Maybe that'll do. If Carlton doesn't get there in an hour, I'm going up myself. You come with me. So just in case, get two sets of packs ready with provisions for three days. And take some shovels, a first aid kit and some extra blankets too. No tellin' what or who we might find up there. Something's goin' on around here, what with both Boyd and Carlton missing, and I want to be prepared."

Maselli turned and started into the back room.

"Oh, Maselli. Don't take John too personally. Maybe on the way up, if the wind's not too bad, I'll explain him to you. He's testin' ya, kid, an' you're doin' just fine. It's sorta tradition here."

Maselli went on about his duties, not having the slightest idea what Norm was talking about.

The hour passed quickly. When Reiter was ready, they set out on the trail Carlton had used two days before. Luckily, the fog had dissipated; the weather was turning cold, and large wet snowflakes were beginning to fall.

The trail moved east for a half mile, then up past Sluiskin Falls to a mostly vertical stretch straight up to the caves. Most of the way, they were sheltered by trees, so they were somewhat protected from the oncoming storm. Here the snow wasn't so deep, and they were able to make good progress. Reiter passed the time by explaining the initiation Al Jameson had given Donnie Whitney and Boyd, and by telling Donnie's story, although he cautioned Maselli to never mention Donnie to John. The knowledge that somewhere on this mountain his brother's body still lay buried ate at Whitney like a cancer. Maselli listened with rapt attention and asked no questions.

The trail grew narrower, and about a mile out it almost died. There were just a few telltale footsteps and some older tire tracks to follow as it turned up mountain.

"I'm bettin' these newer tracks are Jim's," Maselli said. "With this tree cover, it'll take some time to cover these tracks completely."

About a quarter mile below treeline, Maselli suddenly stopped. "Hey, what's that?" He pointed to a roughened area some hundred feet above them, off the trail.

They climbed up to inspect.

They found a large disturbed area and a cavity. "Something was buried here," Reiter said.

It was Maselli who guessed a snowmobile. "Look, Norm," he said, pointing, "here're the tracks, moving up mountain… and here's an exhaust hole where the machine was warmed up." He was pointing to a blackened hole, about a foot in diameter, partially covered with new snow.

"You're right. But why is it here? I can figure out why it's buried; it's not supposed to be here. Maybe a poacher. Think Jim stumbled onto a poacher, kid?"

They looked at each other, worried now. Poaching in a national park was a serious offense. And a poacher would be armed. The guides and rangers had been warned not to interfere with poachers, or worse yet, attempt apprehension; they were supposed to act as if nothing was wrong, and use their radios at the earliest opportunity.

"Look," Reiter said, pointing down slope. "More tracks."

They dropped their packs and moved down ten feet or so, following a set of partially covered tracks where something had been dragged. There were also a couple of depressions in the snow, as if something heavy had been laid down.

"Here," Reiter said, getting down on his knees. "Lightly brush your gloves around. See if there's anything under the loose snow. I'll take this depression; you take that one over there."

Reiter pointed to a spot several feet away. Maselli walked over and dropped to his knees, following Reiter's cue. A few minutes later, he called out, "Norm, I've found something. Come here, quick!"

Reiter rose and ran to where Maselli was kneeling. He dropped down beside him and saw pink snow. He rubbed his gloves over the area. Below the pink area was a darker red. He spread out his hands for a broader sweep and turned up more red snow and some red holes melted into the snow.

"What do you think, Norm?"

"Shit, kid, I dunno. Either this is deer blood... or maybe we found Jim."

EIGHT

Saturday, July 27

Emily Klein returned home at 3:30, to discover Herman had not returned. This puzzled her; he was normally home by now on a Saturday. Was he playing a little game?

The wine from lunch had made her giddy, but now it was wearing off, leaving in its wake the first sensations of a headache. Her eyes felt heavy.

A nap? Why not?

She slept soundly until 5:45. When she awoke, she tottered into the bathroom for her second shower of the day. A half hour later and she was dry, made up and coiffed, ready to dress again.

But where was Herman? She debated calling the office. No, that wouldn't do. Herman would have to come to her.

She began preparing dinner, turning on the kitchen television to watch a "Frasier" rerun while she worked. By 6:30, dinner was nearly ready and Herman still hadn't arrived. Now she was angry.

By 7:30, dinner had been eaten and cleaned up. By 10:30, Emily was very worried. Why was Herman punishing her this way?

She called the office. No one answered. "Where can he be!" she shouted as she slammed the phone down.

Pulling out the telephone directory, she looked up Marge Simmons' number. There were three Simmonses in Kent, so she decided to call all three. She got lucky with the first one.

"Marge Simmons, please."

"This is she."

"Marge, Emily Klein." Her tone was brusque.

"Yes, Mrs. Klein. What can I do for you?"

"Well… uh… Herman must have been delayed. I'm wondering if he might have told you where he was going when he left the office today?"

"I'm sorry, Mrs. Klein. Mr. Klein wasn't in the office today."

"W—what?"

"I'm sorry, but Mr. Klein wasn't there today. Not at all."

"Of course he was! He always works Saturdays. He was there; you just didn't see him. You must have been late."

"Mrs. Klein, I most assuredly was not late!"

"But you must be mistaken. I know Herman was there. He's always there on Saturday."

"Well, he wasn't this Saturday, Mrs. Klein."

There was a long pause. "Look, Marge, I know Herman was there today, and you're going to tell me where he is. Why are you covering up for him?"

"Mrs. Klein! I resent your implication. I may be Mr. Klein's secretary, but that's all I am. I don't lie for him, and I certainly don't cover up for him. If Mr. Klein didn't come home tonight, I would suggest that you are probably more familiar with the reasons for that—and his likely whereabouts—than I."

She hung up.

Emily felt outrage. How dare that little twit lie and then hang up. When Herman returned, she'd make sure he fired that woman. It would be part of Herman's penance.

It was now 11:00, well past Herman's bedtime.

He was with someone!

Emily called Sue Schneider, waking her. Sue was reasonable, asking if there'd been a fight. Emily explained that there had, but that was yesterday. Sue asked if Herman carried identification, and Emily assured her that he did. She asked if Herman had ever done this before, and Emily replied no. Sue then assured Emily that she was sure there was nothing to worry about, that Herman was probably spending the night in a hotel to teach Emily a lesson. She advised Emily to go to bed, that Herman would be back in the morning.

Emily didn't believe her. She pulled out the directory again and started calling hotels. Nothing. Next she tried hospitals. Again, nothing.

Then she called the police.

John Whitney had the makings of an Excedrin headache. And the day wasn't over yet; it was only 5:00 P.M.

He was pacing back and forth at the red snow site. Joe Grogan, having beaten his bout with the flu—or whatever else had been bothering him—was there too, along with Chief Ranger Morris Knauer. They were awaiting the arrival of Pierce County Sheriff Hank Bourdelais—who, given these conditions, might take awhile.

John paced. This day was turning into a beaut.

Grogan came over. The little guide, about ten years younger than Whitney, defied the stereotypical image of a guide by having a paunch above his skinny legs. John ignored him. None of it made sense. A poacher? In this weather? Hell, he wouldn't be able to see more than a few feet.

Could it be the poacher had buried his cache of carcasses along with his means of transporting them? Possibly. But why didn't the tracks go down instead of up?

He was stymied; there was nothing to do but wait. It was useless to follow the tracks in these conditions. They'd be lost at treeline, a short distance away.

The radio on his belt crackled. "Whitney, this is Station…" He freed his radio and acknowledged the transmission. He looked at Knauer and Grogan.

"Whitney here. Seirig?"

"Roger, boss. Sheriff got here about ten minutes ago. I'm sending him up to you with George Stephenson."

"Does the sheriff have a camera with him and some plastic bags?"

"Roger."

"Good! Look, get him here ASAP. I don't know how much longer before this red snow disappears. Some of it's pink now. Put him on our ATV and tell Stephenson to move his ass."

"Okay."

"Any news about Boyd yet?"

"Nope. Just checked with Muir. Doesn't look good. But if anyone can get down in these conditions, he can. You know that."

"Yeah. I just wish the sonofabitch was a little less independent."

"Then he wouldn't be Emery Boyd, boss. Hell, you're the same way."

"Don't start, Noah."

"I'd better give you the latest weather report. Just got it."

"Bad news?"

"Not the best. Supposed to continue like this all night and clear up sometime tomorrow. Winds on the summit are a hundred and fifty, and at Muir seventy-five. Temperature on the summit is minus ten. At Muir, plus fifteen."

"Great! I might as well *buy* the bulldozers. Call the highway department. See if you can get me another day."

"Okay, but I don't think it'll work. They don't own them. They belong to the contractor, and he's got a crew."

"Look! Tomorrow's Sunday! Who, besides us, works on a Sunday? Work something out, Goddammit. Pull some strings. Just get us out of having to pay rent."

"Sure thing, boss."

John paused. "One more thing... Send someone up to the ice caves to help Reiter. I don't care who. I just want Maselli out of there. Shit, by now he'll have an orgy going on, and I'll get letters from parents wondering why their daughters are knocked up. Call off-duty guides, if you have to...Yeah, that's a good idea anyway." He looked over at Mo Knauer, who nodded and made a "me too" sign. "Call them all. Mo's going to call in his rangers too. Sure as shooting, somebody's lost. Shit, I thought this was supposed to be summer!"

"Sure doesn't look like it, boss."

"Yeah, well, I'd sure like to have one of those fancy scientists up here—the ones who say the earth's getting warmer."

He signed off, replaced the radio on his belt and stared at Knauer and Grogan, who were watching him warily. He managed a grin. "Are we having fun yet?"

Saturday, July 27

The radio crackled. "Muir to Station and Whitney."

It was Max Brittain. Both John at the red snow site and Seirig at Paradise acknowledged.

"John, I've got great news! Boyd just got in. He's exhausted and sleeping now, but looks okay."

John let out a whoop and Knauer, Grogan, the sheriff and Stephenson looked around.

"That's great, Max! Did he say where he's been and why he didn't notify us sooner?"

"Didn't get much of a chance to talk to him, John. He mumbled something about the Kautz Cleaver."

"What was he doing there?" John was puzzled; he couldn't imagine why Boyd would have been there. Kautz Cleaver was a rarely-climbed ridge of vertical rock bands alternating with loose, steep slopes of pumice and scree. It divided the Kautz and Success Glaciers at altitudes running from eighty-eight hundred to about thirteen thousand feet.

"Don't know, and it looks like we won't find out till he wakes up, which may be late tomorrow by the looks of him. He was pretty far gone, John."

"Okay, Max. Thanks. If he wakes up, let me know. How is it up there?"

"Pretty bad. Can't imagine it can continue like this for very long. The wind's really blowin'. We've got gusts up to a hundred."

"How're the clients and other climbers taking it? Cabin fever?"

"A little. They're okay. We've got some from the public shelter here. It's over capacity. We couldn't let 'em sit outside. We've got enough food for another day, so we'll be okay."

"Good. Don't let anyone outside."

"No problem. Nobody's gonna be that stupid."

A moment later, "John?"

"Yeah, Max."

"Take some advice. Don't come up here to see Boyd. Chances are he'll sleep through the storm anyway, and it's just too bad out."

"Advice noted, Max. We'll see. I'm gonna be tied up down here for a while."

"Any news on Jim?"

"Not yet. Hank's here looking around where it looks like a poacher had a snowmobile buried, but he just got here."

"That's weird."

"No shit."

"Okay. Muir over and out."

Both John and Paradise signed off.

John secured the radio and turned once more to the scene. Sheriff Hank Bourdelais, a heavy-set local boy known more for his enormous eating habits than for his investigative aptitude, had arrived some fifteen minutes ago. Medium tall but wide, Bourdelais had a meaty face and a broken nose. Wearing a light sheriff's jacket, Bourdelais wasn't dressed for this weather; he wore no boots or gloves and occasionally stomped around to warm himself. Since he'd arrived, he'd asked a few questions, snapped some pictures and taken a few samples of the red snow. Some of these samples he put in baggies; for others he'd soaked some hand towels he'd brought along, then put the towels in baggies. Now he was attempting to take measurements of the tracks left by the vehicle and of the inside of the burial cavity.

"Hank," John said, "do you want us to send for some boots and a jacket?"

"Nah," Bourdelais mumbled. "I'm fine."

"Hank, do you really think those measurements are going to be accurate or of any help? I mean, look at the way the new snow has covered the tracks, rounded them off an' all."

Bourdelais stared blankly at Whitney. "Mmmm," he said, and once more bent over his measurements.

Whitney shrugged and walked over to Knauer, some twenty feet away. "Our Columbo here's not too talkative, is he?"

Morris Knauer, chief ranger for more than twenty-five years, just smiled. He was a short, thin, patient man of sixty-two, nearing retirement. His ranger cap was old, seasoned like him. He'd known John from John's first days on the mountain, Donnie and Emery too.

Knauer knew John as a good friend. Many were the nights they sat by the big fireplace in the lodge, swapping stories over brandies—some even true. Mo planned to retire soon and accept the lodge's long-standing invitation to be its resident sage, his principal duty being to tell stories by firelight to tired climbers and fascinated vacationers.

He wondered how long it would take before he went nuts.

Knauer knew there would be many more such nights with John, and he was glad of it. John's wit, his stature, and his temperament—a little crusty and excitable maybe—made him irresistible. And he was honest and forthright, a man of integrity. Knauer was a little puzzled why John had never married, but John never seemed to be lacking for female companionship—when he wanted it. On the few occasions when Knauer had seen John really lose his temper, he'd seen a rage of frightening proportions. Luckily, those occasions were rare.

Knauer was pulled from his reverie by John's voice. "What'd you say, John? I'm sorry. I guess I was drifting away."

"Goddammit, Mo. Nobody's listening to me around here. Not Colombo over there, and not you. Maybe I'll just go up and talk to the marmots."

Knauer laughed. "There's really nothing to do until Hank is finished. Why not calm down and relax? You've been pacing around here for an hour."

"Relax! Easy for you to say. I've got a missing guide, one hell of a storm on my hands, bulldozers I can't get off the mountain, stranded volunteers, no doubt lost tourists somewhere—which, by the way, technically are your responsibility, but you'll dump the rescue efforts on me—and you tell me to relax? Go fuck yourself!"

"Look, John, maybe I can help."

"How? Do you know where Carlton is?"

"No. But I think I can save you that rental bill."

John quieted. "How? If you can, Mo, I'll be forever in your debt."

"You're already forever in my debt."

"Come on, Mo. I don't have the budget for those bulldozers. How can you help?"

"Simple. I'll just tell the highway department I'm commandeering them for rescue efforts. You said yourself there's a strong probability of lost climbers, and you've got stranded volunteers up at the ice caves."

"Yeah, but they're in no danger, except from Maselli."

"Right. But with this snow, you might have to dig them out of the caves, right?"

"Mo, you're a genius! What can I do for you?"

"Stay down here until the storm's over... and take charge of any rescue operations." He laughed. "You're right. Technically, rescue operations are my responsibility, but I don't have your manpower. So it's a good thing I have some bargaining chips."

"You don't need them, you old beaver. All you have to do is ask."

"I don't mean for the rescue operation. No, I need bargaining chips to keep you down here while this storm is raging. I know you, John, and I know you're just itching to go up to Muir. Aren't you?"

"Oh, for chrissakes—"

"Those are my terms. Do I have your word?"

"Yeah, you've got me by the short and curlies." John walked over to the sheriff, who was flapping his arms trying to beat heat into his bulbous body.

"Well, what do you think, Hank?"

Bourdelais stared at him. "Looks like someone buried a snow-mobile and took it out."

Everyone stood waiting for something more.

John threw up his hands. "No shit, Columbo! Hell, I could tell you that! Don't you have anything else?"

John felt someone's hand on his arm, looked around and saw Mo Knauer giving him a reproachful eye. "Mo, we've been standing around here waiting for Hank's results, and now he tells us what we already know."

John turned back to Bourdelais. "Look, I'm sorry, Hank. Mo's right. I'm just impatient. I want to hear what you've got."

Bourdelais patted Whitney on the shoulder. "These things take time. I can't tell you much. I don't know much. This isn't really my beat; it's the FBI's. I responded because they're up in Seattle. So I'll have to work with them on this. I'll send the samples over to Olympia, to the lab, unless the feds want them sent to Quantico. Do you know Carlton's blood type?"

"It's in our files. I'll have someone get it. Don't you have anything else?"

"Well, I found a torn piece of parka, a white one. Looks like it was torn off a pocket."

Whitney's eyebrows shot up. "Where? Let me see it."

Bourdelais dug into his pocket and pulled out a baggie. He held it in front of John's eyes. "Almost missed it. Found it under some snow where most of the blood is."

John and Mo squinted at the material in the baggie and looked at each other. "That's Gore-Tex," John said. "Parka material. Can you get anything from it?"

Bourdelais shrugged. "Dunno. We'll see what the lab says. If there are some epithelial cells or arm hairs on the inside part, we may be able to get DNA."

Mo nodded. "Well, that's consistent with a poacher. He'd want to blend in as much as possible, and we know Carlton wasn't wearing white."

"I'm going to need Carlton's hairbrush too, for DNA."

"No problem," John said.

Bourdelais rubbed his hands together, opened his jacket and thrust them into his armpits. "It's a snowmobile, all right, but with the fresh snow filling in the tracks, I doubt we can get you the make or year. Need untouched tracks for that." He sniffed. "I agree with Mo. I'd say it was a poacher."

John shook his head. "But that doesn't make sense. How could he hunt in this weather?"

"I think he was clearing out his cache."

"But the tracks go up the mountain, not down!"

"I know, John, and that's troubling. If Carlton caught him, he could have been worried about running into others too. Maybe he went up for a ways until he could find a better escape. I'd like to follow these tracks a little ways and see if they turn back around."

John waved a big hand. "Be my guest, but take Stephenson here with you so you don't get lost or freeze to death. I'm betting you'll be back in forty-five minutes. Soon as you get to treeline, those tracks'll vanish."

"Maybe. Come on, George, let's go take a gander."

John watched as the two trudged up mountain through the deepening snow. "Hank'll be lucky if he can find the fuckin' mountain."

Grogan laughed. "Come on, John. Let's go back to the Guide Service Shack."

Whitney nodded.

Knauer followed Grogan and Whitney. On his third step, something caught his eye. He bent over and picked up a torn piece of yellow waterproof material kicked up by a boot. He looked at it quizzically, then called ahead, "Hey, John. What color parka was Carlton wearing?"

"Yellow. Why?"

Jenny Larson's Dorothy Stratton good looks were devoid of makeup. She sat in her apartment reading a tabloid-like article by her favorite journalist, G. Sherwood Preston, a local reporter for the *Post*, and watching the ten o'clock news. Of the two, the article was the more interesting, something about sex and drugs in the heart of City Hall. While the story was short on facts, it was long on innuendo, something Jenny had come to expect from a G. Sherwood Preston article.

When Jenny heard "Rainier" she looked up. She turned up the volume to better hear the news anchor.

"Authorities here are plagued by a number of problems the freak storm has caused. There is a concern for unregistered climbers on the mountain, although all those who have registered have been accounted for. Winds have been reported in excess of a hundred miles per hour, and temperatures are well below freezing. Rescue efforts are next to impossible in these conditions, even if locations can be pinpointed. There was even a report that famed Everest climber and prominent Seattle lawyer Emery Boyd was lost for some hours, although we are now told that Boyd is safe and resting at Camp Muir, high on the mountain.

"The storm is also creating havoc with efforts to investigate the strange disappearance of a guide lower on Rainier, a disappearance which may be linked to a suspected poacher. Park officials worry that the guide may have been harmed trying to apprehend the poacher. For now, visitors leaving the park are subject to a vehicle search.

"On Mt. Rainier, by the fire in Paradise Lodge, this is Brad Duvall reporting for KSEA."

Jenny sat transfixed while a commercial played featuring the Dell dude. She wanted to call someone, but whom? Emery had once taken her to dinner with John Whitney; he seemed nice enough.

Jenny pulled her flannel nightgown tighter and crossed her legs.

"Oh hell," she said, getting up and walking to the phone. She dialed directory assistance, asked for the Rainier Guide Service, and opted for an automatic connection. John Whitney came on the line, and she identified herself.

"If you're calling about Boyd, I don't know much."

Jenny bristled at Whitney's brusqueness, but she kept herself in check. "Is Emery all right, John?"

"I think so. Haven't seen him myself. He's sleeping."

"What happened to him?"

"Well, apparently the dumb bastard got caught in the storm and barely made it back. But he seems okay; no damage done, although when I get hold of him, he's gonna be hurtin' plenty!"

"Why?"

"Because the stupid fool should've seen it coming. Shit, I was gonna have to send a search party for him."

"Oh, I see your point."

"Yeah, well… Look, I don't mean to be a jerk, but I've got problems here. A friend of mine is missing, and there may be others lost that I don't know about yet. I'm sorry to be abrupt, but I gotta go. I'll tell Boyd you called."

Jenny was holding a dead line, her unmade-up face oddly innocent.

TEN

Sunday, July 28

It was 6:30 A.M. Sunday, and Emily Klein had tossed and turned through a restless night.

Where could Herman be? Why was he doing this? Something must have happened to him.

The police had said they wouldn't take a report until Herman was missing for more than twenty-four hours, unless there were signs of foul play.

Emily rolled out of the bed and went downstairs. Fetching the morning paper, she put a pot of coffee on, then looked out the window to confirm that it was another icky day. Turning to the newspaper, she began leafing through it and spotted Emery Boyd's name on the front page of the Regional section. It seemed that Boyd had been lost during a storm on Rainier, but had staggered in somehow and was now resting in good condition.

Herman.

She shoved the paper aside and walked outside. The walkway down to the lake looked dry; so she decided to put some coffee in Herman's thermos, take a blanket and finish the paper on the terrace.

But where was the thermos? She searched the kitchen.

Had Herman left it outside?

Walking out the back door, she felt the nippy morning air through her coarse flannel nightgown and her nipples stiffened, accompanied by goose bumps on her arms. She moved a little faster, her chubby legs slapping as they came together. Fifty feet from the terrace, she saw Herman's tackle box and signs of violence that confirmed her worst fears.

"Herrrmannn!"

Jerry MacGregor, the spare-tired sixty-year-old captain of Seattle Central's Homicide Division, was lounging at home watching a Mariners-Yankees away baseball game. Lofton had just hit a homer, his twelfth, to give the Yankees the lead. "Damn Lofton, damn Yankees." MacGregor's words were sour as he sipped his beer. His wife, Betty, sitting in the next room reading, overheard him. "What, dear?"

"Nothing. Just this stupid game."

The phone rang.

MacGregor slumped deeper into his chair. Phone calls at home always meant trouble.

"Are you home, dear?" Betty asked. "I wish you'd get some rest."

I wish I could, MacGregor thought. Another new Green River body had been found. The area had been a depository for dead young women since the '80s, and after a long hiatus, a killer was operating again. Gary Ridgeway had been convicted of four of the killings, but now a new body had shown up, a recent kill. These days, about all he knew about the investigation was what the FBI or King County authorities told him, which wasn't much. He was stressed. His predecessor had lost his job over Green

River, and MacGregor knew he was on the hook now, despite his lack of authority on the case. The press and public were blaming him, and the new body just compounded his frustrations.

But there were other sources for his stress: budget cuts, layoffs and lack of manpower in the face of ever-increasing demands. He knew the brass would like him to retire, but forcing his hand would be age discrimination. Instead, they seemed to want to make him so miserable or sick that he'd quit.

"Dear?" The phone was still ringing.

"What? Oh, sorry. Yeah, I'm here."

Betty picked up, listened, then uttered the expected, "Yes, just a moment please."

"It's that woman again," Betty said.

"Yes, Amy, what is it?" Amy Galler was a new promotion, the most attractive detective on the force. While a little naïve, she had a master's degree and hunches as good as gold. Betty, on the other hand, didn't like him working with someone who looked like a younger Sharon Stone. MacGregor knew Betty would be listening closely to this call.

"Hi, Captain," Galler said. "Sorry to bother you at home, but Charlie suggested I call." "Charlie" was Charlie Scott, her partner, a tough and veteran detective of some fifteen years' experience. MacGregor had teamed Amy with Charlie—who but for a recent court-ordered promotion freeze would have been elevated to a vacant lieutenant's position—in the hopes of loosening Amy up. Charlie was the department's free spirit, tough, but loose and fun to work with. He possessed a lively sense of humor and could be counted on for good results.

"Why didn't Charlie call?" MacGregor said, primarily for Betty's benefit.

"Dunno. Do you want to talk to him?"

"No, that's okay. Well, what have you and wonder-boy got that's so damn important it won't wait until tomorrow? Or did you just sense the Mariners were boring me to tears?"

"We've got a strange one, Captain. We're out on Mercer Island. A prominent downtown tax lawyer's disappeared from his waterfront home, and there are signs of violence. His car's in the garage, but the wife says she wasn't aware it was there."

"Where'd she think he was?"

"Well, she says she thought he was at the office or punishing her for an argument they'd had, but she's hysterical. We can't get much out of her."

"Uh huh. Are the lab boys there?"

"Yep, they've been taking samples, shooting pictures and doing their thing, and we've got some uniforms covering the neighborhood. We've also called for an underwater team and some boats to start search and dragging operations."

"So why are you calling me? Sounds like you're following the book."

"We thought you'd want to know. This guy was a big shot, head of the tax department at a big downtown law firm, Terry, Davis & Sherman. You know them?"

"Well, I know Sam Terry, hell of a lawyer, one of the best. And I've had some run-ins with Emery Boyd. Big shot, crafty bastard, dangerously smart. Beat us up a while back. What's the guy's name?"

"Herman Klein."

MacGregor watched with chagrin as Derek Jeter slid safely into second. "Don't know him."

"Excuse me?"

"I said I don't know him."

"Oh, sorry. Well, it's interesting you mentioned Emery Boyd, sir. The wife's almost incoherent. She's being sedated now, but she keeps rambling on about Emery Boyd, swearing that whatever happened to her husband, Boyd's behind it.

"But it doesn't add up. Today's newspaper says that Boyd was rescued yesterday during that big storm up on Rainier. Seems he's a big mountain climber."

"Well, I wouldn't put anything past Boyd. He's mean and nasty, but a hell of a performer in court. The D.A. tried to get him indicted once for subornation of perjury, but the complaining witness disappeared and Boyd had an iron-clad alibi. Think he was off mountain climbing then too."

MacGregor paused. "Finish up there and meet me first thing tomorrow. This is gonna get a big play downtown, so I'd better be involved."

"Right, Captain."

"Also, call out to Rainier and see what you can find out about Boyd's whereabouts during the critical time period. Do you know yet what that is?"

"No. The wife says they had an argument Friday night and Klein was gone when she got up on Saturday."

"What signs of violence?"

"Evidently, Klein went out into his backyard to fish. His poles are still there, but there's dead bait all around, one's even still on the hook, and the poles are scattered around like they got in the way of a fight. Pretty obvious signs of a struggle."

MacGregor frowned as Jeter stole third. "Say, when you check on Boyd, don't say why you're asking. Let's keep this quiet for the time being."

"Righto, Chief."

"And don't call me 'Chief'! I'm not the chief of police, and I'm no Indian!"

"Sorry."

MacGregor hung up and turned around. From Betty's body language, he guessed it would be a while before he returned to the game.

Amy caught her reflection in the doorway and smoothed her shoulder-length blonde hair. Her azure eyes reflected gray in the dreary weather. She adjusted her blazer to cover the Glock, then straightened the badge hanging from her breast pocket. Satisfied that she looked professional but not unduly threatening, she opened the door and walked into the kitchen. The doctor was there with Sue Schneider, a family friend. "How is she, Doc?"

"Resting, finally."

"When will we be able to talk to her again?"

The doctor frowned. "Tomorrow, maybe Tuesday. She's over-wrought. She'll sleep today and tonight, and we'll just have to see how she is tomorrow. I'll stop by on my way to the hospital. But when you do talk to her, I don't want you upsetting her."

Amy smiled. "Doc, I'll do what I have to do to find out what's going on here, but if it's any consolation to you, I can be a soft touch."

"A cop with compassion?" His smile was tired.

Amy turned to Schneider. "When you're done here, Mrs. Schneider, please come outside. I'd like to get a statement from you."

"Mme? I'm just a friend Emily called when she discovered Herman missing."

"I know. But we need a statement. If you prefer, you can come downtown…."

Schneider shook her head. "No, that's all right. I'd rather do it here. Emily may need me. This is all so awful, so terrifying."

Schneider started to cry as Amy opened the door. As it swung closed, she heard the doctor calming her.

Outside, Amy was bathed by sudden, unexpected sunlight and felt her mood lighten. Walking to the terrace, she saw Charlie talking with the lab director, Arnie Trumball, an unflappable, short and squat twenty-two-year veteran.

"Well, Charlie," Trumball was saying, "I think we've got most of it. We looked over the launch area, but found nothing special. That place gets a lot of traffic, and it's difficult making anything out. We also vacuumed the top of the wall and the part of Procter

Lane that runs along it.

"We should start getting some results by tomorrow evening, although the water samples and vacuum bag contents could take up to a week or longer. Depends on the backlog. Anything else?"

Charlie looked at Amy. "I think they ought to vacuum the pier, what do you think? Maybe somebody hopped the piers."

Trumball groaned.

"Yeah, Charlie, good idea." Amy poked Trumball in the arm. "Come on, Arnie, it's not that bad. Look, you've got us for company."

Trumball laughed. "Baby, I'd keep you company anytime. But I'd rather not do it here."

"This is the only chance you'll get, Arnie," she said. "Didn't you hear I'm lesbo?"

"Honey, if I thought that were true, I'd turn in my balls. There'd be nothing to live for."

ELEVEN

Sunday, July 28

Emery Boyd awoke with a start, unsure for a moment where he was. He'd slept fitfully, dreamed of knives slashing, blood running. The kind of dreams he'd had as a kid, or after he satisfied a blinding rage.

He lay still, his eyes closed, sensing his surroundings as he tracked backwards through his mind. Someone might be watching him. Better to have a clear head before he showed any sign of life. He listened for breathing, didn't hear any. But that didn't mean someone wasn't there. He held his breath, listened more. Nothing but the wind outside.

Where was he? The Muir Guide Service Hut. On a bunk. He didn't move, didn't want to chance a squeak from the chain-link fencing beneath him. He moved a toe, felt nylon. He slid an elbow. More of it. A sleeping bag.

He opened one eye, saw gray stone blocks to his left, a wall of it, more above, sloping upward. Yes. Muir. He remembered. His senses and memory were back. He tensed his muscles, ready for whatever awaited him, to fight if necessary.

He opened the other eye and turned his head.

He was alone.

Unzipping his bag, he rolled out, spying his clothes not far away. He was just ready to reach for them when Max Brittain stuck his scabby face through the door. "Well, hi, sleepy head! How's it feel to be among the living?"

Boyd nodded. "Hi, Max," he said, keeping his voice subdued. He made a point of looking around, as if trying to make sense of his surroundings. "What are you talking about?" He rubbed his eyes. "Sorry... just woke up. Guess I'm still groggy."

"You should be! You had quite a time of it, from the way you looked last night. That was some storm. I can't remember when I've seen that much snow in summer." He paused for a moment as Boyd stared at him. "Boy, Emery, you scared us. When you didn't show up, we figured you'd bought it. John was fit to be tied. He wanted to look for you, but was stuck over at the caves."

Boyd held out his hands, slow-down style. "Where am I, Max? Guide Service Hut?"

"Righto, Em. For a while we thought we'd lost you... um... along with Jim Carlton...."

Emery dragged his head up. "What are you talking about?"

"Jim's missing, Emery. He disappeared in the storm."

"How?" He left the mask on his face. Funny, he'd last projected this look at someone's funeral. It worked in both places...

"Yeah. Well... we don't know for sure. He could be lost, like you were... or... well... we think he was murdered."

Time for concern, realization. "What! Damn it, Max! You're not making any sense. Tell me what happened. Jim's my friend too."

Boyd swung his legs around and leaned forward, as if he might spring. Brittain fell back instinctively, bumping his head. "Easy, big guy. I'm tryin' to tell ya."

Even in the dim light, Brittain could see Boyd's eyes were

fixed on him. "Jim was relieved early Saturday morning. You remember; you saw him here Friday night. Well, Whitney ordered him over to the ice caves, and…uh…he never made it. We don't know what happened. Speculation is he came upon a poacher with a snowmobile. There was a lot of blood and a strip of what looks like Jim's parka."

Boyd offered incredulity. Play it out. "A piece of parka? What kind of shit is that?"

"The blood and parka piece were found near where they think the poacher buried a snowmobile."

"Who's 'they'?"

"Whitney, Knauer, Grogan and Sheriff Bourdelais, maybe some others, I'm not sure. Nobody's seen Jim since. They think he took a route that went right by where the snowmobile was buried."

"Were they able to follow the tracks?"

"No. The tracks led up the mountain and were lost at tree-line."

Brittain took a seat on a cot across from Boyd. "Bourdelais drove the blood and parka strips over to Olympia for testing. He took some of Jim's DNA too."

"Strips? You said 'strip' before."

"Yeah. There was a white strip too. They said it looked like part of a pocket." Boyd made his face a mask of confusion. A sudden realization hit Brittain. "Oh, shit!" he said, rising from the cot. "I'd better radio John, tell him you're awake!"

"Max, how long did I sleep? When did the storm lift?"

"Well, let's see. It's 6:00 P.M. Sunday now, which means you were asleep for approximately twenty-four hours—about what I predicted, considering the state you were in. What the hell were you doing on the Kautz Cleaver? Didn't you see the storm coming?"

"Later, Max. Let me get my bearings first. I'm still kinda fuzzy, and now this about Jim…" Boyd rubbed his eyes again. "I'm sorry I jumped at you. Hope your head's okay."

"Oh, it'll be fine. I can understand why you're a little disori-ented, I mean, after what you went through. I can't wait to hear all about it—when you're ready, of course. You didn't sleep very well. You were tossing and turning." He paused. "Why don't you rest a little more. I'll bring in some food, some Gatorade and some coffee."

Boyd nodded absently. "When did the storm lift?"

"About an hour ago."

"Thanks, Max."

"Sure thing, Emery. Say, why don't I get the radio and bring it in here, so you can call John? He'd probably rather talk to you than me anyway."

"Yeah, I'm sure he'll want to chew me out."

"I think you can count on that." Max rose and walked to the doorway, carefully ducking his head to avoid another bump. He stuck his face inside once more. "Say Emery, uh... Parrish, Douglas, Rochet and Sommers are all up here, Diane Edwards too. I'm sure they'd like to see you, whenever you feel up to it."

Boyd shook his head. "Hold off on sending the group in, will you? I'm not feeling particularly sociable right now." Sociable. Maybe with a knife or choke hold...

"Sure. I'll be right back." Another duck of the head and Brittain was gone.

Boyd checked his extremities for frostbite. He felt no numb-ness or pain, but looked anyway. There was none. He listened to the great steady beat of his heart, his control. He stood up and stretched, began putting on his clothes.

Some minutes later Brittain returned, burdened with packages of freeze-dried beef stew, instant coffee and a six-pack of Gatorade under one arm and a bowl and large pitcher of hot water balanced on the other. A two-way radio was slung over his shoulder. Boyd watched as Brittain placed his awkward load down on the hard floor and unslung the radio. His back to Boyd, he began fixing Boyd's meal. When he finally looked up, he was surprised to see Boyd fully dressed, his parka and pack next to him, the pack closed up and ready to go. "Gee, Emery, aren't you going to stick around? You look like you could use more rest."

Boyd reached over, grabbed the Gatorade, took a long swig, then picked up the radio. "I'm sorry, Max. I'm tired and need sleep—in my own bed. I'll call Whitney now. Stick around and listen if you want."

Still stirring the bowl of stew, Brittain sat down. "Boyd to Whitney, come in please."

They heard static, followed by, "Whitney here. Is that you, Emery?"

"Yeah, just awoke from my beauty sleep. Brittain here tells me you've let the mountain go to pot while I was sleeping. Something about you dinging college girls at the ice caves." Noticing Brittain's panic, Boyd smiled and raised his hand.

"You Goddamned sonofabitch. I've been worried sick about you for almost two days; Carlton's missing and presumed dead; a bunch of pasty-faced, whining college kids are stuck at the ice caves, with Maselli trying to get in every girl's pants; extra equipment charges are staring me in the face…. And you have the fucking gall to start cracking jokes?"

"Easy, John, easy."

"Easy my ass! I'm dead on my feet and in no mood for any crap from you. What the fuck were you doing over at the Kautz Cleaver, and why didn't you come in when you saw the storm?"

"Look, I'm sorry about the crack. It was inappropriate, what with Jim missing. Max told me about it. Look, it's a long story, John. I'll tell you when I come down if you're around, or if not, I'll talk to you tomorrow."

"Down! What do you mean, down? You're staying put until I get there, you bastard! And you'd better have some Goddamn good answers, or I'll hit you with a fucking bill for our search and rescue operations!"

"You didn't conduct any for me, John. Look, I'm tired and I want to go home. And that's what I'm gonna do. So you just better get used to the idea. Now, if you're available, I'll meet you in the bar at Paradise in an hour or so and you can buy me a beer. I'll explain then where I was and what I was doing—and from what I hear about this thing with Jim Carlton, I think you'll find it interesting."

"What do you know about Carlton?"

"Nothing, but I may know something about your poacher."

"What? What do you know?"

"When I get down, John, for God's sake, when I get down."

Silence swallowed the line. Boyd glanced over to see Brittain's reaction to all this, and found him sitting in rapt attention, staring at the radio. Whitney's agitated voice came over the radio again. "Boyd, if you're playing games with me, I swear…."

"I'm not, John. Why don't you go have a drink? Sounds like you could use one." He looked over at the bowl of stew steaming in Brittain's lap. "I'll be down as soon as I've eaten."

"How long will that be?"

"Give me an hour."

"All right. But you'd better show up. I swear —"

"I'll be there, John. Just calm down."

"So, how the fuck are you? Frostbite? Edema?"

"Gee, thanks for asking, John." He switched the radio off.

John Whitney, dressed in a red and black wool shirt and black wool pants, looking every bit the lumberjack, put his radio down and sat back in his chair. *Why had Boyd been out in that storm?* Surely, he'd seen it coming. He would have had plenty of time to get back to Muir. *What had kept him?* These questions had been bothering him more and more ever since he'd heard that Boyd had made it back to Muir, and now there was another one: *What did*

Boyd know about Carlton?

Years of mountaineering told John something wasn't adding up.

Thoughts muddled, he glanced over at a picture on his wall: his brother Donnie standing tall and triumphant on Rainier's summit, hand-in-hand with fellow Snowball Emery Boyd. "What's going on, Donnie? What don't I understand?"

TWELVE

Sunday, July 28

Boyd entered the crowded Paradise Lodge bar shortly after 7:30 P.M. Tucked discreetly off the connecting hallway between the lobby and the back dormitory area of the Lodge, the bar was known as a place for climbers, guides, groupies and tourists.

The bar was crowded, but the mood was different tonight. Instead of raucous and cheery, loud and bawdy, the room was filled with somber faces and quiet whispers, reflecting collective concern for Jim Carlton's fate.

As Boyd walked in, heads turned and conversation hushed. All eyes were on him as he made his way to the back table where John Whitney sat alone. As Boyd passed the bar, he nodded to Earl the bartender, as much a fixture in the bar as its dark paneling, and he flashed Earl a raised index finger. Earl nodded and opened a chilled Foster's lager before he followed Boyd to the back of the room.

As Boyd approached, Whitney's glacial blue eyes watched him. He sat quietly as Boyd pulled out a chair opposite him and sat. Earl poured Boyd's beer. "Here you go, Mr. Boyd," Earl said. "On the house. Good to have ya back. We was real worried."

"Thanks, Earl. You always know just what I need."

"Yeah, well, you want another, just raise your bottle." Earl looked nervously at Whitney. "You need anything, Mr. Whitney?"

John said nothing, his eyes still on Boyd. Earl returned to the bar.

Boyd took a long swig of beer. The rich, smooth taste of the great Australian lager was refreshing. Raising the bottle over his head, he didn't check to see if his gesture was seen. Earl would see him; Earl always did.

Earl came back with another. "Also on the house, Mr. Boyd. No way you're buying tonight."

"Thanks, Earl. Obviously, you're happier to see me than my friend here."

Earl made no comment as he turned and walked back to the bar.

They sat in silence, Whitney staring at the half-full bottle he was slowly rolling between thick hands, while Boyd looked around the room. The second beer, he drank more slowly. The first had been exquisite, he thought, almost on a par with a good sexual experience. Well, not really. Boyd liked sex rough, brutal. Not that he couldn't take care of Jenny Larson's needs if he felt like it.

Whitney sipped his beer.

"Well, John, you've been busy."

Whitney nodded. "Last two days."

"I was a little busy myself."

Whitney sat his bottle down. "What the fuck were you doing out on the Kautz, and why didn't you come in when you saw the storm coming? What's wrong with you, Boyd? Looking for a little publicity?"

Boyd watched him. So in command, a showboat. Maybe someday he'd slash John's throat, and as his blood drained away, tell him about Donnie.

Earl made his third uncomfortable trip, this time with two

beers, one for each man. "You two okay?"

Earl turned back to the bar. He shrugged; some had heard Whitney's rising voice.

"I'll ignore the publicity crack, John. You look a little out of sorts. Guess after what you've been through, that's to be expected."

"What I want to know is where were you, and what the fuck were you doing!"

Boyd leaned over and signaled Whitney to do the same. "I was following a man on a snowmobile."

John's eyes flared. "You were what!"

"Easy, John. The only others who need to be in on this conversation are the authorities."

Boyd glanced around at the watching eyes.

It was just after 11:45 when Boyd finally arrived home. Although John, the sheriff and FBI Special Agent Richard Haskins—when they'd finally arrived at ten o'clock—had pumped him for information, Boyd was able to leave only after promising to be available for more questioning the next day. They'd come by his house at noon.

Once home, he threw his gear onto the garage floor, cursing as he watched his pack roll away. He threw his axe down so hard it gouged the cement floor before skidding beneath a work bench.

It took him ten minutes to stow his gear behind the great steel attic door. When he was finished, he trudged into his house, ran some water in his oversized Jacuzzi and poured in some Vita-Bath. As suds began to build, he stripped off his clothes and climbed into the tub.

He lay there in the warm quiet, easing his muscles, playing it all back. Why had it gone so wrong?

They'd discovered some blood, some snowmobile tracks and

some material from Carlton's parka. What were the odds of that?

But so what? There was no connection to him; he'd been seen at Muir the night before. And the storm had covered his tracks. There was no way to trace the snowmobile to him, and it would never be found.

But they'd also found the torn piece off his white parka. What if an arm hair was attached to it? He swirled his arms in the water. They'd need more than a hair to nail DNA; they'd need the follicle too. The odds were in his favor, but still, he was exposed. Well, he'd know soon enough. Besides, he could say he'd lost the parka in the lodge some time ago. That would work. Everyone at Muir had seen him in his red parka.

Bubbles swirled around him, colorful, popping and breaking.

What about Whitney? Haskins and the sheriff weren't problems. They'd seemed satisfied with his story. But Whitney hadn't. Throughout their meeting, Whitney had stared at him. How could a snowmobile get so high in that terrain, and how did one follow it in a fucking blizzard?

He regretted his story now. Maybe if he'd had more time or hadn't been so tired, he'd have come up with a better one. Maybe he shouldn't have mentioned the snowmobile at all. But then how could he explain why he hadn't come in? Whitney was right: he would have seen the storm coming.

Haskins and Bourdelais seemed convinced that the snowmobiler hadn't made it. That high and on the steep terrain around the Kautz Cleaver, they thought he went off over an ice cliff or into a crevasse. He'd agreed with their conclusion, but noticed Whitney shaking his head.

What did that mean?

John would bear watching. Maybe that slash across the throat wasn't too far away. "Let me tell you about Donnie, John..."

Bubbles burst in the silence.

John Whitney was still in the bar, sipping his last beer as Earl was preparing to close. Bourdelais and Haskins were gone. The room was empty except for him and Earl. John was working on a serious drunk, his first in a long while. Usually, he wasn't much of a drinker—maybe a little wine with dinner, maybe an occasional beer. But he was troubled. Emery Boyd was lying: lying to the authorities, lying to him.

Why?

That was the question nagging him. That question and losing Jim Carlton were why he was drinking.

John had no doubt that Boyd had seen the storm coming. He couldn't miss it if he was where he claimed he was. But was he? And why did he wait so long to come in? Tracking the snowmobile? How does a snowmobile get over to the Kautz Cleaver? And why? How could Boyd track it through a howling blizzard? How does one *see* it in whiteout conditions?

So where was Boyd before the storm?

And why did he make up this story?

THIRTEEN

Monday, July 29

The next morning at 8:00, Charlie Scott and Amy Galler were waiting outside Captain Jerry MacGregor's office. Both looked tired and drawn. Amy had stayed up late preparing her report and reviewing those prepared by others. Charlie had done the same.

At 8:15, Charlie asked MacGregor's secretary, the formidable Irena Fiorella, if the boss had called in.

"He'll be here when he gets here, Charlie."

"No shit."

Irena returned to her paperwork.

Jerry MacGregor walked in. MacGregor was big, a beefy man. He looked like what he was—a veteran cop. His trademark cigar jutted from his mouth. He went straight into his office, barely looking at them.   Amy and Charlie swapped curious glances.

MacGregor's voice came through the open doorway. "Get in here."

MacGregor was huddled over his desk, frowning, looking over some papers. They seated themselves.

"Give me your written reports and then tell me what you've

found out. Wait, before you start..." He turned to Amy. "Galler, the next time Charlie here tells you to call me at home, you let him do it. My wife thinks you and I are sweeties, and I don't need the aggravation. Okay?"

Amy nodded but didn't smile. She and Charlie passed him their written reports.

MacGregor paused. "Well?"

"We don't have much yet, Captain," Charlie said. "We've got a disappearance of a prominent tax lawyer in an important law firm...."

"Tell me something I don't know. And speed it up. I'm meeting with the chief in two hours. He wants recommendations on trimming our overhead further and wants to hear about this too."

"Well, Captain, the press showed up yesterday, just as we were leaving—that nosy reporter for the *Post*, G. Sherwood Preston, and a camera crew. Have you seen the paper yet?"

"No. Our delivery boy has the flu or something. His substitute's missed our house two days in a row. What's in there?"

"The usual hype. Some pictures of the house... and... uh... us...."

"Why the hell did you let him do that?"

"Well sir, we didn't see them shoot it. We were tryin' to put off Preston—you know, get him out of there—and they must have shot us."

"What's that slime-ball say?"

"Well, we just told him Herman Klein's name, nothing else. But it seems he's talked to the neighbors. He's reporting that there was a big fight Friday night and that we suspect that Mrs. Klein hit her husband with something and dumped him in the lake. He claims the fight was over another woman."

"Where'd he get that?"

"Most probably from the neighbors. Their statements are in our reports. If they told him what they told us, Preston is making up this other woman crap."

MacGregor's meaty hands shook the reports. "Double check the neighbors again, and don't talk to that sonofabitch unless I personally approve it."

"Yes sir," Charlie said. Amy nodded.

"Now, what do you know?"

Charlie reviewed what was in the reports about the fight Friday night, concluding with, "That's the last time anyone heard of him. Wife claims he gets up early on the weekends to fish— they live on Mercer Island, west side, on the water. As Amy told you yesterday, we found some signs of violence. Looks like there was a fight of some sort down by the lake. Arnie's trying to tell us when."

"What else?"

"Above the terrace, there's a divot on the lawn, maybe from a heavy shoe or boot. And the lab found some rubber scrapes on the top of the wall, where someone probably climbed over. They took samples and vacuumed the wall, sir, along with the pier, the terrace and the grass. Won't have the results for a while though."

MacGregor's eyes stayed on Scott.

"There's a public landing next door. It's possible our perp parked there, hopped the wall and kidnapped Klein, but we don't know. The scrapes could have been made anytime…by anyone. Maybe the lab can give us more."

"What else?"

"Well, the diving and dragging teams are still at it, but they haven't found anything yet. The place is sort of on a point, so current is a factor. Means a wider search. Same for the thermos, if it exists…"

"What thermos?"

"Well, the wife says she couldn't find the thermos. Figured her husband left it outside on Saturday, so she went out to get it. Klein's coffee cup was there, but no thermos."

"What kind of thermos?"

"We don't know. Boss, the wife was bonkers, then a doctor sedated her. We were lucky to get anything out of her. She was apologizing for how she'd treated her husband and ranting and raving about this Boyd fellow and the missing thermos. Could be that it got knocked into the water during the tussle, or maybe it was used to whack him."

"How long are you gonna keep the dive crew on? No overtime, Charlie. Shit, chief sees that, he'll lay me off."

"A couple more days, or until we find something. I don't think the guy's comin' back. His car was in the garage, although the wife says she didn't know it. I don't buy it."

MacGregor frowned, examined his cigar and then stuck it back in his mouth. "Why not? Did you ask her about it?"

"Yes sir," Amy said. "She says she didn't look."

MacGregor nodded. "What else did she say?"

"Well," Amy answered, "she rambled. Mostly, she was wailing that she should have been better to Klein; she shouldn't have punished him; that it was all her fault; how she just knew he was dead…."

"Did she say how she knew?"

"That's when she started yammering about Boyd. But there was something funny about that…."

"Funny how?"

"She knew Boyd was on Rainier; she'd read the newspaper. But she still claimed Boyd was responsible."

"Did she say how she knew?"

"Something about how Boyd must have found out about some file. But that's when the doctor sedated her and wouldn't let us talk to her any more."

MacGregor stared at the reports. "This friend of hers, did you talk to her?"

"Yes. She wasn't much help. Said Mrs. Klein had been rambling on about the thermos, Boyd… and something else that's kind of curious…"

"What?"

"Well, Mrs. Klein was also saying something about Mrs. Schneider's husband, a federal judge, I believe. Thomas Schneider. But he's dead."

"Yeah, I remember," MacGregor said. "Drove off a cliff in the Cascades. Drunk, if I remember right."

"Well, Mrs. Schneider thought Mrs. Klein was out of her mind too. That's why she called the doctor."

"Did you run Boyd down?" His eyes flicked to Amy.

"Yes sir. I called the guide service at Rainier last night. Talked to the chief guide. He confirmed Boyd's been on the mountain since Friday night. Says they almost lost him in the storm."

"Who did you say was asking?"

"I said I was Boyd's girlfriend."

"Good thinking."

MacGregor sat back, mouthing his cigar back and forth in his cavernous jaws. "Okay. Here's what I want you to do: go over to the law firm and talk to Herman Klein's secretary and to Sam Terry. Find out what Klein was working on, for whom, and if he had any enemies. You know the drill. I'll call over there and tell Terry you're coming. Then try to talk to Mrs. Klein again. Get a picture of Klein and have copies made up for the uniforms on the beat. Also, set up a recorder on the Klein telephone in case it's a kidnapping and there's a ransom demand. Leave a uniform there for a day or two. Clear?"

They nodded. Amy asked, "If you think it's a kidnapping, shouldn't we call the Bureau?"

The office went quiet. Outside, Irena's keyboard clicked under her busy fingers. MacGregor took the cigar from his mouth and stared at it. "Like your badge, Amy?"

She stared at the badge hanging from her belt. "Of course."

"Wanna keep it?"

"Absolutely."

"Then don't try to slough off your job as police officer onto somebody else."

"But —"

"Tell her, Charlie."

Charlie twisted uncomfortably, staring at the floor. "We work the investigations, Amy. No feds, no suits. Not unless it's absolutely necessary. We haul our own freight."

Amy colored. "Sorry."

MacGregor regarded her. "Got it now?"

Amy flared. "Yes, Captain. I've got it. So how many pushups do I do?"

MacGregor pulled the cigar out and rolled it between his fingers. "No pushups. Buy us some coffee sometime." The smile crinkled his eyes. "Don't lose your spunk, Amy. It's good on a cop."

Amy nodded.

"Good. I want to see you two again tomorrow, same time."

MacGregor reached for the phone and buzzed his secretary. As they left, Amy heard him say, "Get me Sam Terry."

Once outside the building, Amy steered Charlie to a coffeehouse down the block, where she ordered a big breakfast of eggs, bacon, toast, hash browns and coffee. Charlie just had coffee.

"Forget the FBI thing, Amy. He's dealing with them on Green River. The Feds don't tell us squat, but MacGregor's still on the hook and he gets all the pressure. It's driving him nuts."

"I wish you'd clued me in before the meeting."

"You're doin' all right. Better that you learn some stuff on your own."

"Thanks a lot."

"You're very welcome." Charlie grinned at her.

FOURTEEN

Monday, July 29

A scowling Sam Terry, dapper as usual in his charcoal-colored three-piece suit, white shirt and red striped tie, paced back and forth in his cavernous office, his arthritic back throbbing. The venerable senior partner wished now he hadn't gone out in the rain and cold on that infernal boat. Maybe his back wouldn't be hurting; maybe he could have prevented Klein's disappearance somehow. It bothered him that he didn't know why Klein had tried to contact him.

He'd returned late last night and been shocked this morning to open his newspaper and see the headline, "PROMINENT ATTORNEY VANISHES!" then the byline of G. Sherwood Preston, with the sub-headline, "Police Suspect Lover's Triangle." He'd dressed hurriedly and come immediately to the office, where no one had any answers. His secretary, Helen Voss, told him Klein had tried to reach him on Thursday, but she'd learned later that Klein had said the matter had resolved itself.

What could have happened to Herman? This wasn't like him. Murder? Lover's triangle? It was hard to conjure a lover's triangle involving Herman, his rumpled suit, his melancholy looks.

He was pleased when Miss Voss interrupted a meeting to pass him a message that Jerry MacGregor was on the line. He took the call, hoping for some answers, but MacGregor didn't know much either—or so he claimed.

Instead, Terry learned that MacGregor was sending over two detectives to talk to him and to Marge Simmons. He agreed, of course, but only on condition that he sit in on all interviews. He had to preserve the firm's client confidences, after all. Predictably, there was some argument over that, but neither man's mind changed. They were both too old to engage in idle threats—and too knowledgeable. MacGregor knew what he could legally demand, and so did Terry. MacGregor ended the conversation by asking for as much cooperation as possible, and Terry agreed.

Hanging up, he summoned Marge Simmons. When she arrived, he was at the window, staring at his reflection while his hands massaged the muscles of his lower back. Tall and thin, he looked distinguished, younger than his seventy-four years. As always, he conveyed a calculated image: quiet authority and confidence.

He heard Marge enter and turned around, welcoming her and asking if she wanted coffee. When she declined, he shut the door and sat opposite her, both of them in front of his desk. As she shifted nervously, crossing and re-crossing her legs, he could see that she had been crying. A faint trail of mascara was on her otherwise chalk-like cheek. He reached over, picked up a box of tissues from the windowsill and placed it on his desk near her.

Marge was forty-ish, a plain Jane type, dressed in a nondescript drab-green blouse and dark skirt, and wore the same forlorn look she'd had for years. He recalled hearing somewhere that she'd had a tough life. He knew she was divorced and childless, but knew nothing of the circumstances.

Leaning forward in his chair, feeling the twinge in his back, he took her hands in his. She didn't resist. He noticed new tears welling up.

"That's all right, Marge," he said softly. "Go ahead. That's why I put the tissues there."

She reached for one, and he waited while she dabbed her eyes and gently wiped her nose. When she'd finished, he said, "Let me tell you first how shocked and saddened I am about all this. I've talked to a captain in the police department, and he tells me they don't have much yet. But they're working on it, and I expect they'll have something soon. In the meantime, we'll just have to hope for the best and pray for Herman and his wife."

She blew her nose, a plaintive honk. "Excuse me."

"You know, we operate as a team around here, and I know you're in some distress. Let me assure you that you have the fullest support of this firm—and me personally. I suggest that, soon as you can, you go home. Take some time off. We won't count it as vacation, but I think under the circumstances, it would be appropriate, don't you?"

"I-I don't know, Mr. Terry. I'm just so upset. I don't believe for a moment what the paper is saying about a lover's triangle. That wasn't Mr. Klein. He was devoted to his wife. I-I don't know what could have happened to him. He seemed all right when I last saw him…"

"And when was that, dear? By the way, the police don't believe that lover's triangle crap either. That sorry excuse for a reporter, Preston, was just making it up."

"Oh, thank goodness. I saw Mr. Klein Thursday. He was supposed to be in Friday afternoon, but he had a tax audit Friday morning for the New Beginnings limited partnership and he never made it back. He called from the IRS offices late Friday, saying it was going badly and that he might not be in. He said he'd see me sometime Saturday. But he never showed up."

She started crying again, and once more Terry motioned toward the tissues. When she'd composed herself, he spoke again. "Marge, you decide. If you need some time off, take it, please."

"Thank you, Mr. Terry. I think I will. But I want to stay if I can be of any help."

"No need for thanks. Like I said, we're a team here, and you're a valuable member. Don't worry, if we need you, we'll contact you."

"Yes sir, I suppose you're right."

"Good. Now, before you leave, I want to tell you that the police are sending some detectives over to talk to some of us. They should be here any minute. I suspect they'll want to talk to you, and I know they want to talk to me. Do you feel up to talking to them?"

She nodded, and fished in her purse. "I'm a mess."

"No. You're fine." He paused. "It's possible you might know something that could be useful to them, although I'm sure nobody here and none of our clients had anything to do with Herman's disappearance. What do you think? Would you prefer to talk to them at some other time?"

"I g-guess I can do it, if you really think I should." She dabbed at her eyes, staring into her compact mirror before putting it away.

"Well, I do think it's better today; it could be helpful to them. Then you can go home and get some rest."

"I'll cooperate, Mr. Terry, but I can't imagine I'll know anything of any help. The first I heard of it was when I opened the paper this morning, just like you, although his wife did call me Saturday night...."

"She did? What did she say?"

"Well, she was upset because it was late and Herman wasn't home. She seemed to think I knew something. I told her he didn't come into the office Saturday, but she didn't believe me. She accused me of covering up for him. She's not a very nice woman, Mr. Terry. Uh...I guess I shouldn't be saying that, should I? I'm sorry. I'm just so upset."

"You should feel free to speak your mind here."

"It's just that I've heard her yelling at him before, and she was nasty to me the night she called, although that wasn't the first time." Marge stared at the tissue box.

"I'm sure that's the sort of thing the police will want to know." He moved forward in his seat and held Marge's hands again, feeling the damp of used-up tissues.

"Marge, when you talk to them—the police, I mean—I'd appreciate it if you'd let me be present. There are issues that I'm concerned about...."

Just as Sam Terry was finishing his lecture about the importance of maintaining client confidences, his buzzer rang.

"Mr. Terry?" Helen Voss came on. "I know you didn't want to be disturbed, but there are two police officers asking for you and Ms. Simmons in the lobby. They insisted that I interrupt."

"That's okay, Helen. You did the right thing. Please send them in." He started to hang up, then paused and picked up the receiver. "Helen. Good, you're still there. Please contact Jenny Larson, will you? Have her try to reach Boyd and tell him about Herman Klein."

Sudden shock showed on Terry's face as his secretary related a message. "What! No, I didn't see it. Yesterday's paper?" He slumped over and Marge wondered if he'd topple.

"My God! Is he okay?" He straightened, looking relieved. "Good! Damn! I wish he'd grow up and leave that mountain-man-macho-stuff to people who don't have anything better to do.

"See if Jenny can contact him; I don't know what he can do, but I want him to know. And ask her to have him call me."

Hanging up, he looked at Marge and shook his head. "Boyd was rescued in a storm on Rainier. Evidently it was in the paper yesterday." She nodded. "Well, I guess everybody knew but me.

"Look, the police are here. Relax and remember what I told

you. Let me be your guide. If they ask you if I am your attorney, you should say that I am."

She nodded. Her fingers were twisting nervously in her lap. Self-conscious, she shoved the damp wad of tissues into her purse.

Helen Voss opened the door. "This is Detective Sergeant Charles Scott and Detective Amy Galler."

"Thank you, Helen, that'll be all. Please see that we're not disturbed."

Helen Voss left and shut the door, but not without pausing to stare for a moment with some disdain at a stain of what appeared to be egg on Scott's tie.

Terry walked to the door and extended his hand to Amy Galler and Charlie Scott. "Welcome. Captain MacGregor said to expect you. I'm Sam Terry, and this is Marge Simmons, Herman's assistant."

Charlie took the lead. "I guess Captain MacGregor told you why we're here, and you've probably seen the papers. We'd like to talk to each of you privately."

Terry smiled at him. "Yes, he did, Detective. Here, please be seated." He motioned them all over to a large conference table.

As they were being seated, Amy took the opportunity to take in Terry's elegant and spacious corner office. "Plush" was the only word which seemed to fit the combination of the expansive windows, the mahogany paneling, the oversized wooden conference table and chrome swivel chairs, the antiques and the two oriental rugs overlaying a parquet floor. And the view! The gray waters of Elliot Bay lay before her. Above it, she could just make out the base of the Olympics before their peaks were lost in the massing clouds.

"Ms. Simmons here has asked me to serve as her attorney in this matter and…"

"Oh?" interrupted Charlie. "Does she need one?"

"Detective Scott," Terry said, "why Ms. Simmons may have

asked me to act as her attorney is of no concern to you. I'm sure you understand that a law firm must be guarded about the confidential matters of its clients."

Polished phrases, well seasoned, fitting under the circumstances.

"What you mean is that you *asked* her for permission to serve as her attorney."

"Again, Detective Scott, that is none of your business. If you wish to talk to Ms. Simmons, then you'll do so with me present and you'll respect our clients' confidences." He paused for impact. "Otherwise, as much as we'd like to help you, I'll be forced to ask you to leave. Then I'll call Captain MacGregor."

"Are you refusing to let us interview Ms. Simmons separately?"

"As I said, Detective, if you interview Ms. Simmons, I will be present."

"You realize, Mr. Terry, you're flirting with obstruction of a police investigation?"

"Oh, nonsense." The smile was world-weary, used on neophytes and authority figures. "Unlike you, apparently, I am well versed in the law. I know our rights. Ms. Simmons is entitled to have me present wherever you interview her, whether you like it or not.

"Just so you don't get the wrong idea, however," he added, "let me say that we intend to be as cooperative as we can be. Herman Klein is very important to this firm, and we want him found.

"So, let's not play games, Detective Scott. It's wasting everybody's time. Would you like to call Captain MacGregor, or shall we just get on with it?"

"No," Charlie said, trying to save what face he could. "That won't be necessary. Let's give it a try and see how far we get."

"Good!" Terry said. "Then, what questions do you have for my client?"

Charlie opened his mouth, but Terry jumped ahead of him. "I can tell you that my client didn't see Mr. Klein after Thursday. On Friday, he was at an audit at the IRS downtown offices; he called Ms. Simmons from there and told her he would see her Saturday. We are not at liberty to tell you the name of the client or the substance of the audit, but I'm confident that you can get that information from the IRS, if you feel it is necessary.

"Late Saturday night, Ms. Simmons received a call from Herman's wife as to his whereabouts. Mrs. Klein apparently didn't believe that Ms. Simmons didn't know where Mr. Klein was, and was somewhat abusive. But then you probably already know that Mrs. Klein can sometimes be that way." Terry smiled. "She's a bit imperious, isn't she?"

Charlie looked over at Amy, who shrugged, then he turned back to Simmons. "Ms. Simmons, is that true? You didn't see Klein after Thursday?"

"That's right."

"And Klein told you on Friday over the phone that he wasn't coming in, that he'd see you on Saturday?"

"Yes."

"And he never showed up? You didn't talk to him?"

She shook her head.

"How did... er... does Klein get along with his wife?"

Marge looked over at Terry, who nodded. "Well, I really don't know. Mrs. Klein yells at him, if that's what you mean. Um, Mrs. Klein's not a very pleasant woman."

"Do they argue often?"

"They have arguments, frequent ones, though it's usually Mrs. Klein who does the yelling, from what I've seen. Mr. Klein is more... well... mild-mannered."

Terry nodded sagely. "I agree entirely with what Ms. Simmons just said. Herman is mild-mannered; his wife is not. But surely, you don't think Emily Klein had anything to do with this?"

Charlie shrugged. "Did Klein have any entanglements on the

side that you know of?"

"Most assuredly not!" Marge shook her head vigorously.

"Did he have any enemies?"

"Not that I'm aware of. Well... no."

"Ms. Simmons, you hesitated. Of whom were you thinking?"

Terry said, "Marge, if you know something, by all means, please say so—unless of course it involves a confidential client matter."

"Well, I wouldn't call him an enemy, exactly. But I know he's had a rivalry, I guess you could call it, with Emery Boyd for some time."

Amy and Charlie looked at each other. Terry placed a gentle hand on Marge's. "Marge, they aren't enemies. They merely head different departments within the firm."

"That's why I wasn't going to mention it, sir."

"What department does Boyd head?" Charlie asked her.

"Litigation," Terry said. "Our firm's largest."

"Have they had any confrontations lately, Ms. Simmons?"

"Well... I'm not sure."

Terry lightly tapped the table. "Look, let me short circuit this. I can assure you as managing partner, there is no personal animosity between them. None."

"Mr. Terry, we'll get to you in a little while," Amy said. "Please let us talk to Ms. Simmons."

Charlie regarded Amy. The silent message was clear: *Oh, have you decided to participate now?*

Terry looked at Amy but addressed both of them, raising his hands, warding them off. "But I know both of these men; I've worked with them for years."

Amy nodded. "We'll talk with you privately, sir. Right now, we're interviewing Ms. Simmons."

Charlie smiled at Marge, which only made her uncomfortable. "Ms. Simmons?"

"Well, it wasn't really a confrontation... Our firm's partnership meeting is on August 9, and Mr. Klein was planning to make two proposals. One was to divide the Litigation Department into four separate departments, along practice lines. The other was to merge the Tax, Corporate and Probate Departments."

Terry's face whitened, but his words were measured. "Herman never spoke to me about this. Are you sure?"

"Oh yes, Mr. Terry. I have the proposals and supporting briefs at my desk. I finished them on Saturday."

"We'd like a copy of them, please, Mr. Terry," Charlie said.

"Well… uh… I'll have to review them first… to… uh… make sure there is no confidential client material in them."

"Of course. Now, Ms. Simmons, did Boyd know about these proposals?"

"The merger one, he did."

Terry muttered something under his breath. "What, Mr. Terry?" Charlie asked.

"Just a comment to myself." He looked at Charlie. "It's very distressing to learn of such matters, involving department chairmen no less…from a secretary. I had no idea there were such plans."

Charlie studied him. "Mr. Terry, could this be a motive for foul play?"

"Absolutely not!"

"How can you be so certain?"

"Because I know them. I hired them. I appointed them."

Amy turned to Marge Simmons. "Ms. Simmons, how do you know Boyd was aware of that proposal?"

"Because late Thursday, Mr. Klein met with Mr. Boyd. He said Boyd knew about the merger proposal. He accused me of leaking it."

"Had you told anybody?" Amy asked.

"No! Those proposals were confidential. They were not to be released until…" She hesitated, looking timidly up at Terry. "…Mr. Boyd was gone."

Terry examined a well-manicured fingernail.

"I told Mr. Klein that I resented his accusation. Heck, some secret! He'd already told some of the department heads."

"Can you think of anything else, Ms. Simmons?" Charlie asked. "I mean, did Klein say anything else about his conversation with Boyd?"

"Well, I think what triggered the meeting in the first place—although I didn't know it at the time—was that Mr. Klein learned that Mr. Boyd had appointed Dan Cole assistant department chairman."

"He did what!" Terry's words sliced through the conversation, his eyes like cut glass.

"Mr. Terry, I'm so sorry, but he did. Please don't be angry. You should have a memo or e-mail somewhere. Mr. Boyd did that on Thursday. I think Mr. Klein was concerned that Mr. Cole's appointment might somehow block his attempt to have the department split up—although I'm speculating on that."

Terry sat very still. His eyes cleared. "That's all right, Marge. You just leave it to me. I don't want you concerning yourself about such things."

Charlie turned back to Simmons. "Did Mr. Klein say anything about that subject to you?"

"No, not to me. I heard about it from Jenny Larson."

Charlie flashed a quizzical look at Terry, who nodded. "That's Boyd's secretary…er… assistant."

"Did Mr. Klein say anything else about his meeting with Boyd?"

"No. I just knew there was one because Mr. Klein accused me of leaking his proposal."

Amy leaned forward. "Ms. Simmons, can you think of any other enemies that Mr. Klein might have had?"

"No, but I agree with Mr. Terry: I wouldn't call Mr. Boyd an enemy. They were usually polite to each other. They were just rivals, that's all."

Marge looked back to Terry, who sat quite still. "I'm sorry, Mr. Terry. I'm afraid I gave them the wrong impression."

Terry got up with a reassuring smile, moved over and patted Marge on her shoulder. "It's okay, Marge. You've been through a lot. All this about Boyd really doesn't matter anyway, since he's been up on Mount Rainier through all of this." He offered a courtroom-practiced smile to the detectives. "Have you checked that out? Maybe you should. Boyd had nothing to do with Herman's disappearance."

Amy studied Terry. He had handled himself well, but the fatigue was there. Tough to hide when you're in your seventies. "Yes, sir. Mr. Boyd has been up on Mount Rainier since Friday evening."

"Then why all these questions?"

Amy looked at Charlie, saw him frown. "We have to check everything out, sir," she said. "Klein's wife thinks Boyd was involved."

"I'm sure you're aware of what she's like. She's unstable."

"Maybe. But sometimes if there's a motive, there's a way."

Promptly at noon, Hank Bourdelais and Richard Haskins knocked on Emery Boyd's door, just as John Whitney's car arrived. Boyd opened the door, then waited outside as Whitney strode up the walkway. "Boy, you look like death warmed over," Boyd said, smiling.

John grunted. "Got any coffee?"

Boyd led the three men to his spacious living room and offered them seats. "Wow!" Haskins said, looking around at the luxurious accommodations and spectacular mountain views. "If I lived here, I'd never leave."

Boyd ignored him. "John here needs some coffee. Maybe a transfusion, as bad as he looks. Can I get you anything?"

Haskins shook his head. "No thanks. We won't be long."

Boyd got John's coffee as Haskins walked around the room. "Can you believe this place?"

"Used to be a hunting lodge," Bourdelais said, "then got fixed up. But Boyd's not here that much. He keeps a suite in Seattle."

Boyd handed a large mug to Whitney, then turned to Haskins. "Well, what do you want to talk about?"

"We just wanted to see if you remembered anything else, now that you're rested up."

Boyd rubbed his bristled chin. "No. I think I told you everything I know. It was a blizzard, so I couldn't see much. I suspect you're right that the snowmobile went over the ice cliffs and is buried, or was swallowed by a crevasse. To be up there, the guy had to be lost. As hard as it was for me to get back, I don't see how he could have survived." He watched Whitney drink his coffee. Whitney avoided eye contact.

Haskins nodded. "Now, just where were you when you first saw it?"

"Difficult to say. I'd been over west of Gibraltar and was moving east and down a bit, heading toward Muir. I was having a hard time making my way. I may even have missed Muir and been east a little. I heard an engine and saw a snowmobile moving slowly. It was heading west. So I followed it as long as I could."

Haskins said, "And you think you lost it somewhere around the Kautz?"

"That'd be my best guess, but I could be wrong."

Bourdelais asked, "And you didn't see anybody else? Didn't see anything on the snowmobile?"

"Nope. Conditions were really bad." Boyd paused. "Funny thing, though..." He was staring at Whitney, who sipped and looked up.

"What?" asked Haskins.

"Nothing from Jim's avalanche beeper?" Boyd's mouth curled. *Wanna know what happened to Donnie's, John?*

Haskins and Bourdelais turned to Whitney. He shook his head. "No. Could be he's in too deep or it may have been disabled. Or it could be the batteries. Seems we got a bad batch."

Haskins nodded to Bourdelais and both rose. "Well, that takes care of it." He handed Boyd his card and asked him to call either him or Bourdelais if he remembered anything else. Whitney didn't move.

"John, you coming?" Bourdelais asked.

"No." He sipped his coffee.

Bourdelais shrugged, and Boyd led them both over to the door. When they'd left, he closed the door and returned to where Whitney was seated, sitting opposite him. "What's eating you, John?"

"What are you up to, Emery?"

"What do you mean?"

"You and I both know you gave them a load of shit. You weren't following any snowmobile. Not that high; not over that terrain. You wouldn't have been able to see one or hear one in those conditions, and no snowmobile could have made it as far as the Kautz."

"Well, John, I'm surprised. If you don't believe me, why didn't you challenge me in front of the gendarmes?"

"Because I don't know what you're up to. I know you're lying, but I don't know why."

"That's pretty harsh. Why would I lie to you?"

"That's what's bothering me. What were you doing all those hours?"

"Just what I said. I went over to the west side of Gibraltar, saw the storm coming, waited too long and had a difficult time getting back. Then I saw the snowmobile...."

"Bullshit! You might fool Haskins and Bourdelais with that crap, but you're not fooling me."

"Well, what do you think I was doing?"

"I don't know. You have a snowmobile, don't you?"

"Surely, you don't think I had anything to do with Jim's disappearance? He was my friend too, John." Stiffened fingertips, leaning forward. *Crush his trachea. Watch him drown in his own blood. Let me tell you about Donnie....*

Whitney got up and walked over to the interior garage door. Boyd rose with him, his fingers flexing, then becoming rigid. Whitney opened the door, then shut it again when he saw Boyd's snowmobile.

"Well, thanks for that, John. Thanks a lot." Boyd's eyes flashed for a moment, then his shoulders slumped. "And after all we've been through..."

"Look. I'm sorry," John said, placing his cup on a counter. "But I had to check." His eyes met Boyd's as he passed him. "You're right: Jim was your friend too. I don't believe you had anything to do with his disappearance. But your story is still bullshit, and I don't know why you're sticking to it."

"Maybe your hangover is affecting your judgment, John," Boyd said to Whitney's back. "Go home and rest."

Whitney turned as he opened the door. "Will you be around tomorrow? I'll want to talk to you again."

"No. I got a call just before you arrived. One of my partners disappeared Saturday. I have to go back."

Whitney stared at him, then shook his head. "A law partner disappeared." A moment later, "Some woman called for you Sunday. Are you going to her?"

"Who? Jenny?"

"No. She called too, though. I didn't know this one, and she didn't leave her name. Said she was your girlfriend."

"What?"

"Just what I said."

FIFTEEN

Tuesday, July 30

At 8:00 A.M., Charlie Scott and Amy Galler were outside MacGregor's office.

Ten minutes later, Jerry MacGregor arrived, nodding to his two detectives. Amy wondered if it was the same unlit cigar from yesterday. He waited until they were seated. "Found Klein yet?"

"No sir," Amy said.

" 'No sir,' she says. Seen the paper today?"

"Yes."

"That little worm Preston is claiming Klein's secretary is the 'other woman' in a Klein love triangle. Where'd he get that?"

Charlie shrugged. "He must have talked to her last night, and she must have told him that Emily Klein called her Saturday night wondering where Klein was."

"He describes Simmons as a babe. Is that true?"

"Hardly."

"Is he right about Emily Klein being 'a vengeful, mean-spirited, butch dominatrix'?"

Amy laughed. "You know the rag he writes for, Captain.

That's hype."

"Then why is he telling me all this—in the paper no less— and you two aren't?"

"Sir, there's nothing to this Simmons stuff. You know how Preston is: he takes a grain and builds a wheat field. It's all made up."

MacGregor leaned back in his chair. "Damn shame."

They listened to the clacking keyboard in the outer office.

"Well… I just left the chief…." He fixed his two detectives with a hard stare. "The mayor knows Herman Klein, knows Sam Terry and Emery Boyd too—real well. Thinks they're wonderful people. We've got to find Klein fast."

He let that comment settle; then with a grimace, he crushed his cigar and slammed it down on his desk. "And then in the next breath, the sonofabitch tells me to start thinking about more layoffs! So, what's Klein's wife got to say?"

"We weren't able to talk to her. Doctor's orders. She was still under heavy sedation late yesterday. Probably can today."

MacGregor swept the remnants of his mashed cigar into the wastebasket. "Better get on it."

"Yes, sir," Amy said.

He turned to Charlie. "Okay. Brief me on yesterday. Terry called. He wasn't pleased with the interview, especially the questions about Boyd and Klein. He called the chief and the mayor too. The chief ordered me to tell you two to cool it, that there's nothing there. But I want to hear your report."

Charlie covered their interviews at the law office, reading and flipping pages in his notebook.

"Doesn't sound like much," MacGregor said, when Charlie finished. "And Boyd's got an alibi. Just to be thorough, go over this Boyd thing with Mrs. Klein anyway."

Charlie nodded.

"So, there's Klein's wife. What else you got?"

"Well, we want to interview Terry, some of the other department chairmen and some of the office staff." Charlie waited, but MacGregor had no comment. "I expect Terry will insist on being present for all interviews, like he did with Simmons."

"Are you gonna talk to Boyd?"

"If he's around."

"Hold off. That'll just stir up Terry again, and he'll start phoning people I don't wanna hear from."

Charlie nodded, pocketing his notebook. "Okay. Then, we need to check with the IRS about Friday's audit...."

"So, as of now, you're telling me you've got squat."

"So far. We don't have the lab results back yet. My money's on the wife, especially with the fight the night before. I think it was murder."

"Go on."

"The dragging and diving operation is spreading out. Trouble is, what with Klein living on the point, it's damn tough to gauge where the body could be."

"When's he likely to float?"

"Hard to say. Water's cold, and of course Lake Washington is fresh water, and we don't know if anything was in his stomach. He was sorta thin, so it could take a while."

"So, I've got nothing to tell the chief or the mayor except that the dragging operation—expensive as that is—is likely to go on forever?"

"Guess so, Captain."

"We can't run that crew forever. The cost will kill us. You've got two days."

Charlie said nothing.

"Amy? What about this thermos?"

"Nothing yet, Captain. We don't know what Mrs. Klein meant."

He sat back, fingered a new cigar, slid its band off. "Okay. I've asked Randall Barts to look into Klein's finances. See if there's anything weird there. He should have something by tomorrow." Barts was the department's accounting attack dog, a shy, mole-ish man of about forty.

"As for Preston, I don't want you two talking to him. That's what I get paid for."

The two detectives stood up.

"One straw you can clutch at: you'll have some lab results today by five o'clock."

At ten o'clock, after a dreary breakfast during which neither detective spoke much, just sat there sipping coffee, Amy and Charlie left to interview Emily Klein. As they were leaving the diner, they were hailed from behind by a lurking, smirking G. Sherwood Preston. The rail-thin, red-haired reporter closed with them. "Don't give him shit," Charlie said under his breath.

"Just where are Jack and Jill off to?" Preston smiled his commiserating smile, the one he used in funeral homes and hospitals.

"Beat it, snoop. We've got nothin' to say to you." Charlie stared him down.

"Aw, c'mon, Charlie. Still smartin' over that picture? I thought you two looked pretty good standing there with big shit-eating grins on your faces."

"A well-known tax lawyer disappears, and you show us grinning. Well, piss off."

"What if I have something to trade?"

"Like what? Pictures of Marge Simmons in a terrycloth robe? If you had anything, you'd have put it in your rag. You don't have squat. That Simmons stuff is crap and you know it."

"Well, it's selling papers, Charlie." He flipped open his notebook, pencil scratching. "And you guys don't have anything. That'll look good tomorrow."

Charlie moved a step closer, then checked himself. He waved

Preston off. "Print what you want."

"I will. But you'd better smoke something out soon, Charlie, or I'll make you look like fools. Nothing like reporting the truth, is there?"

Amy held Charlie back. "Cool it, Charlie. MacGregor said he'd handle this snake. Hit Preston and you're tomorrow's headline."

Amy turned to Preston. "Lay off. We're working on it; we get lab results today."

Charlie's head snapped toward Amy, his face showing shock. "Shut up, Amy! Don't talk to this asshole! You'll be all over his yellow sheet."

"We're gonna be anyway, Charlie," Amy said. "Preston can find out with just one phone call. You know how many glory hounds we have in this department."

Preston, natty in his double-breasted blue blazer, his ginger moustache waxed and curling up, flipped his notebook to a clean page. He began scribbling. "Amy? Galler, I presume. The female wonder. 'MacGregor's folly,' someone said. Nice."

Charlie ripped the notebook out of Preston's hands, tore off the cover sheet, wadded it up and threw it on the ground. He tossed the notepad back at Preston, bouncing it off his blazered chest to the sidewalk. He grabbed Amy by the arm. "Let's go."

"He's laughing at us, Charlie. You should have kept your cool."

"Fuck him."

When they were far enough away, Charlie let go of Amy's arm, then pushed her against a wall. He pressed in close. "Do you know what you did? You deliberately violated a direct order from the captain, and you gave that scum-bucket his lead story for tomorrow."

"Get off me, Charlie, or I'll break your arm."

"Do you know where he was going? Did you even think? He was on his way to see MacGregor. He's probably in his office right now. And do you know what he's saying? He's saying you told him we get the lab reports today. Mac will know that information came from us. Then Preston will lead Mac on to make him think we said a lot more, and Mac will then have to give confirmations or denials—which will put more shit in Preston's trough. It'll all be in tomorrow's paper. Mac, the chief and the mayor will all want our hides. Nice play, Amy!"

SIXTEEN

Tuesday, July 30

As they approached the Klein residence, Amy waved to the uniformed policeman sitting in his car, drove through the wrought iron gates and parked. With some tension between them, she and Charlie walked up to the door and knocked. Emily Klein opened the door.

"Mrs. Klein," Amy said. "Detective Scott would like to check something in your backyard, if you don't mind, and while he's doing that, I'd like to talk to you, if you feel up to it."

Emily seemed glad to see them. "I was hoping you'd come by. I feel much better, and my doctor's given me a tranquilizer. He said you'd probably be back today. I'm sorry, do come in. Have you found out anything?"

Amy wondered just how many tranquilizers Emily Klein had taken. She seemed very calm. After getting ripped up by Charlie, a tranquilizer sounded good.

As Charlie moved toward the back of the house, Amy wondered how much damage had been done to their relationship. Emily led Amy to the breakfast table, asking again if there'd been any news. Amy said they were awaiting a lab report and the lake operations were continuing. She noticed a tear on Emily's cheek. "Are you all right?"

Emily nodded. "It's the *Post*," she said. "How can they say such things?"

Amy went to the kitchen sink and got a few sheets from a hanging Brawny roll. Emily Klein took them, dabbed her eyes, and looked dolefully at Amy. "They don't know anything, Mrs. Klein," Amy said softly. "They're just trying to sell papers. The reporter who wrote that article doesn't care whether what he says is accurate, or who he hurts. Maybe it would be better if you didn't read the paper for a while."

Emily dabbed her eyes. Amy gave her a moment to compose herself. "You know," Emily spoke through the paper towel, "usually I'm such a strong person. This isn't like me. Most of the time, I'm very much in control, too much so, Herman says."

Amy saw her wince at the reference to Herman. "Well, it's a common reaction, Mrs. Klein. Don't feel bad about it."

"I'm just so angry... at the *Post*. There's not an iota of truth to what they're saying. There was no other woman, not for my Herman. And I feel so helpless..." Her head sank into her paper towel.

A moment later, she'd composed herself. "You wanted to talk to me?"

"Yes. You were deeply upset Sunday. We need a statement from you, if you feel up to it."

She nodded. "I understand."

"Good. What I'd like to do then, is just sit here and talk. I've got a tape recorder in the car I'd like to bring in. It'll help me make sure that I get everything down right, and it may prevent additional trips back as the investigation progresses—although I can't guarantee that."

"A tape recorder?" Emily's voice shook a little, overriding her medication.

"Yes, ma'am. It's standard procedure. If I take notes, I might not write something the way you said it. Do you object?"

Emily shook her head. "No. I don't have anything to hide."

"Mrs. Klein," Amy said, getting up from the table, "I probably should mention that you don't have to talk to us. We hope you'll cooperate, of course, but you don't have to. We think you may have some information that might help us find out what happened to your husband. You may not even be aware that the information you have could be significant, but we hope you'll be open and frank and tell us what you know."

"Okay. Go get your recorder."

Amy was back and set up in minutes. "Mrs. Klein, tell me about the argument you and your husband had Friday night."

"Oh, well... Herman and I yell at one another all the time. Well... I yell at him anyway. Anyone can tell you that—especially the neighbors. But that particular argument happened to be outside. You see, we were eating outside, taking advantage of some decent weather. It really wasn't a big deal though, our argument, just some raised voices."

"What caused the argument?"

"That's a long story. I suspect you're going to ask me if there is anyone who might want to hurt Herman, and I'd probably have to answer yes. But I can't be sure."

"I'm sorry, I don't understand. Are you talking about Emery Boyd?"

She nodded.

"Mrs. Klein," Amy said, "you'll have to speak up, the recorder can't register a nod."

"Oh, I'm sorry." She stared at the recorder, so foreign in her kitchen. "Yes, he's the one, if he found out what Herman knew.... But I don't see how he could have.... And besides, wasn't he up on Rainier when Herman disappeared? At least that's what someone told me." She paused. "Or did I read that in the newspaper?" She sighed. "Oh, it's all so confusing."

Amy waited, watching the recorder enfold her words for the record.

"Maybe Herman is just trying to scare me. I was pretty rough on him, you know." She paused, reflecting. Her voice softened. "I hope he comes back. I didn't mean those things I said. I was just mad that he'd lied to me."

"Lied to you about what, Mrs. Klein? I'm sorry, but I'm not following you."

"Well, he lied to me about the documents, where they were. He made a slip of the tongue and I found out."

"Mrs. Klein, why don't you start at the beginning and lead me through the story?"

"Well, Herman told me Thursday the documents were in a safe deposit box. But Friday night I found out he'd lied about that; they were sitting on his desk."

"Are you referring to your husband's proposals for the annual partnership meeting?"

"You know about that?"

"Yes, although I haven't seen them yet. You were giving your husband advice about the matter?"

"Oh, yes, Herman had to talk to someone. Who else could he turn to? His information could have sunk the firm."

"How could the proposals sink the law firm?"

"No! Not the proposals! The information Herman had."

Amy wondered if the pills were talking. "What information?"

"Well, that Emery Boyd had something on Judge Schneider. He used it to win a big case—that EAC stockholder suit."

"What!"

Emily flinched, and Amy caught herself. "Are you saying Boyd blackmailed a federal judge?"

"Yes. Herman had proof!"

"I thought the documents you were talking about were your husband's proposals to the partnership," Amy said.

"Oh, no! Those are different. See, Herman was going to

present his evidence to Sam, along with his proposals to change the firm. He was going to force Boyd out of his leadership position and maybe the firm. Then he was going to consolidate three corporate departments, so he'd be Sam's likely successor." She talked to the tape recorder, wanting it right.

"See. He didn't want the information to be made public, or for Boyd to even know about it. He feared Boyd might claim that Herman and Sam had been in on the blackmail, and that could ruin the firm. Herman thought Sam would find some other way to kick Boyd out without a public disclosure."

"I see. Your husband had a secret file that he was going to use against Boyd and get his partnership proposals passed, and this file is what the argument between the two of you was over?"

"Yes. He lied to me about where it was."

"In his office, as opposed to a safe deposit box?"

"Exactly."

"Now, which file are we talking about?"

"Judge Schneider's confession! He wrote it right before he died. Herman found it."

"Have you seen this confession?"

"Well, no. But Herman told me about it."

"Does anyone else know about this confession?"

"Not that I know of."

"And you say it's in your husband's office?"

"It was as of Friday night. In the Schneider estate file under 'Miscellaneous.' That's what we were fighting about."

Amy paused for a moment. "When did Mr. Klein find this confession?"

"Several months ago."

"Why didn't he use it sooner?"

"He was trying to find out what Boyd had on Judge Schneider. Herman is very thorough."

"Did he find anything?"

"No. Just that Boyd probably got whatever information he

used from the bar association investigation before Schneider's confirmation. Boyd was one of the investigators."

"Did Boyd know what your husband had?"

"I don't see how he could have."

"Mrs. Klein, do you believe Emery Boyd had anything to do with your husband's disappearance?"

"Well, at first I was positive that he did. But if he was on that mountain, I guess he couldn't have, could he?"

"Mrs. Klein, when did Judge Schneider die?"

"January 10, 2002. See, Herman was handling the judge's estate. He found the confession when he was cleaning out Schneider's office desk drawers."

"Why didn't your husband go to the FBI?"

"Because it would ruin the firm!"

"Can you think of anyone else who may have wanted to harm your husband?"

She stared at the recorder again. "No."

"During your argument, did you strike your husband?"

"I slapped him. And I guess I threw some plates at him. Oh, wait, I think one of them hit him. At least he yelled as if it had. But he wasn't hurt."

"Are you sure?"

"Of course I'm sure."

"Mrs. Klein, do you have any life insurance on your husband?"

"Well, sure. We each have a policy on the other."

"For how much?"

"A million dollars. Then the firm has some more on Herman. I'm the beneficiary of some of that, I think, and so is the firm, but I don't know the details. You'd have to ask someone there." She paused. "You don't think I did anything to Herman, do you?"

Amy said nothing.

Tears welled up in Emily Klein's eyes again. The Brawny towel dabbed. "You can't believe that! I'd never hurt Herman!"

"You admit you struck him."

"Yes, but he wasn't hurt!" Tears, hot and relentless.

Amy gave her a moment to recompose. "Mrs. Klein, did you tell Mrs. Schneider about this confession?"

"I tried. But she wouldn't believe me. That's why she's not here today. She got mad and left."

"Mrs. Klein, that whole story about Boyd was made up, wasn't it?"

Emily's head snapped up and anger flashed through her red, wet eyes. "No, it's true! It is! I swear it! Herman was going to show Sam the proof before he... he..." Sobs racked her. She raised her hands to ward off Amy like one would an attacker. Amy shut off the recorder and got up from the table.

She walked outside and down to the terrace where Charlie was sitting, looking bored, staring out into the gray water. As she neared, Charlie looked up. "Well, am I free yet?"

Amy smiled and sat next to him, patted his knee. "I owe you an apology. What I said to Preston was dumb, and you were right."

"I've done worse. What happened in there?"

"I've got it on tape; we can listen in the car. I don't know if she's nuts or not, but I'll tell you—I don't think she's responsible for her husband's disappearance."

"Why?"

"Call it a hunch."

"What about the thermos?"

"Damn! I forgot to ask."

Charlie smiled. "Back to it. Finish up and let's get out of here. I can't wait to hear that tape." He looked at the weather. "Plus, it's going to rain again."

Amy headed back up to the house.

Charlie was driving now, the windshield wipers beating a steady rhythm. After adjusting the car's defroster to melt away condensation, he popped the tape into the car's player. As he did so, Amy pulled out her cell phone, pointed to it and beckoned Charlie to pull under an overpass. When the car came to a stop, Amy exited and called Sam Terry.

Terry was in the office and took the call, saying he'd sent the proposals over by messenger. "Just useless garbage," he said. "Didn't stand a chance of passage. Can't understand why Herman wasted his time."

Amy asked about life insurance on Klein. "We have a million on him and he purchased another half million through us for himself and his wife," he responded. "I've decided to postpone the annual meeting. The firm's in turmoil. The meeting would be counterproductive. Look, we need Herman back. Why can't you find him?"

"We're doing the best we can, sir. We'll learn something soon."

"You'd better. I've got friends in high places, you know."

"Yes, sir. I've heard."

By the time Amy returned to the car, Charlie had finished the tape. Amy briefed him on her conversation with Terry and asked him what he thought of the interview.

"Jesus!" he said, as he pulled into traffic. "She's bonkers. I don't believe that bullshit for one minute. Murder's a lot cheaper than divorce. She gets the house, all the investments—I assume Klein stashed away a tidy sum. Plus, she gets at least a million and a half in life insurance." Scott laughed, "It's the classic spousal murder. Either it's a fit of passion or simple 'follow the money.' Either way, it's the wife.

"Besides," Charlie added, "unless something comes up on

that IRS thing, the only person who didn't like Klein is Boyd, and he's clear. Who else has she got to pin it on?

"So she invents this 'confession'—which we'll find doesn't exist—and plans to finger Boyd. But she can't foresee that he's gonna get lost in a mountain storm. She's screwed."

Amy sat in silence as the wipers maintained their steady cadence and a hard rain beat on the roof.

SEVENTEEN

Tuesday, July 30

Amy and Charlie arrived back at headquarters at 2:00 P.M. and found Post-it notes on their chairs. MacGregor wanted them ASAP. They went upstairs, where a suspiciously friendly Irena Fiorella smiled at Charlie. "I wouldn't want to be in your shoes."

"You're not smart enough to pass the detective exams."

From inside MacGregor's office, they heard a growl. "Whenever you have the time…" Amy followed Charlie in. "You know, kiddies," he said as they entered, "my doctor says I have high blood pressure. You two ain't helping."

They sat opposite their boss, waiting.

"Which one of you talked to Preston?"

Charlie stared at his shoes. "I did," Amy said.

"What did you tell him?"

"W-well—"

"Did you tell him we suspected the wife?"

"No, sir. I did not! And I'm not sure I do."

MacGregor's eyes bored into her.

"Sir, you didn't confirm that, did you?" Charlie asked.

"I told you not to talk to him. What part of my order didn't you understand?"

"I didn't say anything intentionally, Captain," Amy said. "I don't remember exactly what I said. Preston was on us for answers, and we weren't giving him any. I think he said our silence was confirmation of something, and that was it. Ask Charlie."

Charlie nodded.

The silence tore at Amy. She was conscious of her badge, recently polished. Maybe she didn't measure up…

"No more mistakes, you hear?" MacGregor said quietly.

"Sorry, sir," Amy said.

"What did you learn from the Klein woman?"

Amy told him about the life insurance, which caused his eyebrows to lift. Then she moved on to the Schneider blackmail confession and Emily's claims that Herman was about to tell Terry. She played the tape.

MacGregor drummed thick fingers on his desk. "Interesting."

"Okay," he said, taking up a cigar. He regarded Amy. "What's your take on it?"

"Well, Captain…" Amy paused, "…I admit her story sounds a little far-fetched, what with Boyd having an alibi. And there is the money thing…"

"But?"

"But we need to check out that Schneider client file."

"How do you propose we do that?"

"I don't know. I think we have to check with the DA. See if we can get a search warrant. We can't just ask Terry for it. And I wouldn't trust him anyway if what Emily says about potential damage to the firm is true."

"And if we do that, it becomes a federal matter, right?"

"Yes, I suppose so."

MacGregor rolled the cigar from one side of his mouth to the other. "How about you, Charlie? Think wife?"

"Yes."

"Look, Captain," Amy said. "We need to check out Boyd's alibi. Mrs. Klein's likely to make noise about Boyd, maybe even talk to Preston, although I doubt that. But she may talk to some other reporter. She really hates Boyd. And apparently, so did Klein. We've gotta check it out."

MacGregor looked interested. "You mean like see if he was really lost in a storm?"

"Exactly."

"Go on, I'm listening."

"Then there are a couple of other things...." Amy looked over at Charlie. "We need follow-up interviews with Mrs. Klein and Marge Simmons, and we need to talk to other law firm personnel."

"You already interviewed Klein and Simmons. What more do you need?"

"Well, if Charlie's real charming..." Amy laughed, but it sounded brittle, "...maybe he can get Marge to take a look at the file and tell us if the confession is there."

"What about Terry?"

"It's her choice if she wants to be represented or not. If Charlie's real sweet... maybe she'll cooperate."

Charlie pulled a face. "What do you want me to do, Amy? Seduce her? Claire wouldn't like that."

"No. Just be kind and understanding."

MacGregor said nothing.

"As for Mrs. Klein, she was on tranquilizers. I want to try again when she's not so medicated. Plus, she said her husband talked to Schneider's clerk and a David Dawson, who investigated Schneider for the confirmation process. I'd like to talk to them."

"What about this thermos?"

"It's missing. That's what drew her outside. She thought maybe her husband left it there." Amy paused. "Then, of course, we need to check out the audit Klein was attending."

MacGregor nodded. "Are you finished, or is there more?"

"That's it for now."

MacGregor eased back in his chair. "Okay. Carry on for now. Let's assemble here at five o'clock, and we'll call Trumball. We'll discuss it further after that."

They rose to leave.

"Amy?" She turned. "You screwed up with Preston, but your tape makes up for it. I like where you're going."

Charlie shook his head. "Typical. She falls in a barrel of shit and comes up smelling like roses."

EIGHTEEN

Tuesday, July 30

At five o'clock they called Arnie Trumball, MacGregor putting him on the speaker phone. "Okay, Arnie, what have you got?"

"Several things, Mac. We've got a trace of type O human blood, Klein's type, on the live-well. It had dried before the rain. We estimate the fish T.O.D. to be between 4:00-7:00 A.M. Saturday. Sorry. We can't get much closer than that."

"What else?"

"For fingerprints, just Klein and his wife."

"What else?"

"On the wall, we found rubber, a hard type—typically found on boots. We also found fabric; looks like wool, the kind you'd find on any of a hundred types of wool pants. Not sweater material, though. This wool was coarse."

"Like on mountaineering pants?" Amy asked.

"Yeah," Trumball said, "could be."

Amy smiled at Charlie.

MacGregor asked, "Anything else?"

"A few synthetic blond hairs, like from a wig."

Amy said, "Where'd you find those?"

"On the terrace and on the wall."

MacGregor asked, "Anything else?"

"Yes. We found some denim fibers in the parking area, near the wall. Found some of the synthetic hair in that area too. Same type we found on the terrace and wall."

"How about lip prints on the cup?"

"Nothing."

Charlie added, "Anything in the divot area?"

"No."

Charlie again. "Anything on the pier?"

"Nope."

Amy asked, "Can you be more specific about the rubber material?"

"Not really. It's a real sturdy type that's pretty common, used on all kinds of boots: hiking, climbing, wading—all the outdoors stuff. Very common."

"Anything else?" McGregor asked.

"Yeah. There was a scratch on the terrace, three feet from the divot, which was positive for metal particles. It could be a knife, or some kind of blade, but it was heavy gauge."

MacGregor kept the questions coming. "No footprints?"

"No. Found a lot of the same wool fibers, though: on the grass, on the wall, on the terrace, and in the launch area where vehicles would be parked."

MacGregor asked, "Anything else? Any other blood?"

"Some on the wall. It was protected from the rain. Type O. Oh, we also found some human cells in the live-well. We're doing DNA on everything we can."

"How long will that take?" McGregor demanded.

"Few days."

Charlie chimed in. "Anything near the water?"

"No, nothing."

MacGregor said, "What happened then?"

"I'd guess somebody struck him with something and either dumped him in the lake or took him over the wall to a waiting car."

MacGregor pushed. "You said the mark on the terrace was from some kind of blade. Why not a stabbing?"

"Not enough blood loss, Mac. But it had a blade. You can tell by the width of the scrape and by its edges. A hammer would have been wider, with edges less angled."

"Don't mountaineers carry large hammers with blades? Could it have been something like that?" Amy suggested.

"An ice axe or maybe an ice hammer? I suppose so. Both are heavy gauge, both have blades—one's just bigger than the other. It's a possibility, certainly not inconsistent. Yeah, it could have been an ice axe. Why, got a suspect?"

"Maybe." Amy sat back in her chair.

Charlie asked, "Find anything more in the landing area?"

"Yeah, more rubber. But hell, half the people walking around the city are wearin' the stuff."

MacGregor added, "Any other trace evidence?"

"Oh, yeah. Shit, almost forgot. We found cotton fibers, looked like camouflage. Found it in the terrace area and also on the wall. Also found a garbage bag tie in the parking area, although you might expect that, considering it's a public landing."

MacGregor said, "Is that it?"

"Yep."

"Thanks, Arnie, I appreciate your help. As always, you're fast and thorough."

"We've been busy. Olympia was jammed up, so we took on their Rainier problem too. But we gave you priority."

"What's going on at Rainier?" MacGregor asked.

"Suspected poacher, somebody missing. That sorta thing."

The conversation over, MacGregor took the mangled cigar he'd been chewing and dropped it into the wastebasket. "I think Amy may be on to something.

"Charlie, I want you to follow up on this Boyd-Schneider thing, all the stuff Amy mentioned before, and with Barts on the financials. Plus, I want you to do the follow-up interviews with the law firm people and talk to the IRS. Then I want you to interview Mrs. Schneider, but go easy on her. I don't want the feds in this thing. Understood?"

Charlie nodded.

"Good. Now, from what Arnie's told us, this appears to be a homicide. Anyone disagree?"

Silence.

"Good. Now let's focus it. Klein was murdered by someone he knew. There's no robbery, and the body was taken away.

"For suspects, we've got the wife and Boyd, so far. Obviously, there are problems with Boyd. And we may have a third, the client in that IRS matter. Charlie, get on that, the sooner the better.

"Now, the visibility on all this, pressure from above, the press, not to mention Sam Terry. It demands an all-out effort. Check out everything and anything. And above all, don't speak to the Goddamn press! Any questions?"

"Captain?" Amy said. "So far you've only said what Charlie's doing. What's my role?"

MacGregor smiled. "You're gonna be on Rainier. Starting tomorrow morning, you'll be finding out just what the hell Boyd's been doing for the last several days."

"Sir?"

"We've got to bust that alibi to get a search warrant on Boyd. And I don't want Boyd to know who you are or what you're doing. I don't want that kinda heat just yet."

Charlie was grinning. "Does makeup freeze?"

NINETEEN

Wednesday, July 31

I-5 traffic was sparse, and Amy was cruising in her Honda Prelude, some light rock on the radio. As she drove she went over the last few hours: returning the Glock to Inventory, checking out a snubbie .38—easier to hide—then selecting an array of holsters. Right now, the snubbie was on her ankle. It was odd driving with the extra weight on her right leg, odder still to be without the familiar press of the Glock under her arm. And the badge and I.D. were now secreted in a pocket in her purse. Naked. Icons gone. Except for the .38, all she had was her cover story.

"Keep going over it, Amy," MacGregor had said. "Add a couple of small intimate and real things, but don't get too cute. Complications will bring you down."

"Got any pictures of nieces or nephews?" Charlie had asked.

The Honda maintained a steady sixty, the sort of driving a bookkeeper and tax advisor would do. She ran her cover story, checking it for detail. "Yeah, a couple of nieces up in Minnesota—they'd like it here, all the water, the outdoor activities, the warmer temperatures..."

As she drove, her senses took in the green forests, black pavement, fast moving gray clouds, and the freshness of wet moss and fir. Somewhere in those dense rainclouds were mountains, big ones. An old song, Tom Jones crooning. She backtracked over her college accounting courses. A lot of it had stayed with her. She glanced at her reflection in the rear-view, running a hand through her hair. No make-up, no hair spray. Just how a bookkeeper and tax advisor for a supermarket chain would look. Rain now drowned out Tom's rich tones. She turned up the volume.

As she entered the park and bought a week's pass, she felt the excitement of her first undercover assignment. *Calm down*, she told herself. *You're a bean-counter now. No assertiveness, no authority.*

The drive through the park was spectacular. The rain forest was dark and dank, the Nisqually River just beyond, wide, strewn with boulders miles from the glacier's mouth. Several times she stopped and stared at the many waterfalls cascading down along the winding road. Several miles in, at the four-thousand-foot level, she came to an opening, a long bridge spanning the monstrous Nisqually Glacier. She looked left and almost drove into the rail. Way up above was the mouth of the glacier. It looked like a lava flow, black, rough, pocked with crevasses, massive. It disappeared into the clouds. She stopped on the other side. There was a sign. The glacier was a mile deep, a mile wide. The bridge, first constructed in 1909, so high above the river, had been washed out twice by glacial flows.

She parked in the crowded Paradise lot and waited for a lull in the rain. Through the windshield she saw the great lodge shimmering a hundred yards ahead. Impressive, even with the rain distortion. And there could be a killer about. She looked around, seeing no hint of a mountain. Just gray.

The rain kept coming. The humidity was building, the windows fogging. She started to sweat. Breathing deep, she pulled her parka around her, grabbed her belongings and made a break for the lodge. She was sopping wet before she reached it.

Check-in was easy, although Amy felt anxious tendering only her driver's license and credit card—no cop I.D. here! The charges would put a dent in her limited credit card; she hoped MacGregor was prompt in approving her expense report.

Amy checked her room out. Rustic, very much so. Vulnerability from a window ten feet from the bed and from flimsy locks. She'd have to rely on the .38, and it would have to be concealed, possibly taped behind the bedside table when she was sleeping. And she needed soda cans for an alarm system. She stood in the sounds of the rain, looking at the grayness outside. The thought came again: *was a murderer lurking?* A cold shiver rippled down her spine. She left her assorted packs and walked back to the lobby. As a detective she would have studied the Paradise layout map intently. Now she moved casually. All the time in the world...

As the rain pounded the timbers, she glanced at her watch. Late afternoon. Plenty of time to explore the lobby, the shops, the bar. Get her face out there, ease into the casual consciousness of the crowd. Insert her presence by osmosis. Instinct had her gravitate to the Guide Service Shack. She made the quick dash in the rain.

"Frank Maselli, at your service." He leered at a dripping-wet Amy Galler. Maselli's eyes had spotted her as soon as she entered the Guide Service Shack.

Amy's reflex was to shoo him away, but she reconsidered. This puppet might dance. She let him talk her into a drink when he was finished at the counter.

While she waited, Amy walked around the Guide Service Shack, scanning the pictures on its pine walls. There were a lot of them, covering a wide expanse of time. Immediately in front of her was a pyramid of captioned pictures of the current guide staff, several individual shots and a group shot including Frank Maselli. Capping the pyramid was a tall, good-looking athletic man identified by a brass plate as John Whitney, Chief Guide and President of Rainier Guide Service, Inc.

Moving down the row, Amy saw guide staff pictures from past years. In a 1970s grouping, she saw the name Emery Boyd. He was one of three gangly lads portrayed in triumph, arms raised and hands joined. The legend read, "The Snowballs," and the other youths were identified as John and Donnie Whitney.

Moving back to the current pictures, Amy couldn't find Donnie Whitney. To her right, she found expedition pictures, many of which showed Boyd and John Whitney, but no Donnie.

As she started to turn, Amy felt a hand on her shoulder and swung around.

"Oops," Maselli said. "Sorry. Didn't mean to startle you. Dried out yet?"

"Do you always sneak up behind people?"

"What'cha thinking about? Me, I hope."

Turning back to the pictures, she pointed. "I'm curious. I see pictures of John Whitney, but only one of Donnie, who I assume is his brother. How come?"

"He disappeared a long time ago. I don't know much about it, and Whitney doesn't talk about it, or if he does, not to me. Whitney's sort of… well… you know… distant. So," he said, shifting gears, "where'd you say you're from?"

"Didn't."

"C'mon, pretty lady," he said, "I don't have much time…"

Amy frowned. "I doubt you need much time."

"Nah, you got me all wrong. Look, it's just after 4:30. I was hoping to sneak out…" He looked around. "Whitney and most of the guides are attending a memorial for a guide who was lost during the storm last week. So we're short-handed. I'm gonna have to work till 5:00. How 'bout you moseying over to the lodge bar and I meet you there?"

"Sorry about the guide," Amy said, then she nodded. "That sounds good. I just checked in. That'll give me time to dry off and change clothes."

A half hour later, dressed in a red sweater over bell-bottom jeans, Amy walked into the dark, cave-like lodge lounge. She carried a small nylon backpack with a handle on top. Tucked within it were notebook, pen and wallet, while her cop accoutrements—I.D. and badge—were zippered into inside compartments.

She'd wanted Maselli to arrive first, so he could pick a table with lots of regulars eager to gossip. Although the bar was crowded, she had no difficulty spotting her mark; Maselli was in the middle of the room, draped over a chair in the center of a throng of people. Drinks, a scattering of wet napkins and peanuts. Mountain-man types and their rowdy ladies were laughing at something Maselli had said. He spotted Amy and beckoned her over.

His left arm clamped around her waist, he asked her name, then presented her to the group. Names flew at Amy as Maselli nuzzled, groped and pulled her onto his lap. Amy pushed off him and pulled up a chair. A woman in a blue parka smiled at her. "Don't let him get to you. He tries that with everybody."

"With men too?" Laughter, quick and easy.

A burly man in his fifties stood at Amy's shoulder. His nametag read "Earl."

"What can I get you?" Earl said.

Amy turned back, saw beer and wine on the table. "Uh. Mineral water and lime?"

Earl nodded and returned to the bar. Maselli frowned. "Thought you wanted a drink."

Amy smiled. "Never been here before. Worried about the altitude. Taking it slow."

The woman in blue smiled at her. "Not a bad idea. Especially with Maselli around." Someone said, "Where you from?"

"Seattle. Got a few days off. Thought I'd try the mountains for a change."

The woman in blue sipped some wine. "Some climbing?"

"I wanted to do some trails…" Amy looked out the window, frowned, "…but now… well… I don't know…"

A short, thin man sitting next to the woman in blue said, "Well, don't worry. The only constant here is the changing weather." Several people nodded.

Charlie answered on the third ring.

"You ought to see this place!" Amy said. "Fifty rustic rooms that make the Holiday Inn look like the Ritz! A bed, a table, a chair, a tiny bathroom. Jeez! The place even has mice!"

"What'd you expect? It's a convenience for the climbers, that's all."

"Well, from the looks of the dining room and the lobby, which are stupendous, I expected there would be some modern conveniences."

"You're spoiled, Amy. Look, I gotta hurry. What did you find out?"

"Give me a sec. Gotta organize my notes." Amy had a pile of them. Once she'd broken the ice, and made it clear to Maselli that he wasn't going to score, she'd found her companions chatty and open. Liquor flowed like glacial water, loosening lips and greasing gossip gears, although Amy stuck to mineral water. Nobody questioned her cover, nobody asked for tax advice. She made many trips to the restroom, scribbling notes in the stalls. If anybody noticed her pattern, nothing was said about it. As the alcohol flowed, others made these trips too.

Amy heard Charlie's impatient breaths. "Okay. Here goes." She rattled off bullet points: bad storm Saturday; mysterious snowmobiler; vehicle cached not far from Paradise; probable poacher; missing, presumed dead guide Jim Carlton; blood, yellow parka strip and white parka piece found near poacher's cache, all sent to lab; location of cache near trail Carlton took; Carlton wore a yellow parka; Boyd seen high on the mountain at 1:00 A.M. Saturday; Boyd lost until late Saturday afternoon, and Boyd's parka color was red.

Charlie chuckled. "What's your hurry? Got a hot date?"

"You said you were in a hurry, and I haven't eaten yet. The restaurant closes soon."

"Ah. So how does all this relate to Boyd?"

"I don't know. I'm keeping my mind open. But Boyd was definitely seen high on the mountain early Saturday morning."

"Great."

"Huh?"

"Then he's clear, right?"

"You said Boyd was a wild goose chase."

"Yeah, well… Marge Simmons just called me. I talked to her earlier today. She's at home. I tried to get her to take a look at the file, but she said she'd have to think it over."

"What did she want?"

"She wants me to come over."

"Great! Give her the personal touch."

"She's all worked up by what Preston is saying about her and Emily Klein. Did you see the paper today? Preston's suggesting now that maybe Marge Simmons and Emily Klein were in cahoots—lovers maybe—trying to get the insurance money."

"I really hate that worm."

"Me too. Anyway, when we got past discussing Preston, Simmons went on and on saying she just can't believe Mrs. Klein had anything to do with Herman's disappearance. She swears they were close, in an odd sort of way."

"What?"

"Yeah. She says they argued, but the fights weren't serious—just bickering. Everybody says Emily Klein is a ball-buster."

"Well, get off your ass and go see Marge. Find out if that file exists. Maybe there's a hole in the alibi."

"What are you talking about?"

"Well, Boyd was seen up on the mountain early Saturday morning, but not again until late Saturday afternoon. What if he was able to get down the mountain, kill Klein, dump the body and return?"

"Look. I don't want to be around when you run that by Mac."

"Hey, just keeping my mind open."

"Well, come home. I think all that fresh mountain air is bad for you."

"What fresh mountain air? So far, all I've seen is rain. No, I'm gonna stick around here. So what else have you learned?"

"Not much. I spent the morning over at the law firm, but didn't really learn anything. Also, I looked at Klein's proposals for the partnership meeting. I'm sure Boyd wouldn't have appreciated Klein's gesture, but he might have been amused by it. Neither Sam Terry nor any of the partners to whom I spoke thought they had any chance. Big deal!"

"Well, there goes that notion."

"Yup. Then, as I said, I went to talk to Simmons. I charmed her a little, and she decided she didn't need Terry present. We talked for a while, then I asked her to look for that Miscellaneous file. I told her we thought some important documents might have been stashed there which had nothing to do with Schneider's estate. I asked her to just look and tell me if anything was there. I plan to have a search warrant drafted up so if she says something's there, we can get it before a judge immediately."

"Good idea. Did she say anything else?"

"Well, there's no question Boyd and Klein didn't care much for each other, but it seems to be petty office politics, no reason to kill somebody.

"Then I looked into this IRS thing. It turned out to be a criminal tax fraud investigation. No one seemed mad at Klein though, except for the general partner, the guy on the hook. But I checked him out. The guy passed out drunk in the bar of the Four Seasons about 10:00 P.M. Friday and slept it off in a room the hotel provided. His car didn't leave the garage all night."

"Nothing but dead-ends."

Charlie paused. "Had another run-in with Preston."

"Charlie, you didn't hurt him?"

"No, but I wanted to. I think that leech must wait for me, stake me out or something. He was wearin' a Goddamn rain suit. His bow tie was soaked and his moustache looked like a clump of seaweed."

"What happened?"

"Oh, I gave him hell about what he's writing. But he doesn't care. He wanted me to confirm that we've narrowed our investigation to the wife and someone at Terry, Davis & Sherman. I told him to fuck off."

"Good. What'd he say?"

"That it wasn't a denial. I split and ran back to tell Mac in case Preston went to see him again."

"How did Mac take it?"

"How do you think? Christ, you'd a thought I turned over our files. Then we went to see the chief…"

"Oh, no."

"Oh, yes! And together, the three of us called the *Post*'s editor-in-chief."

"Shit."

"They argued about the First Amendment and police inefficiency. Of course, nothing got resolved."

"What are you doing tomorrow?"

"Mrs. Klein again, then Sue Schneider. Maybe Dawson and Schneider's clerk."

"Maybe you should check with Arnie, Charlie."

Charlie hesitated. "Aw, shit, Amy. I'm running ragged already. If Boyd's got an alibi, what's the use?"

"There's that time gap... See what Arnie knows."

Charlie grumbled but capitulated. They signed off, agreeing to talk tomorrow at the same time.

Amy looked at her watch: 9:25.

Maybe the dining room was still open.

TWENTY

Wednesday, July 31

The dining room was nearly empty. A few remaining couples were paying their bills or gathering their gear, and the staff appeared to be cashing out.

Amy walked down the three entry stairs, making her way under the high ceilings, the expansive windows, the dangling brass chandeliers and the marble columns and between the rows of red-and-white checked tablecloths.

She walked down one of the room's three long corridors toward the kitchen, her clopping footsteps echoing on the linoleum. As she neared the kitchen door, a young waitress looked up from her station behind a pillar. She pointed Amy to a table. The table was large; it would easily accommodate six. There was only one place setting, but the waitress quickly prepared another as Amy sat down, her back to the kitchen.

"You'll have to order fast, ma'am. The kitchen is ready to close."

Amy scanned the menu, then ordered spaghetti and meatballs. As she waited, she glanced at the map and historical narrative on the placemats. In a moment, the waitress was back with a bottle of Merlot, but before Amy could say anything, she was gone again. Shrugging, Amy poured herself a glass of the wine she hadn't ordered.

Two minutes later, her food arrived. Amy watched the salad, spaghetti, rolls and cheese being placed on the table and nodded her thanks. As the waitress disappeared again, Amy heard footsteps echoing off the walls.

The kitchen door opened again. "Oh, Mr. Whitney! Good. Your food's all ready. I'll bring out your plate."

Not looking up, Amy heard only an answering grunt, gruff, not friendly. The waitress disappeared, returning quickly with more plates of spaghetti, salad, and rolls, and set them down opposite Amy.

Amy looked up to find a towering rock of a man, middle 40s or so, dressed in black wool mountain pants and a black-and-red-checked wool shirt. He took off his dripping khaki rain suit. He was easily recognizable from his pictures. Wavy brown hair and chiseled features, broad shoulders and a trim waist.

"Hello," she said as he sat down. "My name is Amy."

Whitney hunched over his meal.

"I understand you're John Whitney, the local personality around here."

Knife and fork in big hands.

"Sorry you have to eat so late. Long day?"

No response.

"Well, at least you could be sociable."

He looked up and fixed his piercing blue eyes on her. "Hey look, lady. I'm in no mood for bullshit. It's been a bad few days, and I'm not lookin' for a date. If you're waitin' for me, you'll just have to march your sweet ass outta here."

Amy's jaw dropped. "Why, you insufferable, arrogant shit-head! If I wasn't so hungry, I'd dump this spaghetti in your lap. I'll go sit someplace else." She tossed her knife and fork onto her plate, piled some bread and her salad plate on top and stood. She started walking.

"You're gonna piss off Camille."

Amy whirled. "What did you say?"

"Camille. She's gonna be pissed." He nodded to the kitchen. "More cleanup. She wants to get home."

The kitchen door opened and the waitress peered out. She looked first at Amy, then Whitney. Her face showed confusion.

Whitney waved his fork at Amy. "Come back. We don't wanna put Camille out. She works hard enough. Right, Camille?"

The waitress stood still. Only her eyes moved.

Amy hesitated. She looked at Camille, then back at Whitney. Camille met her gaze. Whitney's was on his fork, busy twirling spaghetti. He took a bite, chewed, then rubbed a napkin over his mouth. "How's my wine? Pretty good?"

Amy's eyes fell on her half-empty glass on the table. Whitney freshened hers and poured some for himself. "Shame to waste this stuff. Come back."

'I don't need your wine or your company."

"Yeah, we established that. Look. I'm sorry. Like I said, it's been a bad week, capped off today by a memorial service for one of my best friends. It's no excuse, but it is an explanation. I over-reacted. Okay?"

Camille smiled and shut the kitchen door. Amy stood still. "You think I was waiting for you?"

"You knew my name."

"Yeah, it's plastered all over the place. Who doesn't?"

Whitney nodded, sipped his wine. "Damn, that's good." He looked at Amy. "You're right, it is. And I said I was sorry. Let me make it up to you."

"What do you have in mind?"

"Buying your dinner and sharing my wine, for starters."

Amy set down her plate. Whitney smiled and stood, extending a hand. "Now let's do this right. I'm John Whitney. And your name is Amy?"

"Amy Galler."

"Well, Amy Galler, I'm pleased to meet you. Maybe you'll brighten up a day which badly needs some light. Let's sit down."

Amy sat, withdrew a tissue, and blew her nose. "Sorry. All this humidity."

"Yeah, it gets to you. Been a bad summer for that."

Amy took a sip of wine. Camille came out again, and Whitney caught her eye. "Can you bring us another bottle? Then you can go home. I'll lock up."

Amy started to object, but stopped herself. What the hell. It was late. Maybe a little lubrication would get Whitney talking.

Camille brought another bottle, a corkscrew and their bills. Whitney took the bills, added a fat tip, signed and handed them back to Camille, who smiled. "Thank you, Mr. Whitney! Have a great evening." A quick smile at Amy, then she was gone.

Whitney studied her. "So what do you do, Amy? Haven't seen you around here."

Amy tucked into her spaghetti. "Bookkeeping and some tax work for a supermarket chain in Seattle. King's Market. Know of it?"

Whitney nodded. "Yeah, they're all over Seattle, Tacoma and Olympia, although I have to admit, I try to avoid those places."

"Our markets?"

"No. Cities. I like it up here."

"I can see why." She laughed. "No, I guess I can't. Can't see much of anything today."

"That's for sure. So why are you here? Vacation?"

"Just a few days. I'm in the Seattle headquarters, never been up here. Thought I'd check it out, maybe do a little hiking."

He nodded, then reached for the bottle. She watched him pour the wine, assessing him from a cop's vantage point, finding it a little exciting from behind her accountant façade. Whitney glanced at her, saw her watching him. A smile. "What are you thinking?"

"Are all you mountain men like Maselli? I mean so obvious, so lecherous."

Whitney laughed. "So you've met our local Romeo."

"Just briefly."

John shook his head. "I don't know why I let that guy sign on. All I get are complaints. Maselli is over the top, always.

"Don't get me wrong. We get groupies here. If you give 'em what they ask for, they want to be yours forever; if you don't—or if you do and don't come back—they complain."

"So never date a mountain man." Amy's face bore a wry, quizzical smile.

"Sorry, didn't mean it that way. But you know what I mean, don't you? I've got a lot of attractive, rugged men up here, living a lifestyle that's sexy and romantic. Some of it goes with the territory."

"Are you like that? Love 'em and leave 'em?"

"Why?" he asked, his eyebrows arching. "Interested?"

"Nope. I'm into more sustained relationships."

He smiled. "I'll have to share my tax returns."

They were starting the second bottle. "So tell me, John…"

Whitney was chewing some garlic bread. "Fire away."

"I saw pictures of you in the Guide Service Shack, pictures of the whole staff, but only one of a Donnie Whitney. Something about 'Snowballs.' Is he your brother?"

It was like he imploded, turning in on himself, lost to her.

"I'm sorry. Am I going where I shouldn't?"

He sipped his wine and stared out the window. "My brother. He died a long time ago."

"I am so sorry. I didn't know."

He nodded. "See… there was this race…"

The second bottle was almost finished. John had drunk more than Amy, his pace picking up during the race and Snowball stories. But she was feeling the effects too.

"You said earlier that you attended a memorial service today. One of your friends. Did something happen to him?"

John took a sip of wine.

"We don't have to talk about it."

"No... no. I probably should; it's probably good for me. I lost my good friend, Jim Carlton, during the storm."

"What happened?"

"We don't know for sure. We think he ran into a poacher... The poacher had a snowmobile; he'd buried it. We think Jim caught him as he was firing it up..." He rotated the glass in his big hand. "...and he... well... he got rid of Jim." He looked out at the black night. "Poaching is a very serious crime, Amy. Those guys are nuts, and very dangerous."

"Did they find your friend? Or the poacher?"

"Just snowmobile tracks, blood and pieces of two parkas. Blood's Jim's. Our local sheriff and the FBI guy had it analyzed. The yellow parka strip was Jim's too." There was a hollow laugh. "We were calling him Big Bird." He took a breath. "The other one was white, looked like a pocket. Good camouflage in a snowstorm, huh? The tracks went up the mountain. We think the poacher, his snowmobile and most probably Jim's body ended up in a crevasse somewhere. Boyd says he was trailing a snowmobile way up on the mountain, but..."

"But what?" She set her plate aside, keeping the question casual.

"I don't know. Something's just not right about that." John looked around, eyes calm. "Quiet, isn't it."

"A big empty place and just us." She felt his eyes on her.

"I really am sorry, y'know. About the way I came in and spoke to you."

Amy smiled. "Hey, we're on a new level, right? You're gonna show me your tax returns."

"Let's finish off this bottle."

She watched him pour.

"Another dead soldier," John said.

"So, what's not right about it, John?"

"Jim's death, y'mean? Well, nobody else saw him, but mainly it just doesn't feel right. Live and work up here for a lifetime and you develop instincts." He waved a big hand in a cutting gesture. "Can we talk about something else? And truth be told, I'm a little drunk."

Amy watched her hand go out and cover his. It just happened, no thought. "With good reason."

"Yeah."

"How about we talk about what you have in mind for me tomorrow?"

His hand went over hers. "Now you're talkin'."

Later that night, Amy unwrapped a roll of quarters and fed them into a drink machine. She got herself six sodas. Back in her room, she popped them, emptied the sodas down the toilet, then went to her locked front door. Carefully, she stacked the empties into a pyramid. Anyone trying to enter would find themselves on the wrong end of a .38 snubbie loaded with hollowpoints.

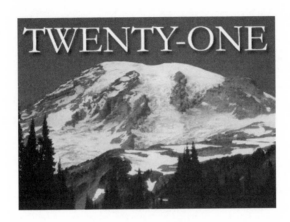

TWENTY-ONE

Wednesday, July 31

"You know, Emery…" Sam Terry said, over dessert and coffee at Il Terrazzo Carmine, tucked neatly into the old-time aura of Pioneer Square, "…this whole Herman thing has made me see the need for succession planning."

Boyd started to speak, but Terry raised his hands. "I won't go over again my surprise and disappointment about learning from others of your—what would you call it?—turf battle—yes, I think that best describes it—with Herman. We've been through all that." The old man sighed. "That's not my point.

"What I'm saying… is… maybe if firm succession had been dealt with earlier, this whole thing between you two wouldn't have happened."

"Sam, I told you it was one-sided, not a 'dispute' at all. And don't be so tough on yourself. Yes, succession planning is important. But Herman was just making a power grab, and a sneaky one at that." He shoved aside his dessert plate. "I only found out about it myself just before my vacation."

"You mean just before you named Dan Cole your assistant?"

"Bullshit, Sam. That's legit. I should have done it a long time ago. It had nothing to do with Herman's little games."

"Look. Whether it was appropriate or not, it's done. I'm not going to undo it. That would be embarrassing for you, for me, and especially for Dan."

Terry's manicured hands encircled his coffee cup. "This is just awful. Gossip, rumor, shock. I don't think anyone's doing any work. Police investigations, newspaper articles... This sort of thing only happens to other people... to other firms. Not to Herman. Not to us!"

Boyd nodded.

"Well, you couldn't have picked a better time to make a controversial move. Everyone's forgotten about it already; it's old news. But, as I said, I think we need a plan for contingencies."

Terry paused. "Anyway, I've postponed the annual partnership meeting for the time being. I'll reschedule it in a few months. But this time, two weeks in advance, I'm going to submit a detailed agenda..."

"Good idea, Sam. No surprises."

He nodded. "And item number one will be succession planning—beginning with managing partner."

Boyd was silent, expectant.

"Now, Emery, I think you know who my first choice is. But this damn mountain climbing concerns me. I need to be sure that my successor will be around. We need stability."

"Mountain climbing is no more risky than sailing, Sam. It's just that you don't do it."

"There may be some truth to that, Emery, but it's a feeling I have. I'll have to give it serious consideration."

"Well, just be sure that you consider all I've meant to this firm. I'm the man for your job, Sam. And you know it."

"I will not make this decision lightly."

"Good."

They sat, eyes fixed on each other. Then Sam drained his coffee, fished his money clip from his pocket and placed cash on the table. "Well, I must be off. I assume you'll be around a while. I'm sure the police are going to want to talk to you—especially since Marge said you and Herman were practically enemies. Hell," he said, shrugging his shoulders, "they're talking to everybody else! You may even enjoy the experience: one of the detectives, Amy Galler, is a stunner."

Boyd did a Groucho with his eyebrows, and Terry smiled. "I've got to be in L.A. the next two days," Boyd said. "Emergency meetings with that new client I told you about. Next week, I don't know where I'll be. I don't have much scheduled. I may try to fit in the vacation I lost."

Sam Terry nodded and walked away.

Boyd watched him go. Old men die easy. A good tap with the spine of a book on the fourth vertebrae could do it. He used a fork on a dessert crumb.

TWENTY-TWO

Thursday, August 1

Amy slept fitfully, tossing and turning. She was tired, but couldn't sleep; her aching head reminded her of all the alcohol she'd had last night. A bad practice for an undercover cop. Amy had known she should stop with the first bottle, but she hadn't wanted the evening to end.

She looked at her watch: 6:30, then glanced at the soda cans. She rolled over, her thoughts turning once more to John, as they had for much of the restless night.

She couldn't remember when meeting a man had caused such a stirring within her; it surprised her, scared her and excited her. It hadn't been just his looks, tall, rugged. That had been evident from his pictures. John radiated self-confidence; he was a force. His place was on this mountain. He made her feel safe. She smiled at that. She was the one with the .38. John was rough, sure; maybe a little uncivilized. So what? John could be depended upon; his honesty and goodness showed through. Too bad she looked so plain for the job. She wanted to knock him dead.

Several times during their dinner—which had lasted until

almost midnight—she'd felt herself losing concentration, a bad thing. And heat, something she hadn't experienced in a long time.

And John had felt something. Or had she just imagined it? She sat up in bed, running a hand through her hair. She forced herself to focus. There was the strong possibility of a killer out there; she'd better stay sharp.

John was coming by at noon with a picnic lunch to show her some of his mountain. A sudden thought caused her to leap out of bed. *The weather!* A few steps toward the window told her the entire area was encased in a deep, gray fog. Rain was still falling. "Shit! We can't go out in this!"

But John had come in last night wearing rain slickers. Could they still go out? She turned away from the window and pulled some Motrin from her purse. Taking three, she moved to the bathroom, where she cupped her hands under the open spigot, then sloshed the little orange pills down.

She brushed her teeth, took a shower and dressed. Pulling on her new wool pants over the neoprene long-johns she'd purchased, and forsaking a bra, she chose a T-shirt and wool sweater to wear to breakfast. She knew that in the sober light of day she should go over the notes she'd hurriedly scribbled late last night, but she decided that task would have to await a big breakfast and coffee. She stared at her cluster of packs. She was on duty. She slipped the .38 snub into an IWB holster and pulled the sweater down over it. Her I.D. and badge went into a zippered compartment of her day-pack, which she'd use as a purse. She tossed her wallet in as well.

By 7:15, the dining room was bustling. Most of the fifty or so tables were already filled, and Amy was surprised to learn there was a waiting list. God, she thought, why are all those people here so early, and in this weather? She asked the hostess, who told her that a couple of buses had just come in, and some others had come up from the hotels and motels outside the park.

The hostess, a pleasant, plump woman of forty or so, told her she would have to wait a half hour for a table for herself, or she could join one of the singles tables, which were reserved for those who were alone or didn't mind sharing with others. Guides and staffers usually occupied these tables, the hostess said; there were four of them, all in a row, in the back on the right side. The last one, Amy noticed, was the same table she'd occupied with John. She selected it.

Amy studied the people at other tables. The elderly, the ones she guessed had come by bus, were dressed normally: slacks, blouses or open-neck shirts, some sports jackets, loafers or sneakers. At some of the other tables sat families. Tourists, she decided, probably some of those who'd come up from below. Then there were the more hardy groups, people dressed like her in wool, wearing mountain boots. Across the back of many of their chairs hung rain gear of various types, colors and price ranges, even some garbage bags.

The mountain could be climbed, or at least hiked, in this weather.

There was a young woman at Amy's table, an attractive brunette, about twenty-six or so. Amy studied her, using her academy training. Despite the woman's green woolly mountain garb, she didn't fit in. Her full plate of food was untouched and she was staring out the window, distracted, sad. She looked up as Amy sat, then quickly looked away. "Hi," Amy said in a friendly tone. "Mind if I join you?"

"Help yourself," the woman said, briefly glancing back again before she turned once more to look outside. Amy noticed red-tinged eyes.

"I'm Amy Galler. What's your name?"

"Uh… Sherry Brannigan."

"Been here long?"

"No."

"Your food's getting cold. What's the matter, not hungry?"

At that moment, Camille, the waitress, appeared and greeted

Amy, asking how dinner went last night. Amy laughed and said she'd drunk too much wine.

As Camille gave her a menu, Amy watched Sherry turn back to the window. Camille poured a cup of coffee. "Thank you. This should kick-start my day."

Camille noticed Sherry's untouched plate and asked if everything was okay, if she could warm anything up. Sherry looked at her plate. "Yes, please," she said, her voice pleasant. "Could you? I'm sorry. I guess I'm lost in my thoughts… like in the fog outside."

"Well," Camille smiled, "don't worry about the fog and rain. Those clouds are low. I'll bet if you go another five hundred feet up, maybe a thousand, you'll have sunshine." Her smile broadened. "Then again, it might be snowing. It's like that up here. You just never can tell. When you're done, go over to the ranger station at the end of the parking lot. They always have the latest weather conditions and predictions posted—but beware, predictions up here aren't always reliable, and the weather can change real quick."

Amy filed it away. "Really?"

"You better believe it. This mountain's got so many different climate zones, even a slight change of conditions can totally change the weather. That's why it's best to pack so you're ready for anything. People who get in trouble usually aren't geared right; maybe they dress for what they see here and then they get a thousand feet up, and it's totally different. Or it changes suddenly. But you know, I'd be willin' to bet it's sunny up there today." She smiled reassuringly at Sherry.

Amy sipped her coffee. "Will there be many people up there on a day like this?"

"Oh, yeah. This stuff…" pointing outside to the fog and rain "…doesn't stop most people. Just look around, you'll see people planning their trips."

Camille left with Sherry's plate, promising to return in a few minutes. As soon as she was gone, Amy turned to her tablemate. "So, where are you from, Sherry? Here for a while?"

"Portland," she said. For a moment, she said nothing more. Then she shrugged and looked at Amy. "I'm sorry. I don't mean to be rude. I'm coming out of a relationship. I figured I needed some time away, and I'd never been up here. If I can't get away from my troubles here, where else can I go?"

Tears filled Sherry's eyes. Amy reached over and squeezed her arm. Sherry withdrew inside herself. Amy pulled out a packet of tissues. She handed them to Sherry, who took one and blew her nose. "I'm sorry," Sherry said, "I wasn't gonna do this today."

"Naw, that's okay. Sometimes you need to get it out of your system. Look, I'm up here by myself, too. I just got in late yesterday afternoon. What say you and I become friends?"

Sherry blew her nose again. "Thanks… er… Amy, was it?" Amy nodded. "I'd like that." Amy extended her hand.

They spent the next two and a half hours getting acquainted, eating their breakfasts of pancakes, eggs and sausage washed down with several cups of coffee. But Sherry didn't talk much about herself, and from time to time she slipped back into her sadness.

Despite Sherry's reluctance, Amy was able to learn that Sherry was a sort of a "girl Friday" in a small office in Portland. She had four weeks of vacation stored up, so after her breakup, which she wouldn't discuss, she'd taken off. After spending a small fortune—like Amy—on mountain gear, she'd headed for Rainier, a place where she thought she could heal.

Amy told Sherry the story she'd been telling everyone else: that she was a bookkeeper and tax advisor for King's Market, who was taking a few days off to explore. She said she didn't know how long she'd be here, but through the weekend for sure.

"So, Amy," Sherry said, "is your job boring? I can't imagine working with figures all day."

"Nah, I love it. I like the exactitude of accounting. You know where you are—or aren't."

"Different from love." Sherry looked down.

Amy nodded. "Very different from love."

As they talked, the two women decided they had much in common. Both were young, single career women, who needed some time away. Both were novices at mountaineering and thought they'd been taken when they bought their mountain gear, particularly when they'd realized later that despite spending hundreds of dollars on a variety of items, neither had bought any rainwear. They laughed at this, a rallying of Sherry's spirits, and Camille glanced over and smiled.

"So when did you get in, Sherry?"

"This morning. I spent the night in one of those cheap motels outside the park."

"It must have been hard, sleep I mean."

"Yes. I took a couple of aspirin, read a while."

"So, you have a room here now?"

"Unfortunately not. They're full. I'm kinda hanging around, hoping for a vacancy." She pointed out the window at the weather.

Amy pushed aside her coffee cup. "Look, Sherry, why not bunk in with me? Store your stuff anyway. If you get a room, great. If not, I promise I don't snore."

A smile found Sherry's mouth. "Deal."

For a fleeting moment, Amy wondered whether Sherry's staying with her would be a problem—if things worked out well with John, for instance, or if Sherry saw the .38. The soda cans wouldn't be a problem; they were always smart when traveling. Well, she'd just have to manage those matters when—if—they developed. Wanting to get to know her better, she invited Sherry along on the planned afternoon hike. But Sherry declined, saying she needed to hang around in case a room became available. Besides, she said, she could use the time alone. Amy nodded. "Not too much time alone, Sherry. It could work against you."

They left the dining area around ten and stopped at the desk for a key for Sherry. Then they ran through the rain to the Guide Service Shack to look at rain wear. Maselli was there, but if he saw Amy, he gave no clue. Amy guessed she'd been dismissed, an incomplete pass.

Amy bought red rainwear, while Sherry chose yellow. They laughed that they wouldn't be hard to spot, even in fog. Now appropriately dressed, they ventured down to the ranger station. The handwritten forecast pinned on the doorway called for more wet weather. Disappointed, Amy returned to her room, while Sherry walked to the Visitor's Center, a metal and glass building at the west end of the parking lot which strangely resembled a spaceship from a fifties science fiction movie.

Once in her room, Amy checked it, looking for any dislodged hairs she'd placed as traps. She sat down at the wooden table and skimmed through her notes. She was surprised she'd learned so much so soon. Much of the information she'd not written down. Some was only peripherally relevant, like the general history of the Whitney-Boyd relationship: how they'd met; the "Snowball" story; Donnie's tragic disappearance; the shared conquest of Everest in his memory, plus an assortment of anecdotes from their mountaineering journeys together. John had been talkative once they got past Donnie and Carlton.

John had shown a sensitive side when talking about his brother. Surprising in a man so rugged. His depth of feeling had stirred her.

They hadn't talked much about her, but then that was the plan. Just her cover story. Her cop training had served her well.

She began tearing used note sheets from her pad, stacking them off to the side while she fumbled in her purse for her good pen, the medium-point rolling ball she used for keeper notes. These were second-stage thoughts incorporating logic or theory with tidbits of information. She studied her notes, then began writing.

Item: Boyd told Whitney he'd been following a snowmobile

through the storm. No one but Boyd had seen it, but tracks had been found, along with blood and parts of two different parkas. No one saw Boyd from about 1:00 A.M. Saturday until late Saturday afternoon, nearly seventeen hours later.

Item: The FBI and local sheriff believed Jim Carlton was dead, killed by the snowmobiler on the trail. They'd run lab tests— Trumball?—to confirm the blood and yellow parka were Carlton's.

Item: Whitney thought the snowmobiler was a poacher, who most likely died in the storm, if Boyd was to be believed. Something bothered Whitney about Boyd's story. What was it? Whitney had referred to instincts. Was there more to it than that?

Amy stood up, dropped her notes on the table and stretched her arms and shoulders. Theories and facts swirled through her head, looking for connections. She spread her legs and bent her torso forward and down, to a point where she could almost flatten her palms on the floor.

She straightened up and returned to the table. She tore off the sheets she'd just completed and spread them out before her. She pulled together the summary she'd prepared last night for her conversation with Charlie. Arranging her notes chronologically in a fan around her, she leafed through the stacks.

For a heading on the clean pad, she wrote: "Things to Consider." Then, underneath it: "Boyd unseen 17 hours."

She put the pen down, shuffled some notes and cradled her head in her hands. Bad sleep was catching up with her. In those seventeen hours, couldn't Boyd have descended, driven to Seattle, killed Klein, and returned?

She wrote out her question, then another underneath it: "Where's Herman Klein's body?"

He could have dumped it in Lake Washington, of course, or taken it out to the woods somewhere, but it might be found. He wouldn't have wanted to gamble on a possible DNA or evidence link if the body was discovered.

Wait! DNA. Arnie Trumball had said they were running tests. If the blood on the wall was Klein's, it meant his body was taken away. Why carry the body over the wall to dump it in the lake? She made a note to have Charlie follow up with Arnie.

So what did he do with the body?

Her eyes moved back to the table, focusing on the guidebook she'd bought in the lodge's gift shop yesterday. The cover picture was an impressive view of the Nisqually Glacier from just below the suspension bridge. Her thoughts returned to her drive up, how she'd been mesmerized by the glacier, by the power it possessed. Power enough to wash out that bridge—twice.

She stared at the picture. A river of ice, yet not the color of ice. Dirty and black, pockmarked with gaping crevasses, it bore the dirt and grit of the ages. She wondered what secrets the glacier held, what animals and artifacts it entombed.

The thought insinuated itself, real and ugly, like much of her work. A familiar tension tightened her, and she looked at the door, confirming it was locked. She had been here before, this developing matrix of fact and theory. It always existed, and it frightened her. The .38 was comforting in her holster.

Item: Why not bury Klein in a crevasse? An ace climber like Boyd would have no trouble finding one. It'd be so easy; all he'd have to do is figure out a way to get the body there.

Item: How? He couldn't carry it far. If by snowmobile, he'd have to hide it in advance, in a secure but easily identifiable and reachable place, probably not far from a road. John had said the poacher's snowmobile was buried not far from Paradise, just off a trail.

Of course!

Item: So how did he get the snowmobile up there? Did he have a truck? There wasn't any snow below snowline; he must have brought it up some other way. But was this really a problem? If he'd decided to kill Klein in advance, he could have hidden it anytime, maybe even in winter, when the whole area would be snow covered. She made a note to find out if Boyd owned a truck.

Item: But why kill Carlton? On her pad, she wrote: "Carlton." Next to that, she wrote: "Poacher."

Carlton had to be killed; it wasn't planned, it just happened, caused by a chance encounter. Carlton knew Boyd. He'd blow Boyd's alibi. He had to die.

On her notepad, underneath "Poacher," Amy wrote: "Emery Boyd." Then she circled the two of them.

So far so good. It had symmetry to it. It felt good.

Item: Have Charlie check with Arnie: Were any wig fibers found at the Carlton scene? Boyd might have removed the wig, or the snow may have made them too hard to see. No one had mentioned any wig fibers, but it was worth checking.

Sitting back, Amy stared out the window again, ignoring the fog. She eased her head, felt the popping of sinew in her neck and shoulders as waves of stress were released and her muscles relaxed. She got up and slowly paced.

"Okay," she said aloud and took a deep breath, exhaling slowly. She walked over to the window and turned around. "Now he's got two bodies, when he's planned on one. So he takes both with him. Why?"

She moved back from the window, toward the door. "This one's easy. He doesn't want Carlton's body discovered either. It's just as easy to dispose of both at the same time. Everyone will assume Carlton was lost in the storm."

Returning to her pad, she wrote, "No body, no proof," and drew a connecting line to Carlton.

She doodled with the pen, the notion of a poacher developing not because there was any proof, but to fill the logic vacuum.

But why had the yellow parka been cut into a strip? Her pen flew across the page. How important was that? Could it be so Boyd wouldn't get blood on him?

And why was she the only one to see all this? Because those investigating didn't know about Herman Klein—the cause for it all.

Amy scribbled her conclusions, circled them and drew an exclamation point. She put her pen down and sat back.

But how to prove it? Her stomach went queasy. She would be coming under the scrutiny of a killer. A crevasse could be awaiting her. She shuddered.

She glanced at her watch: 1:05. "Oh, shit!" She gathered her notes, looking around for someplace safe. Her eyes fell on the excursion pack, the one she'd probably never use except maybe as a suitcase. She opened the pack's front flap, dropped the notes inside, and refastened the plastic clips. She grabbed her parka, raingear and backpack, and went to the door. She paused, ducked into the bathroom, threw water on her face, and toweled off. She bumped the .38 against the sink. Uh oh. Belt wouldn't do: John might hug her. Ankle wouldn't do either: mountain boots. She tucked it into the day-pack, zippered the compartment, then slipped into the pack's straps.

Once outside, she saw Sherry coming the other way.

"Oh, Sherry, hi," she said hurriedly. "I'm sorry… forgot you were coming. Make yourself at home. I'm afraid I left the room a little messy. Look, I'm late. If anything gets in your way, just throw it in a pile, will you? I'll clean it up when I get back. Sorry!"

Sherry put her stuff down and looked around. Not so bad. Just a few clothes spread around. She walked to the window and watched the rain. She thought about her and Amy arriving without rain gear and winced at their naiveté. That salesman had sure seen her coming.

She turned away from the window and her eyes fell on the excursion pack standing in a corner. *An excursion pack? For a novice hiker?* Maybe Amy had been taken even worse.

Rain gear. Anything else I forgot? The Guide Service Shack was open. Maybe she should check. Amy had said to make herself at home.

She opened the pack's front flap and began pulling out clothing, looking for things to purchase. Something else: papers. She put the papers on the table and went back to pulling out clothing, mentally comparing what she'd brought with what Amy had.

Wool socks. She'd buy them today.

She stuffed the clothing back where she'd found it and reached for the papers, ready to shove them back into the pack. Her eye caught the top page. Slowly, she thumbed through the rest. She put the notes on the table and pulled up a chair.

TWENTY-THREE

Thursday, August 1

"Captain…" Charlie Scott added, finishing his briefing on yesterday's activities "…there's one more thing."

MacGregor waited. He had fidgeted through Charlie's "lack of progress" report, as he called it.

Charlie was discouraged too. Like his boss, he was aware of the statistics: most murders are solved, if at all, within the first week of the investigation. That wasn't going to happen here, not the way this investigation was going. He pressed on.

"That Simmons woman… you know… Klein's secretary… well, she called yesterday and asked me to come over…" He paused, seeing MacGregor's eyes come alive.

"Yes?"

"So I did… last night… right after I got off the phone with Amy."

MacGregor sat upright. "Was Terry there?"

"No, I…"

His boss lunged forward in his chair. "Goddamn it! Terry told you he represented Simmons—as her fucking lawyer, Charlie! He demanded to be present for all conversations with her. Am I going to have him on my ass for this too?" He rubbed his neck. "He's calling me twice a day now. He's asking for progress reports and berating me for no results. What's more, the sonofabitch is talking to the chief and the mayor on a daily basis too.

"Jesus Christ." He stared at his desk, lost in thought. "Isn't this Green River crap enough? Ever since that new body was found, I haven't been able to get any sleep. The feds are running it, but everyone's beating on me. I don't need another problem, Charlie."

MacGregor eyed his detective. "My stomach needs a rest. It's in knots. I'm constipated." He saw Charlie smile. "Let me get out of this, Charlie."

"I think it's all right, Captain. After all… she called me. I asked her if she wanted Terry present."

"Did you have her sign anything waiving her right to counsel?"

"Well… er… no…" Charlie back-pedaled, "I-I guess… well… I didn't think about that."

MacGregor shook his head. "Are you still dragging?"

"Yes, sir, but they've got diddly. They've moved it a-ways, following the current, but they still haven't found anything. They'd like a couple more days."

"No way. Close 'em down today. With the budget problems we've got, I can't afford to keep a project like that going forever."

"But sir, I don't think it's been enough time. There's still…"

"Close it down. We'll just have to wait for Klein to float."

Charlie stayed mute.

"Well, anyway," MacGregor said a moment later, "back to Simmons…"

"I don't really think there's a problem, sir," Charlie said. "She was very friendly."

"Charlie," MacGregor said, "anytime the police go nosing around a law firm, there are problems. You know that. If Terry…

or should I say... *when* Terry finds out... he's gonna chew that woman out to within an inch of her life. Fast as you can say, 'I'm fucked,' Marge Simmons will cover her ass by saying you tricked her, just sweet-talked your way into her house and pried her mouth open. Then Terry will call the mayor and the chief again... You can guess what'll happen next..."

"Sorry, Captain. I'll get her to sign a waiver."

"Did you see the paper today?"

"Yeah. Preston is rubbing your face in the... uh... shit-pile again, if that's what you mean. Maybe you ought to talk to Preston, or better yet, his editor again."

"I'm going to, the editor, not Preston. She's relatively new. Name's Chancey LaRue. There's a name for you." He shrugged and broke cellophane off a cigar. "I'll give her a call when we get through here. So, what did Simmons have to say?"

"She's going to look in that Schneider file, the Miscellaneous portion, where Emily Klein says the confession is located. She'll let me know if there's anything in there. I stayed up late last night working up a search warrant draft so we can take it over to the D.A. if there's anything there. I want to act fast, but not before I know something's there. She should call me soon."

"Doesn't she know what's in that file?"

"No. She says she always adds a 'Miscellaneous' folder to any file she works up, but she doesn't remember ever looking in that folder in connection with the Schneider estate."

"So, is that all we have?"

"Well, so far. Until I talk to her again."

"Let me see that draft search warrant." Charlie pulled out a folded document and handed it to his boss. MacGregor pulled the cigar out of his mouth and put it in the ashtray. A few minutes later, he nodded. "Good job. The D.A.'s office ought to appreciate your saving them the time and expense. Call Simmons. If she says there's something there, see if she'll make a copy for you. If she won't, I'll call the D.A. and explain. I'll tell him you're on your way over and that we need to get before a judge right away."

"But Captain, that's a client file. What about Terry? Don't you want that search warrant before you see the document?"

"No. Fuck Sam Terry. Marge Simmons is an employee of the firm. If she gives us a copy, that's her problem. Look, I don't know if there's anything to this Boyd-Klein thing or not. I don't want to go to the D.A. unless we have to. He may decide it's a federal matter. So, if she says something's there, you see if she'll make a copy. If so, you run over and get it, and take a waiver form with you."

"Right. But what if she mentions Terry, wants to talk to him?"

"If Simmons wants to talk to Terry, don't try to talk her out of it. I don't want Terry telling the mayor we bullied her. We'll revert to plan B and go with the search warrant."

"Yes, sir."

"Call her now."

Charlie reached over and dialed Marge Simmons' number as MacGregor leaned back in his chair and stared at the ceiling. After several rings, he hung up. "Voicemail," he said.

"Call her at home. Make sure she went in today."

Charlie dialed her home number. Again, after several rings, he hung up. "She must be in the office. I'll try her again in a little while."

"Has Emily Klein gotten an attorney yet?"

"Yeah. Dick Anthony."

"Good! Score one for us. He's somebody we can work with. Call him. Tell him you want to meet with his client. See if you can get Schneider's wife there too. Let's have her listening to what Mrs. Klein says. See if anything opens up."

"Do you think there's something to this Boyd thing?"

"Who knows? Are you going to be talking to Amy tonight?"

"Yeah. About nine o'clock."

"Good. Tell her to soak up as much information as she can. First thing Monday, I want her here, with you, in my office."

TWENTY-FOUR

Thursday, August 1

G. Sherwood Preston stood in the rain on the sidewalk across from police headquarters, sipping lukewarm coffee from a large Styrofoam cup. His black double-breasted London Fog raincoat was wrapped tightly around him. He stood with his back to police headquarters, admiring his reflection in a shop window, but frowning at his drenched, drooping moustache. He had a good vantage point; he could observe his appearance while at the same time keeping a lookout for Charlie Scott or Amy Galler. He hadn't seen Galler the last few days and wondered if she was sick, but Scott had certainly been busy. He'd been following Scott around, hoping for a break.

He needed a big story. His editor, Chancey LaRue, was fed up, calling him lazy and a tabloid journalist; claiming he wouldn't know a good story if it fell on him. She'd accused him of not checking out facts, of not probing deep enough, of backing away from confrontation. The humiliation ground deep inside him. His mind tracked back to when he was a freelancing stormtrooper for grocery store magazines. So he hadn't originated each story. So what? His stories had been eminently more entertaining than what his competition had produced. He'd expanded reports of Nicole Simpson's drug use and her frolicking with young men to claims that she'd been hooking and dealing; he'd hypothesized that Bill Clinton might have given Monica herpes; that the Clintons might have smoked dope with Chelsea; that the Kennedys were America's most notorious crime family, supporting that story with a litany of alleged crimes, some documented, some rumored— some made up. His stories sold a lot of magazines, which was why the *Post* had hired him. Four years ago, when the *Post* had needed to strengthen sagging revenues and re-assert itself in the Seattle marketplace, he'd been brought in to liven the old lady up. The *Post* liked the gossip he'd routinely dug up for his magazines; they wanted to broaden the paper's appeal, sexify it.

And circulation rose—dramatically. Sure, other newspapers and some of the radio and TV stations decried his steamy, sex-filled gossip, but that was just free publicity, which translated into even more sales. He was the most-read reporter on the paper. He felt entitled to star treatment as a savant, respected for his talent and his journalistic charisma.

Instead, the last year had been pure hell.

A new editor—and a woman at that—the hookerish-sounding Chancey LaRue, had been hired to run the City Desk. Chancey LaRue didn't like him; she'd told him so, in fact, and she liked less his style of journalism—what she called "scurilism."

A disaster. This kid, for she was all of twenty-nine, this *neophyte*—who was reputed, though she denied it, to be "involved" with the publisher—had no concept of what made a newspaper work, of what sold papers. Her hot body combined with her too-pretty face and pliant smile, not to mention her blue eyes, bleach blond hair and full lips, offered hints that she was somebody's toy. Indeed, the publisher, Wayne Malcolm Huston, seemed to spend an inordinate amount of time "in conference" with Chancey. Office gossip about the two was rampant, and speculation ran on what "special" uses Huston's conference table served.

Professionally speaking, LaRue talked of "standards" and "professionalism," but what did she know of such things? She claimed to have worked for the *New York Times*, but Preston knew there was a bug in her soup. He'd checked up on her and learned that she'd worked there just two years and hadn't held any editorial positions. She'd been a cub reporter only.

He stared at his reflection, his moustache. He'd need to work on it. At first, Preston tried to ignore Chancey. But she threatened him, said she'd fire him if he didn't comply with the changes she wanted. Then she'd denied him a raise.

That had been the last straw, or so he'd thought. He'd stormed angrily up to the publisher's office, planning to settle the matter once and for all.

How wrong he'd been; his strategy had backfired mightily. Huston, a duplicitous family patriarch, whom Preston had long felt ran the paper as a hobby, refused to take his complaints. He said he was "comfortable" with Chancey LaRue; he liked her instincts, her drive and her "mission"—whatever the hell that meant. Adding insult to injury, he said the paper—and especially Preston—had been moving away from the style of journalism he wanted: one focused on the unvarnished, unadorned truth. He said Chancey was the right person to get things back on track.

It was a slap in the face. He'd argued, for sure; he reminded the doddering old windbag of the great leaps in circulation the paper had experienced since he—not to mention his style of journalism—had arrived. And Huston gave him his due. But then, he commented acidly and in a condescending tone—not unlike LaRue—that quantity wasn't as important as quality.

Enraged, he railed at Huston, and when that failed, he tempted fate: threatening to quit, to take his notepad across town. But Huston just smiled, saying that was always an option. Expressing his hope that Preston and Chancey could find a way to work together, he urged Preston to make a cooperative effort.

Failing that, he said—in what came as a final blow to Preston's ego—he'd have to give Preston his walking papers.

After that disastrous meeting, Preston tried working with LaRue, tried meeting her "standards." But he'd been fighting a losing battle.

So he needed a story, one so important that his presence—his rightful place—in the forefront of Seattle journalism could not be denied—even by his tits-for-brains, uncreative editor and the lecherous old fool who catered to her.

The Herman Klein story just might be his ticket. Prominent lawyer, prestigious law firm, strange disappearance, no body; the story had it all—well, almost. He hoped he could dig up a good scandal, preferably related to sex or money, to go along with it. His tabloid experience led him to expect that with power, money and foul play came greed, sex and debauchery. These elements were probably lurking behind this story too. If not, maybe he could add them, make them up if necessary—assuming he could find a way to get by LaRue.

He suspected Klein's disappearance or murder could prove much more interesting than the Green River story. Green River had been covered for years by everybody. There was a growing frustration associated with Green River; no one knew what was going on. Ridgeway had confessed, but now there was a new body. Copycat? Who knew? No, the new body was intriguing, but interest would wane unless more bodies showed up.

The Klein case had added advantages: Preston was at the ground floor on this one, not like Green River. And it certainly didn't hurt that so many other media outlets were distracted by the Green River developments. Handled right, he had this case largely to himself.

Preston wiped his moustache and discarded his coffee cup. He stood in the rain waiting, while torrents of water ran down the front of his stylish raincoat onto his black patent leather shoes.

He glanced at his watch: 9:30. How much longer before Charlie Scott came out? He wondered if he had time for another cup of coffee and a doughnut.

He'd made the decision to follow Scott, at least during the daylight hours, a couple of days ago. He'd been peppering the police in his columns about their lack of progress on the case, but that, and the speculation about a three-way between Klein, his wife and Marge Simmons, was about all he had so far. He knew there'd been an argument the night before Klein disappeared, knew blows had been struck. He knew also that Mrs. Klein had called Marge Simmons and confronted her. He'd been running that nugget for a few days now, but had little else. Learning of the contentious IRS meeting from a secretary at the law firm and the IRS auditor, he'd run that story too, hoping he could find a way to work in some fraud—always a bankable subject. And fraud there apparently was, except the party involved, the general partner, the only one with any motive, had no opportunity to kill Klein. Today's paper had ruled him out and again focused on the several-day-old suspicion of sexual hanky-panky.

The police didn't seem to have any real leads except the wife. He thought Galler might be a better source than MacGregor or Scott, both of whom were tight-lipped, but he couldn't find her. Where the hell was she?

So here he stood, waiting in the rain, hoping Charlie Scott would take him on a merry ride. That Scott might not appear, or if he did, that he might not lead him anywhere interesting, were very real risks. But what else was there? He wondered if his instincts were slipping. If he didn't find something new soon, he would join the police in looking the fool.

And how Chancey LaRue would love that.

While G. Sherwood Preston was rain dancing, Charlie Scott, seated in the dry comfort of his office, was on the phone with Dick Anthony, Emily Klein's attorney. He had first called Anthony at his office, but was told he was at the Klein residence. Calling him there, Charlie was even more pleased to learn Sue Schneider was present.

He'd known Anthony for six or seven years, ever since Anthony had taken on the case of Charlie's cousin, a tough 1st Avenue beat cop accused during an Internal Affairs investigation of drug money skimming. Charlie was impressed with Anthony's methods then, particularly his persistence and his willingness to go out on a limb for a case he believed in, even though eventually a sting operation proved Charlie's cousin was guilty, a conclusion Charlie, despite the strains on family ties, had never doubted. While he had no sympathy for his wayward relative—indeed he'd always held him in contempt and secretly celebrated his dismissal from the force—he was pleased that Anthony kept the family name from being tarnished further by a criminal prosecution. He liked Anthony and regarded him as a lawyer who could be trusted—a rarity, in his experience. MacGregor liked and respected him as well.

Charlie requested an interview with Mrs. Klein and Mrs. Schneider together.

"Does this mean you're starting to give some credence to Emily's claims that Boyd is responsible for Herman's disappearance?" Anthony asked.

"Let's just say we're checking it out, Dick. Mrs. Klein was on medication when Amy talked to her before. Amy had trouble following her. It might help if I can hear it again step-by-step. And I think it would be useful to have Mrs. Schneider there too. I'd like her take on what your client says. It might open something up, if you're willing to take the chance. What do you say?"

Anthony laughed. "It's not a wager when it's a sure thing, Charlie. I'd be happy to have Emily answer your questions. She has nothing to hide. Just let me be present and you can talk to her as long as you wish."

"Good," Charlie said, "then I'm sure she'll have no objections to Mrs. Schneider hearing it all too, will she?"

"Absolutely none. In fact, Emily's already told her most of it. You may be surprised at her reaction now. You may be further surprised to learn that Emily is considering consenting to multiphasic polygraph testing, assuming we can agree on who'll conduct it and what questions will be asked.

"You're a fair man. Does that sound like a guilty conscience to you? If she passes, will you let her off the hook?"

"Let's see how the interview goes first. We've cleared suspects before on the basis of polygraph material—as I'm sure you're aware—but usually only when it's been conducted with police involvement, and even then, only where it can be corroborated by objective evidence. If it's all she's got… well, I don't know."

"Good enough, Charlie. My client's innocent. Come on out."

Charlie called Marge Simmons again and caught her this time. After a few moments of small talk, he asked if she'd looked in the file.

"Yes. But there wasn't anything there."

"There was no file?"

"No. There was a Miscellaneous file, but there wasn't anything in it."

"Nothing at all?"

"No."

Charlie resisted the temptation to curse. "Where was the file located?"

"In the Schneider estate file in our file room."

"Can you check to see who accessed that file recently?"

"I thought you might ask that, so I did. The only people who checked the file out were Mr. Klein, Gary Gallagher and... Emery Boyd."

"Emery Boyd? Really?"

"Yes. But don't get too excited..."

"Why not?"

"Well, because Gary Gallagher is up for partner. A decision will be made at the annual partnership meeting."

"So?"

"Well, he's a litigation associate. He did some work for Mr. Klein on the estate file, researching potential litigation."

"I'm sorry, Marge, but I'm not following you. What's that have to do with Boyd checking out the file?"

"Well, just that it's not unusual at all for a partner, especially a department head, to check out some files an associate up for partner has worked on. It's done all the time."

"When did he check it out?"

"About two weeks ago."

"Well, that's significant!"

"Not necessarily. Remember, the partnership meeting was just around the corner. Besides, Mr. Klein checked it out again, after Mr. Boyd returned it. He asked for the file the day before the audit, two days before he disappeared. It was on his desk, but I'm not sure he looked at it. I put it back in the file room on Saturday."

"So you don't know whether he saw it or not?"

"No, I don't. Not really."

"Was it exactly as you'd placed it on his desk?"

"No. It had been moved over to the right side, like out of the way. I suppose he could have looked at it, but then again, I may have moved it myself. I just don't remember. But the folders were in the carton just as I'd left them, or at least as far as I could tell. There were no folders sitting on top of the carton, like they'd been pulled out. But then again, Mr. Klein is neat. He's very good about putting things back where they belong."

"So you don't think Klein got into the file, right?"

"I said I don't know. I assumed at the time that he had. I mean, the carton had been moved and all. That's why I returned it to the file room."

For several minutes more, Charlie tried gently to shake Marge from thinking there was nothing strange in Boyd's having checked out the Schneider estate file, all to no avail. As they spoke, he sensed Marge's cooperation waning. Sure enough, with some abruptness, she said she had to go. She said she was feeling guilty about working behind Sam Terry's back and thought she ought to talk to him. Charlie advised her to use her own judgment, reminding her she had his telephone numbers. He thanked her and terminated the call.

He headed upstairs to brief Captain MacGregor.

TWENTY-FIVE

Thursday, August 1

MacGregor's briefing took longer than Charlie had expected and was not pleasant. Just as he arrived at MacGregor's office, sidling past Irena, MacGregor was wrapping up his phone conversation with Preston's editor, Chancey LaRue. He'd tried to talk to the editor-in-chief, a man named Cutter, but had been shunted off to LaRue instead.

The phone call hadn't gone well. MacGregor railed at Charlie about abuse of First Amendment rights and the things he'd like to do to "that Goddamn cocksucking bitch" and her "puppet" G. Sherwood Preston.

When MacGregor finished with Preston and LaRue, Charlie reported his Simmons conversation. MacGregor nodded, winding down. "So Boyd's out. It's the wife."

"I don't know, boss. Boyd checked out the file. Maybe Amy can pierce his alibi..."

"No. We've got nothing on Boyd. Wish we had."

"Arnie Trumball says blood DNA at Klein's was his own. On Rainier, it was the missing guide's. Amy thinks Boyd took Klein's body to Rainier and that the guide saw him. That would explain the weird stuff there: Boyd had to protect his alibi."

"Really? And how are you going to prove that?"

Charlie left and drove through incessant rain to the Klein residence. Lost in thought, he failed to notice the green Toyota following him. Nor did he see it pull off the street and park several hundred yards up from the Klein residence as he pulled into the driveway.

Charlie was escorted by Dick Anthony into the spacious kitchen. Emily Klein and Sue Schneider were already seated at a large breakfast table spread with sandwiches, coffee, ice and soft drinks. Everything was set for a long afternoon.

It didn't take Preston long to figure out where Charlie was going. When Scott reached the Mercer Island Bridge, Preston dropped further behind Scott's car to avoid detection, and once they were on Klein's street, he lay back still further. Noticing a wide berm north of the Klein residence, he pulled over and shut off his engine.

He waited a few minutes to be sure Scott was inside the house before he grabbed his notepad, directional microphone and portable recorder and ventured out of the car. He left his raincoat sitting on the passenger seat; it was too bulky for stealth work. Hugging the foliage on the side of the road, cursing the rain, he made his way to the open gate of the Klein property. Next to Scott's sedan was a black Jaguar, which he knew from its tags belonged to Dick Anthony, the defense lawyer. There was also a station wagon next to the Jag. He made a note of its license tags.

The wife must be in serious trouble. Why else would she have brought in a heavy hitter like Anthony? Yet something didn't fit: the meeting wasn't being held at police headquarters, where interviews with principal suspects were usually conducted.

Walking carefully down the slope toward the pier, he crept to the wall and peered over. From here, he could see the entire backyard and the back of the house. He focused on the house, looking for movement.

Within minutes he spotted several people sitting at a table behind a large picture window. He could make out Scott and another woman, a blonde. Mrs. Klein wasn't a blonde. Who was this woman? Squinting in the rain, he looked for a better vantage point, but found none.

Could he get inside? There had been an open garage door on the east side of the house. The picture window revealing Scott and the blonde was on the northwest side of the house. If everyone was in that room, he should be able to enter through the back of the garage—assuming the interior door was not locked. His directional mike was powerful; he wouldn't have to be that close. He readied and tested his equipment. He had three micro-cassettes, three hours of recording time.

Tingling with anticipation, he made his way along the wall to the driveway. Then he was through the gate, crouching low, moving by the station wagon to the open garage door. He removed his sodden loafers to avoid leaving wet footprints, and carried them with him. He tip-toed over to the interior door. Wiping the wet soles of his shoes on a tarp hanging nearby on the wall, he placed them next to the door.

Preston could hear his heart pounding from the adrenaline high. He was taking a big risk opening the door. But risks and rewards, the end justifying the means, were how big stories were broken.

He placed his ear against the wood, listening for sounds on the other side. Hearing none, he took a deep breath, said a prayer and opened the door.

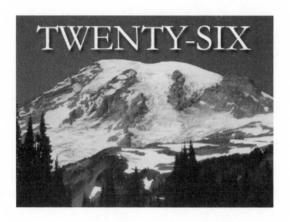

TWENTY-SIX

Thursday, August 1

Preston looked at his watch: 2:30, time to get out of there. Things were winding down now, questions and answers becoming repetitive. He was now at high risk.

But what a story! Blackmail. Murder. Intrigue. Greed. Power. Everything but sex.

And G. Sherwood Preston, courageous, crusading reporter, avenging voice of the people, scourge of the high, mighty and crooked, had bagged it. This story was his ticket to Pulitzerland. And he'd rub Wayne Huston's and Chancey LaRue's faces in it.

Get out now.

Preston stretched each leg. Slowly and carefully, he got to his feet. Blood tingled in his legs.

He bent over to pick up his microphone and recorder, and a micro-cassette tumbled out of his breast pocket to the tile floor below.

Thwap!

Oh, shit! They had to hear that!

Preston scooped up the cassette and his equipment, even as

he was moving toward the door. Clutching the offending cassette, he edged the door open. Slipping out, he closed it, bent to retrieve his shoes, then hurried through the garage out to the driveway. Crouching low, once more cursing the rain, he raced across the pavement out to the street.

He looked for shelter. It made no sense to run for the car now. If Scott came out, he couldn't help but see Preston legging it down the road. No, he had to hide fast. He'd return to the car later.

But where to go? The landing was out; that'd be the first place Scott would look.

Instinct took him. *Go away from the landing. They wouldn't expect that.*

He ran. Ahead was a chest-high cement block wall surrounding some trash containers. In front of the wall was a row of pine trees, and behind it more trees stretching down the roadway, fronting the next-door-neighbor's wall.

Legs pumping, chest heaving, Preston slid down the berm pressed as close to the trees as possible. He dove for cover. He lay face down and motionless in wet gravel. His lungs ached. His knees and feet were raw.

He wanted to look, wanted to rise up and peer over the wall. At any moment he expected to feel the strong arm of the law yanking at his collar. But he forced himself to lay still until his breathing normalized. Several minutes later, having heard nothing but his own ragged breathing, he got up on his bruised knees. He inched up the low wall to where he could see.

No one was there.

How much time had passed? He looked at his watch: 2:40. Only ten minutes since he'd stopped recording. And now he was stuck. Wet, cold and hurting, he couldn't start back to the car until Scott and Anthony left; he couldn't take the chance of being seen. A shiver shook him and daggers stabbed his knees.

Pulitzer territory.

In the kitchen, everybody heard the odd clatter in the laundry room. Scott whispered to Emily Klein, "Is anyone else here?"

When she shook her head, he asked, "What's in there?"

Anthony whispered, "There's a laundry room, then a small mudroom, leading to the garage. I came in through there." He turned to Emily. "Did you close the garage door after I came in?"

"I don't know," she whispered, her hand at her throat. "I don't think so."

Scott cleared his coat from his holster as he and Anthony moved to the laundry room. On top of the dryer on the far wall was a pile of clothes. On the floor next to the dryer lay a few scattered items which apparently had fallen. Charlie picked up the fallen clothing and saw it was mostly a collection of blouses. Looking between the dryer and the washer, he saw a belt with a large brass buckle on the floor. Smiling, he picked it up and showed it to Anthony, who nodded.

Returning to the kitchen, Charlie smiled and held the belt up before he dropped it to the floor, where it went "Thwap." As everyone relaxed, the two men retook their seats.

A few moments later, Charlie and Anthony left to speak privately in the living room while the two women remained seated. Sue turned to Emily. "I'm still having trouble believing it," she said, her voice strained. "My husband *blackmailed?* I mean, I know there's just no other explanation... But my word, I *lived* with that man for years. What on earth could Boyd have found?"

"Who knows, Sue? It may have been before your time."

Schneider was staring out the window, thinking. She turned back to her friend. "Well, it certainly fits. It explains so much: Tom's strange, distracted behavior; his wild mood swings; his depression; his drinking; his hatred of Boyd—everything!" She began to cry again.

Emily put a reassuring arm around her friend. "Sue, I can't thank you enough for coming. I think even Detective Scott sees it now." She disengaged her arm. "But...you know, well... Sue, if Boyd killed Herman... uh... he may have killed Tom too."

"*What?*"

"I'm sorry... maybe I'm getting carried away. But think about it..." Another pause. "Let's say Boyd became increasingly nervous that Tom was going to spill the beans—either to you or to the authorities." Sue sat staring at Emily, her complexion pale. "Okay, we know Carmody was with Tom the night he died, and Carmody—and the restaurant for that matter—say that Tom wasn't drunk. So where'd he do his drinking? There's really no other place between the restaurant and... well... *Sue, what if Boyd was at the restaurant?* Maybe *waiting* for Tom?" Her eyes grew wide. "*Sue?*"

Sue Schneider's eyes rolled up and she slipped out of her chair. Emily screamed, and Scott and Anthony both ran back. Applying wet towels and rubbing Sue's face and arms, they soon roused her. They eased her back into a chair.

"It's entirely my fault," Emily said. She turned to her stricken friend. "Oh Sue, I'm so sorry. I never meant to hurt you."

Both men looked at Emily, Scott angry, Anthony puzzled. "I think you'd better tell us what happened, Mrs. Klein," Scott said.

As Emily explained, Sue Schneider twisted her wedding ring.

Charlie leaned forward. "Mrs. Klein, you're not doing anyone any good with this, certainly not Mrs. Schneider here, nor yourself. Let me explain something to you: causing the death of a federal judge is a matter for the FBI, not the local police. Now I assume that when Judge Schneider died, there was some sort of federal investigation..." He looked at Sue Schneider, who nodded.

"That's what I thought. Now, if you or Mrs. Schneider have anything to tell the FBI, do so. But understand, that won't help us here. In fact, it may sidetrack us. This investigation—not that one—should be your primary concern, Mrs. Klein. You're still a suspect. Do I make myself clear?" Emily nodded, for once at a loss for words.

"Good! Dick, do you have anything to add?"

"Charlie, you're being a little harsh. We covered a lot of ground here today, and I think we've all learned a lot. We left them here alone and in an emotional state; it's only logical that they'd continue discussing things. I'm just sorry that Mrs. Schneider, who was so helpful to us here today, was distressed. I hope she bears no hard feelings."

Everyone looked at Sue, who turned to Emily and forced a weak, embarrassed smile. "No, I'm fine," she said.

Charlie wound it up. "Mrs. Klein, before Mrs. Schneider fainted, your attorney and I were discussing where we go from here. I told him that after today, I... well, I believe your story." He saw her react and held up his hand. "Now, you understand, I'm just part of this investigation. My word doesn't necessarily govern here. But if you are willing to submit to a multi-phasic polygraph examination before someone mutually agreed upon, and you pass...." He paused again. "Then I think you'll have little to fear in this investigation."

As Emily and Sue hugged, Scott suggested that Emily consult with her attorney about the polygraph, and he gave Anthony the numbers where he could be reached over the weekend.

Charlie wanted to get out of there. He didn't care for the magpie nagpie Emily Klein, but he did believe her. Claiming a need to return to his office, he headed for the door. He was unable to avoid a cloying magpie hug.

A wet, cold and ailing G. Sherwood Preston watched with glassy eyes from his bunker. He watched as Charlie's car drove north toward the interstate. He'd about given up on the detective, thinking he'd decided to stay for dinner, as unlikely as that seemed. What could Scott have been doing in there so long?

He didn't have the slightest idea, nor did he really care. He just wanted to get home to a hot bath, some dry clothes, and some band aids. All of the elation he'd felt at having locked up the biggest story of his career, the story that would finally put that bitch, Chancey LaRue, in her place, had long since dissipated. What once had been a beautiful Saville Row suit, one that had cost him a month's wages in London, was now a rag. His stockings were shredded. He thought he had a fever, although it was hard to tell, what with all the shivering from the wet and cold. Only his dreadful fear of a felony conviction had kept him in this hellhole.

After Charlie Scott left, Preston had to endure another miserable half hour before Anthony too departed. Then he struggled to his feet and found his balance. He took a tentative step, then another, as pain shot through his feet and joints. The once-elegant G. Sherwood Preston worked his way up the road. Someday, he told himself, he'd forget all this; he'd just remember the Pulitzer glory that would soon be his.

TWENTY-SEVEN

Thursday, August 1

The sound of the buzzer on his desk broke Captain Jerry MacGregor's reverie. For the past half hour, he had been daydreaming. He felt terrible, had felt that way all day. He knew his health was deteriorating; his age and lifestyle, the weight, the bad eating habits—the cigars—all left him barely able to cope with the pressures he faced. Maybe Betty was right: maybe it was time to go.

Irena stuck her face in the doorway. "Captain, didn't you hear me buzz? Are you all right?"

"Yes, I was ignoring it. Who is it?"

"Sam Terry."

"Again?"

"Yes. Want me to tell him you're unavailable?"

He sighed. "Thank you, no. He'll just call me at home."

"I think you'd better put a stop to that, sir."

"Yeah," he said absently, "maybe I'll shoot him."

The light on MacGregor's phone began flashing a moment later. He watched it for a second and then picked up.

"Hello, Sam," he said. "What's up?"

You're intentionally interfering with a client relationship. That's actionable."

"Sam, what in hell are you talking about?"

"You know damn well what I'm talking about: Marge Simmons!"

"Oh, that."

"See?"

"Sam, she called us."

"You tricked her. Got her to look in one of our confidential files too. I've told you before there's nothing to your cockamamie Emery Boyd theory, and now you've gone behind my back to one of my clients. I'm going to talk to your superiors about this, and if it happens one more time, I'll have your Goddamn ass!"

"Sam, I thought you wanted Klein found."

"You know damn well I do! But I'm not about to let you go prowling around in our files. I'll put a stop to that, by God! I'll file a lawsuit if I have to."

MacGregor gently replaced the phone. He looked up to see a worried Irena filling his doorway. He reached for one of his pills and looked for something to wash it down. There was only this morning's stale coffee.

"What do you want?" he asked.

She held up the vial of pills. "I'm worried sick about you. And I'll tell you this: if you won't take care of yourself, your wife and I will. I'm calling her. Maybe she can do something with you, make you see what you're doing to yourself. I'll be damned if I'm gonna sit here and watch you kill yourself." She wheeled around and stomped back to her desk.

MacGregor nodded. "I'm sorry."

She came back. "You're ready for a stroke or heart attack any day now, and I won't sit back and watch that happen."

"Look, I know I've got a problem."

"Yeah, a medical one. I'm gonna call your doctor and get you an appointment. And then I'm calling your wife."

"Call the doc. I was gonna call him myself. Please don't call Betty."

"She needs to know." She turned and a moment later he heard her dialing.

He leaned over his desk and put his head in his hands.

"Where the hell did you get this?" a disbelieving, lush-lipped Chancey LaRue scrutinized the freshly bathed G. Sherwood Preston. "I've never heard anything like it. Were you in the room?"

"No, my source was."

After finally reaching his car, he'd gone straight to his apartment, where he'd soaked in a hot bath while he worked out the story he would use. The easiest way to explain the tapes, he decided, was the classic "highly placed undisclosed source close to the investigation." A reporter's need to protect his source was sacrosanct within the newspaper community and accepted by the general public. The only real issue would be the tapes' authenticity, and on that score, the tapes spoke for themselves. Any one of the participants could verify the content—how could they deny it?—or if necessary, a scientific examination would nullify tampering. As for the tapes themselves, he would insist on keeping them in his custody. If the newspaper insisted on having them analyzed, he would agree only if he was present and the tapes, and any copies or transcriptions made from them, were returned to him for safekeeping. He wanted to keep these tapes as close to his vest as possible; they were proof that he'd committed a crime. He wasn't about to let anyone else get them.

Preston knew he could be subject to a court order to produce the tapes, but if that happened he would refuse and risk a brief incarceration, in typical heroic reporter fashion. Such unpleasantness would increase his stature—martyr him, so to speak. He'd find himself on talk shows giving speeches on the sanctity of the First Amendment—possibly writing a book.

After his bath, he called LaRue, who, as luck would have it, was still at the office. Asking her not to leave until he got there, he said he had something important on the Klein case and suggested that she hold the headline for tomorrow's paper. As he expected, she demanded details. He made her wait.

Confident and cocky, he stiff-walked into LaRue's office without knocking and seated himself, not without pain, in a chair opposite her desk, then began setting up his recorder. Without any explanations, except to identify the participants, he played portions of the tape for her.

"Who is your source?" LaRue inquired early on.

"Can't say."

LaRue continued listening, fascinated. A little later, she reached over, stopped the tape and said, "Sherwood, something this explosive, implicating one of this city's leading citizens, can't go to press without my knowing who the source is. Surely, you understand that. We could be sued."

"Bullshit! Sued for what? They're tapes! The source is irrelevant. The tapes speak for themselves. They say that the police *suspect* Boyd; they *don't* say he *murdered* Klein. And that's just what I'm going to write."

LaRue glowered. "If that's the way you write it up, if Legal and the editor-in-chief, maybe Mr. Huston, all approve it, then we'll see. But you better hurry."

"How long are they going to be here?"

"I don't know. It's 8:00 now. Deadline is 10:00. But if it's really good, who knows? I'll check and see, tell them what you've got and we'll see what they say. Okay?"

"All right, I'll have it for you in an hour."

"Good. And Preston..." she said, as her stilettos spiked to the door.

"What?

"Keep it simple, straightforward. Don't embellish."

Preston muttered "Fuck you" and collected his tapes.

TWENTY-NINE

Thursday, August 1

At 6:30 P.M., an exhausted Amy Galler, in the company of John Whitney, was just stumbling through the fog and rain bank that still hung over Paradise Lodge. She was tired beyond words and desperately conflicted. Blindly she followed her leader, hoping that around each bend, over each rise, would be the welcome sight of Paradise. She found herself thinking only of a bath, bed and sleep.

For his part, John seemed to have as much energy as when they'd started. She admired his stamina, one of the many things she admired. For John, she knew, this had been a stroll.

John had predicted she'd be tired; he'd told her early on he doubted she'd want to have dinner with him. She thought that meant a pass was coming, a prospect she wasn't sure she'd mind. But now she understood better. She was too exhausted to eat.

John had said all day that she was doing just fine. "Your primary problems are lack of proper caloric intake and the fact that you're not breathing properly," he said during one of their rest stops. "On an average day, a mountain climber will burn about eleven thousand calories. What did *you* eat today?"

"I skipped lunch but had a big breakfast."

"I'm surprised you made it a mile," he teased, giving her a candy bar from his day pack. As she'd clawed it open, he said, "Don't expect too much. These may tide you over for a while, but they won't do the job that a hearty meal will. You'll feel a quick pick-up, but it won't last. And it'll disappear just as fast as it comes on. Here," he said, handing her several more, "take these too. If you run out, I've got more. I kinda thought this might happen. Next time, eat like a horse."

He'd shown her how to power-breathe. "It's really simple," he explained. "Just force your exhale. Don't worry about the intake; it will take care of itself. It's the exhale that's most important. Most people use only about a third of their lung capacity. Before the lungs can be filled, they must be emptied. Here, let me show you."

Exaggerating for the purpose of instruction, he exhaled in a loud whoosh. Amy mimicked him, and they both started laughing. But he'd insisted she practice, saying he wanted to be able to hear her from a distance. After a while, he said, the breathing would become second nature.

At first, she thought John was enjoying making her sound like a mule. But the more she practiced, the more air she had.

Next, he'd taught her the pause-step. "You want to avoid constant upward motion, which is too tiring. With the pause stroke, your pumping leg gets a little rest each step. That will help save energy for the more tiring trip down."

"What? How could going down be more tiring?"

He demonstrated the difference in range of motion and stresses on the leg from upstroke versus downstroke. But the proof was yet to come. Amy had been tired going up, but nothing like coming down—when each step was dreaded.

John said she'd be sore tomorrow but that the best tonic was another trip. He volunteered to be her guide.

Tired as she was, Amy had to admit that this afternoon had been one of the most special, most beautiful of her life. She'd seen pictures of mountain vistas, but never anything like the panoramic beauty she saw here.

Shortly after they'd left Paradise, they broke through the seemingly impenetrable fog and rain bank. Above it, the sun had been bright and warm, requiring the shedding of jackets and application of a thick layer of sunscreen.

"You know," John said during a rest break at Panorama Point, while Amy had been looking out over the sea of fog, broken only by the islands of St. Helens, Mt. Adams and Mt. Hood, "this is the best day since the storm. Often when it's raining at Paradise, it's like this—sunny—up here. But this summer, even the upper reaches of the mountain have had steady rain, fog, drizzle and snow. I just hope today's weather means that's over."

"For the tourist trade?"

"No. I'm worried about the glaciers."

John's face was serious in the slanting sunlight. "What do you mean?" she asked.

"You know that a glacier is a river of ice, right?"

"Yes."

"Well, depending on water levels and the mass and weight of the ice, portions of it float or rest on the bottom. If the water level grows too high, the glacier shifts."

"So?"

"Look at it this way: If you have a full glass of water, then fill the glass with ice, what happens?"

"You have a mess."

"Exactly. And it's the same with glaciers. If the ice moves, you can have huge avalanches, as ice cubes the size of buildings shake loose. Or, if the water spills over, you can have raging lahars—mudflows. A lahar can be fifty feet high or higher and move at great speed, knocking down trees, rocks, anything that gets in its way. Do you remember when you came into the park, seeing a long stretch of dead trees at Longmire?"

"Yes, I do. Was that the result of a lahu?"

"'Lahar,'" he corrected, smiling. "But yes, that's exactly what it was, about seventy years ago."

"But you said lahars knock trees down. Those were still standing, just dead."

"Yes, that's because at lower levels the flow spreads out. Those trees suffocated. At the higher levels though, that sucker would have been awesome!

"Did you notice the Nisqually River, the river that runs from the glacier to Puget Sound? It runs adjacent to the park road."

"Yes."

"Well, as you leave, take a closer look. There are rocks there, twenty miles or more from the mountain, that are as big as a house. How do you suppose they got there?"

"You mean..."

"Yup. Lahars come in all shapes and sizes. That's why I'm so worried. No telling what heavy rains on those massive glaciers might do. If the rain continues, we'll close the park."

As they climbed, John pointed out mountain wildlife, both plant and animal. Amy took great delight in the high-pitched scream of the beautiful, furry marmot, and thought the little mouse-like pika, with such big ears, was "cute." And the smell of the mountain meadows, so full of flowery delights, had been like fields of potpourri.

They'd traversed up the east side of the mountain to the ice caves. The caves were breathtaking, translucent blue ice sanctuaries, nearly transparent in some areas. Without a word, John took Amy into his arms, and she shivered, not with cold, but anticipation. A first tentative kiss grew into a long lingering one. Surrounded by ice, Amy felt herself melt into John's lean, hard body.

Moments later, when they finally separated, breathless and flushed, they fell back. Neither spoke, but promise and expectancy were electric between them…

"You know how long I've wanted to do that?"

"No longer than I have, John."

"Better wait, I guess. Want your parka on?"

"No. You've sent my blood heat up ten degrees."

John smiled, but there was something reflective in his eyes.

Later, when they were resting Amy's jellied muscles, she followed up on his look. "John?"

"Mmmm?"

"Back in the ice cave—"

"Just thinking about that myself." He touched her cheek, a surprisingly tender gesture. For a moment it knocked Amy off guard.

"No, I mean I thought I saw a look in your eyes. Is something bothering you?"

"Bothering me?" He shifted his weight, looked down.

"You had the same look the night I met you. Just once in a while."

He smiled. "Over the spaghetti and meatballs."

"Yes."

"Over the wine."

"John?"

"I know, I'm dodging. Fact is I'm not comfortable with Emery's story about what happened out there."

Amy waited.

"Emery's a first-class mountaineer, good as I am, but don't tell him that." He gave a quick smile, then it was gone.

"But what he said bothered you."

John pulled at his boot. "As a matter of fact, yes."

"What bothered you? Look, I'm sorry, this is your business—"

"No, it's okay. It's just that all his talk about following a poacher through a blizzard, it doesn't sit right. He knows I know it doesn't sit right."

"So what will happen?"

John stood up, smiling, and reached for her hand. "We're old friends, we'll do what old friends do—talk."

"Well," Amy said, feeling stress, interrogating someone she was now deeply involved with, "I can understand him getting lost. It's so wild up here, and fog and storms…"

"Could happen, I guess."

Amy took in the words that were obviously for her benefit. "So he really could get lost? You could get lost?"

"Like I say, it could happen." John stared off toward Mt. St. Helens. He seemed as distant as its ruined peak.

Amy didn't push. Not the time. And John wasn't the man. Amy was skilled at assessment. She was called upon to judge people every day: who was lying; who would cave under the right pressure; who would kill when a weapon was in hand. Life and death assessments. She read John as honest and loyal, deliberate, one who would not be pushed; someone who would be slow to make a judgment, but once made would stubbornly defend it with grit and determination. Not someone to be trifled with.

Which led to the problem, what had been bothering her all day…

Training and instinct said to ward this man off, use him, do whatever was necessary to pry information from him, but remain objective, distant. Her heart wouldn't let her. She wanted to wrap herself around John Whitney, smell the heat, feel the strength, taste the danger. Emotions and reason in conflict, her resolve was breaking down.

They'd made it to the snowbank surrounding the lodge. She had stumbled down the embankment, glad for John's supporting hands.

Reaching bottom, John swooped her up into his strong arms and carried her over to the entrance. "I'm going now," he said, as he released her. "I've got to check in—see who Maselli's accosting. Then I've got to see a few people. See you tomorrow? Same time and place?"

She nodded. They kissed, this time briefly. Her fatigue and conflict were taking their toll. As they parted, their hands lingered.

John walked a few steps and turned. "Any chance you can stay next week?"

The question surprised her. Would she still be a cop? Too tired to think. "Don't know. Work, you know."

"Well, think about it. Boyd is due in sometime Monday, and he and I have to meet, but if you're around, I'll re-arrange my schedule so that as soon as he and I finish our business, we can be together."

"Good luck with it."

Amy went directly to her room. She forced her way over the exhaustion and checked the hair traps. *Broken hair at the door. Broken hair at the bathroom door.* Quickly she checked the excursion bag: *hair dislodged.* It took her a few moments to recall that Sherry had come to the room. The hair traps had been innocently broken by Sherry. But what was with the bag? Amy opened it and noticed the crime notes had been rearranged.

Wearily, Amy retrieved her .38, took it into the bathroom, and placed it on a towel beside the tub, careful to fold over the edge so the gun wouldn't get wet. She undressed and climbed in, turned on the tap, and stood back while she waited for hot water. There were tortured groans from the pipes, then steam began rising. She flipped the switch for the shower, shuddered at the first touch of cold water, then sighed as it became hot. Her legs were shot. She sat down groaning, then slid into a reclining position, letting the shower's soothing hot spray pound her.

Out of the shower and dried off, she picked up the .38 and looked longingly at the bed, which last night had seemed so hard and uncomfortable but now looked so inviting. Instead of flopping down, she called the front desk and asked for Sherry.

"Hi, Sherry," she said once they were connected. "You got a room, huh?"

"Yes, no sweat. There were several cancellations."

"Great."

"You sound exhausted."

"I'm dead on my feet. Do you have plans for dinner? I'll tell you all about it."

"I was kinda hoping you might be free. What time?"

"Why don't you call me in about an hour? Is that okay? Can you wait?"

Sherry laughed. "No problem. Sweet dreams. I'll call you in an hour."

Amy hung up and walked over to the bed, tucking the .38 under the pillow. She sighed heavily when her head hit the foam rubber; then she was out.

Wayne Malcolm Huston, elderly but spry publisher of the Seattle *Post*, looked up from the printout he'd been reviewing, cynicism etched on his face. He looked first at Preston, seated next to him, then at the others sitting around the large oval mahogany conference room table. Only Preston, who'd been eagerly and nervously awaiting his reaction, returned his gaze. Huston returned to his copy of the document that all present, except for Preston, were studying.

Preston looked at his watch: 9:45 P.M., fifteen minutes to deadline. How much longer before someone said something?

The lawyer, Turner K. Chapman, would be first, Preston guessed. Lawyers liked to talk. This one was nicknamed "Chip," although Preston had no idea why. Chip was a small, overweight, balding, mousey-looking man, about fifty, whose Armani suit was wasted on him. He had, to Preston's knowledge, never been in a courtroom handling real work. But that didn't stop him from being a show stopper. Preston knew Chapman's favorite word was "No."

Next to Chapman sat Evan B. Cutter, the editor-in-chief, a

disheveled, boorish man of about forty-five; someone who, despite his position in the organization, seemed out of place in an office. An Armani wouldn't save him either, Preston thought. Cutter was reading also, but as usual was in an agitated state: legs moving, arms moving, and teeth chewing on his lip. Cutter looked as if he was about to have a heart attack. But then, Cutter always looked that way.

Next to the publisher, on his left, was the office brown-nose, Preston's nemesis, Chancey LaRue. As usual, she was positioned next to Huston, where she could hang on his every word and second every statement.

At 9:55, the lawyer, Turner K. Chapman, looked up. "Do you expect us to approve this for publication tonight?"

"Yes, Mr. Chapman, I do. I've played portions of the underlying tape to Miss LaRue. She can verify the article is correct, and— "

"Wait a minute," Chapman interrupted. "You mean nobody's listened to the *whole* tape?"

"Well, er… Mr. Chapman," Preston said, "the tape is over two hours long."

Chapman turned to the publisher. "Wayne, before we even consider publishing this article, I want to listen to the whole tape. How do we know there aren't portions which contradict what's in this article? All we have is this man's word." He gestured toward Preston with a dismissive wave. "An article of this type…asserting serious charges against a prominent member of this community, not to mention the bar… Well, we need more. I do not believe it is reasonable for this paper to publish such potentially libelous material without at least some verification or confirmation. Thanks to the Supreme Court, we don't have to do much before we smear a public figure like Boyd, but we damn sure have to do something. If we were to print this, and it turned out not to be true, Boyd would claim the newspaper's recklessness in not even listening to the entire tape, or doing any checking at all, was malice. He'd martinize us."

"What sort of verification do you need, Chip?" Huston asked.

"Yes," chimed Chancey LaRue, ripe lips moving. "What sort of verification do you need?"

"For starters, how about verifying these people on the tape are who Preston says they are? I'm not saying you have to turn over *every* leaf, but I'd think you might want to know that. Or maybe get a confirmation from, what's their captain's name?"

"MacGregor," LaRue and Preston said simultaneously.

"Yes. Well, anyway, confirmation of the tape contents from him, or even this Detective Scott, who Preston mentions in the article, would give me more comfort." Chapman continued, "Wayne, Boyd's a partner in one of this city's most prestigious law firms. We're practically saying he *murdered* one of his part- ners."

"He did!" Preston blurted.

Both LaRue and Chapman shot Preston angry looks. "Shut up, Preston!" LaRue snapped, her face red. "We don't know any such thing. And your article doesn't say that. It says the police are investigating him, or at least it will when I get through with it."

Huston held up his hands, a silent command. "Now let's just everybody cool off. Chip's right, we need more before we can go to press with this. I've known Sam Terry for years, and I've met Boyd. They're influential and they're tough, serious litigators. We've got to at least verify that the people on this tape are who Preston says they are, and that the tape contains what he says it does." He paused for a moment. "Now, I don't see how we can do that right now. So we'll wait."

"Yes, we should wait," said LaRue.

Huston said, "Besides, I think this might be better for Sunday."

"Yes, Sunday," LaRue added.

"Chancey, please," Huston said, deviating from tradition. "I have an idea this could lead to something interesting..." He turned to his editor-in-chief, who was busy nibbling on the skin around his thumb. "Evan, didn't we do an article—maybe more than one—on this EAC decision of Schneider's?"

Cutter jumped at the sound of his name. He nodded.

"That's what I thought. I think you may remember it too, Chip. You were worried about that one too."

Chapman nodded. "We were implying improper influence. For obvious reasons, I fought that, and as I recall, we substantially watered down our comments."

"Hmmm, yes, I think you're right," Huston said. "Well anyway, Preston's story, if it holds up, lets us resurrect all that, get back into this Schneider thing once more. Hell, he's dead now. As I recall, Chip, you can't libel the dead."

"No, you're right, but I urge extreme caution here. We can't libel Schneider, but we can sure as hell libel Boyd."

"Point well taken."

"Yes, good point!" said LaRue.

"Well, we'll just be careful," Huston said. "As long as we stick to what's on the tape—assuming it's verifiable—and couch it in terms of a 'police investigation,' I think we'll be all right. Don't you, Chip?"

"I'd have to give you a guarded yes, Wayne. But I want to pre-approve the article when it's re-written. We're on slippery and dangerous ground here."

"I think we all know that, Chip," Huston said. "And yes, I want you to pre-approve any articles which point accusing fingers in Emery Boyd's direction."

"Yes." LaRue made a note with a flourish.

Huston turned to his editor-in-chief. "Evan, why don't you have someone pull out everything they can find on that EAC case? I want to be ready to go with this stuff next week, assuming Preston here can satisfy Chip. Let's get someone to back him up. I want Preston to stay on top of this Boyd thing, and I want his byline on everything. This is his story, and if it works, he gets the credit. By the same token, if he's wrong, he pays the piper. That's the nature of responsibility and the public trust."

"You know," Cutter said, "something about this bothers me. Like everybody else, we reported that Boyd was lost in that Rainier storm. How can Boyd be there and out on Mercer Island killing his partner at the same time? And where's the body? The police still haven't found one, have they?"

"Good point," said Huston. "Preston, what do you say to that?"

"Well, as my article points out, the police think maybe Boyd wasn't on Rainier the whole time, and wasn't lost in the storm. They're not sure yet. They've got a detective out there now, trying to pierce his alibi."

"Do we know if they've found anything?" Huston asked.

"No, sir. They're being very tight-lipped."

Huston appeared pensive, Chapman too; both were frowning. Lest his partial victory be lost, Preston added, "But I don't see that his alibi is our problem; that's a problem for the police. They can't very well charge Boyd until they break his alibi, I suppose, and the lack of a body may be an obstacle for them. But we're not saying he did it. As you've all made very clear, we're just saying they're *investigating* him. It's all on the tape. We're just reporting what they're investigating."

Chapman said, "Preston's right, Wayne. Boyd's alibi is a problem for the police, not us. If they're investigating him, we can report that. The police will have to beat his alibi before they can charge him. While the lack of a body is a problem, they might be able to overcome that with circumstantial proof. But that's not our problem either. We just need to verify that they're investigating him. We can report that he appears to have an alibi."

Huston turned once more to Preston. "Well, Preston, looks to me like you've got some work to do. Get on it. If you can verify this tape to Chip's satisfaction, we'll run your article, at least in some form."

Preston smiled and stroked his freshly groomed moustache. He'd suspected his article would be watered down somewhat—after all, a lawyer would be picking through it—but it sounded like it would be largely intact. And the paper was prepared to support him with follow-on material under his by-line. His Pulitzer was still in sight.

Huston turned to him. "Preston, you know how to work a modem, don't you?"

"Yes," he said. "Why?"

"Because, assuming you can authenticate your tape, you're going to need to take a laptop with you, so you can write your copy and review what else Evan here and his troops come up with for you. If this thing pans out, you're going to be mighty busy."

Preston looked confused. "I'm sorry, sir. I don't understand. Why do I need a laptop and a modem? I've got DSL at home."

"Why, Preston!" said a laughing Wayne Malcolm Huston, "I'm surprised you had to ask. I thought it was obvious: you're going mountain climbing, my boy!"

A stunned G. Sherwood Preston barely heard the predictable echo.

Amy Galler was drawn out of a deep sleep by a shake. "Amy? Are you going to eat?"

She sat up and looked around. Didn't have a clue where she was.

"Amy?" Sherry was standing in front of her. "Sorry. I tried calling you, tried knocking, then remembered I had a key. I knocked over your soda cans, but you didn't wake up. Do you want to eat or go back to sleep?"

"Sherry," Amy said, as if for reassurance. Her head was clearing, but when she moved, her legs felt like rubber. "Let me throw some water on my face. I better eat."

Sherry stepped back as Amy got up and made her way into the bathroom. She shut the door. Running water, the flushing of a toilet. The door opened and Amy peered out. "Look, why don't you go get us a table. I'll be down in a minute. I've got to dress, and there's no sense you just standing there. I promise I won't fall back asleep."

Sherry nodded and left. When she was gone, Amy sighed. Transferring the holstered .38 with Sherry present would have blown her cover. She put on jeans, the belt holster and a loose sweater. Her badge and I.D. were still in her pack. She plucked some hairs, grabbed her bag, set her alarms and was out the door in minutes.

Sherry was at the last table on the left, and the restaurant was full. Camille was their waitress, and she'd left a menu for Amy. Amy gave it a quick glance, then caught Camille's eye. "Coffee, please, a pot of it."

Camille took one look at Amy's face and smiled. "You're gonna be sore tomorrow."

Amy nodded. "I'm sore now." She looked at the menu. Several minutes later, she was sipping coffee and had ordered a steak. No wine tonight. Sherry hadn't wanted any, and Amy was worried about dehydration. She'd guzzled her first glass of water. She handed Camille her menu and smiled at Sherry. "Hope things weren't too messy in my room."

"No, not at all. You're tidier than I am."

Amy waited. Give her a chance to talk. The excursion bag, the notes…

"Amy?"

"Yes."

Sherry shook her head. "I don't know how to say this—"

"Say what? What's the matter?"

"Look, are you really a bookkeeper?"

Amy watched Sherry as Camille brought them salad and rolls

and re-filled their water glasses. As soon as Camille had left, Amy said, "Why don't you tell me what's bothering you?"

Sherry looked away, then looked back. She was playing with her fork. She took a deep breath. "Okay... Don't be mad."

Amy poured more coffee and waited.

"See, I was looking out the window, at all the rain and fog, then I glanced over and saw that big excursion bag you bought. That made me think, gee, maybe I forgot to bring something more than just raingear. Maybe I should compare what I brought with what Amy brought. So I opened the pack."

Amy rubbed her temple. "Did you look at the papers?"

Sherry nodded. "Please don't be mad. I wasn't snooping. I just..." Tears formed.

Amy sighed. "It's okay, Sherry. Don't get upset. I understand. And I don't think you were snooping." She sipped her coffee. "I probably would have done the same thing. Hell, neither one of us knew what we were supposed to bring up here."

"But who are you?"

Amy leaned forward. "Stay cool, okay?"

"Okay."

"I'm a homicide detective and I'm here on an undercover assignment."

"Jesus, Amy—"

"Cool, I said."

Sherry quieted.

"But you must have had some idea. From my notes..."

"Yeah, but it's one thing to read, it's another to hear it out loud."

Amy smiled.

"Are you checking on John Whitney, you were with him today?"

"Enough, Sherry. We'll talk outside."

"Okay."

"Look, I can't tell you all, and forget the notes. Technically, I could have you taken into custody and away from this investigation."

Sherry's eyes grew big. "Really?"

Amy nodded. "Count on it."

"I understand. It's okay, Amy."

"Good. Let's eat."

Outside, they found a bench at the side of the lodge.

"So if it's not John Whitney, then who?" Sherry asked.

"I'm investigating a friend of his, for a murder in Seattle, although there may be more to it than that."

"Emery Boyd."

"You know about Boyd?"

"Yeah, from your notes, that and the fact his picture's plastered all over the Guide Service Shack. I went over there to buy some wool socks. I realized when I saw your stuff, I needed some. I had some time to kill, so I looked around. He and John Whitney are famous."

"Okay, Sherry. Stay out of things. All right?"

"But I've seen your notes. Can I help?"

"Absolutely not! You're a civilian." Amy put her head in her hands. "Oh, Christ, what a screw-up."

"Don't worry, Amy. I won't say anything. I promise."

Amy stared at her, realizing her own life could be in Sherry's hands.

Sherry poked her, eyes shining. "So, tell me about John Whitney."

Back inside her room, Amy went immediately to the excursion bag and pulled out her notes, cursing herself for not taking them with her today. She'd been afraid they'd get wet. Hell, she should have locked them in the trunk of the car. Charlie would be furious. And just wait until she told him about John Whitney...

Tired as she was—bone tired, the kind of tired that had already muddled her brain and dulled her senses—she had to tell him. Charlie was her partner; sharing information kept them both alive.

Notes in hand, she sat at the table and reached for the phone. Claire answered. Charlie was out. But he'd left a message.

"What is it?"

"Let's see, I wrote it down somewhere… Oh, yes, here it is… It says, 'Nail Boyd!' It's underlined twice. Does that make sense to you?"

Amy stood in the quiet of her room. John had said Emery Boyd would arrive Monday. The earlier queasiness came back hard, and she rushed to the bathroom and vomited up her steak and rolls.

THIRTY

Friday, August 2

Amy awoke before her wake-up call after a fitful sleep. Every movement during the night had been painful, and worry had troubled her dreams. Awake, the muscle and joint pains were stabbing, nearly crippling her movement. And the conflicts, embarrassment, fear and guilt remained.

It was foggy and warmer outside, the air heavy and brooding.

A hot shower and some difficult stretches helped loosen her muscles and relieve some of the soreness, and may have helped clear her head. She'd planned to call Charlie, talk through her conflict with him, but after the scalding hot water, the relief from her stretches, she dismissed that option. She knew what Charlie would say; she knew what she should do.

But she had other plans.

Her cover was blown, like it or not. But blown it was. It wasn't intentional; it had just happened. Going home was not an option. She was professional, and Charlie had said, *Nail Boyd.* She'd tell John tonight, when Sherry wasn't around, then gauge his reaction. If he cooperated, she'd insist on propriety; if he felt betrayed, well, that was bound to happen at some point anyway. Either way, she'd pry out whatever information John had. She hoped he'd cooperate willingly and understand that his integrity as a witness was keeping her away. And what if he had no information? Well, that might be too much to hope for.

So how mad would Captain MacGregor be? She was a cop in the field, trained to make judgments on the fly. MacGregor had praised her intuition, her hunches, so what was different now? John had to be told, it was just that simple. Sure, she could call MacGregor, but he wasn't here. He hadn't met John, wasn't familiar with the context. She'd be on the phone all-damn-day.

That she couldn't tolerate. And there was something she wanted to do.

Dressing as quickly as her sore muscles allowed, putting her cop stuff in their usual places, she stiff-walked to the dining room to meet Sherry, who was already at a table and had coffee waiting. Ordering immediately, she told Sherry that she was in a hurry and had to attend to some business away from the mountain. She wouldn't be late for the one o'clock rendezvous, however, and she confirmed where they'd meet.

"Are you sure I can't help you?" Sherry asked, a hurt look on her face.

"Sherry, we talked about this. I can't involve you. I just can't. It's too dangerous, you're a civilian, and you're not trained. Now, I'm sorry, but I have to do this alone. We can't talk about this any more."

"But surely I can help in some way."

"If you want to help, say nothing about what you saw or what you know. After it's all over, I swear I'll tell you all about it. Okay?"

"I told you I wouldn't say anything."

"And I hope you meant it. I also hope we can still be friends, just like before."

"Sure."

"Great! Then you'll still go with us today?"

"Absolutely. Assuming the weather cooperates." She looked outside.

"Yeah, it looks dreary. But don't worry about that. I'm sure it will be fine. We'll go over what we need later."

"Where are you going to be?"

"Don't ask."

Leaving the lodge at 8:30, she hurried to her car, lugging her camera and purse over her shoulders. Pulling out the map she'd bought in the gift shop and using the general directions the desk clerk had provided, she traced what she believed to be the route to Emery Boyd's cabin.

Skate Creek Road was easy enough to find and follow, and the "bend" the desk clerk had described was quite pronounced. Her only problems were the bumps and the standing and running water in low spots. Several times, as her Honda Prelude bottomed out in a trough or plowed through water, she wondered if this could really be the right road. She was about to look for a turnout, to try somewhere else, when she discovered Boyd's sawdust driveway. The mailbox next to it bore his name.

Her first view of the cabin took her breath away; she stopped the car and just stared. "Jesus! Some cabin—that's a mansion!" she murmured. She felt around the front seat for her camera. Sitting in her car, she snapped an occasional strategic picture, then drove the rest of the driveway, parking just in front of the garage doors.

With no search warrant, there wasn't much she could do except nose around. The idea intrigued her. Amy wondered what Charlie would do if he were here alone. Sightseeing would be her explanation if anyone should catch her. But there wasn't much chance of that: the cabin was in the boonies; Boyd wasn't there, and he was single. She doubted Boyd had a housekeeper, and no other vehicles were in the driveway. Technically, Amy was trespassing, but so what? This place was an attractive nuisance; anyone who owned a place like this should expect gawkers.

Climbing out of her car, she walked around the front yard. The oppressive wetness of the air, much more intense here than at the mile-high Paradise, caused her sinuses to fill, and she felt a sneeze coming on. She pulled some yellow Kleenex tissues out of her back pants pocket. Blowing her nose helped and the sneeze was stifled. Stuffing the used tissues back in her pocket, she didn't notice that one slipped out and fell to the ground, where instantly it became sodden.

Moving up to the wooden deck fronting the massive house, Amy shuffled her feet in the wet grass to clean off any mud. To be sure she wouldn't leave muddy tracks on the wood, she scraped her boots on the edge before stepping up. Once on the deck, she walked directly to the front door, where there was a large brass loop knocker centered at eye level, but no doorbell. Just to be sure there was no one home, she banged the knocker on its brass plate. There was no response.

She walked to the furthest window and pressed her face close to the glass, using her hands to shield the glare. Window by window, she moved to her left. In a couple of places, her nose touched the glass, leaving an oily smudge. "God, what a place," she said into the quiet.

She tried the front door and wasn't surprised to find it locked. Now she moved to the side of the lodge, then to the back, finding more large picture windows, more decking, more impressive views—this time of Lookout Mountain looming above. Peeping through windows where drapes weren't drawn, she saw again glimpses of a large, well-designed, well-furnished cedar palace. She tried the two back doors as well as the one on the side of the large, oversized garage. All were locked.

Deciding there wasn't much more to do, she returned to her car and climbed back in. As she started her engine, her eyes caught her electronic garage door opener, and a thought flashed. She'd heard once that there were only a few frequencies for these things and that once in a while you could open someone else's garage door using your own control. She punched the button.

To her surprise, a garage door rumbled open.

A tired Charlie Scott was having a busy morning. He'd been up late last night meeting with some friends and hadn't gotten to bed until 2:00. Claire had been asleep by then but she'd left a note saying Amy had called. Amy had nothing new to report and would call at seven tomorrow evening. Good. That would give him an excuse to be home early, something that would make Claire happy.

Six A.M. came early, and Charlie struggled out of bed, feeling wasted. He went through his routine of reloading his pistol, palming home the clip, and adjusting his holster. It was a routine that kept gun-shy Claire happy. Arriving at the office, he was told that MacGregor wouldn't make their seven o'clock meeting; he'd been ordered by his doctor and his wife to take the day off and rest. "Great. Thanks for calling me," Charlie gritted, furious at Irena for costing him some sleep.

So what to do now? He thought about going back to bed, but his conscience wouldn't let him. It was too early to set up appointments. He gathered up his files and carried them to the diner.

Returning at nine, Charlie began making calls. First up was David Dawson. He arranged to meet Dawson at his office in the Rainier Bank Building at 9:30, explaining he was trying to track down Herman Klein's movements in the several weeks before his disappearance. Next was John Carmody, Schneider's former law clerk, now an associate at Booker & Boggs. Carmody seemed suspicious, said he'd talked to Klein only once, some time ago, and couldn't see how anything they'd talked about related to his disappearance, but he agreed to meet anyway. Richard Haskins, the FBI agent, was next, but Haskins referred him to Pierce County Sheriff Hank Bourdelais. Bourdelais reluctantly agreed to an afternoon meeting.

As he walked out of the building, on his way to Dawson's office, Charlie found G. Sherwood Preston waiting for him. "Hey, Preston, looking a bit ragged, aren't we? What happened, get busted in a public restroom?"

Preston smirked as he followed him. "Just wait till you see what we're printing Sunday. You'll be calling me looking for hand-outs."

"Yeah? Well, don't bet on it. What're you gonna print? That Klein was captured by aliens?" He laughed, amused at his own joke.

"How 'bout that Emery Boyd is your man?" Preston chided. "That he killed Klein because of law firm politics and because Klein was gonna bust him for improperly influencing a certain federal judge, now deceased? Wanna guess who the judge was?"

Charlie lost his smile. He grabbed Preston by the lapels of his raincoat and shoved him up against a wall.

"Whatsa matter, Charlie?" Preston chortled over a bunched-up collar. "Hitting a nerve?"

"Where'd you get that information, you little worm? Tell me, or I'll pull that Goddamn moustache right off your ugly face."

"Easy, Charlie, we're in front of your building. What better place for me to build a case for police brutality? And I'm no lawbreaker. Hell, Charlie, I'm a guardian of the First Amendment, don'cha know? I'm just asserting my rights. Who knows, maybe I have a photographer stationed across the street."

Scott looked around, saw no one. He released Preston.

Preston smoothed his lapels. "Look, Charlie, maybe we can work together on this. I need things, you need things. You're burdened by a bunch of rules and regulations. I'm not. You scratch my back, I'll scratch yours."

"I'd get fleas. You're not burdened by the truth either, scum-sucker."

"Do we have to be so personal, Charlie? I suppose you're right though, in a way. Technically, I'm not burdened by the truth. But then think about it, neither are you. Face it, do you really care about the truth? Or is it reasonable doubt that concerns you?"

"Preston, what are you talking about?"

"Just this. Look, you know Boyd did it; I know Boyd did it. But there's a difference: you can't do anything about it unless you can dispose of reasonable doubt. Right? I mean, if you were only concerned with truth, you could blow the son of a bitch away now and feel justified in doing so."

"So what?" *Where was this conversation going?*

"Well, as long as Boyd has an ironclad alibi and there's no body, face it, Charlie, you have no case. This, despite the fact that you know he did it. Now I'm in a totally different position. I don't have to have proof beyond a reasonable doubt. I can work with speculation, as long as I'm not malicious. You know how hard it is to prove malice against a newspaper, Charlie? It's damn near impossible. All I have to say is that I have a source and everything's okay."

"Well, I'm sure as hell not going to be your source."

Preston smiled, the tips of his moustache moved up, and Charlie saw yellow teeth. "Charlie, you're way ahead of me. Just hear me out." He paused as Scott watched him warily. "Now, let's say I have a source and refuse to identify him, a refusal which is a matter of pride and ethics in my line of work...."

"You'd go to jail for contempt of court."

"Yeah, for a short while. When's the last time you heard of a newspaperman rotting in jail for longer than a few days for refusing to reveal a source?"

Charlie shook his head. "I don't follow those things, Preston. Frankly, I don't hold your 'profession,' as you call it, in very high regard."

"Well, you should. We hold police officers in high regard."

"Bullshit. All you want is a story, no matter who gets hurt."

"Let's not debate that; it's not germane. What is, however, is what I was saying: we don't stay in jail long, and while we're there, we just build our reputations. In a way, I welcome the opportunity. All I need is one trip to jail—just one—for a source, and everyone will know that I can be trusted when I say I won't reveal my sources. It'll open all sorts of new doors for me. Heck, I'll have phones ringing off the wall. I'll be on Larry King."

"Well, I won't be your source. Get lost."

"I don't need a source. I've got one. How do you think I learned about your meeting yesterday with Emily Klein, Dick Anthony and Sue Schneider?"

Charlie repeated his lapel-grab and wall-throw and leaned in close to the skinny reporter's face. "How'd you learn about that, you greasy maggot?"

"You haven't been listening, Charlie. I told you: I have a source. Now, unhand me. You're making a scene."

Charlie released Preston and stepped back. Again, Preston smoothed his lapels. "Want to hear what was said in the meeting?" He recited a few details, just enough to prove his point.

Charlie was stupefied. *Who could have talked?* Emily Klein: that nagpie just couldn't keep her beak shut. "Preston, you print that stuff, I'll have your ass."

Preston showed his yellow teeth again. "Charlie, don't make promises you can't keep. Give me one good reason why we shouldn't go to print? Maybe I'll reconsider."

"Because you'll jeopardize a police investigation. We're having a hard enough time digging up evidence; the one thing we have going for us is the suspect doesn't know what we got. If you tip Boyd off, it'll just make our task more difficult." He forced himself to calm down. "You don't want him to get away with it, do you?"

"Again, Charlie, we have different points of view. Believe it or not, I don't care." He let that sink in. "What I do care about, is a good story. And I've got one. Now, the only way you can get me off it… is to promise me something better. What do you say?"

Charlie hated to admit it, but Preston was making sense. Still, he wasn't ready—or authorized, for that matter—to give Preston the satisfaction of hearing it. "I'm not even supposed to be talking with you. It'll be my ass if I get caught."

"You won't, Charlie. Remember, I always protect a source."

"You can't protect me from a polygraph."

Preston laughed, on secure ground. "There are laws against that now, Charlie. I don't think they can force you to do that any more."

"Yeah? Well, I'm no lawyer. And I know *they* think they can. I'll have to think about it, maybe talk to MacGregor."

"Why's he have to be involved? Let's keep this between us. Less chance of a problem that way."

Scott was silent for a moment. "I don't know. If MacGregor ever got wind that I fed you information, what he'd do to me would make the Green River killer look like a boy scout."

Preston slapped Charlie on the shoulder. "He doesn't have to know."

"Keep your fucking hands off me. And how the hell do I explain your stories? MacGregor—and the brass above him for that matter—will know the information came from the investigation. And that's me."

Preston stroked his moustache. "You've already got that problem. How you gonna explain Sunday's paper?"

Charlie blinked. "I don't know. I'm gonna have to think about it."

"Well, don't think too long. My article's set to run Sunday. Here," he said, pulling out a card, scribbling on the back of it, "these are my numbers. Give me a call if you make up your mind before we go to print."

"Yeah, well, don't hold your breath." He shoved the card in a side pocket of his jacket as he walked away.

"Want to tell me where you're going?" Preston called after him.

"Fuck you."

"I thought you'd say that. Well, so long, Charlie. Say hi to Amy Galler up on Rainier."

Charlie stopped again. But Preston was already walking away—a little hop in his step now.

Preston walked to the end of the block before he stopped, turned around and looked to see if Scott was out of sight. He was beaming, almost floating. He could hardly be happier with the way the conversation had gone; he'd gotten his confirmation all right—in spades. And from the horse's mouth, no less. Even that little shyster Chapman would have to approve going forward with the article now.

Delighted with himself, he reached into his breast pocket and turned off his voice-activated recorder.

Amy entered the open garage. She stood for a few minutes, afraid to move, concerned about alarms.

She took a few cautious steps and turned around. Outside, nothing had changed; the same birds still sang; the same trees rustled in the light breeze. Everything was normal.

But if that was the case, then why was she breathing so heavily? Why was she so on edge, ready to spring out of her shoes? She knew. Fear of Boyd. Her throwing up had proven that. Gun in hand, she struggled to calm herself. Deep breaths helped. Over and over, she repeated to herself that there was nothing to worry about; she would be all right, no one was coming to get her.

Alarms. Electronic sensors? Looking around, she couldn't see any telltale control pads or mounted discs. Again, she assured herself she was in the middle of nowhere, that her fears were groundless.

Still, her stomach twisted in knots.

The first things she noticed once she calmed were the vehicles in the garage: a massive YukonXL; a newish-looking snowmobile, and an ATV with trailer attached. She studied the trailer. Maybe that's how he got the snowmobile up there: the ATV and trailer were ideal.

On the wall shared with the main body of the house, in front of the staircase, she saw several keys hanging on a rack. She walked over for a closer look. One key was clearly imprinted with the name "GMC," while the others bore the imprints of "Yamaha" and "Honda," corresponding to the nameplates on the gasoline tanks of the snowmobile and ATV. She took the Yamaha key off the ring, walked over to the snowmobile, inserted it and turned it to the indicated start position.

Nothing happened. The battery was dead.

Popping the gas cap, she peered inside. The tank was empty. She walked to the back of the vehicle and saw a rag hanging out of the exhaust pipe, no doubt to keep spiders and other insects out.

The snowmobile was resting on a wood platform. Next to it was another one, this one empty.

She looked up and saw a row of switches on the wall. She flipped them one after another. Two of the four switches flooded the garage with light. Satisfied, she walked over to the empty platform and squatted next to it. There were two deep troughs in the wood, running along its length. In the center, there was a small dark puddle. She dipped the tip of her thumb and rubbed it against two of her fingers.

Oil.

Did Boyd own two snowmobiles? Was the second one buried on the mountain? With Klein, perhaps?

Three colored containers were on a shelf.

Aren't some snowmobiles and ATVs two-cycle engines? Like lawnmowers, isn't it necessary to mix oil with the gas? She thought so.

She walked over to the three containers. One label read "Honda," one read "Yamaha," and one read "Arctic Cat."

There had been two snowmobiles!

Holstering her .38, she pulled her camera off her shoulder and took shots of everything she'd seen.

Inserting the key into the ATV, she turned it, and the powerful engine surged. But it wasn't as loud as she'd expected. Had Boyd had it muffled? She turned the engine off and walked back to the key rack. As she started to replace the keys, a sudden thought struck her: *Which keys had been on which hooks?*

Did it make any difference?

She distinctly recalled that each key had been placed on a hook; no hook had two keys. Why would this be, if their placement made no difference? *Damn.* She wasn't focused. She should have memorized positions before she'd removed the keys.

Wait. Why not shake Boyd up a little, play a little mind game? He'd have no way of finding out who'd been here. He might panic, make a mistake.

She dropped the Honda key to the garage floor, then placed the other keys all on one hook. Anxiety rippled through her, then was gone. She was playing this right.

Satisfied, she moved to the trailer to inspect it more closely. Sure enough, the wooden bed bore scratches about three feet apart. She found an old yardstick and measured the distance between the runners on the Yamaha. Comparing that measurement with the marks on the trailer bed, she found them nearly the same.

She walked outside and retrieved her purse from the car. Returning to the garage, she removed her notepad and a pen and jotted herself a note: "Check vehicle registrations."

So far, she had ignored the stairway on the left side of the garage. Now, she climbed it and found at the top a locked steel door with no knob. *Steel? Why would anyone put a steel door in their garage?*

How did the door open? Putting her shoulder to it, she gave the door a tentative shove.

Nothing happened.

Returning down the stairs, she looked around for a flashlight. Finding none, she went back to her car for some matches she kept in the glove compartment. She reclimbed the stairs to the door. It took three matches before she saw the keyhole in the upper right-hand corner.

Where was the key?

Was Herman Klein, or some trace of him, up there? Was Boyd a souvenir collector, a ghoul, someone who—like so many serial killers—played with his trophies?

She was convinced the doorway held answers she needed. Maybe the key was inside the house. Up to this point, she hadn't tried that door.

She trudged down the steps and walked to the door leading to the main part of the house.

It was unlocked.

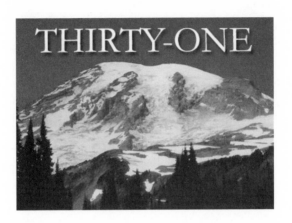

THIRTY-ONE

Friday, August 2

David L. Dawson didn't think his meeting with Herman Klein had anything to do with Klein's disappearance. Klein had merely asked some questions about the bar association's fitness investigation of Thomas Schneider. Dawson said he'd referred him to Emery Boyd, Klein's partner. With a sniff of his upturned nose, Dawson asked how this information could be relevant to Klein's disappearance.

"I'm not sure it is," Charlie said, "but I've got to check everything out, you know."

"Well, if that's all, then this meeting is over. I told Mr. Klein that my files were destroyed and the bar association's are sealed away in Chicago. I said he needed to talk to Mr. Boyd."

"Do you know what Boyd found, if anything?"

"No, I don't. As I told Mr. Klein, Mr. Boyd wasn't very cooperative. He didn't share any of his specific findings with us, if there were any. He just concluded that Schneider was fit, though it damn well took him long enough."

Charlie asked what Klein's reaction was when Dawson

referred him to Boyd.

Dawson thought for a minute. "You know, that's interesting...
I would have thought he'd be overjoyed, Boyd being his partner
and all. But he seemed a little sour. His reaction wasn't what I
expected."

Charlie thanked Dawson and left.

Next up was John Carmody, but before that meeting, Charlie
stopped at the take-out counter at Ivar's Indian Salmon House,
under the I-5 bridge. His mouth watering and stomach growling,
he decided it was worth the diversion. There just wasn't much
better than Ivar's broiled salmon and corn bread.

While eating, he called Dick Anthony. "Dick, that big-
mouthed client of yours has talked to the *Post*. Preston is threatening to go out Sunday saying we suspect Boyd, and lay out the
whole scenario."

"What?"

"Yeah. He stopped me this morning in front of my building.
He knows everything—*everything!* It had to have come from some-
body at our meeting. It wasn't me, and I'm sure it wasn't you. And
I don't think Sue Schneider is the type. That leaves your client,
Dick. I'm mad as hell."

"She wouldn't do that, Charlie," Anthony protested. "She
knows she's not out of the woods yet. I can't believe she'd want
to jeopardize her credibility with you now. I mean… the timing's
terrible."

"Yeah, well, I'm tellin' you: Preston knows, and he got it from
someone at the meeting. He says he's got a source. Now you tell
me: who else could that be, Dick?"

"Well, I'm not ready to say it's my client."

There was a moment of silence, broken only by heavy, excited
breathing from Anthony and by Charlie's chewing. Anthony said,
"Look, I'm gonna call Emily right now. Just cool down. There's
got to be some other explanation."

"There better be, Dick. I'm not ready for that information to be public."

"I'll get back to you, Charlie."

"No, I'll call you. I'll be out of the office all afternoon." He hung up, wolfed down the rest of his lunch, then drove cross-town to the offices of Booker & Boggs.

Instead of sending a secretary, John Carmody appeared at the receptionist's counter to usher Charlie to a waiting conference room. As they walked, Charlie sized the young lawyer up. The circles under Carmody's eyes, the somewhat detached, lost-in-thought visage, the flat butt and small paunch splitting the unneeded suspenders, signified that Carmody probably met or exceeded the legendary sweatshop work hours required of worker bee law firm associates.

Carmody led him to a small, windowless conference room with spare furnishings and monotonous walls. Contrary to some law firms, it was apparent that Baker & Boggs didn't waste profits on trappings. There was a small table, four chairs and a coffee service, and not much else.

Feeling claustrophobic in the cramped room, Charlie got right to business, asking Carmody to describe his discussion with Klein. Carmody repeated the conversation nearly verbatim, his mind apparently a trap. As Carmody spoke, Charlie wondered if he was one of those bright, egg-headed nerds he'd always hated in school—teacher's pet because of his powers of retention. "Amazing," Charlie said aloud, when Carmody finished, his version dove-tailing tightly with what Emily Klein said Klein had told her about it. "How do you remember everything so clearly?"

"I have what some people call total recall," Carmody said. "Others call it a photographic memory. In school, all the other kids hated me; I was teacher's pet."

Charlie smiled. "Did Schneider say anything else about Emery Boyd, other than what you told Klein?"

Carmody shook his head. "Say," he said a moment later, "you don't think Boyd had anything to do with Mr. Klein's disappearance, do you? You're asking about the judge, Boyd and what I told Mr. Klein. That leads me to believe you suspect Boyd. You think maybe he had something to do with the judge's death too?"

"John, I'd be real careful about speculation like that," Charlie said. "You know the law of libel a lot better than I do. No, I'm just checking everything out and, as I said, you're on the list."

"Well," Carmody said, "the reason I asked is… there is something I didn't tell Mr. Klein…"

"What's that?"

"Well, Mr. Klein asked me if I could identify any of the lawyers with Judge Schneider in the restaurant, and I said no, that I hadn't paid any attention to them."

"Yes. So?"

"Well, I saw Boyd that night. He pulled into the parking lot as I was leaving."

"I'm tellin' ya, Mo, Goddamn it," an irritated John Whitney was saying while pacing around the chief ranger's office, "you gotta shut it down. You gotta call the superintendent. It's too damn dangerous. I was up there. I canceled all our trips today, sent everybody down."

"John, come on," said Mo Knauer, sitting calmly at his desk, his hands folded in front of him, "don't you think you're exaggerating?"

"No, damn it. Mo, it rained all night up there, and it's still raining. Everything's turning to slush, movin' around. I swear to you, Mo, something's gonna happen."

"You don't know that, John. Nobody does."

"Mo, those glaciers can't take this much water this time of year!"

"So you want me to have the superintendent evacuate the park, send all these nice people home, based on what? Your *instinct?"*

"Mo, I've been on this mountain a long time…"

"So have I, John." Knauer sat back, his wooden chair squeaking on rusted rollers. "I was here long before you. I've seen rain high on the mountain before, and it's never caused any problems."

"But it's hot too, Mo. We had months of rain, then a heavy, wet snow, now heat and more rain. The glaciers are unstable."

"John," Knauer said in a withering tone. "Look. I'm concerned too. But I'm not ready to tell the superintendent to close the park." He sighed audibly. "Just relax a little. It's been a bad week. You're a little excited."

John's pacing stopped and he leaned forward, his hands spaced across the front of Knauer's desk. "I inspected the Nisqually, the Emmons and the Ingraham early this morning, probably at the coolest point of the day." His fists closed into tight balls. "I'm tellin' ya, Mo, there's too much movement up there."

Knauer pushed back, clearing space between himself and Whitney. "John, I've been in contact with our Muir station all day. The reports I'm getting are that everything is stable."

John's fist pounded the desk, startling the smaller, older man. "Well, they're wrong, Mo. They're fucking wrong!"

Knauer jumped up, his eyes blazing. "Goddamit, John! I won't stand for this. I won't let you intimidate me in my own office. If you're going to act like a spoiled child, you get the hell out of here. I am not your subordinate; you have no authority over me. I do not appreciate your bullying."

John straightened, but his eyes and tight fists retained the fury. Knauer continued, "Whether you believe it or not, John, I take my responsibilities—my job—seriously. I think the park is safe."

John started to speak, but Knauer waved him off. "Now you may not agree with me, and you're entitled to say so. I respect your opinion. But I've made my decision, and it stands. You'll just have to accept it. I expect you to treat me with some respect, not come around here pounding on my desk, threatening me. We've been friends a long time, John. Don't ruin our relationship now."

Whitney whirled and left the office, slamming the door behind him. Knauer, feeling tight and restless, walked out to the parking lot a few seconds later and watched his good friend—he hoped that description still fit—leave.

When Whitney disappeared from view, a worried, frowning Mo Knauer returned to his office. For the tenth time that morning, he pulled out his radio and called the Muir Ranger Station.

Amy was just as impressed—overwhelmed really—by the inside of Boyd's house as she had been by its exterior. It was certainly a man's domain, all wood with large, masculine furnishings and appointments. No doilies or knick-knacks here; mostly skins, brass, iron, steel, wood and glass. It could use a woman's touch, she thought.

The living/activity area of the great room impressed her the most. It was dominated by a large stone walk-in fireplace, one so big and well used that Amy suspected there was no need for a furnace. A large iron grating, fully six feet high, spanned the entire width of the opening and then some. On either side of the fireplace, some fifteen feet in front and at an angle, were placed large, oversized Early-American-style couches. Antique-looking tables, carrying large, heavy brass lamps topped by bulbous, multi-colored, amber-dominant Tiffany shades, attended the two couches. On the wood floor was a large oval Moroccan rug, colored in various shades of earth tones. Several tall bookcases ringed the room, filled with books, magazines, trophies and decorative paraphernalia, much of it in copper. Four winged, high-back, fabric-covered chairs were spaced elsewhere in the room, two with chrome extended-arm reading lamps, and two with small brass lamps with domed shades atop thick, carved oaken tables. A weighty, winged wrought iron chandelier, bearing a multitude of pine cone bulbs, hung on heavy cables from the ceiling pinnacle. Amy was struck by how much she was reminded of the cozy, comfy Paradise Lodge.

In the study area, two large picture windows framing Lookout Mountain formed most of the south wall, while books in crammed cedar cases covered the west and north walls, plus the area below the south windows. Two sets of waist-high back-to-back bookcases to the east completed the sense of a separate room. An oversized pine desk with matching chair stood in the center of the room, facing south, and a black Dell digital monitor sat on a desk side-arm, the tower below it. Golden cedar paneling covered all the wall surfaces in the lodge, but it was here in the study that the cedar was most striking because of the illuminated southern exposure and the contrasts between the multi-colored books and the glowing wood. The study was a professional's dream.

Sitting in Boyd's chair, Amy opened his desk drawers and found supplies, bank account, accounting and various corporate records, but no keys. She turned to the side-arm and powered on the computer, but turned it off when she saw it was password protected.

Moving into the master bedroom, she stopped in her tracks at the sight of the 9mm on the bedside table. Her hand went to her holster, and she looked around as fear sharpened her senses. She picked up the HK and slid out the clip. Hollowpoints. A shudder ran down her spine. She emptied the clip into her pocket, wiped it down with a Kleenex tissue, then popped it back in place. She racked the slide, ejecting the slug there. She felt the weight of the bullets against her leg and touched her holster once more.

There was a picture on the table, a young woman. Amy picked it up with the tissue. The picture was torn, as if someone had been cut out. She looked around. No pictures of Boyd's father.

Was this his mother? She put the picture back.

She went to the walk-in closet. There were a number of suits and some casual clothing, but not the inventory of climbing and outdoor equipment she'd expected. She searched the chest of drawers, but found no attic key. There was a stack of albums in the corner, some with dried leather bindings. She thought about leafing through them, but the fear left from the 9mm, the reminder that Boyd might be a calculating killer, made her claustrophobic in such a confined space.

Walking through the laundry room, Amy found a hamper piled high with dirty clothes. Dumping the hamper on the floor, she sat beside the pile and sorted through clothing, looking for things left in pockets. She found nothing of interest, and no attic key.

She started to leave when a thought struck her: she turned back to the pile of clothing and, opening the washer, threw them in. Adding some soap and setting the controls, she turned the washer on.

In the bathroom on the Jacuzzi ledge, she found a Lawrence Sanders hardcover, the cover leaf marking a page. She pulled off the cover leaf, reversed it, and reset the book so it marked no page. Then she moved the book to the kitchen and placed in on the counter.

For several minutes, she searched the kitchen drawers and cabinets, looking for the key. Giving up, she looked at her watch: 11:45. Time for lunch. Opening the refrigerator, she took out a bottle of water, some sealed lunch meat, some bread and a squeeze container of mustard. She made herself a sandwich and ate it at the counter. When she'd finished eating, she returned her fixings to the refrigerator, then wrestling the appliance out, she reached around and unplugged it before shoving it back into place.

Returning to the garage and the frustrating steel door, she had another idea. For several minutes, she opened drawers and cabinets until she found a heavy-duty screwdriver and a hammer. Then, climbing the steps, she took the screwdriver, placed it into the slot where the steel door met the doorjamb and pounded on it. Next, she placed the screwdriver in the key slot and pounded some more. Finally, she pounded the screwdriver at an angle across the face of the door, wounding it as deeply as possible, just for the appearance.

It was time to leave. Remembering a box of rags in the garage, she selected one, then spent the next several minutes retracing her steps, wiping everything she'd touched. By the time she was done, it was 12:20.

Amy chucked the hollowpoints out the passenger window as she wound around a hairpin turn on the road to Paradise. She was whistling. The clouds were rising; it was going to be a good, but hot, day.

And, she thought, as she cut off her whistle, a difficult night.

THIRTY-TWO

Friday, August 2

"You've cut the guts out of it!" screamed a distraught G. Sherwood Preston as he completed reading the revised feature for the Sunday paper, his audience the assemblage of Turner K. Chapman, Evan B. Cutter and Chancey LaRue, all seated with him at the conference table in the editor-in-chief's office. "What's going on? I proved my story to you; I let you listen to the tapes of the meeting and my conversation with Charlie Scott. Why'd you chicken out?"

He rose from his chair, unable to contain himself just sitting, and paced the room, shaking his head, taking short steps, while he strangled the printout in his hands.

"Calm down, Sherwood," Chancey said. "Insults aren't going to win you any concessions here. We had some concerns with your draft—which Chip will explain—and there's a strategic aspect to our decision."

"What strategy?" asked the still-pacing Preston, now stroking his moustache with his free hand.

"I'll get to that in a moment," Chancey said. "But first, Chip will explain his concerns." She turned to the lawyer.

"We... I am uncomfortable with this Boyd-Schneider stuff," Turner said. "I think it's close to libelous, and Boyd is a very dangerous adversary."

"Libel? All I said was that the police suspect an illicit connection between Boyd and Schneider. That was the motive for killing Klein."

Turner nodded. "That may be true, Sherwood. But we don't *know* that. And to our knowledge, nobody's investigating Schneider's death, despite what you claim in your draft. Your speculations go too far."

"But they think he blackmailed Schneider. You heard it on the tape."

"No, I didn't. I didn't hear anything of the kind. What we heard was Mrs. Klein say Mr. Klein suspected it. That's a big difference."

"But it's the same thing."

"No, it isn't, Sherwood."

"No, it isn't," echoed Chancey. She looked at Evan Cutter, who nodded while sucking on his Mont Blanc.

Preston opened his mouth but was shut down by Chapman's raised hands. "Don't!" he said. He turned to Chancey LaRue. "Chancey, please keep your patronizing comments to yourself. I'm trying to explain this to Preston so he'll understand my concerns. I'm trying to take some of the emotion out of all this."

A look of "who—me?" crossed Chancey's face. Her mouth opened, ripe lips pouting, but she too was cut off by Chapman's raised hands. She sat back in her chair.

"Thank you," Chapman said. He took a deep breath. "So all we know for a fact is that Emery Boyd is a suspect in the Herman Klein disappearance. Everything else—motive, blackmail, et cetera—is speculation. We do know there was some office intrigue; we can print that. We all know people have killed for less. But the further we go out on this Boyd-Schneider limb, the thinner the branch we're sitting on."

Preston waved his printout in the air. Chapman warded him off. "No, let me finish."

Preston dropped his arm to his side.

"Thank you," Chapman said again. "Now, under the law of libel, an important aspect is the burden of proof. If we get sued, we have the burden of proving the statements are true."

"But it *is* true," Preston said. "The police do suspect Boyd blackmailed Schneider—if not actually killing him."

Chapman rolled his eyes. "Well just how do we *prove* that, Sherwood? You've told us that you insist on keeping the tapes—which I think are ambiguous at best. But even so, you say that if you're pressed, you won't turn them over. And you won't reveal your source. So just how do we meet our burden of proof? What's our evidence?"

"Yes, how do we prove it?" echoed Chancey LaRue.

Chapman shot her a look before turning back to Preston. "You don't expect Detective Scott to come to our rescue, do you?"

"I don't know. He may."

"I don't believe that, Sherwood," Chapman said. "Not after listening to that tape. Scott doesn't like you. If you get sued, he'll fry your ass—the paper's too." He took a deep breath. "We're just being careful, Sherwood. Boyd's a tough and nasty adversary, and you'd better believe he knows the law of libel."

"Yes, indeed," chimed Chancey LaRue.

Throwing the now balled-up printout to the floor, Preston lunged at the table, at a point directly across from LaRue, whose disdainful smirk now gave way to a startled gasp. "You gutless cunt!" he raged, his face purple, as everyone sat stunned. "If you were a man, you ball-less hump, I'd put your head where everybody knows it belongs—up your ass!"

Evan Cutter jumped up and moved to protect LaRue, while Chapman bounded out of his chair to restrain Preston.

"Enough!" shouted the burly editor-in-chief. "That's enough!"

Everything freeze-framed for a moment, then Cutter turned to LaRue, who was frozen against the back of her chair. "Chancey, leave the room. I'll talk to you later. You're not helping us."

LaRue's jaw dropped.

"You heard me. Get out! I'll talk to you later."

"You can't do this. I'm his editor. He works for me."

"He did and maybe he will again. We'll talk about that later too."

"Well!" she huffed. "We'll just see what Mr. Huston says about this!"

"Be my guest, Chancey," said Cutter. "But for now, get out."

Chin up, LaRue rose with an exaggerated dignity and left the room. As soon as she was gone, Cutter beckoned Preston to sit down. Taking his cue, Chapman released Preston and returned to his chair. Preston stood for a moment, muttered something incoherent, shrugged, then he too sat down.

"Now maybe we can finish this up," Chapman said. "Thank you, Evan."

Cutter nodded and resumed popsicling his pen.

"I'm sorry," Preston said. "I just lost it. I don't know why I let that insipid woman get under my skin. But she does."

"She's aggravating, all right," Chapman said. Turning to Cutter, he smiled. "Evan, I hope you and Mr. Huston have a good relationship."

"Me too." He laughed nervously.

"Well, we can worry about that later. Sherwood, do you understand now why I had to make some editorial changes?"

"Don't you mean gut my piece?" Preston picked up his papers. "Look, I'm not a lawyer… I understand why you're being conservative, even if I think you've gone too far. But what's this about strategy? What did you mean?"

Cutter put a hand on Chapman's arm. "I'll handle this." He

turned back to Preston. "It's really very simple, Sherwood. We don't want to shoot our wad on one piece. We want to tease a little, build up momentum. We think this has staying power if we can keep stuff flowing."

"I get it," Preston said, nodding.

"The public loves a good soap opera. This thing has potential. If we play this right, we could have a pot-boiler."

"Or the lawsuit of the decade," Chapman inserted.

Cutter laughed, raising his hands in a surrendering gesture. "Okay, Chip, okay... I understand. We'll be careful, I promise you. And you'll see everything before it goes to print..."

The lawyer nodded, and Cutter turned to Preston. "Sherwood, how do you feel now? Better?"

He nodded. "But if I'm going to be up on Rainier, how am I going to direct the story?"

"We'll give you Jessie Barlowe, our legal beat reporter. It's your story, your byline, but she's going to ghost-write."

"Jessie?" responded Preston. "She's perfect. She knows everybody in the legal community."

"I agree. I want her to build this Boyd-Klein thing up, research the EAC decision and do an in-depth background on Herman Klein and his wife, Schneider too."

"Fantastic!" Preston fingered a drum beat on the table. "Now that's what I call support." He extended his hand first to Cutter and then to Chapman, whose continued concern was apparent from the deep furrow of his brow.

"Now," said Cutter, "let's discuss what trade-offs we can offer Detective Scott..."

Fifteen minutes later, they opened the conference room door and were surprised to find Wayne Malcolm Huston and Chancey LaRue—her chin high—standing there.

Elation left their spirits like air from a pierced balloon.

THIRTY-THREE

Friday, August 2

John was late, so Amy and Sherry spent the extra time sitting in the dining room, snacking, sipping coffee and chatting. Finally, John arrived at 1:30, tense and preoccupied. Signaling the women to remain seated, he ordered a cola from Camille and pulled up a chair. Once he was seated, Amy made the necessary introductions, but was troubled by John's seeming distraction, bordering on rudeness.

Had John learned why she was here?

Looking at Sherry, she sensed John's coolness was making her friend uncomfortable. Sherry excused herself to the bathroom, and Amy was glad for a moment alone.

"What's wrong, John? You're in a different world. Same problem?"

He shook his head. "I'm worried about the mountain. The glaciers... all this water. Mo won't shut the place down."

"Mo?"

"Mo Knauer, the chief ranger. He thinks the glaciers are fine, but he hasn't seen them. I have. I went up early this morning."

"Doesn't he have people up there? Can't they look at them and radio down?"

John nodded. "That's just it. Mo says they're telling him the glaciers are fine. But they're wrong. They're unstable as hell, all this water and heat. Not usual for this time of year, the water anyway."

"What are you going to do?"

"Not much I can do. Mo's got the authority here. I've pulled out all our people from Muir, cancelled today's climbs."

"Isn't there anybody you can talk to?"

"Just the superintendent. But he'll bow to Mo. No point in calling him."

"So, you want to cancel today? If so, that's okay, but I'd still like to see you tonight..."

"No, no point in canceling. The exercise would do me well. Get me off worrying about the glaciers. I'll take you two to Ranger's Roost, outside the park."

"What's that? A ranger station?"

"Yeah. It's sorta a landmark around here. See, many years ago, this ranger carried up materials some sixty-five hundred feet to build a station on a cliff overlooking Rainier. It's got some amazing views, but the trip up is pretty rigorous."

"Why is it a landmark?"

"Well, maybe that's not the right word. It's a place of some mystical significance for those in the know. You see, shortly after the ranger built the place, he fell off the cliff to his death."

"Is it safe?"

"Oh, yeah."

Sherry returned, and Amy filled her in on the change in plans. When Amy told her about Ranger's Roost, Sherry's eyes grew wide.

"John says it's safe, Sherry."

John nodded. "And the views are spectacular, although the trail's a bit rugged. Lots of wildflowers, some good vistas of the

Tatoosh Range to the south. Then, at the Roost itself, you've got a fantastic view of Rainier." He smiled. "Lovers really like the place."

Sherry cocked an eyebrow. "Maybe I should leave you two alone."

John laughed. "No, Amy needs a chaperon."

He outlined the gear they'd need, and the women went to their rooms to pack. Amy used her day-pack again, and stuffed her gun, badge and I.D. inside. Fifteen minutes later, they were on their way.

The unmarked trail began at a turn-off two miles east of Lookout Mountain. The trail was rugged, gaining altitude quickly, via switchbacks, and the three climbers were soon peeling off layers as the exertions and the humidity took their tolls. Numerous water and rest breaks were required, not so much because the women were out of breath—although Amy certainly was—but because they lost so much fluid during the climb.

The exercise tortured Amy's aches and pains and her thigh muscles tired quickly, while power breathing did little to soothe the oxygen cravings of her lungs. Sherry, on the other hand, seemed fit. During a rest break, she confessed that she ran daily in Portland, often in the mountains. John had noticed her superior conditioning; several times he commended her for her strength and endurance and once commented that if she ever tired of Portland, he could use her on his guide staff. John laughed and said he was always looking for attractive female guides; they were good for business.

While Sherry got compliments, John teased Amy about lagging behind. Although his tone was joking, John's words stung. Convincing herself that she was losing John to the fitter of the females, she dropped even further behind, feeling drained and sorry for herself.

Like yesterday, John used rest stops to describe the flora and wildlife which lined the trail; it was much different here, far below the snowline, from what Amy had seen higher on Rainier. The wildflowers were taller, thicker and of different varieties, with brighter colors, a contrast from yesterday's climb as between Monet and Van Gogh, but both worth the view. And the fragrances today were dominated by forest smells: pine, damp bark and dirt. Along the way, John pointed out red-tailed hawks, bald eagles, marmots, rabbits, owls, pileated woodpeckers, hanging bats, pine martens, and other birds and animals.

During one rest break high on the trail, Sherry turned to John. "So, John, was Emery Boyd really lost during that storm?"

John looked at Amy. She shook her head. When John turned back to Sherry, Amy flashed her a stern glance and made a cutting motion across her throat.

"Apparently, he was," John said. "Why?"

"Just seems strange, that's all, him having grown up on this mountain."

Amy made another cut-throat motion, staring daggers at her friend. John had his back to her.

"How do you know about Emery Boyd?"

"Guide Service Shack. Everybody's been talking about it."

"Have you met Frank Maselli?"

"The good-looking boy? Oh, sure."

John nodded. "Figures." He stared off toward the Tatooshes. Took a breath. "Let's just say… during a storm… when everything around you is white, including the air… it's awfully difficult to get your bearings." He picked up his pack and strode off up the trail.

Sherry and Amy hurried to catch him, but Amy soon fell back, her strength and attitude waning. Before long, Sherry and John were out of sight, having crested a ridge some two hundred feet above her.

Amy was exhausted. She was alone now, sore and abandoned. She dropped to a flat rock, shrugged out of her pack, and put her head between her knees. For several minutes, she sat rocking, oblivious to the beauty around her.

And that was how John found her. Silently, easily, he scooped Amy off her rock, kissing her tears away as he carried her off the trail to a bed of flowers, sparkling in reds, oranges, yellows and shades of purple. As he lay her down, then moved alongside her, she pushed him away. "We can't, John," she said. "We've got to talk about something."

John gently covered her mouth, then he was kissing her. Amy tried to turn away, but her breathing was rapid, her effort half-hearted. She moaned, then clutched at John as passions overcame her.

They made love, oblivious to their surroundings, ignoring everything except their craving for each other.

They made it to the top, which was only just over the next ridge, some fifty minutes later, and found Sherry sitting on the station's balcony, which hung out over a five-thousand-foot drop. Sherry was sitting, leaning against the shelter, admiring the panoramic view. The clouds over Rainier had lifted, and Rainier was spread out as if on a brilliant canvas.

Sherry climbed over the shelter's rail, grinning, and rushed into Amy's arms, whispering into her ear, "You go, girl!"

Amy said nothing. Her legs were shaking and her knees felt weak. She didn't know how she'd made it up over that last ridge; the last few hundred feet had been a blur. Her thoughts had been a mixture of joy and anguish, guilt and fear. Her body ached but tingled too. She was wracked with worry.

John and Sherry helped her to the rail, then boosted her over. She crawled a few feet, careful to stay away from the balcony's edge, then leaned back against the wall. In front of her was the most spectacular scenery she'd ever seen. A sharp intake of breath, and she was staring. She shrugged out of her pack, letting it fall next to her.

John and Sherry scrambled over the rail and took seats next to her. John pulled water and candy bars out of his pack and passed them around. He pointed to a spot a thousand feet below him. "Paradise," he said. "Above it and to the left, the Nisqually Glacier. To the left of that, the white cliffs you see, that's the Kautz Ice Cliff. It looks small from here, but those cliffs are three hundred feet high. Above Paradise and to the right, those are the Paradise, Cowlitz, Williwakas and Ingraham glaciers. You can't see Camp Muir, but it's on the lower left of the Cowlitz Glacier."

Sherry and Amy marveled at the view, while John closed his eyes and enjoyed the tranquility of their isolation and the after-glow of lovemaking. Without opening his eyes, he found Amy's hand and gave it a squeeze. After a moment, she pulled her hand away.

"This is amazing," Sherry said. John nodded. Sherry turned to him. "So, just how does somebody follow a snowmobile through a whiteout?"

Amy almost choked on her candy bar. She pushed off the wall and glared at Sherry, who ignored her.

John didn't answer. He was staring at the mountain. He got up and walked to the rail. A few moments later, a distant, dull rumble rolled up from the canyon, starting as a whisper, like drums in the distance, then louder, like the thunder of an oncoming storm. The resonance swept across the canyon, growing ever louder, deeper and more insistent. John's eyes were wide.

"John? What's wrong?" Amy asked.

John said nothing, his attention riveted, his face taut.

Amy looked out over the canyon. "What's that noise? It sounds like an airplane…"

There was movement on Rainier. Something blurry, out of focus. Amy looked at John, saw recognition and fear in his face. He slammed his hand on the rail. "Oh my God! Look!"

He was pointing at Rainier's right flank. The deep, bass drum roll was growing louder. Amy wondered if the earth was shaking. John was looking at her, his face a stricken mask. Over the roar, he yelled, "The Ingraham's broken loose!"

Across the ten miles of space, above and to their right, Sherry and Amy saw first wavering lines of grey, black and shimmering white, then billowing white clouds soaring upwards like blown flour. Around and ahead of the clouds, trees flattened like dominoes, as if blown by a pyroclastic blast. The eruption accelerated and moved down, destroying all in its path, then it passed over and behind an eastern ridge, leaving in its wake only a settling cloud and the din of its passage.

Amy gasped, while Sherry stood gaping.

"C'mon!" John shouted, leaping over the side rail to the ground. He bounded over the ridge and down the trail, running headlong.

It took John some twenty minutes before, panting heavily and soaked in sweat, he made it to his vehicle. Not pausing to catch his breath, he swung the door open and reached for his phone, glad for his long-range antenna. Hurriedly dialing ranger headquarters, he shouted for Mo Knauer. In seconds, he heard the distressed voice of the chief ranger. "John, is that you?"

"Yeah, Mo. What do you know?"

"Not much. We're not sure what happened."

John heard fear and uncertainty in Knauer's voice, both unusual for the hardened ranger. Knauer continued, "Something let go, but we're not sure what. I don't have anybody in the area. Several of my people are heading out to Stevens Ridge Road now."

"Look, I saw it, Mo… from Ranger's Roost. Mo, the Ingraham's let loose! Can't tell how much of it, it was hard to see… maybe that's a good sign. If it went straight down the Muddy Fork to the Cowlitz River, the way it looked before I lost it, we may have dodged a bullet. But check the Box Canyon area by

Marsh Lake… where the trail and Stevens Ridge Road both cross over the Muddy Fork… And you better check the campsite a mile from there… the picnic area… Cougar Falls too."

"Jesus, John, you were right, and I didn't listen! There could be hundreds of people in there."

"Stay calm, Mo. We don't know how bad it is. From what I saw, we may be okay. Have you called for assistance?"

"Yeah, I called Olympia, Tacoma and Seattle. But I couldn't tell them much, just that something awful had happened. They're sending support, ambulances and body bags, that sort of thing. Seattle's sending choppers; they should be here shortly." He paused, "John, how big was it? Tell me straight."

"I really couldn't see very well, Mo. I'm tellin' you the truth. I was pretty far away. I saw trees going down; I saw what looked like a lot of water, ice and debris…. It was movin' real fast, but I lost it when it hit the narrows on the Muddy Fork. From where I was, I couldn't see how high it was running. It was following the Muddy Fork, Mo, but who knows? Keep your fingers crossed. The Muddy Fork and Cowlitz are straight shots, by and large, and pretty isolated. With some luck, if it stayed mostly within their banks, we might get out of this with just some minor damage, maybe a lost roadway or bridge."

"At least we had the rotten weather going for us," Knauer said.

"Yeah. I'd hate to think about it if the park was jammed."

"I wish I'd listened to you."

"Goddamnit, Mo! You don't have time to sit and stew. You've got to coordinate everything." He heard his friend take a deep breath. "If you'd believed there was any real hazard, you'd have acted. Hey, buddy, nobody's God out here."

"Thanks, John…"

"All we need is luck and a little planning. What are you doing about the campgrounds, trails and picnic areas in other areas of the park?"

"I've ordered—or the superintendent did at my request—all of them, well… those below any glacier spillways, closed."

"Good, what about a survey?"

"Well, the choppers should be here soon. I've called all my people together, and I just sent some out. We're gonna do a foot survey."

"Good. How many do you have?"

"Twenty right now. I've called for volunteers; I should have a lot more by tonight. I'm scheduling a meeting at the lodge for 7:00. Can we use your people? We've got a lot of ground to cover."

"Sure. I'd like to take some of my people and focus on the campgrounds, picnic areas and trails. I'll put everybody under your command, and we'll take radios."

"Great, John."

"Go easy on volunteers, Mo. We don't want a lot of half-drunk tourists running around. We'll be saving the saviors. Keep the number small for tonight, and make sure they're all good people."

"I agree. We'll only take the best tonight, and they'll work in teams. We'll keep somebody at the lodge tonight, organizing for tomorrow. We'll have some make-work projects, you know, to keep do-gooders busy."

"Good thinking. It's gonna be a long night."

"We've had a few of those lately."

"Never a dull moment on this mountain, Mo."

"Yeah, well, I appreciate your help, John…"

There was a moment's silence. John said, "Always, Mo," then hit the "End" button.

THIRTY-FOUR

Friday, August 2

Back in the lodge lobby, Amy was sitting with Sherry in front of one of the two large fireplaces located at opposite ends of the room, waiting for Mo Knauer to finish talking with a group of men. When he'd dropped them off, John had left Amy instructions to see Knauer if she needed to know his whereabouts. The desk clerk had identified him for her.

"Okay, Sherry," Amy said. "Just what the hell did you think you were doing? You promised me."

Sherry shrugged and looked at her. "Don't be mad, Amy. I was just trying to help a little."

"We discussed that. You can't help. Give me one good reason you shouldn't be taken into custody."

"I'll give you two. One, we're friends; two, it was a natural question. C'mon, Amy. Everybody knows Boyd claims he was tracking the snowmobile through the storm. I think it's a reasonable question. I'm surprised nobody else has asked it."

Amy shook her head.

"Look, Amy, I promise I'll stay out of it. If I screwed you up,

I'm sorry. I won't do it again."

Amy was studying the groups clustering in front of her. One group, the quiet ones, guides and rangers, Amy guessed, spoke in hushed tones. Her training told her these people were experts used to emergencies; they knew what was ahead—many hours of tiring, dirty toil and the likelihood of unpleasant, maybe dangerous surprises. The louder groups, Amy decided, were tourists, rubberneckers who thrived on excitement—the people who probably bought hockey fight tapes.

It was only 6:45, fifteen minutes to Knauer's showtime, and fifteen minutes to Amy's promised call to Charlie. She was hoping to get Knauer alone, to find out what John was doing and when he would return. He'd said he would be leading a search and rescue mission and didn't know when he'd be back.

So much was going through Amy's mind. Not just the issue of what to do about Sherry, but what to do about John. So much for the best laid plans… How was she gonna resolve this mess? One thing hadn't changed: the need to talk to John. But when would she be able to do that? She didn't want to think about the upcoming talk with Charlie, and the thought of Captain MacGregor made her feel nauseous.

What would John's reaction be?

Would he cooperate?

Was the relationship over already?

So many questions, so few answers.

She saw Knauer break free and head toward the dining room. She caught him at the steps and tugged at his elbow. He turned, frowning, a harassed, worried man. "Yes?" he said, then before she could speak, followed with, "Look, ma'am, I'm giving a status report in…" he glanced at his watch, "…seven minutes. I'd like to get a Coke."

"No. You don't understand," Amy said. "I'm not one of them. John… I mean… uh… John Whitney told me to see you."

The old ranger's eyes softened and he smiled. "So you're the

little lady he's been talking about?" He grabbed her hand and
began pumping.

"He said something? About me?" Amy was surprised.

"Both last night and a while ago. Made quite a nuisance of
himself. He's quite taken with you. Let's see… Amy? Amy
Galler?"

She could only nod.

"A bookkeeper, from Seattle, right? Well, you certainly don't
look like a bookkeeper. What are you doing up here, Amy? Just
getting away?"

She nodded.

Knauer's eyes turned quizzical. "You were with John today?
Up at Ranger's Roost?"

"Yes."

"What did you see?"

"Not much. Mostly, a cloud of white and trees going down."

"Yeah. With a bad one, whole chunks of forest can be flattened and carried away."

"Not many trees went down… But we were pretty far away,
you know, and it disappeared behind a ridge."

"That's what John said. That's encouraging. Maybe it was
contained by the ridges."

"Have you heard from John?"

"Not in a while. He called me to say the road and bridge are
out, but that was it."

"Oh."

He saw concern painted on her face. "Now, don't be worried.
John's the most knowledgeable and experienced man in these
parts… well, next to me, maybe. He's in no danger. That boy
knows how to take care of himself."

"When do you think he'll be coming back?"

"Can't really say. Depends on what he finds. Fog's set in, so
we can't get the copters up. But I wouldn't expect to see John
tonight, probably not tomorrow either."

"Can I help?"

"Not really. You just sit tight for now, okay?" He flashed a warm smile, then turned and clattered down the steps into the dining room.

At 7:00, a tired Emery Boyd, his suit looking as if he'd slept in it after two long days of business meetings, was sitting in the lounge of the Irvine Marriott, sipping an Amstel Light and eyeing the pretty, long-legged, redheaded waitress in the short—very short—black miniskirt who was serving him. He was awaiting the arrival of the two men from Hartsfield Industries—its chairman and CEO, Marvin Hartsfield, and his in-house lawyer, Barry Bowman—who were taking him to dinner. His plans called for him to return to Seattle tomorrow for an evening with Jenny Larson. Then he'd spend a full day in the office on Sunday, before resuming his vacation Monday or Tuesday, assuming Sam Terry would let him go.

Now, as he sat sipping his beer, smiling at the young waitress—who seemed to be eyeing him back—he glanced over at the television and saw Paradise Lodge. Puzzled, he asked the bartender to turn up the sound.

"No one knows what caused today's massive mudflow, although officials suspect a major glacial shift, perhaps caused by the sustained, unusually wet, warm weather. And no one yet knows the extent of the damage, or if lives were lost.

"It's dark now, and much of the park is encased in fog, preventing aerial surveys. Crews are out on foot, led by park rangers and guides, and a call is going out for experienced volunteers.

"Only time will tell the legacy of this cataclysm—a true phenomenon of nature—and the extent of death or destruction it has left behind in this, one of our nation's premier national parks. For now, though, officials aren't speculating. All we can do is watch and wait.

"For NBC and KING 5 News, I'm Gerald Baldwin, at Paradise Lodge on Mount Rainier."

The bartender must have noticed the stunned look on Boyd's face. "Hey fella, you okay?"

Boyd made no response, but turned and walked rapidly to the lobby phones. Dialing the lodge, he asked to speak to Mo Knauer, but was informed Knauer's meeting was still going on and that he couldn't be disturbed. He asked for Whitney and was told that John was on the scene. Frustrated, he left word that he was on his way and would check in as soon as he arrived.

Next he called Jenny Larson. She wasn't pleased at the change in plans, but he was insistent. With a despairing sigh, Jenny said she'd inform Sam Terry. She wished Boyd luck and ordered him to be careful and to call at his first opportunity.

Turning from the phone booth, he saw Hartsfield and Bowman enter the lobby. Hurrying to them, he explained the emergency that forced him to cancel dinner. Hartsfield offered his jet, stationed at the airport, and as Boyd went up to grab his bags, Hartsfield called his pilots.

Amy was on the phone with a somewhat glum Charlie Scott. After some obligatory teasing and small talk, focused tonight around the glacier's collapse and whether Amy might somehow have been responsible for it, they turned to business.

Charlie told Amy her joyride was over. They had a meeting with MacGregor on Monday at 8:00, and it was not likely to be a pleasant one. He said MacGregor's blood pressure and temperament had been raging and he hadn't come in today, on doctor's orders. Charlie feared that unless they had a lay-down case by Monday, MacGregor would blow.

He gave Amy a briefing, saying that while he believed Boyd was the perp, he doubted they'd ever be able to prove it—they had no evidence.

"Did you talk to Arnie about the Rainier scene?" Amy asked.

"Yeah. It was Carlton's blood. The white parka stuff yielded nothing."

"Damn. No wig threads either, I gather?"

"Nope." There was a moment of silence.

"My turn?" Amy asked.

"Not yet." Charlie paused, "There's more…" He took a deep breath. "Our old buddy Preston jumped me this morning… He knows about Boyd… Knows it all… Says it'll all be in the paper on Sunday."

"Oh no! How'd he find out?"

"Damned if I know. Says he has a source."

"Who?"

"He won't say. At first, I thought it was Emily Klein, but I talked to Anthony and he swears it's not."

"Do you believe him?"

"Yes. She's taking a polygraph on Monday. I told her if she passes, I'd probably let her off the hook. Anthony's right: she wouldn't jeopardize that. She may be a big mouth, but she's not stupid."

"Well, who could it have been?"

"You aren't gonna believe this…" he paused, sucked in another deep breath, "…but I don't think there is a source. I think Preston eavesdropped on a meeting I had with Anthony, Sue Schneider and Emily Klein. Anthony agrees."

"What? How?"

"I think that wormy weasel snuck into Klein's house during our meeting."

"Come on, Charlie. The guy's a snake... but breaking and entering? No story's worth a felony rap."

"I know... but it fits."

"How? What makes you so sure?"

"We heard a noise. Anthony and I got up to check it out. We thought a belt must have fallen off the washer or dryer in the laundry room next door; we found one on the floor. One of the outside garage doors was open, and..."

"Oh, no."

"My sentiments exactly. Can you imagine what MacGregor's reaction is gonna be?"

"You haven't told him?"

"No, he's ill, remember? He didn't come in today."

Amy was lost in her own thoughts; a sudden fear was dawning on her. "Charlie, does Preston know where I am? That I'm still on the case?"

"Yup. Told me to say hi to you up on Rainier."

"Oh, shit! You can't let him print that. It'll blow everything."

"Well, what can I do about it?"

"There must be something... Why did Preston tell you he knew all this? Why didn't he just go ahead and print it?"

"He wants to deal. Says he's going with it if I don't work with him."

She mulled this over. "Hell, Charlie, what's the harm? He already knows everything. Maybe you should trade with him."

He laughed. "Are you gonna tell MacGregor that? I'm in enough trouble already. MacGregor's gonna have my ass..."

"Well, you're right about that."

"Thanks. The way I see it, I'm hanged if I do, hanged if I don't."

"Yeah, but it just may be the best way out, a compromise of competing interests."

"What the hell are you talking about, Amy?"

"Just this. If Preston prints that we suspect Boyd of blackmailing Schneider, the FBI will step into the case and take it over. Right?"

"Yeah. So?"

"So, we'll lose the case and Preston will lose a source—you. Both sides lose. But if he doesn't print anything about Schneider, then we keep the case and he keeps his source. And, since this benefits him more than us, you have him delete any reference to me. That way, maybe I can finish up here."

Amy could hear Charlie breathing.

"Charlie?"

"How are you going to stay undercover when Sam Terry knows about you? He met you, remember? Don't you think he'll tell Boyd? Maybe he has already."

"I'm not worried about Boyd. I'm worried about John Whitney. Besides, my cover's already blown. It was an accident."

"An accident?"

"Yeah. The how's not important. The only thing that's important is that I get to John Whitney before he finds out who I am."

"What's Whitney got to do with this? Isn't he the chief guide up there?"

"Yeah. He doesn't buy Boyd's story, Charlie. But I don't know why yet. Something about instincts. I'm certain he'll tell me, but I need a few days. John can't learn why I'm here yet, not before I tell him... the right way."

"What's this 'right way' crap? You sound like you've got something going with him."

"He's Boyd's best friend, Charlie. They practically grew up together." Now she paused and took a breath before continuing. "And I do. I need time to work it out, explain why I'm here, you know. If John finds out before I can tell him, he'll feel betrayed. Not only will I lose him, but I'll lose his cooperation on Boyd. Charlie, Whitney is the key to breaking Boyd's alibi."

"Have you gone fucking nuts? Have you compromised this investigation by getting involved with a key witness?"

"Easy, Charlie…"

"Easy, my ass! He's a *witness,* Amy. Jesus! You're breaking every damn rule. You could get suspended. Don't you know that?"

"Yes, Mother Hubbard, I do. Believe me, I didn't intend it. It… just sort of happened."

"Happened, my ass! You're a cop."

Amy waited for more hysterics. Instead, some moments later, Charlie surprised her. "Boy, we're a pair, aren't we?"

"Yes, we are."

He remained quiet for another moment. "Amy, this is wrong; you know it. You can't win. If you tell him first, Whitney will clam up. If you tell him after, he'll never forgive you for using him. And even if you get him to testify, he'll be crucified on cross. You've conflicted him and jeopardized what little case we had."

"Too late, Charlie. I've got to play this out. I wanted to tell John tonight, but now I can't reach him."

She heard a heavy sigh on the other end of the line. "Jesus, I hope for the best for you, Amy. You know that. If things go wrong, if you need a shoulder to cry on, you know where to turn… Claire and I will be here for you. You're family."

Amy burbled something which sounded like, "Thank you, I love you too," and put the phone down.

She pulled out a tissue and blew her nose. As she picked up the receiver, she heard Charlie say, "Okay… I'll do it… Strike the deal with Preston. But there's still one little problem…"

"What?"

"What the hell do I tell MacGregor after he picks up his Sunday paper and sees what a fucking canary I've become?"

Amy laughed. "Give him the dilemma we were in—minus the part about John and me—and tell him you were so worried about his health, you didn't disturb him at home."

"Disturb him at home? This will *kill* him. Can you imagine him opening his Sunday paper and there's my smiling eight-by-ten?"

Struggling against laughter, Amy said, "C'mon, Charlie, knock it off. Have you got anything else to report?"

"Yeah," he said, "I do." He told Amy of his call to Haskins and his meeting with Sheriff Bourdelais. "Bourdelais doesn't buy our theory. He says Boyd's a fine, upstanding citizen, a hero. Forget Bourdelais; we won't get any help there. If it hadn't been for that mudflow, which took him away, I'm not sure I wouldn't have spent the night in the hoosegow."

"So there's no chance we can get a search warrant for Boyd's home?"

"Are you kidding? Hell no." He paused. "Why?"

"Just curious," Amy said, trying to sound unconcerned, kicking herself, hoping Charlie would let the question go.

"Bullshit, Amy, I know you better than that." There was a moment's silence. "What are you up to? What did you learn?"

"Not much, I'm afraid. I've spent most of my time with John."

"I'll bet."

"I'm serious, Charlie. He's not buying Boyd's story."

"So why're you so interested in whether or not we can get a search warrant for Boyd's home?"

Amy grimaced and remained silent.

"Amy? Talk to me."

"I just think... well... there might be some evidence lying around there." Pulling the phone away from her ear, she took a breath. That was so lame.

"Bullshit, Amy. You're lying."

He knew her too well.

"Why a search warrant?" he repeated. "And why at his house specifically? Why not the office or the Sorrento?" Only her silence responded.

"Amy?"

Silence.

"You've been there, haven't you? You broke into his fucking

house, didn't you?"

"You think I'm that dumb?"

"Didn't you?"

"Charlieee!"

"I *knew* it! I don't fucking believe this!"

"I didn't actually *break* in, Charlie. I was nosing around outside and tried my garage door opener. It worked. So I sort of… well… took that to be something of an invitation…"

"That's about the dumbest thing I've ever heard. MacGregor will have your badge. Mine too, probably."

"He can't find out, Charlie. Ever."

"Well, I'm certainly not gonna tell him. What if you left something behind? What if somebody saw you?"

"Nobody did, and I want Boyd to know somebody was there. I planned it that way; I made sure he'll know. I'll just deny it was me, even under oath."

"What do you mean, you made sure?"

She explained she'd moved some things but refused to elaborate.

Charlie remained silent for a moment. "That may work. Everything's been going so well for Boyd, maybe a few mind games will shake him. Maybe he'll make a mistake. But what about fingerprints?"

"I wiped the place down."

"Well, I'll keep your secret. You can count on that. So tell me… what'd you find out?"

"I'd rather not say, Charlie. If I do get caught, you can deny any knowledge of what I did."

"Okay. But can't you just hint at what you found?"

"It's circumstantial. But there's another place I want to look. It was locked."

"So what do we do now?"

"John. He's got to break Boyd's alibi. But there is something else you can do."

"What?"

"Check to see if Boyd has registered any snowmobiles, ATVs or trailers. Check with dealers in the area too. Also, check any gun registrations."

"Okay. Why the ATV and trailer?"

"Because that's how Boyd got the snowmobile into the park."

"Okay. But that means he'd need a trail. You can't just ATV a snowmobile up the park roads, can you?"

"Damn. You're right. I didn't think of that. I'll have to look for that some other time."

"Good. Look. I gotta go. I have to call that news reporter slime-ball Preston. To think I thought I'd have a free night with Claire…. Fat chance."

"No rest for the weary, Charlie."

"You haven't made it with this guy, Whitney—right?"

Amy hung up.

THIRTY-FIVE

Saturday, August 3

On his midnight arrival at Sea-Tac, Emery Boyd raced to his car and switched on his radio. Most of the newscasts were devoted to the catastrophe, but there was precious little hard information yet about casualties or damage. Deciding there was little more to be learned from the media, he dialed the Paradise Ranger Station and asked to speak to Mo Knauer.

Knauer came on the line. "Emery, is that you?"

"Yeah, Mo. I should be home in another forty minutes; then, a few minutes to change and I'll be ready to help. What's going on?"

"We can really use you. We're spread pretty thin. John and a few guides are surveying the campground, picnic and trail areas where Stevens Ridge Road crosses the Muddy Fork, and of course, Box Canyon just above. Then I've got several other people at Cougar Falls and below. I figure if somebody got swept away, it was probably where Whitney is. I need to know how close to the campsites and picnic areas it came. If close, we'll have to concentrate more of our efforts down below, maybe at Cougar

Falls. I'll use tourists, with maybe a few guides, to look below there along the Cowlitz River to the park boundary, maybe beyond. I've asked Whitney to take his group as high as Fan Lake. It's possible that so close to the mouth, the flow was high enough there to crest the ridge before it shot down the Muddy Fork. We'll check it out."

"Sounds good, Mo. It was the Ingraham, huh?"

"Yeah, middle part of the lower glacier. We're lucky it didn't fan out, you know, shoot off to the side over the Cowlitz to the Paradise Glacier. I wouldn't want to think about that."

"It was confined to the Muddy Fork?"

"Looks that way. I've issued instructions to close everything beneath the glaciers for now."

"Have you had any reports yet?"

"Whitney's called in several times. So far, so good. He checked out the Marsh Lakes; apparently the flow didn't reach that high. So maybe it isn't as bad as we first thought. All that ice may have made it look worse than it is. He called just a while ago from the picnic grounds, said the water didn't quite reach there. So that's fantastic. John's on his way to the Box Canyon patrol station, another place people like to camp. Then he's going to cross over to the back-country campsites. Hopefully, because of that high east ridge on the Muddy Fork, there's no problem there. I'm a little worried the flow could have crested that ridge higher up and crossed over to Twin Falls Creek. If so, it would have moved right through the back-country campsites."

"Well, Mo, if it didn't crest the ridge at Fan Lake, I doubt it could have crossed that ridge. Do you want me to head up there and take a look? I could go up the Paradise Glacier, cross over to the Williwakus and then make an easy traverse to Fan Lake and report back. I'll need a radio, of course, but I can probably make it over there in about two and a half hours. What do you think? It might save some time, and maybe then John won't have to cross the Muddy Fork; it's gonna be a bitch."

"Good idea. Stop by and pick up a radio. I'll call John and let him know what you're doing. But he'll still need to cross the Muddy Fork. Even if the flow didn't make it over the ridge, some campers could still have been caught. Maybe John will find some signs one way or the other."

"Okay, but crossing the Muddy Fork higher, just below Fan Lake, might be easier. There should be less flow by now. I'll see what it looks like. Maybe I'll meet John at the campground."

"Great, Em. Hey, thanks again. I'm glad to have you."

"Thanks, Mo. Say, any new word on Jim?"

"Bourdelais says it was his blood we found. He's dead. We had a nice memorial for him. FBI is letting Hank run the show. We think Jim's body and the poacher's are in a crevasse somewhere on the Kautz or South Tahoma Glaciers."

They talked for a few minutes more and then hung up. Boyd arrived at his home some twenty minutes later. Pulling into the garage and leaving the door open, he jumped out of the Mercedes and walked briskly to the light switches, flipping them on. Removing his attic key from its hiding place, he opened the heavy steel door, then left it open as he changed clothes and grabbed gear appropriate for a two-day trip under difficult mid-mountain conditions. Ten minutes later, he was dressed and ready. Turning to the door, he saw deep scratch marks, like claws, reflecting from the light behind him.

He dropped his pack and gear and examined the door more closely.

He spun around, facing the room. Anger seething, fear making him sweat, he checked the room, searching for any evidence of entry. Nothing seemed out of place or missing.

What about the main house?

He looked at his watch: 1:45. There wasn't time to worry about the house now. And he couldn't call Bourdelais yet; he needed to check the place before he brought anyone in—especially a police officer. There'd be time later.

He grabbed his pack and gear, locking the steel door behind him. Replacing the attic key, he dropped his gear in front of the ATV and reached to hang his Mercedes key on its designated hook.

He stepped back. The Honda key was missing. No, it was on the floor.

Scanning the garage, he looked for things moved, out of place. His breathing was rapid, his hands sweaty. He could feel his heart pounding.

Everything seemed normal.

None of the vehicles were gone; they didn't appear to have been moved. What had this person done with the keys? They were just some car keys, an ATV key and two snowmobile keys....

Make that *one* snowmobile key.

He stopped. Was there any other evidence that he owned two snowmobiles?

He glanced at the spot where the Arctic Cat was usually parked and saw an oil spot. He moved to a cabinet, pulled out a rag and wiped at it. He spread some sand over it.

Now there was oil on his fingers. Absently, he wiped it on his wool trousers. A thought struck him and his eyes searched the shelves. There it was, the Arctic Cat oil.

He yanked the half-empty container off the shelf and placed it in the ATV's storage container. He'd dispose of it on the trail.

Within minutes, he was moving across his front yard toward the trail to Longmire.

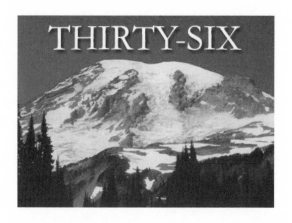

THIRTY-SIX

Saturday, August 3

By 4:00 A.M., John Whitney and his band of six guides had surveyed Box Canyon and begun preparing for their crossing of the Muddy Fork. Having found no problems at the picnic ground, they'd followed the trail up to Box Canyon, where a low swinging bridge spanning the narrows of the Muddy Fork was now gone, as was the Stevens Ridge Road highway bridge just below, both lost in the deluge.

Curiously, the flow and the extent of the damage were not as great as John had feared. But one worry still haunted him: had the main body of the flow crossed the ridge higher up? Had it swept through the remote campsites a mile away on the *other* side of the Muddy Fork? If so, that would explain the lack of overall destruction so far found, but it would mean disaster for anyone unlucky enough to have been near the usually popular remote campsites. There would have been little warning, just a swiftly growing rumble before death came riding in on a hundred foot wave. There would have been no escape: anyone unfortunate enough to have been in the path of the flow… was just gone.

Reporting his position and findings to an ever-more-relieved Mo Knauer, John was ready to cross the Muddy Fork. He was pleased to learn that Boyd was here and was now making his way up to Fan Lake. He hadn't tried to contact Boyd yet; there hadn't been any need.

The crossing would still be hazardous, requiring careful preparation and execution, because the water, while not as high or wide as expected, was still raging. But it would be manageable, and John's group was well trained. Even now, Max Brittain, George Stephenson, Noah Seirig, Norm Reiter and Diane Edwards, the lone woman in the group, were preparing slings and harnesses.

Joe Grogan, perhaps feeling some guilt at having been sick the day Jim Carlton was sent to the ice caves, volunteered to be the beach-ball-on-a-line who'd cross the rampaging waters first. Grogan's rough, tumultuous journey, requiring three hundred feet of line and the straining muscles of the group, took just over a half hour. Somewhat battered and bruised, Grogan made it to the other side and secured his line around a tree. As Whitney tied on a harness, he heard the squawk of his radio over the roaring of the water. Frowning, he stepped out of his harness and moved up the steep embankment to a quieter spot. He untied the radio, unwrapped it and heard a familiar voice: "Boyd to Whitney, come in, John."

"Whitney here," he replied.

"Hey buddy, what's up? You and Dianecommuning with nature?"

"So, you do exist. How 'bout that? Where are you? We're just crossing the Muddy Fork. Bridges are gone, road too."

"I've just finished at Fan Lake. Looks pretty good. It didn't cross the ridge. I found some back-country types up there. They'd had the scare of their lives, but no casualties. I sent them back to Paradise, told them the media was so starved for news, they'd be treated like heroes."

"Yeah, I bet. Well, that's good news, Emery. How high did it get there?"

"Looks like about three hundred feet on the ridge just to the north of me, John. Kinda hard to tell in the dark. Looks like a lot of trees down and ice all around—some the size of houses—but at least it stopped short of the top."

"Could it have crossed the ridge on the other side, toward Twin Falls Creek? The water would have hit that east side pretty hard, down where the Muddy Fork turns south."

"Yeah, I know. Can't say yet. Looks like it might be close. I'll have to head southeast to get a look. Probably take me an hour or so. Crossing the Muddy Fork up here where it's narrow won't be a problem. I'll just tie up to a tree and let the water carry me."

"Crossing the Muddy Fork here is not gonna be as bad as I expected either. The ice and debris seem to have passed. It's just water now."

"Good. Did you find anything down there?"

"Not so far. Looks like nobody was around. Guess we'll see when we get over to the remote campsites."

"Well, maybe I should move west then instead of crossing. You're gonna beat me to the remote campsites, and the campers I met said the flow crested the small ridge immediately south of the Ingraham mouth. I'm worried about Williwakas canyon. I'll check it, then follow the creek and either cross the Muddy Fork on your rope or wait there for you."

"Good idea. Just wait for us at the confluence of the creek and the Muddy Fork. No need to get wet, if you don't have to. If the campsites are okay, we'll be coming back."

"Sounds good. Say, John, have you heard anything from the ranger group down on the Cowlitz River?"

"Yeah. They called an hour ago. Said there's plenty of water, some ice and a lot of trees down, but so far no bodies in the debris snags. They're going to hole up down there for the rest of the night, and look again in daylight."

They signed off after Boyd volunteered to call in a report to

Knauer. Turning his radio off, John re-fixed it, then returned to his group. As he approached, Diane Edwards saw him coming and moved to meet him. "We're ready, John," she said. "You going first?"

"Yeah," he responded, moving past her down the steep embankment. "That was Boyd on the radio. He's at Fan Lake, heading down Williwakas Creek."

He saw disappointment in Edwards' eyes, and laughed. "Don't worry, Diane, you'll get your chance. If everything goes as planned, he'll meet us in two or three hours."

"Is it that obvious?" she asked, turning away, her face flushed.

"You've carried a torch for him for a long time."

"Not just him," she replied, a wistful look on her face.

Thirty minutes later, John's group had crossed the Muddy Fork River and was converging on the remote campsites. He said a quick, silent prayer when he saw that the area was untouched.

Several groups of stranded, scared campers were at the campsites, eager for a way back to Paradise. John called in his find to Knauer and reassured everybody that help would be along at first light. Cautioning the campers to sit tight and not stray, he and his party helped them build campfires.

On the return, it took another forty-five minutes for his tired and hungry crew to traverse the Muddy Fork once again. An hour after that, they met up with Emery Boyd. The first light of dawn was evident high on a west ridge, but darkness prevailed everywhere else.

His ATV parked some fifty feet away, Boyd was cooking breakfast on an open fire on a high peninsular outgrowth at the confluence of Williwakas Creek and the Muddy Fork. Looking up as John's wet and dead-on-their-feet group stumbled in, he greeted them and invited them to eat. There was a brief scurry as packs were dumped, opened and meal kits rooted out. Emery and John briefed each other.

Boyd reported that the flow had surged over the falls into the Williwakas canyon, but most of the overflow had been ice, not water, so there had been little damage further below. And he'd found no trace of any hikers or campers. After John briefed Boyd on his group's good news, they called in their report to a greatly relieved Mo Knauer.

Knauer suggested, and Emery and John concurred, that the group should pitch their tents and catch some rest. Once breakfast was completed, they set up their tents.

Noticing how Diane Edwards kept looking hopefully at him, Boyd suggested to John that they share one tent and offer the other to Diane. John agreed, saying he needed to talk to Emery anyway. He broke the news to the disappointed Edwards.

In their tent, unrolling their sleeping bags, Emery said, "Say, John, who is this woman Mo says you were with on the Roost?"

"Leave it alone," John growled. "We'll talk about her later. There's more important stuff first."

"Ranger's Roost, huh?" Boyd persisted. "Mighty pretty up there, private too… Good views, flowers, a little soft grass… Who is this creature, John? Usually, they get the wham, bam, thank you ma'am routine. She must be unusual to rate the Roost."

"I said we'll talk about her later."

"It'll wait a minute, John. Just tell me her name."

"Oh, hell!" John said. "It's Amy, okay?"

Boyd stood quiet, still, hulking in the confines of the tent. His eyes carried a feral look, and his fingers had stiffened. "What's the matter?" John said.

Boyd stared at him. "Amy, like in Galler?"

"You know her?"

"A Seattle police officer."

Whitney looked puzzled. "No. She's a bookkeeper for a super-market chain."

Boyd shook his head. "No, she isn't." His eyes bored into Whitney. "She's a homicide cop, John."

John sat back. He was remembering Amy's probes, her friend Sherry's question right before the Ingraham blew out. Nausea took him.

"She was asking about me, wasn't she?" Boyd said. He was sneering. "You had no clue she was using you, did you? She's investigating me, John."

John had a wild look in his eye, and his fist was clenched. He burned a flashlight into Boyd's face. "Okay, friend. That's it. You're gonna tell me what the fuck is going on... *right now!*"

Boyd watched John through dead eyes. "She's investigating the disappearance of my law partner, Herman Klein. She's trying to break my alibi." He shook his head. "God, you're so pathetic. She's using you, John. It's that simple."

The tranquility of the early mountain morning, the rushing sounds of water over rock, the birds singing, the winds rustling down the valley and through the leaves, all were disturbed by an anguished wail, a "Thwack!" then more unmistakable sounds of violence.

At ten o'clock, Amy was having breakfast with Sherry in the dining room. She was quiet, nervous, worried, hardly touching her food. Sherry was trying to draw her out. She was chattering away when she wasn't stuffing food in her face.

Amy looked around. Everywhere else, a spirited optimism was prevalent; people were friendly and chatty. The good news of the day was all around: the preliminary results of the aerial and ground surveys had been better than anyone expected. No serious casualties had been reported, and the damage was far less than expected. The desk clerk said Mo Knauer was estimating the park could be back almost to normal, excepting roadway and bridge repair, in a few days, assuming the good weather held and the number of volunteers stayed high.

But Amy felt as if there was a dark cloud over her. She'd felt this way ever since she'd talked to Charlie. She needed to talk to John.

She looked to the door and saw to her delight a determined-looking, somewhat disheveled John Whitney approaching.

She snapped to attention and waved. Sherry turned, saw John and waved too. Sherry got up, saying, "I'll leave you two alone," and walked away. As she passed the oncoming Whitney, Sherry smiled and said, "Good morning, John, you look like you've seen some action," but received no response. He was gone before the bruises and blood registered.

Amy rose to greet him, noting the bruises. Rough climbing... "Hi there," she said, raising her face for a kiss. "You look done in."

John bypassed her upturned face, took her by the shoulders and held her at arm's length. His hands were trembling, his voice shaking. "Emery Boyd is here. Why did you use me, lie to me? Did chasing him mean that much to you?"

John's fingers were digging in. Amy felt impaled on them. "John! You're hurting me."

"No more than you deserve."

Boyd wasn't due until Monday! "John, let me explain. We need to talk."

He shook his head. "I don't want to hear anything from you."

Looking into his furious eyes, Amy reexamined the puffiness and discoloration just below his right eye, a slash and a lump on the left side of his jaw. There was a jagged tear down the front of his shirt, blood around the edges. Another slash on his right upper sleeve, more blood there. Realization sank in. "John!"

All eyes were on them. The din of the room, so loud, cheerful and carefree just moments ago, had imploded into a suffocating silence.

"Don't deny it," John said. "I know who you are and why you're here. And I'm just one of your tools." His hands shook. "All those questions, all that interest… It was professional, not personal. And I thought you were interested in me." He slapped her. "All in the line of duty, eh?" He turned and walked a few steps, then turned around. "Sluts are amateurs. You're a whore."

John left, not looking back, shearing through the ugly silence.

THIRTY-SEVEN

Saturday, August 3

When Emery Boyd arrived home at 9:15 A.M., he stripped and showered, hoping to wash away the memory and traces of battle. Only partially successful, he filled up his tub, poured in some Vita-Bath and watched as the cleansing bubbles rose. As he watched, he replayed the morning's events.

John's attack had caught him off guard. Amy Galler must have really had him by the balls. If she'd had such an effect on John, maybe he ought to look her up. Yeah, some night in the dark, some place where nobody would hear the screams coming out of her. Split her crotch on a knife, maybe. He lay unmoving in the swirling waters.

He'd reacted instinctively to John's lunge, but caught John with only a glancing blow of his own. Then people were falling on them, even as Boyd's knife caught John's ribs, pulling John and him apart. Max Brittain tried to patch things up, tried to explore what had happened and force them to reconcile, but John had stormed off, not saying a word. It was left to Boyd to explain. He'd called it teasing that got out of hand, said it would all blow over in a few days. He should have realized how tense and tired John was; he should have known when to quit. No big deal. Just give John a few days.

Yeah, give John a few days... To live, maybe...

He lay back, covering his face with a washcloth. He felt the soothing heat soak into his pores.

He'd left soon after. The bulk of the work had been done; the group could carry on without him. He left his radio with Brittain before mounting his ATV and roaring off.

Now, watching the water swirl, bubbles bursting dry, a thirst welled up. He climbed out of the tub and gathered up his clothes. On his way to the kitchen, he stopped in the laundry room and raised the lid on the washer. There were clothes in there. He reached in and touched them: wet. He looked at the hamper: empty. He didn't remember doing any wash...

Moving into the kitchen, he called his cleaning service in nearby Elbe. They told him they hadn't been there in a month.

No change occurred in Boyd's face.

He picked up the book on the kitchen counter, the one that was supposed to be in the bathroom. What was it doing in the kitchen? He opened it and saw that the flyleaf had been reversed.

He smiled.

THIRTY-EIGHT

Saturday, August 3

G. Sherwood Preston arrived at Paradise at 10:20 A.M., tired but eager. Last night's meeting with Charlie Scott had lasted much longer than he'd planned, but had been well worth the effort. Four times over the course of their two-hour meeting in a downtown hotel bar, he'd excused himself for a hurried tape change. As the evening wore on and as Charlie became drunker, the information he'd passed on was better and better.

In the beginning Charlie spoke in hushed tones, dodging, while his eyes scanned the room like a felon looking for cops. Eventually, he'd stated his demands, which were fairly simple: no mention of Judge Schneider or Amy Galler.

The first one made sense; any hint of a connection to Schneider, and the FBI would come storming in. Everybody would lose.

But why so sensitive about Galler?

So she was undercover on Rainier, trying to pierce Boyd's alibi.

He sensed that Charlie was more concerned about keeping

Galler out of the story than he was about Schneider. This intrigued him and fueled his determination to get to the mountain.

Charlie had loosened up after a few quickly downed double scotches. To keep him talking, Preston, who had been sipping mineral water, lied: about the content of the article, and about his ability to negotiate. Despite his growing sense that Amy Galler was the key, he pressed the Schneider-Boyd button, saying he was being asked to give up a lot and that the Schneider story was ready to run. The presses would stop only if Charlie gave full cooperation and promised an exclusive.

Charlie, in his intoxicated state, had fallen for his blather. Among other things, he revealed that Carmody had seen Boyd in the Salish Lodge parking lot the night of Schneider's death and that Amy believed Boyd was the poacher on Rainier. He disclosed Arnie Trumball's findings, said they pointed to Boyd killing Klein and taking the body to Rainier. Carlton was a casualty necessary to protect the alibi.

Preston still pressed, but Charlie was slurring his words badly and weaving in his chair, denying that he knew anything more. He said Preston would have to talk to Amy. Promising to make the agreed adjustments to Sunday's article and extracting a promise from Charlie to keep the information flowing, Preston brought the meeting to a close. After calling a cab for the unsteady Scott, Preston had left the bar and gone home, where he set his alarm for seven.

Arriving at Paradise, he parked in the south lot, leaving his bags and equipment locked in the car. He wanted to get the lay of the land before he started lugging in gear and setting up shop. He entered the lodge and walked to the desk, where he had to pull on the clerk's sleeve to get some attention. He shouted his name and asked for his reservation. Without even looking at the register, the clerk snapped that it would be at least an hour until he could be accommodated; he suggested Preston get a bite to eat while he waited.

He didn't protest. The drive up from Seattle had made him hungry, and his new jeans felt loose around the waist. Entering the dining room through its double-doored entrance, he stopped to marvel at the high ceilings and expansive windows. If the food matched the setting, he'd be lucky indeed.

Then his eyes found Amy Galler.

Galler was seated at a table in the far left row, about mid-room, next to another very attractive woman. Galler was talking to an older man. Whatever they were saying, Galler didn't look happy.

Preston was delighted. Not here ten minutes, and he'd made contact. *No time like the present*, he thought. He'd just mosey over and find out what was cookin'.

Amy felt sick. Stunned by John's broadside, she'd been late in rushing after him. John was gone before she could recover. She'd sunk into her chair, her shoulders shaking.

Sherry and Camille arrived to comfort her. Camille left, then returned a moment later with a fresh cup of coffee. A silent, worried glance passed between Camille and Sherry, followed by Sherry's whispered assurance, "I've got her." Sensing there was little more she could do and worried about her table duties, Camille disappeared back into the kitchen.

Gradually, the room settled down; conversations resumed. But it took several more minutes before Sherry was able to stabilize Amy. Sherry handed her friend a napkin, telling her to wipe her eyes and blow her nose; it would make her feel better. Amy complied and sank back in her chair, her hands cradling her face. Sherry watched, unsure what to do.

Amy knew she was the subject of every conversation in the room. Reaching out, she found Sherry's shoulder and squeezed it.

"Get me out of here."

Before Sherry could move, there was a new presence at the table, a worried-looking Mo Knauer. "Amy? Are you all right?"

"I'm okay."

"Did you see John? I heard from the desk that he was here. Was he hurt? Did he say something?"

"He sure did!" Sherry said angrily. "And when I see him…"

Amy grasped her arm, silencing her mid-sentence. "It's all right, Sherry. I had it coming."

"Had *what* coming?" asked Knauer. He looked at each of the women, concern on his leathery face. "What the hell's going on around here? Boyd and Whitney fighting, trying to kill each other, then leaving their group; now I come looking for you—since I can't seem to find either of them—and I find *you* in tears."

Amy looked at Knauer through swollen eyes. "John and Emery Boyd were fighting?"

"You'd better believe it! You mean John didn't say anything about it?" Knauer paused. "Was it about you?"

She stared at her crumpled tissue.

Knauer leaned over. "Well, are you gonna *tell* me about it? Jesus! They damn near killed each other. Tore up their tent and the campsite, had to be restrained… What's this all about? I've never seen them—either of them—that angry, especially at each other. They've always been… well, like brothers."

Amy looked up. Somehow, she managed to find her voice. "Mo, can you give me a little time? I can't talk about it right now. Okay?"

Before he could answer, a new voice, a familiar one, broke in. "Well, well, well! Amy Galler. Just who I was looking for. We need to talk… Care to introduce me to your friends?"

Once again, Amy Galler became the object of all eyes in the room. The sound and sight of G. Sherwood Preston sent her lunging out of her chair. She dodged a restraining arm from Sherry and went quickly up the aisle toward the exit. She narrowly missed a startled Camille, approaching a table with a tray of plates. Sherry's concerned, "*AAAAMY?*" went unheard.

THIRTY-NINE

Saturday, August 3

"No prints, Emery." Bourdelais leaned back and took a generous sip of his warm beer. "You know," he said, nodding at the mug, "this may have been the cruelest trick."

Boyd laughed. "That was my reaction too. By the time I discovered it, I was on to the gamesmanship of it all. It's as if that was the whole purpose."

"Maybe. I don't know… I just don't get it… Why would someone break in here… and just leave calling cards?"

Boyd shrugged. "Yeah. I know." He took a sip from his mug, knowing his beer was colder than Bourdelais'. It was one of several he'd stuck in the freezer after re-plugging the appliance. "Maybe what he wanted was access to my attic; maybe the games were a payback for not being able to get in."

Bourdelais put his mug down. "You really think so?"

"Who knows? Those marks on the door sure as hell look like he was earnest." He shook his head. "Doesn't figure, you know? There's nothing up there but gear."

Bourdelais nodded. "That doesn't make much sense, though.

I'm thinking vandalism."

"I'd expect to see more damage. Wouldn't you?"

"Yeah, normally." He drained the rest of his beer and wiped his mouth with his sleeve. Boyd walked to the refrigerator and removed another tepid can.

"You never know," Bourdelais continued, pouring his second one. "Could be some star-struck tourist, I suppose… maybe some groupie looking for souvenirs. Or…" he said pointedly, "…maybe it was one o' your women-friends."

Boyd gave him a half-smile. "No, Hank, don't think so. That's John. My women tend to have more class."

"Well, I hear a woman's been the source of *some* problems around here lately…" Seeing no immediate reaction, he added "…like maybe between you and John, for instance?"

Boyd sipped his beer. "News travels fast, doesn't it? That was John's problem, though, not mine. Who told you about it?"

"Mo. He says you and John were goin' at it, a slugfest. He said John left you, went to see her and slapped her around a little. I hear she was a wreck."

Boyd smiled. He walked back to the refrigerator and removed another beer from the freezer. "Go on."

"Not much to tell. Mo didn't see much. But he said John was pretty rough on this woman and that it had something to do with what happened between you two."

Boyd laughed.

"There was a reporter fella mixed up in it too…"

Boyd's mood changed. "What reporter?"

"I dunno. Somebody from the *Post*. Mo said that just after John left, he went to talk to the girl—you know, to try and calm her down and find out what happened. Well, anyway, while he was talking to her, this reporter fella shows up, says howdy, and the girl goes nuts. She ran outta there.

"So, Emery, what happened? Did you make a play for John's girl?"

Boyd shook his head. "No, Hank, nothing like that. John's been under a lot of stress. I think I just caught him at a bad time and said the wrong thing, you know how it is."

"There's another possibility, I suppose…"

"What are you talking about, Hank?"

"Your mysterious intruder. I was just thinking… This might be stretching things, I suppose, but I had a little visit yesterday from the Seattle P.D., Homicide Division."

"What'd they want?"

"Not they. He. Detective Charlie Scott. Anyway, Scott was asking about you."

"Why me?"

"Well, seems they're investigating the disappearance of your partner, Herman Klein, I think his name is—or was, I guess, since it was Homicide who was askin'. This Scott fella was interested whether there was any link between Klein's disappearance and our problems here… you know…"

"Really? Where'd Scott get a wild idea like that?"

"Don't know. But don't worry, I straightened him out. I told him you're one of our most respected citizens and he was way off base."

Boyd put his mug down. "I don't get it, Hank. I mean, didn't he know I was up on the mountain when Herman disappeared?"

"Yeah. That's why he came to see me." He put his mug down on the counter and faced Boyd, a smile on his face. "You'll love this one, Emery. Scott thought maybe you came down the mountain, drove to Seattle, took care of your partner…" Seeing Boyd's surprise, he laughed, "…then returned to dump the body on the mountain somewhere, killing Carlton in the process—maybe because he saw you."

"That's preposterous!"

"That's what I said. Do you know this Detective Scott?"

"No, but I know the name. He's been asking stupid questions about a number of people in the office. Did he say why they're checking on me?"

"Just that your partner's wife has been mouthing off. According to Scott, you and Klein weren't the best of buddies. Evidently, she thinks there's more to it."

"Herman and I weren't very close, Hank. Hell, I'm a litigator and he was an accountant; we never had much in common." He sipped his beer.

Bourdelais nodded. "That makes sense."

"But there wasn't any real trouble between us. Just a few minor political squabbles, you know, like you'd expect between two department heads: who gets which office; arguments over firm resources; who gets which secretary, that sort of thing."

Boyd watched him. "You know, I can't help but wonder why the police aren't taking a long, hard look at Herman's wife. Hell, everybody knows they were always fighting. That's where they ought to be looking."

Bourdelais said nothing, just listened.

"Well, enough. You said there was another possibility... I don't see how a visit by this Seattle detective translates. Do you think there's some relationship?"

"I don't know, Emery. You know big city cops better'n me. Maybe this Detective Scott came out here to get the lay of the land... you know, check things out."

"But why, Hank?" He was delighted at the direction Bourdelais' speculation was taking. "That'd be an illegal search."

"Yeah, but sometimes big city cops play games... you know... to shake people up... even plant stuff." He paused. "Maybe it's a good thing you called me. Just to protect yourself."

Boyd nodded. "I'm glad I called you."

Bourdelais drained his mug, then set it down firmly. "Let's take a little walk outside. See if we find anything."

Following Bourdelais, Boyd heard him belch as the contents of his belly shifted. Bourdelais stepped off the deck into the soft grass. Spotting something in the grass ahead of him, he lumbered over to it. Pausing for a moment to adjust his pants, he bent over, then straightened up and returned to the deck. He opened his hand to show a soggy yellow tissue, somewhat drained of its color. "Don't s'pose you left this here?"

"No."

"See, I *told* you it was a woman." He thrust the soggy tissue into a plastic bag and then stuffed the treasure into his jacket pocket. "Evidence, Emery. Don't want you to think Pierce County's best and brightest doesn't follow scientific methods."

He looked around the yard again. "So, somebody—probably a woman—stood here and cased the joint." He turned and pointed toward the nearest window. "Bet she snuck a peek inside."

They walked to the front window. At the edge of the deck, Bourdelais bent over again, this time looking at a smudge of mud. "Just as I thought. She scraped her shoes right here just before she stepped up. Let's see if there's any prints or smudges on the window. If so, she was here during the day. Probably had to shield her eyes to peer in."

He moved over to a front window. Suddenly, he laughed and turned to Boyd. "Here's a nose print, smeared though."

"Amazing, Hank."

Bourdelais stood upright, satisfaction evident. "Experience helps. I've got a camera in the car." He walked to his vehicle.

"Say, Hank, you gonna be long? I was up all night. Do you mind if I hit the sack? You're done inside, aren't you?"

Bourdelais looked up. "Yeah. Go ahead. I'll let you know later if I find anything else."

FORTY

Saturday, August 3

A dejected Amy Galler stayed in her room all afternoon, ignoring knocks at her door and phone calls. She wasn't ready to talk to anyone yet, not until she'd reached John.

But John wasn't answering his phone either. She'd called him on the hour both at home and at the office, leaving messages at both places. As the afternoon dragged on, she decided to call Charlie.

Claire answered, sounding curt. She said she'd get him.

He picked up the phone a few moments later and moaned something that sounded like "Hello." Amy asked what was wrong.

"Hangover. Worst one in years. Been in bed all day."

"What happened?"

"Preston... last night... awful drunk..."

"Damn it, Charlie! Preston is here! I need to know what you told him."

There was silence, followed a moment later by a sick-sounding moan, then rustling noises. "He's *there*? What's he doing there? He's not supposed to be there."

"Tell me about it. What did you tell him?"

There was some stammering, mumbling.

"Charlie, damn it. Talk to me. What did you say?"

"Gee, Amy, I'm not sure. I'm trying to remember... We had a long talk and too many drinks." He coughed into the phone. "He's pretty slippery, you know, and he got me pretty drunk. I'm afraid I... well... I may have told him quite a bit... I'm having a little trouble remembering. But I think I told him more than I wanted to."

"What?"

He took a breath. "He just kept coming at me, Amy. He knew so much already, and... and he kept demanding more."

"So you just spilled your guts. Is there anything you didn't tell him?"

Scott's silence answered her question.

"Aw damn." She listened to breathing. "Great, Charlie. What do I do now?"

"Do you want me to come out there?"

"No. You've done enough."

"Maybe you should get out of there, Amy. You're coming back tomorrow anyway. What's another few hours?"

"I'm staying, at least tonight."

The silence was unpleasant. "Look, I'm sorry about Preston. Maybe I shouldn't have told him all that I did. I can't change that, and if I hadn't told him what I did, he wouldn't have agreed to leave you out of his article.

"Look, Amy, the key to Boyd's alibi is there. Preston knows that; he knew it before he spoke to me.

"He's got a source, Amy," Charlie pressed. "Somehow he found somebody. And it's a real good one."

"A source? I thought you said he listened to your conversation with Anthony, Schneider and Mrs. Klein. What happened to that theory, Charlie?"

"I dunno. Maybe so. I forgot about that. Anyway, last night it sounded like he really does have a source."

"Yeah. Someone high up in the police department? Closely associated with the case?"

"Amy, that's not fair. Look, what's wrong? Did Preston do something? Did he blow it for you? If he did, I'll drive up there myself and strangle the bastard."

She didn't trust herself to talk.

"What is it? What's happened?"

She told him everything, her voice breaking as her hurt poured out.

Charlie listened until Amy seemed spent. "Amy, I'm really sorry. Why don't Claire and I come out? Sounds like you could use a couple of friendly faces."

"No! I got myself into this; I've got to find a way out."

"But Amy, there's another consideration: Boyd. He knows you're there. And he knows someone broke into his house. You're in danger."

Anger was building in Amy, a slow hate directed at the man who'd cost her so much. Charlie's comment had snapped her downward spiral. Boyd was laughing at her; he thought he'd won. She wouldn't let that happen. And no more throwing up in fear, by God.

"I'll be fine," she said.

"What are you planning, Amy?"

"Nothing."

"Did you hear me? You're in danger."

"I'll handle it."

"Amy?"

"I'm okay, I said."

"I don't believe you. I'm coming out there."

"Don't you dare! Believe me, Charlie. I don't need you here, and I don't want you here."

"Well, what are you gonna do?"

"I don't know yet. But I know one thing: I'm up for this."

FORTY-ONE

Saturday, August 3

Emery Boyd struggled awake a little after 6:00 P.M., frustrated by how long he'd slept. After showering and dressing, he dialed John Whitney's home, connecting only with his answering machine. He left a message asking John to meet him at Paradise. If John couldn't make it, he urged him to call tomorrow at home or Monday in Seattle.

The trip to Mo Knauer's office took a little over ten minutes; it was 6:55 when he arrived. Knauer looked tired and haggard, but he was glad to see Boyd. He said he'd been worried about both Boyd and Whitney, although Bourdelais had called and said Boyd was no worse for wear. "Have you talked to John? I tried to call him, but he's not answering."

"No."

"What happened between you two? You're like brothers."

Boyd laughed. "Hell, Mo, brothers fight. Look, it was no big deal. We were a little tight and edgy, maybe I touched a nerve. I was teasing John a little, and he snapped. It happens. I'm sure that when he comes down from his high-horse, all will be forgotten."

"Good," Knauer said, relieved.

"Anything new on the lahar?" Boyd said, changing the subject. "What's the damage? Any casualties?"

Knauer's tired face brightened. "So far, so good. No casualties yet and only minor damage. But survey crews are still out, mostly working lower levels, so I guess it's too soon to say we totally dodged the bullet. Of course, there's road damage and the lost bridge over Stevens Ridge… That'll take about six months, I'm told. But otherwise, it's looking good."

"What about the glacier? How's it look?"

Knauer shook his head. "We don't know. We can't get close yet, and we can't tell much from the air. We're keeping everything below the Ingraham closed, except for the survey crews of course, but whatever condition it's in, it shouldn't worsen, what with the break in the weather. Hopefully, it will stabilize a bit."

Boyd nodded, and Knauer continued. "Biggest problem now is keeping tourists away. We're posting rangers and signs in danger areas."

"So we don't know anything about the glacier?"

"Not really. Whitney's group moved up a little higher after you and John left. They said things were shifting and moving around, but the water level appeared down. A lot of water was displaced, so I'd expect an extended settling period, maybe a few smaller flows as the ice shifts. That's why I'm keeping everybody away."

Boyd nodded. "Anything else going on?"

"Well, there's a reporter up here from the Seattle *Post*, asking about you."

"About me?" He feigned incredulity.

"Yeah, he showed up this morning about the time of the ruckus in the dining room. Boy, I don't know what you said to John, but he really took his girlfriend apart, and in front of everybody. Then that reporter showed up and all hell broke loose."

Boyd laughed. "Keeps the place lively, anyway. What happened to John's girl?"

"Don't know. Her girlfriend, Sherry somethin', was looking for her. Last I heard though, she hadn't found her."

"Sherry?"

"Yeah. A real looker."

"Did they come together, this Sherry and John's friend?"

"No. I think they met here."

"How about the reporter? Is he still around?"

"Don't know. Haven't seen him in awhile."

Boyd looked at his watch. 7:10. "Want to get some dinner?"

"Let's go to Anderson's," Knauer said, referring to a restaurant two miles west of the park entrance. "I don't want the media bothering us while we eat."

By and large, the bubble of G. Sherwood Preston's first day's optimism was deflating; it wasn't completely busted, but it was leaking air. Nagging self-doubts, which had often plagued him during his tabloid days, were resurfacing.

Everything depended on twos, it seemed: the alibi and the body; find either, be a hero; find neither, be a goat. Galler and Boyd; Galler and Whitney; Whitney and Boyd. Numerically, according to this logic, he'd come up with less than one.

He'd started his first day well enough, feeling happy, fresh and full of the hunt. His reporter's instincts honed, he'd sprung headlong to the scent of his prey.

And promptly fallen on his ass.

His bold decision to approach Amy Galler had proved a mistake, one which set the tone for the day. On reflection—oh, the vision of hindsight!—he realized that his timing couldn't have been worse; he'd barged right into the teeth of a buzz saw.

No, the morning had started as a disaster. He'd seen Amy only briefly and now couldn't find her.

Left to forage on his own, Preston didn't learn much. Few, if any, knowledgeable people would talk to him.

It was all so frustrating. People up here seemed to treat Emery Boyd as a god. Time and again, after cornering a likely prospect, he faced mocking laughter when he suggested that Boyd could have been anywhere but lost during the storm. And the more questions he asked, the more close-mouthed or sarcastic the source became.

Why was everyone so certain Boyd was on the mountain the whole time? Could the cops be so wrong? Christ! He'd gone out on a limb on this thing; he couldn't be wrong. He remembered Geraldo's opening of the Capone vault. His fate would be worse.

Mulling this over, Preston realized there was only one way out: to retain his focus and shoo away the nagging insecurities. Tenacity was how he'd survived the tabloids; tenacity was how he'd succeed now.

Amy was the key. Well, Amy and Emery Boyd. He had to talk to Amy before he confronted Boyd.

Where was she? What had she found out? MacGregor wouldn't sanction one of his detectives spending a week up here just on a whim. He would have recalled Amy if all she'd found were dry holes.

It was 8:00 P.M. He picked up his phone and tried Amy's room again. No answer. His stomach churned; he hadn't eaten since early afternoon.

Entering the dining room a few minutes later, he saw Amy sitting with Sherry Brannigan at the last table on the right, by the kitchen doors. And likewise, she saw him. He saw her slink down in her seat. Too late—she was his now.

As he scurried through the crowded room, he kept his eyes glued on his target. He saw Amy speak to Sherry, and saw Sherry rise and leave the table, taking a route which avoided him.

He took a seat opposite her. "I'm here and there's no avoiding me. As you may know, I'm working with Charlie Scott. We have a deal. If you won't talk to me now, the deal is toast. You, he and MacGregor can read everything in the *Post* tomorrow."

Amy pushed her plate away and signaled the waitress, handing her a signed credit card receipt. Then she looked up at him. "Well, it doesn't look like you'll just go away."

Preston recapped what Charlie had told him, stretching things a bit, as Amy frowned and winced from time to time. Completing his summary, Preston said he was ready for her side of it—all off the record, of course.

Amy just looked at him.

"Come on, Galler," he said, leaning over, moustache twitching. "You don't want to jeopardize the deal Charlie and I reached, do you? How do you think MacGregor will react, reading everything in the paper?"

She smiled. "Mr. Preston"—her tone was calm and confident—"any deal was between you and Charlie. God knows what possessed Charlie to talk to you at all—I suspect to protect my cover. But, as you may have noticed this morning, my cover is blown. So things are a little different now."

Preston looked perplexed. "What do you mean, your cover is blown?"

"Boyd is here. He knows about me, why I'm here, what I'm doing. I'm leaving tomorrow. So I don't see why I should talk with you at all. Do you?"

Preston's confidence sagged, leaking as blood drains from a nicked vein, slowly but steadily, draining energy as it escapes. "Well... uh... it's not quite as simple as that," he said, realizing that his voice had lost its authority. "One phone call from me and the story changes. Right now, there's no mention of Schneider. I can easily change that. The FBI will be all over this case. You, Scott and MacGregor will be out on your asses, doing errands for the feds."

Amy smiled. "Yes, that's probably true, but who loses more?

Better make your call."

"Huh?"

"If you lose us, you lose your source. Maybe Charlie buys you having somebody else, but I don't. I think you got your information from breaking into the Klein house and overhearing a conversation Charlie was having. If you lose us, your source dries up."

She smiled as if holding a trump card. "So in other words, I'm calling your bluff. Go ahead and print your story, all of it. Then be prepared to back it up when Boyd sues, which he will. If I'm right that you got your information from overhearing conversations at the Klein's residence, you can't use that because it will result in your prosecution. Charlie will say he talked to you just to get information from you; he'll say he only followed along the path you'd already determined. What's more, I'll testify that I told you tonight your information was inaccurate, but the record will show that you decided to print anyway. So let's see how you fare with no source and no back-up. Now, I'm no lawyer, but I think Boyd can show malice enough for a verdict."

"You don't think I will, do you?" Preston smirked, masking the panic rising in his chest.

"Oh, you don't understand... I don't really care."

"Look," Preston said, flashing his yellow teeth. "Maybe we're getting off on the wrong foot. You know, we should be working together. I help you; you help me. We both want the same thing; we just have different perspectives, different circumstances, if you will, and different opportunities. Why can't we work together?"

For several moments, Amy studied him, saying nothing. Finally, she broke her silence. "I don't see what we get out of all this. So far, it's been us giving you information. What have you given us? What will you give us?"

So this was the key to opening her up. Amy was a bargainer, a trader. Okay. That was his forte.

"You know, Amy..." Preston said, and saw her cringe at the

familiarity, "…so far you're right. I have been feeding off you—well, Charlie anyway. It's time I started doing my share."

"So how do you propose to do that?"

"Well, Boyd's got to be feeling pretty secure. All you've got is circumstantial evidence—and pretty weak at that—going to a motive. I figure to shake him up a bit."

"How?"

"Simple. I'll confront him; tell him what I think happened. Then I'll measure his reaction. I'll fill you in on all the details, and we can figure out what to do next."

"I don't think Boyd rattles that easily."

"Oh, I'll rattle him. I'm good at that."

Amy nodded. "You know, Preston, if we're right, Boyd's a dangerous man—and I don't mean lawsuits. Aren't you afraid maybe he'll arrange a… convenient accident?"

"Believe me, Amy," Preston said, twirling his moustache. "I've dealt with more dangerous people than Emery Boyd. Besides, he can't do anything to me. His whole thing is security, careful planning. That's how he's gotten away with all this, maybe back as far as Aimsley Castle…" He saw Amy's eyes flash. "So you know about him too."

"No comment."

"Well, we'll work on that later. My point is that Boyd works from plan, not spur of the moment. I'll come at him from a blind side."

"Aren't you forgetting Jim Carlton? I don't see how Carlton fit his plan."

"That's different. Boyd didn't have a choice if he was going to protect his alibi. No, I don't think he likes spontaneous violence. He's methodical; all good trial lawyers are—they have to be."

"Yes," Amy said. "But they're also quick on their feet. I wouldn't make too many assumptions when it comes to Emery Boyd. I have a feeling we're dealing with someone who's an adapter. You could be in danger."

"Well, let me worry about that. What do you say? Deal? First I produce and then you do?"

Amy shrugged. "We'll see." She rose and walked away.

At the registration desk, the desk clerk handed her a pile of messages. The last one was from Emery Boyd. The note was simple: "Talk. Bar at 9:00," and was signed.

Amy looked at her watch: she had fifty minutes.

Sipping from a glass of scotch and holding a steak to the side of his face, John Whitney was miserable. Not usually a drinker of hard liquor, the scotch tasted awful. Ignoring his ringing phone, he sat sprawled over a stuffed leather chair as a baseball game played on his TV. He wasn't watching; he didn't know who was playing.

He'd tried sleeping, tried music. Nothing forced the pain or questions away. Amy had deceived him; Emery had lied to him.

Why?

Amy had captured his heart, then stomped on it. She was investigating Emery for the murder of his partner. She thought Emery was the poacher. She'd used him, lied to him.

Had Emery killed his partner? Had Emery killed Jim? Could he be so wrong about someone he'd known so well for so long? Emery had twisted him up emotionally. Emery, his near brother.

Why?

He gulped more scotch and gagged, resisting the urge to throw up. Draining his glass, he stumbled to the bar for another. As he poured, he lay the right side of his face on the ice block in the sink. The scotch missed his glass and ran along the counter.

If he couldn't freeze out the questions and the pain, he'd drown them in amber.

FORTY-TWO

Saturday, August 3

Amy visited the lobby restroom before meeting Sherry in the bar. She spent several minutes primping in front of the mirror. As she ran a brush through her hair and gazed at her reflection, she was glad she'd decided to wear a loose black sweater and jeans. Casual and relaxed was just the image she wanted to portray to Emery Boyd, and the snubbie felt good on her belt.

Even though the bar was crowded, she spotted Sherry immediately, noticing that her friend had changed into a tight red sweater and a short black skirt. Sherry was trolling.

Sherry was sitting at a table along the wall, engaged in conversation with two people, a pretty, dark-haired woman Amy didn't know, and a guide John had identified as Joe Grogan. Sherry saw her and quickly separated herself, moving her beer to an empty table in the back of the room. As Amy passed the bar, Earl, the smiling, hulking bartender, caught her eye. She thought for a moment, then ordered a dry white wine. One wouldn't hurt her, and it might steady her nerves. Earl wouldn't let her pay.

The table Sherry'd selected offered privacy plus a view of the bar, just what Amy wanted. Taking the seat next to the wall, Amy explained she was meeting someone.

"Who? John?"

"No."

"Who?"

"Sherry, you promised."

"Yeah, but surely you can tell me. Hell, all I have to do is just sit here and wait. C'mon, Amy."

"I'm meeting Emery Boyd."

Sherry's eyes looked like saucers. "Can I sit nearby?" She looked for a nearby table.

"No. I don't want you anywhere near me. You understand?"

"Aw, c'mon. This is exciting."

"No, Sherry, it isn't. It's dangerous." Amy's tone was firm and her eyes were steady. "I want you to leave in a few minutes."

"Will you talk to me afterwards, fill me in?"

Amy gave her a look.

Sherry sighed. "Okay. So tell me about this reporter. The guy gives me the creeps. What's he want?"

Amy sipped her wine.

"Well, if you won't talk to me about Boyd and won't talk to me about this reporter, will you talk to me about John?"

"What do you want to know?"

"What are you going to do?"

Amy sighed. "I don't know. I'm gonna keep trying him. Sooner or later, he's got to talk to me."

"Want me to try?"

"No!" Amy saw Sherry deflate. "Look, Sherry, I know you want to help, but you can't. I'm sorry. This is something I have to work out with John, and nobody can help me. I've already screwed this thing up enough. Nobody but me can do anything about it."

Sherry took a sip from her beer. "He'll come around."

"I don't know. John's a mountain man, you know, proud,

strong, set in his ways. He'll talk to me, for sure; I'll see to that. But whether anything more comes of it…" She slowly rotated her wine glass. "So, how long are you staying?"

"A while. I've got plenty of time. I really enjoyed that hike with you and John. I'd like to do some more of it. And who knows, maybe I'll meet somebody…"

Amy laughed. "You've made progress. Just stay away from that Maselli character."

Amy and Sherry were so absorbed in their conversation that Sherry didn't notice the tall, imposing figure who entered the bar. She didn't see the bartender welcome him, hand him a beer and point to their table, nor did she notice as he worked the room. But Amy saw him coming, and she grabbed Sherry's arm. Sherry turned, and the man was at her side.

"You must be the lovely Sherry," he said, addressing her with a practiced smile. "Allow me to introduce myself. I'm Emery Boyd."

Sherry's eyes grew wide, and she looked at Amy.

"I'm sorry," he said, "I see from the looks on your faces that you weren't expecting me." Smiling still, he looked at Amy. "Didn't you get my message?"

"Yes… uh… I did. I'm sorry, I lost track of the time." She sat back and glanced nervously at Sherry, who was leaning forward now, her legs crossed, devouring Boyd with her eyes, vamping him with a teasing smile. She kicked at Sherry's shins but missed. Glancing up at Boyd again, she saw that Sherry's attention had not gone unnoticed.

Boyd's eyes were dead, like those of a vulture sitting on a fence watching a dying squirrel. His stance wide, dressed powerfully in a black silk shirt covered by an open, oversize, black, wood-buttoned Pendleton jacket, over well-worn black jeans adorned by a wide black leather belt and an enormous silver buckle, Boyd looked every bit the predator.

Amy's eyes narrowed. She would keep him on her left, her right hand free for quick access to her .38.

"And your last name, Sherry?"

"Uh… Brannigan," she said. "Sherry Brannigan." Her smile deepened.

He extended his huge hand, enclosed Sherry's and held it for an uncomfortable—for Amy—length of time. Sherry seemed delighted.

"Don't you need to be somewhere?" Amy said.

Sherry ignored her.

"Ah," Boyd said. "I see you know who I am. That must mean Amy here…" He paused and looked at Galler now. "I hope you don't mind the familiar, Amy. I think we do know something of each other."

Amy sipped her drink, willing herself to stay calm. She raised her glass, catching Earl's eye.

"At any rate, as I was saying… that must mean that Amy's been talking about me." He glanced at Amy again, and his smile disappeared. "I'm not sure I like that. How about it, Amy?" he said. "Have you been telling stories about me?"

Boyd released Sherry's hand, stepping back to let Earl put Amy's glass down and pick up the empty. He smiled at Boyd, who gave him a pat on the back.

Boyd turned back to Sherry. "You know, being known has its disadvantages. You find people say the strangest things about you. Frankly, I don't know where they get some of their ideas. May I join you, or is this an inconvenient time?"

Amy gave Sherry a head-shake, and Sherry rose. "Oh, don't go," Boyd said. "I'd like to get to know you better."

Sherry looked at Amy. "I'll leave you two alone. I'll just sit over here." Sherry gave Boyd an inviting smile. Amy thought of catnip.

"Well, Sherry," he said to her back. "I hope Amy hasn't colored your judgment of me. I suppose I should ask for equal time." He turned back. "Maybe I should sue for slander."

"I assure you, Mr. Boyd," Amy said, "as unaccustomed as you are to hearing it, we were discussing another topic altogether."

"I'll bet," he said. He picked up his mug and drained a third of it. "I'm sorry if I caused you some discomfort earlier today… Well, not really… You see, I don't particularly like people using my friends against me. And as a lawyer, I practice full disclosure. John needed some enlightenment." He gave her his practiced smile.

"So you decided to be the avenging knight."

"Something like that. See, John and I have been friends a very long time. I didn't think he'd appreciate being used. John's an honest guy—not too bright, maybe—but honest. If John has a fault, he's too trusting, too easily misled. I thought I'd better set the record straight on why you were interested in him. Judging from his reaction," he said, rubbing his jaw, "I'd say John didn't appreciate your using him. But then, maybe you're a better judge of that."

His smile darkened.

"Well, from the bruises I see, looks like John was more upset with you, although maybe you're the better judge of that."

"Oh, I am. I am." He sat back, rotated his mug on its coaster, then met Amy's eyes. "John's like a brother. We've had spats before, but they never last. And neither will this one. By tomorrow, John will have forgotten about it—and about you."

Amy maintained her cool. "Well, it's water over the dam now. I thought I'd get something useful from John, and I did."

"Oh, really? Well, I'm sure John will be glad to hear that."

The Intimidation Tactic. She'd expected him to try it. He'd seized upon her weakness immediately.

"Look, Mr. Boyd," she said, sipping her wine, "this is all rather uninteresting history. Why did you want to meet?"

"Hitting a little too close to home?"

She smiled. "Not at all. Sorry to mislead you. I just don't like wasting my time."

Boyd leaned forward. "You know, if there's anything I do well, it's judge the credibility of people. You're lying. You're bleeding on the inside, trying to keep it from showing." He sat back again.

Amy laughed. "You're very much mistaken, Mr. Boyd." The smile left her face. "And you know, I'm a little surprised. I would think that a man in your position wouldn't want to make too many mistakes when dealing with someone like me."

"Right." He drained another third of his beer. "I thought it was usual practice for the police to inform a suspect that he was the target of an investigation, especially before something as illegal as a warrantless search of the suspect's home. Did I miss something, or have the rules changed?"

"I'm sorry," Amy said, shrugging, "I have no idea what you're talking about."

Boyd leaned forward, and his voice became a whisper. "Or maybe you just decided to violate them, huh? I'm wondering if I should take steps to protect myself..." He paused a moment. "Maybe a complaint to the mayor?"

Amy shrugged. "Go ahead. I really have no idea what you're talking about. It is our practice, constitutionally required as you know, to advise a suspect of his rights before we interrogate him. Inasmuch as this is your meeting, not mine, I don't think that rule applies. Be that as it may, if you'd feel more comfortable, I'd be happy to so advise you of your rights."

"I think it's a little late, considering your invasion of my home. Don't you?"

Amy's eyes held his. "Did someone break into your house? I'd have thought you'd call the sheriff."

"Oh, I did, Amy. I did. That's how I know it was you."

"I don't follow, Mr. Boyd. I don't even know where you live." She paused. "Give me some credit here. You talk about your ability to judge people. Well, remember, I'm trained for that too. You're lying. If you could link me to a break-in at your house, I'm sure the local authorities would be hauling me away. Instead, here I sit."

Boyd raised his mug in salute, drained it, then signaled Earl. In a moment, another mug appeared.

Boyd watched Earl walk away, then turned back to Amy. "Your yellow tissue, the one you used when you blew your nose? It gave you away. That and your nose prints on my windows. Oh, and there was a footprint... So, may I ask what you think you found? And do you realize that with the proof our sheriff has of the break-in, you've blown anything you might get from a warranted search, not that you could get a warrant?"

"Mr. Boyd, I haven't been to your house, and I sure as hell didn't break into it. What makes you think I'm the only person investigating you? Are you aware the *Post* has sent G. Sherwood Preston up here? I understand the paper's printing an article about you killing Herman Klein tomorrow."

She saw Boyd twitch, a slight involuntary movement of an eyebrow. She pressed in. "You know, maybe I should talk to Preston some more. I mean, he told me he has all sorts of interesting information about you and Klein; about you and Judge Schneider; even about you and Aimsley Castle." No twitch this time. Under control. "Let's see, did I get their names right? Maybe Preston knows something about your snowmobiles too. Yes, I think I'll have to look him up. Listen, I appreciate your telling me about the break-in. It opens all sorts of interesting possibilities. I can find out who did it, cut him a deal."

Boyd skewered her with a cold stare. Amy met his eyes, as her arm slid down close to the snubbie.

He leaned in again, his Pendleton jacket taut over powerful shoulders. "Don't bullshit me, Galler. As far as Preston is concerned, I'd suggest you caution him about the law of libel. Let me assure you, anyone who passes along bad information is just as guilty—and liable, I might add—as the person who prints it. And you'd better believe I'll sue."

"Well, Mr. Boyd, it certainly looks like you're going to get the opportunity." She smiled. "Make sure you read the paper tomorrow… for that matter, every day next week. I understand the *Post*'s going to give it a run."

"Yeah, we'll just see about that."

She raised her glass to him.

Boyd watched her. "Tell me, Amy. I'm amazed by all this. Do you think you can get an indictment? You've got nothing: no body, no motive—nothing. I'm wrapped tight in my alibi. You're not being realistic. Have you considered Emily Klein? I'll bet you any number of people will tell you she's threatened him. Have you checked her out? I mean… Why me?"

The Persuasion Tactic. She'd expected he'd try that too. And at the same time he was applying *The Fishing Tactic.*

Clever.

"She's taking a polygraph Monday. Will you?"

"Why should I? You've got nothing on me. Not even enough to get by a charge of harassment."

"Then file it. I suspect the *Post* would love it. Look, if you think I'm going to sit here and tell you what we've learned, go fuck yourself."

Nothing changed. Boyd sipped his beer. It frightened her.

"You made a mistake, Mr. Boyd. Don't be too hard on yourself. Most murderers do."

"You're very smug, Detective Galler. Experience should tell you that's a mistake. Anyway, may I expect then to be arrested at any moment? Do I have time to put my affairs in order before you cart me away?"

"I don't make those decisions, Mr. Boyd. But if I were you, I wouldn't plan any trips."

Boyd ran a fingertip around the rim of his beer mug. "If you've done your homework, you must realize I can be dangerous."

The Threatening Tactic. "Should I take that as a threat?" Amy pulled back her sweater, made sure Boyd saw the snubbie. "Do you know what it means to threaten a police officer? Oh, of course you do; you're the famed attorney, aren't you? Explain to me just how I should take that."

"Take it as a promise." He got up, silver belt buckle gleaming.

"Oh, Mr. Boyd?"

He turned around.

"Did you make the same promise to Herman Klein?"

As he left Amy's table, Boyd's eyes found Sherry Brannigan. She was watching them. He pointed to his watch and held out five fingers. Her eyes moved to Amy, then back again. She gave him a slight nod. Then he hurried out of the bar, ignoring all the clutching arms and hails from friends or admirers.

Boyd walked down the short corridor to the lobby. Heads turned.

Boyd was oblivious. Used to adulation, he was no longer intimidated by it. Space was what he needed, space and quiet. He kept walking.

Galler had been tougher than he'd expected. He hadn't had many dealings with female police officers; he'd been on unfamiliar ground. He wondered if he would have fared better if he'd prepared for a man. He wished he could've caught her privately, like he'd imagined in the tub. But with the noise she'd made, her disappearance now would be awkward. He'd have to wait.

Exiting the lodge, he walked out into the parking lot. It was a beautiful night: there was a full moon highlighting his mountain. But his mind wasn't on such things; he was assessing the damage.

She'd gotten to him. But what made it worse was the certainty that she knew it. Had she told him anything he could use?

A mistake. Was she bluffing? They'd been on the case for a week, and he'd not been interviewed. They had no body, no way to crack his alibi.

Did they?

He heard footsteps behind him. He stopped, turned around and saw a thin man with a ginger moustache, dressed in blue jeans and carrying a pad of paper, scurrying toward him.

"Are you following me?" Boyd asked. The man stopped in his tracks. Stepping forward hesitantly, he seemed nervous; his eyes darted around and he avoided eye contact, while he fumbled with a pad and fished around his pockets for something.

"Are you Emery Boyd?" the thin, edgy man finally managed, looking up after having found a pen.

"And who might you be? No, wait. Let me tell you." Boyd reached into his left breast pocket, removed a little recorder and switched it on, showing the red light to his interviewer. "You're G. Sherwood Preston, from the *Post*, right?" He enjoyed the thin man's startled nod. "Please speak up, Mr. Preston, the recorder can't pick up a nod."

Preston cleared his throat and acknowledged who he was.

Boyd stepped forward and Preston stepped back. Boyd dwarfed the reporter. "And I bet you're going to tell me that you're about to print an article saying I was somehow responsible for the disappearance of my law partner, Herman Klein, then ask me if I have a comment, right?" Boyd's eyes were hard, and he stepped closer to Preston.

Preston's eyes grew wide. Shrinking away, he focused on the recorder and froze. He nodded, struggled for words, then cleared his throat. "Y-Yes, I… uh… I was. Would you… uh… like to make a statement?"

Boyd smiled. "Well, since you haven't asked me anything, nor told me anything, what would I possibly want to comment about?"

Preston fidgeted; his tongue wouldn't shake loose. Why did

Boyd have to stand so close? *He was so big!*

"Well, for the record," Boyd said, "since you won't tell me what you're going to print, nor who your lying sources are—that is, if you in fact have any—I'll make a statement. Have you got your recorder? Is it going?"

He saw shock in Preston's face, and he smiled again. "I'll take it that most of your supposed information has come from Detectives Charlie Scott and Amy Galler. Right?" Preston's lack of a response answered him. "Well, let me tell you something. I bet you don't know that Amy Galler has a reason for bad-mouthing me, do you? You see, she's in love with my best friend, and I've sort of broken up their relationship. If you don't believe me, ask Mo Knauer, the chief ranger. Better yet, ask John Whitney.

"Now, as for Charlie Scott, he got his information from either of two sources: Emily Klein or Amy Galler. Galler, I've already discredited. As for Emily Klein, she's always hated me. For years, she's pushed her husband mercilessly. She's abusive, and she's threatened him. Ask anybody. Herman and I have never had any problems, just the usual sort of petty things generally associated with running different departments of a law firm. You know: allocation of secretarial staff, office assignments, that sort of thing.

"But that wife of his is another story. She's driven, deceitful, maybe dangerous, although it's my guess that Herman just got fed up with her and took off for a while."

He stared hard at Preston, who hadn't taken a note. "Am I getting through to you? I'm telling you that I had nothing, absolutely *nothing* to do with the disappearance of Herman Klein, and the only people who say I did have their own axes to grind. I suggest you check that out."

Preston opened his mouth, but Boyd waved him off. "I'm not done yet, Mr. Preston. I've just told you the facts: I had nothing to do with Herman Klein's disappearance, and the only people who say I did, well, they have their own reasons for making those statements. But there's more, which if you'd done your home-work, you'd already know. I have an alibi, a solid one. If you don't believe me, again, just ask around.

"You see, Mr. Preston, in the context of what I've just told you—what I've just recorded here, I might add—if you print your article and it contains any link between me and the disappearance of Herman Klein, I'll sue. And I'm gonna prove that your faulty investigation into the true facts, despite my pointing them out to you, goes way beyond simple negligence; it smacks of reckless disregard, Mr. Preston, or for a layman like you… *malice*. If I were you, I'd think long and hard about that. I guarantee you that I'm going to read your article tomorrow. And if I find one thing out of whack in it, I'm going to file the biggest libel suit the *Post* or you have ever seen."

Boyd was moving past the open-mouthed G. Sherwood Preston, even before he'd finished. With his last word, he switched off his recorder and dropped it into his breast pocket. He was well on his way back to the salacious Sherry Brannigan before a stunned G. Sherwood Preston even turned around.

FORTY-THREE

Sunday, August 4

The western bank of the Cowlitz River, deep within the Pinchot National Forest, about a half-mile south of the park boundary, was patrolled this morning by Senior Guide Max Brittain and his crew of five volunteers. They had covered in excess of half a mile, and the spirits of the tourist volunteers were still high. Brittain expected it would be another two hours before the tourists wore down and began whining.

Now, rounding a heavily wooded bend, Brittain noticed that two of his charges had stopped and were standing, pointing to a spot five feet in from the edge of the river. "What's the matter?" he asked, trying to follow where they were pointing. "Did you find something?"

"We're not sure," a computer salesman from Ohio said. "There's something shiny next to that rock in the shallows. See?"

Brittain's eyes followed the salesman's sausage-like finger into the churning waters. In the slower-moving, clearer area near the shore, he saw a bright, shimmering object bouncing against a large rock. "I see it," he said, already dreading the cold, glacial wash.

"Any idea what it could be?" asked the other volunteer, this one a contractor from Connecticut.

"Nope," Brittain said, wrapping a rope around his waist. Tying it off, he turned to the two volunteers. "Wrap this around a tree twice and hold on to it. Don't let me be pulled to the center." As they did so, he stepped into the icy waters.

Immediately, his legs went numb. The water was deeper than it looked. By the time he'd reached the rock, the water was over his knees and a strong current was tugging at him, trying to draw him into the center. Just as he reached the shiny object, it began to slide around the left side of the rock. Grasping at it, he lost his footing and the current caught him. As the shock of total immersion into thirty-three degree water stunned him, his remaining volunteers jumped to the rope and began pulling. Inch by inch they dragged him out of the current and into the shallows. Once on the bank, he plopped down and caught his breath while a couple of volunteers rubbed warmth into his arms and legs.

Someone said, "What is it?"

His hands numb, Brittain shrugged, thinking he'd lost the object in the current. But looking down, he noticed that his left hand was closed tight. "Open it," he said to the guy on his left. "My hand's numb. I don't know if I've got it or not."

The contractor opened Brittain's hand. The object was there. "What is it?" the contractor asked.

"An avalanche beeper." Brittain looked puzzled. "This shouldn't be here."

"What d'you mean?" asked an accountant from Des Moines.

Brittain's scabby face darkened. "People carry them when they're up high, in case they fall into a crevasse or get buried in an avalanche. That can't happen down here. This had to come from up above."

A silence fell over the group. The accountant broke it. "Wow, it looks like a Zippo lighter. What's it made of, stainless steel?"

"Looks like it," said Brittain. "That's unusual too. Usually, these things are plastic." He turned it over. "There's an inscription here." A moment later, "God damn!"

"What is it?" someone asked.

Brittain looked at his group. "Have you ever seen *The Twilight Zone?*"

The insistent ringing of the phone brought Amy fully awake, although it seemed she'd been awake most of the night. She glanced at her watch and was surprised to see it read 9:15. She grabbed at the receiver and mumbled, "Hello."

It was Sherry. She wanted to meet for breakfast.

Joining her in the dining room some twenty minutes later, Amy was surprised to see her friend so giddy. After they'd ordered, she said, "Okay, what gives?"

"Guess where I spent the night?" Sherry was grinning.

Amy stared at her. She remembered Sherry flirting with Boyd. Catnip. Amy's mouth dropped. "You didn't."

An answering grin. Amy stared at her.

"Aren't you going to ask me how it was?" She shifted in her seat. "God, I'm so sore."

"No. I don't want to know." Amy paused. "Sherry. Are you nuts? After all your promises… after I specifically warned you to stay away… and with all you know about Emery Boyd… Are you out of your fucking mind?"

"I thought you'd be happy."

"Don't give me that. *Happy?* Where'd you get *that* idea?" Amy took a breath. "That does it; I'm taking you in."

"Why?"

"Because you're interfering with a police investigation."

"No, I'm not. I'm trying to help. If you take me in, I'll tell everybody you asked me to sleep with Boyd, that I was just doing what you wanted."

"You'd be lying."

"So what? Lies aren't always bad. You lied to John...."

"That was in the course of duty."

"Me too."

"What do you mean, 'me too'?"

"I'd be lying in the course of duty. The duty of helping you."

"That's ridiculous."

"Look, Amy, I didn't do anything more than you did." She cocked an eyebrow, held it for an instant, then smiled. "Guess I'm over my slump, huh?"

Amy ignored her last comment. "There's a big difference, Sherry. Boyd could be another Ted Bundy."

"And if you could do something to put a Ted Bundy out of business, with little risk to yourself, wouldn't you do it?"

"Little risk? The guy's a killer."

"Yeah, and everybody in the bar saw me leave with him. What's he gonna do? Slash me up in front of witnesses?"

Camille arrived with heaping plates of flapjacks. As they buttered and drenched their cakes in syrup, Amy said, "Well, it was reckless, Sherry. Really dumb. It could have gotten you killed."

"So, you're not gonna take me in?"

Amy put down her fork. "Christ! I shoulda known you'd do something like this. I saw the way you were looking at him. Is this out of your system now?"

Sherry nodded.

"Then I won't take you in. It would just create more problems for me anyway, and I'm in deep enough." She stared at Sherry. "But I'll do it if that's the only way I can get you off this kick."

"No problemo. I mean it. Besides, Boyd hurt me a little."

"What do you mean, he hurt you?"

"Trust me, you don't want to know. He likes it rough. 'Nuff said. I won't be doing that again." She winced as she adjusted her position again. Amy's face flushed and her eyes dropped to her plate. "You aren't gonna believe this, but Boyd keeps a gun by his bedside. It scared the hell out of me. I made him move it."

Amy played dumb. "Lot's of people do that. Paranoid, you know."

"Really?" Sherry took a bite of her flapjacks. "Say, you remember that question I asked John right before the glacier erupted? About following a snowmobile through a blizzard?"

"Yes."

"Well, I got Boyd talking about mountain storms, not that one in particular, but storms in general. He says they're so strong they blow all tracks and sounds away, that you can't see your hand in front of your face. He called it a whiteout, everything's white."

Amy dropped her fork. "So how was he following a snowmobile?"

"Exactly."

Was that what was bothering John?

They left the dining room and walked over to the lobby gift shop, where they each bought the *Post*. G. Sherwood Preston had been true to his word. The front-page headline was: "Firm Politics Probed in Klein Case."

Underneath, Preston's byline read: "Police Ponder Role of Prominent Attorney in Disappearance."

"Oh boy," Sherry commented, as they left the gift shop and strode down the hallway toward their rooms. "I'm glad I got out before he saw this."

"Oh, I don't know," Amy said. "Emery Boyd might enjoy notoriety. It keeps his name in the press, and if he beats the rap, he looks invincible."

When they got to Sherry's room, they hugged, exchanged addresses and phone numbers and promised to stay in touch.

In her room, Amy plopped down on her bed to read Preston's

article. It was more understated than she'd expected. It reported that Boyd was a principal suspect in the disappearance of Klein, all right, but there was no mention of Schneider and only the hint of a link to the deadly poacher.

More troubling, however, was the article's reference to "a source close to the investigation." The article mentioned Charlie but didn't say he was the source. Big deal, MacGregor would make the connection. She dreaded tomorrow's meeting all the more. The article, the blown cover, John… She'd be lucky to keep her badge.

She dialed John and left a message this time. "John, if you're listening, will you please pick up? I need to talk to you. It's very important."

Nothing.

"John, I know I hurt you. I'm sorry. Believe me, I was going to tell you Friday night... I never got the chance. Boyd got to you first."

The message machine clicked off and she redialed. Another message. "John, I'm going to have to talk to you sooner or later. I'm sorry, but I do. Please John, let me explain.

"Believe me, John, I never expected to fall in love with you. I really was going to tell you everything Friday night.

"John, I have to return to Seattle. I don't know when I can return. Hopefully, you'll do the fair thing and at least hear me out. You owe me that, John. Think about it."

She left her phone numbers in Seattle and hung up.

Nine A.M. found G. Sherwood Preston at the Guide Service Shack. The man at the counter—Maselli, according to his name tag—wanted to know if Preston was the reporter asking all the questions about Emery Boyd. Preston confirmed that he was, and inquired where Boyd was. Maselli said he'd stopped by the Guide

Residence at 7:00, saying he was on his way to Camp Muir.

Why not tour Boyd's grounds, assuming he could find them?

After stopping at the gift shop, Preston went back to his room. He pulled out the phone book, looked up Boyd's address, then logged on to MapQuest and wrote out the directions. He stuffed his computer into his pack, then sat down to read his article. While he wasn't happy with the editing, he took solace in the pieces he knew would follow. He tucked the paper under his arm, grabbed his pack and walked out to his Toyota.

It was 12:15 before he finally found Boyd's house. When he got out of the Toyota, he pulled out his pack and slipped his arms through its straps. He felt more comfortable with his "stash" on his body.

He walked up to the front door and knocked. No response. Satisfied, he turned around, and with his back to the house surveyed the area. If Boyd was the poacher, he'd have needed a way to get his snowmobile up the mountain. Preston doubted that Boyd had just driven it up on the back of a pickup.

The forest here was dense and dark. It would be relatively easy to hide a trail, maybe a grave, and make them invisible. He struck out along the treeline heading generally east. A quarter mile out, hidden by a large tree jutting into the yard, was a clearly defined trail bearing fresh wheel tracks. Pulling a camera out of his pack, Preston shot some pictures, then began walking his find.

The trail was like a long, dark corridor in a cave, but instead of rock formations, all around were high Douglas fir, impenetrable underbrush and moss. Mosquitoes nipped at him, cobwebs entangled him. There was no sunlight and no sense of direction. Only darkness. Preston had never seen a forest so ominous.

He snapped a picture, not because he wanted the shot, but for illumination. But how many flashes did he have? He needed flashlights. Maybe it would be better to return later with Amy Galler.

Satisfied, he turned.

An immense man stood silhouetted four feet away.

"Hello, Mr. Preston. How nice to see you again."

There was something in Emery Boyd's hand.

The still quiet of the rain forest was pierced by a pitched scream followed by a soft thud.

FORTY-FOUR

Sunday, August 4

Emery Boyd dropped Sherry Brannigan off at the lodge at seven o'clock, then parked in the lot and removed his day-pack, skis and poles. Not finding any takers in the Guide Residence, he struck out for Muir alone, using the long hike for reflection.

The only wild cards in the deck were Amy Galler and John Whitney. He'd counted on the police checking out his alibi; he hadn't anticipated that the detective they'd send would compromise his best friend. And John wasn't buying his story.

John was right: there was no reason for a poacher to be on the Kautz, especially during a storm, and no way could he have tracked him through a blizzard. He'd have to monitor John carefully, make a determination for better or worse. And soon.

Making good time to Muir, he arrived at 10:10 and checked in. There were only two rangers around, and Muir was deserted. Most of the routes were closed. Then he went to his cache, retrieved the torn white parka strips and placed them in his day pack. After eating an early lunch out under the sun on the high snowfields, he changed boots, slung his axe and strapped on his skis, departing for Paradise before noon. The trip down took only twenty minutes. Stashing his gear in the Yukon, he walked over to the Visitor's Center to buy a paper. He took the paper back to his Yukon and read it in the parking lot.

The article wasn't bad. Certainly it didn't contain everything the police suspected, but he knew there was precious little proof, so he figured the paper was being cautious. Still, he'd give their general counsel a call and make some noise, maybe send him a copy of his taped interview with Preston. That would make them even more careful.

Turning into his driveway, he was surprised to see a beat-up green Toyota parked there. He opened his garage door and drove the Yukon in before investigating further.

The press card on the front dashboard was the giveaway.

Returning to his garage, he grabbed his ice axe and electronic control, then shut the garage door. He circled his house and found no sign of Preston. Next, he scanned his yard toward the trail. *Could Preston be there?*

He walked to the trailhead.

Finding Preston was easy, killing him and disposing of the body and car nearly as simple. One quick tap on the top of the head and Preston was gone. The car and body he sent over a steep cliff high in the rain forest foothills, using the Toyota's hitch to transport his trailer and ATV for the return trip. Before the car went over, however, he set it afire using gasoline and Preston's own paper, a nice irony, he thought. Smoke from the fire was lost in rain forest fog.

When he returned home, he opened Preston's pack and found his treasures. He suspected Preston's tapes were the originals.

He'd enjoy that call tomorrow.

A bleary-eyed John Whitney, covered in foul-smelling sweat,

racked with a headache and an upset stomach, awoke at 2:00 P.M. For half an hour, he lay on his couch, where he'd passed out last night, and buried his aching head in pillows. Then he staggered into the bathroom and threw up. Over and over he retched, continuing long after everything in his stomach was gone. Finally, having exhausted the urge to retch and lacking the strength to stand, he crawled to his shower and turned on the cold water tap.

Forty-five degree water caused him to yell, but it helped bring him back to reality. Then Maalox calmed his stomach and Motrin began working on his aching head. Bran flakes and an hour in the sauna added the final touches to his sobriety program.

As he doctored himself, he thought of Amy. He had a right to be upset, but he shouldn't have struck her and he should have let her explain. If she really meant so much to him, he owed her that.

He thought of Donnie too. So much hope, such great potential—all lost.

And Boyd? They'd have that talk, and it wouldn't be pleasant. He was forming some disturbing conclusions about Emery Boyd, but he needed to see the truth in Boyd's eyes.

Turning to his message machine, he cranked up the volume and pressed "Play." There were a number of messages; the tape was almost full. Many were from Amy. But it was her last message, the one pleading with him to contact her, to give her a chance to explain, that moved him most. He heard the emotion in her voice, the longing, and he felt her pain. He tried to call her, but learned she'd checked out. Rewinding the tape, he wrote down her Seattle numbers.

There were also messages from Boyd and Mo Knauer. Knauer's last message, one left this morning, intrigued him. "John, this is Mo again." Knauer sounded excited. "You've got to meet me tonight. It's important. We've found something… Something of Donnie's… in the wash. And there's more. Read the *Post*."

There was a pause, some mumbled voices in the background, then Knauer continued, "Uh... I've got to go. Some brass from Washington are here. How 'bout dinner at Anderson's... at 8:00. Be there, John. It's important."

Donnie? Mo said they'd found something of Donnie's? *In the wash? What the hell?*

He dialed Knauer, but he was unavailable. He slammed the phone down, then stormed around his home talking to himself.

What could they have found?

From where? The Ingraham? How?

He looked at his watch: 5:45.

John threw on his jacket and went quickly to his car.

John Whitney was already seated, sipping a mineral water with lime when Mo Knauer, Special Agent Rich Haskins and Sheriff Hank Bourdelais entered Anderson's Homestyle Restaurant. Seeing John at a corner table, they headed straight over, ordering a drink from the waitress as they pulled out their chairs.

John rose and shook their hands. "Mo, you said you found something of Donnie's, that it's somehow related to this story in the *Post*. I don't get it. I don't see any connection at all."

Knauer looked surprised. "Jeez, I'm sorry, John. You misunderstood my message. You're right, there's no connection. I didn't mean to imply there was. I wondered if what's in the *Post* might have something to do with what happened between you and Emery, between you and Amy. Haskins here says Amy's a cop."

"Wait," John said, looking at Knauer, ignoring Haskins and Bourdelais. "I didn't come here to talk about Boyd. I want to know about my brother."

"Later, John. These two can't stay. Let's take care of them first."

Bourdelais chimed in, "This'll only take a minute. Then we'll leave."

John looked at them, frowning. "Okay," he said. "If it doesn't take too long." He turned to Knauer. "But Mo, I want the whole story, all of it. Right?"

"You'll have it."

Haskins nodded to Bourdelais. "John," Bourdelais began, "Seattle P.D., a Detective Charlie Scott—the one mentioned in the article—contacted me about Emery. They think he may have killed his partner and buried his body on the mountain somewhere. They think Boyd may have been the poacher, that he may have killed Jim to cover his alibi."

Bourdelais paused to let the waitress bring their drinks. When she'd left, he continued, "But all they have is a circumstantial case, and a weak one at that. They think they have a motive, but the issue is opportunity. Boyd's alibi appears strong.

"I laughed at the idea, practically threw Scott out of my office. But now, what with the bad blood between you and Boyd—the fight and all—and this Amy Galler working the case too, I need to ask you about Boyd's alibi."

John said nothing. His breathing was ragged.

"I need to know, John. If you know something, it would be bad to protect Emery.""Look. I don't know anything. Amy and I never discussed this Klein thing or Boyd's alibi. Boyd and I never discussed it either."

Bourdelais looked perplexed. "I don't understand, John. If that wasn't the cause of your spat, what was it? The girl... uh... Galler?"

John's anger flared. "Let's just say..." he drummed his fingers impatiently "...Emery made the wrong comment at the wrong time. I was tired and maybe a little stressed. I overreacted."

Bourdelais and Haskins looked skeptical, Knauer too. "John, you aren't covering for Emery, are you?" Bourdelais asked.

"I told you, I overreacted. Hell, Hank, it happens."

"Overreacted to what, John? You're being evasive."

"Jesus!" John took a deep breath. "Okay, I'll tell you all about it. Then maybe you'll leave me alone."

He looked up, caught the eye of the waitress, and ordered another mineral water. "It's like this... Amy comes up here... arranges to meet me... Not just meet me...she comes on to me, see?" He paused. "She tells me she's a bookkeeper on vacation... Gets me to take her up on the mountain.... Makes a play for me... or... maybe puts me in a position to make a play for her... You know what I mean... Well, I fell for her. I mean, I'm starting to think I've got something special here, you know?"

He made a fist, lightly beat it on the table, "Well, anyway... We go up to Ranger's Roost, get to know each other some, and I'm thinking how great she is. Then the Ingraham busts loose right in front of us.

"So anyway, I'm out on search and rescue, busting my hump, wearing myself out... all the while thinking what will be waitin' for me when I get back." His laugh was ugly.

"Then Boyd shows up... Tells me Amy's a cop who's using me...to get information on him. I mean, shit, Hank! Here he is, big fucking stud and all, can have his pick of anybody he wants, and he tells me my girl is only interested in me because of him!" He saw Bourdelais start to say something, and he waved him off. "Look, I know... it's different. But to add insult to injury, he says all this with a shit-eating grin on his face. Hell, I just lost it, that's all. Maybe it was the grin that did it."

John looked up. "So, Hank," he snapped, "you satisfied now?"

Bourdelais nodded. "Yeah. I'm sorry we had to ask."

John nodded.

"John," Bourdelais said, "we also need to ask you about this alibi thing. Do you have any reason to question Boyd's version of where he was? I mean, I'm no expert. It sounds good to me. What do you say?"

John sipped his mineral water. "I don't know. I wasn't there."

"John," Mo Knauer said, "I'm gettin' the feeling there's somethin' you're not sayin'."

"Mo, Goddamnit! I wasn't there. I didn't see a damn thing."

"John, we know that," said Haskins. "But you can make judgments based on your experience. Could Boyd have come down, killed his partner and then returned with a snowmobile to dump the body? Could he have killed Jim Carlton?"

John stared at them. "Aren't you going to ask me if he caused the lahar too? I mean… how the hell should I know? He says he was following the poacher; I'll accept his word on that. Okay?"

Haskins nodded to Bourdelais. "Okay, John," Bourdelais said, "that's what we needed. We'll leave you two alone."

They rose to leave, and Knauer got up with them. John stayed in his seat, didn't offer his hand.

As soon as they'd gone, Knauer beckoned the waitress to bring menus. "Sorry about that, John," he said.

"Fuck 'em. All I want to hear is what you found."

Knauer sighed and pulled the avalanche beeper out of his jacket pocket, passing it over.

John's eyes opened wide. He picked it up, turning it over in his hands, as tears welled up in his eyes. "Where was it found, Mo?" he said, his voice barely a whisper.

"In the Cowlitz River, about a half-mile down from the park boundary. You're seeing it just as it was found, John."

John fixed Mo with a quizzical look.

"Open it, John."

John snapped its top open, looked inside. His face twisted. "Where are the batteries?"

"I don't know. That's just the way it was found. I checked."

"But this cap's never supposed to come off, unless it's taken off."

"I know."

FORTY-FIVE

Monday, August 5

In the Seattle *Post*'s executive office conference room at 8:00 P.M., Turner K. "Chip" Chapman, Evan B. Cutter and Chancey LaRue were awaiting their publisher, Wayne Malcolm Huston. They were nervous: urgent meetings called by the boss were always bad.

Huston burst into the room. "Has anyone found Preston?"

Everyone looked to someone else.

"Damn it, is no one going to answer me?"

All eyes turned to Chancey LaRue, who seemed to be struggling to find her voice. "Uh... N-no sir. Not yet."

"Why the fuck not?"

Huston never used four-letter words.

"Well, sir," LaRue said, her voice a whisper, "I tried. Nobody knows where he is. He hasn't checked out, but nobody's seen him."

"Did you send someone to find him?"

"Well, no. I thought he'd call in."

Huston slammed his hand on the table, causing LaRue to

jump. "Cutter, did you send someone to find Preston?"

"N-no, sir. You made it very clear the other day when Chancey and I had our little falling out, that this was Chancey's story. I thought..."

Huston shook his head. "Chip," he interrupted, "surely, after your call from Boyd and that tape, you checked up on Preston?"

Chapman froze. No one spoke; they awaited the next outburst.

Huston shook his head. "The story tomorrow... will be a *retraction* and an *apology* to Emery Boyd. On page one."

Audible gasps, but no one spoke. Huston turned to LaRue. "Chancey, clean out your desk. You and that lunatic G. Sherwood Preston—God! May I never hear that name again!—are through, kaput, out of here. You're both fired."

"B-but, Wayne, er... Mr. Huston..."

"You heard me. I want you out of here. You and that damn reporter of yours came close to ruining this paper. If Boyd sues, you may have yet."

Sobbing, her hands covering her face, Chancey LaRue, ex-echo box, ex-editor and ex-confidant to the top man, fled the room, slamming the door behind her.

Huston spoke into the ugly silence. "I've just had a rather shocking phone call... from the chief of police and the mayor. The police are dropping their investigation of Boyd and issuing a statement exonerating him." Huston raised his hand. "That's not all... There's an IA investigation into the actions of Amy Galler; she's been suspended, and Charlie Scott and Jerry MacGregor have been taken off the case. MacGregor's retiring. Health problems, they say." He took a breath. "The chief feels we assisted Galler and Scott in, and I'll use his exact words here, 'conjuring up such an obviously trumped-up case.' He says the statement they'll issue tomorrow will reflect that.

"So, it appears that we're about to be exposed as part of a malicious conspiracy to assert false charges against a prominent member of a leading law firm. I think you can all acknowledge what that may mean: the other papers will have a field day at our expense; the police will try to dump as much on us as they can, and we may face litigation from Boyd despite our retraction and apology.

"So LaRue and Preston have to go. I'm just wondering if that action and the retraction and apology are enough...."

Some thirty seconds passed. Finally, Chapman found his voice. "Uh, Wayne..." he said, "...you know I'm not one to criticize your actions unnecessarily—"

"Good! And you'd be wise to keep it that way!"

"But sir, there is something else to consider..."

"What?" Huston said. "This better be damn good."

"It's just that I'm thinking of our litigation posture, sir. I mean, we don't know—as you say—that the retraction and apology will satisfy Boyd. Again, with the police and all the other papers clamoring for our necks, he may file anyway. My point is, we got our information from the police. We need Chancey LaRue on our side, rather than hostile, if a lawsuit is filed. I mean, I don't mind dumping on Preston; we were all squeamish about him, that's why we did such a heavy edit job. But we need to show we supervised Preston, and that's Chancey. She could side with Preston and screw us. We need her on our side. We need to be able to show that if any wrong was done, it was by Preston, despite our efforts. We have to be concerned for punitive damages. Insurance will cover Boyd's compensatory damages. But punitives come right out of P & L."

A minute went by, and another, then Huston looked up. "Chip, you're worth every damn cent I pay you."

Emery Boyd sat at his desk, looking out at his mountain shimmering a golden orange in the late twilight. Sam Terry had just left his office, and Boyd was jubilant. With the police statement and an expected apology and retraction from the paper, his problems were over. He and Terry had discussed filing suit anyway, but decided against it. They didn't need the distraction, and since it would be two years before the statute of limitations ran out, maybe they would receive some favors from the city or the paper in the interim.

He smiled. Sam had even suggested that with all the media attention the police action and the papers were going to generate, maybe Boyd should be someplace else for a few days. The press of media attention today had been constant and unrelenting; tomorrow it would be even worse.

Sam's suggestion fit his own plans. He wanted to take John's temperature, make a decision, carry it out. John still worried him.

And John wasn't answering his phone. He'd find him tomorrow.

He called Sherry Brannigan. A nice piece, that one. Bent over a chair, crying out. The thought made him smile. How much more could she take? She agreed to meet him at the lodge bar at ten, but warned him she might still be too sore to go home with him. *Wanna bet?* he thought. He looked at his reflection in his window, gave it his charm smile.

His last call was to Mo Knauer.

"Where do things stand?"

"Still looking good, Emery. But we'll need a few weeks for the glaciers to stabilize. Still got most of the higher areas closed off."

"Have you seen John, Mo? I want to patch things up, but can't reach him."

"I had dinner with him last night. He's in Seattle now, trying to patch things up with Amy." Knauer hesitated. "Did you know she's a cop?"

Alarm bells registered. "Yeah," Boyd said. "She was interviewing people here. I guess she came out to see if I was really on

Rainier a week ago last Saturday. One of my partners is missing, and his wife—a real bad-ass—has been trying to deflect attention away from herself. She told the cops it must have been me because her husband and I ran different departments in the firm. It's all bullshit. But I guess Amy Galler lied to John about what she was doing. Maybe that's part of why he got so mad at me. I told him who she was."

He was thinking about John and Amy together and missed what Knauer was saying. Something about Donnie Whitney. "Sorry, Mo. What was that?"

"I said I know John is anxious to get on the Ingraham because one of our survey crews found Donnie's avalanche beeper in the Cowlitz River."

"You're kidding."

"No. I gave it to John, and he got pretty excited. He thinks maybe his brother's body can be found, that maybe it slid down in the Ingraham's underbelly. He wanted to go up right away, but I ordered him to wait until the glacier stabilizes."

Boyd said nothing. He was staring out the window. The mountain was darkening.

Knauer continued, "But that's not all. The batteries were missing. That really got John going."

"What?"

"I said the batteries were missing."

"Well, maybe the survey crew took them out. Or, maybe all that time in the glacier, they got knocked out."

"I checked with Max. He found it. He says the top was fastened."

Boyd terminated the conversation.

He picked up his letter opener, tapping it on his desk top. It was bad enough that John was with Galler; now he'd be thinking about those batteries too. The mountain hadn't taken them; Boyd had removed them.

But had he locked the lid?

He must have. How else could it have become locked?

Could John find the body after all these years?

Doubtful. It might have been preserved by the cold. More likely it was ground to pulp and dispersed by glacial action.

He looked down at his desk. Craters and chunks of wood dotted the surface. His fine Spanish letter opener was bent. He threw it into his wastebasket and wiped the wood chunks to the floor.

John would return soon. He never stayed away more than a few days unless he was on expedition.

And Emery Boyd would be waiting for him.

At 10:10 P.M., Emery Boyd strode into the Paradise Lodge bar and found Sherry seated at a cozy corner table.

"I guess I should be up front," Boyd said. "You and Amy Galler are friends, so I'm sure you know by now who she is and what she was doing here."

Sherry nodded. "Maybe we shouldn't discuss Amy, Emery. She is my friend, even if she lied to me."

"Fair enough. But you should know that the police have dropped their investigation. They've exonerated me." He smiled one of his smiles. "The whole thing was silly."

Sherry nodded. "I heard on the radio. That's good news, although I feel bad for Amy."

"Yeah. Well…" He paused. "Maybe I'd better stop there."

Sherry nodded again.

"So, do you know when John's coming back from Amy's? I want to go climbing with him."

Sherry gave him a quizzical look. "Well, that's odd."

"What? That I want to go climbing with John?" Boyd laughed. "He won't stay mad at me long."

"No. That you think John's visiting Amy. He's not. I saw him early this morning."

Boyd cocked an eyebrow. "Really?"

"Yes. He was carrying a big pack and all sorts of gear. He looked like a moving van on two feet."

Boyd leaned forward with an intensity that sent a shiver through Sherry. "Are you telling me the truth?"

"Of course I am. Why would I lie?"

Boyd stared hard at her, then sat back and looked at his watch. He drained his beer and stood up.

"You leaving already?" Sherry grabbed her coat. "Changed my mind. Can I come too?" She gave him a seductive smile.

"Uh, look, Sherry... I don't think I can tonight. I... uh... had a hard day, and I need to get up early tomorrow. How about a rain check?"

"Don't worry, Emery," she said, "I won't keep you up that late. Besides, I bet I can relax you."

"Not tonight. Maybe this beer didn't agree with me, I don't know. I just want to hit the sack."

"But it's only 10:25. Surely, you can stay up another hour." She showed concern. "What's the matter? Did I say something?"

"No. I want to see you again. I just don't feel well, you know?" He was placing a ten on the table.

"Wait, Emery," she said. "I'm not sure how long I'm going be here. This may be the last chance."

Boyd was now several feet away. He turned and shrugged. "Well, if I don't catch you here, I'll come down to Portland and look you up. Don't worry, I'll stay in touch."

He walked briskly away. In moments, he was out the door.

"Damn," Sherry muttered. Clenching her fist, she pounded the arm of her chair hard enough that a couple two tables over looked up at her. She ignored them, rose and left the bar, neatly sidestepping and swatting the outstretched arm of Frank Maselli.

By ten-thirty, Amy Galler was working on a drunk. She was alone in her apartment, cursing the police department and mayor, feeling sorry for herself, damning Emery Boyd and calling John Whitney every half hour.

Financially, she was okay. She was still on salary, at least for now, and she'd saved some money. But how to restore her good name? It would be months before the IA investigation was over, and tomorrow, the publicity train would run her over like a squirrel in the road. She was a marked woman; she needed to get away.

Damn the chief of police; damn the mayor! Why hadn't they stood up for her in the wake of Sam Terry's pressure? She knew the answer: she'd broken the rules; she'd gotten personally involved, acted irresponsibly. The other side had power and connections; she had none.

The phone rang several times, but she didn't answer.

Where to go?

Maybe she could stay with Sherry. Go back with her to Portland.

The doorbell rang. Charlie and Claire were peering through the glass.

She wobbled to the door, carrying her wine. As the door swung open, Claire began to cry.

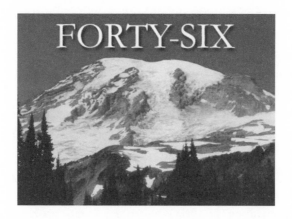

FORTY-SIX

Tuesday, August 6

John Whitney was getting used to the weirdness, the bluish wet glimmer of a futuristic dreamscape; he'd been surrounded by it for over thirty hours. It was the danger he found most unsettling, the prospect that at any moment he could be crushed or washed away by a sudden collapse or deluge. He'd been inside glaciers before, but this one was different. It was vibrant, creaking, groaning—falling—all around him. There were passages, tunnels shooting off in all directions, through which periodically torrents of ice and water would cascade. Blocks the size of boxcars would suddenly break loose and drop, making a soft thud that shook his footing, causing mini tsunamis and sending tremors through him and the fractured ice surrounding him. More than once he'd had to scramble—crampons, hammer and axe working furiously—high up a wall of blue ice in a desperate race to save his life.

Early on, he'd set up a base camp one hundred feet high on a sub-surface ledge in the mid-to-lower Ingraham, from which he could branch out; a place offering relative safety and room to stash his gear. From this perched hub, he explored systematically, unburdened by his pack. Eyes and ears alert, he was ready at any moment to duck, dodge or climb.

Twice, after covering all the surrounding passages, he'd changed his base camp, moving further up mountain. Each time, though, he selected another high ledge much like the first. Only twice did he go topside.

There really hadn't been any other choice for him; he'd known that when he saw the beeper, saw that the batteries were gone. He'd lied to Mo; he had to. Knauer would never approve of what he was doing.

Only Donnie and Emery Boyd had been on the same route, yet Boyd said he hadn't seen Donnie. But Donnie's beeper had been found below the Ingraham, the same route Boyd took. Donnie didn't remove those batteries; he wouldn't have risked a safety disqualification.

Did Emery Boyd kill Donnie and dispose of the body here?

Conflicted, John remembered how Boyd had raced back up the mountain without even grabbing a parka when he learned of Donnie's disappearance. *Was that an act?* He remembered the trip to Everest, how Boyd had pushed and prodded him in Donnie's name. *Had Boyd been laughing at him all the while?*

Old loyalties died hard in John Whitney; only proof would resolve his inner conflict.

Amy awoke from a restless night of tossing and turning to a raging hangover and a bad case of the sweats. The Advil she'd taken, after getting rid of Charlie and Claire, hadn't helped much; the headache and stomach upset were in full swing.

In the kitchen, she got the coffee going before she popped three more Advil, washed them down with Pepto, and wobbled back to bed. Covering her head with pillows, squeezing them tightly to her temples, she waited for relief.

Some fifteen minutes later, after the pain had thankfully lessened, she got up and fetched life-giving coffee. Today, she left the newspaper outside.

Charlie and Claire had tried to be helpful, but their sympathy and words of encouragement hadn't penetrated her depression. They'd urged her to defend herself, but she hadn't made up her mind. She'd visit Sherry first, maybe follow her to Portland for awhile.

It was still early, just after six. There was still time to get away before the press flocked to her door. Feeling better now, she showered and packed her bags, then stuffed them into her car. A cold assessment of her sobriety caused her to throw her personal weapon, a Sig Sauer P229 .40 caliber, into her shoulder bag. Suspended, yes; defenseless, never.

On arriving at Paradise, Amy parked and lugged her bags to Sherry's room. Thankfully, Sherry responded to her knock.

From the anguished look on Sherry's face, Amy knew she'd heard the news. The paper was sitting on the bed. Over Sherry's shoulder, Amy could just see her picture on the front page. They hugged each other, then dragged Amy's belongings inside.

Sherry led her to the bed and had her sit, after first snatching the newspaper away and dropping it to the floor. "Amy, what are you going to do?"

Her lower lip quivering, Amy whispered, "I don't know."

Sherry bent over and gave her another hug. She sat opposite her friend. "I'll help any way I can. You know that."

Amy managed a tight smile. "I know. You're about the only person I know who's been as alone as I feel. I thought maybe we could spend some time together."

Sherry nodded. "John?" she asked gently.

Amy shook her head. "No. I never reached him. I doubt he called back, but frankly, I haven't been answering my phone. If he wouldn't talk to me before, I don't know why he would now." She pointed to the newspaper.

"Well, I can guarantee John doesn't know anything about all this. He went climbing yesterday. Maybe when he comes back…"

Sherry moved over to the bed and sat down. Cradling her friend's head on her shoulder, she said, "It's okay, honey. We'll watch out for each other."

They sat for a long time, holding on to each other.

FORTY-SEVEN

Tuesday, August 6

Emery Boyd had spent most of the night searching the topside portion of the lower and middle reaches of the glacier. It was slow going, given the many crevasses and jagged surfaces. With the glacier's collapse, its surface had become more ragged, rough and perilous. Despite his heightened sense of caution, he kept a constant vigilance on a wide area around him, looking for any telltale beams of light. Shortly before dawn, exhausted, he pulled his sleeping bag off his pack and bedded down for a few hours, hoping for better luck during the day.

Awakening just after seven, he found fog. He ate hurriedly and continued his search.

He guessed that John had started at the bottom, exploring crevasses as he made his way up, hoping his brother's body had slid down some sort of sub-glacial chute like the avalanche beeper must have done. John had a big head start, which meant he was probably somewhere in the glacier's lower middle by now. Boyd headed there.

So far, rather than searching below, he'd concentrated on

inspecting the glacier's surface, looking for signs. But now a massive crevasse loomed in front of him. Over three hundred feet across, he guessed it might take an hour to traverse in these dangerous conditions. He decided to risk the underbelly.

Slamming the shaft of a spare axe into the snow, he affixed his rope to its head, harnessed up and lowered his pack, then himself. As he dropped, his mind's eye pictured Jonah in the belly of the whale.

He'd been in glaciers before, but never seen anything like these conditions. The glacier was a bowel of death. Like John before him, he was frightened by the maze of collapsing passages, by the eerie blue hell around, above and below him. As he heard the creaks, groans, thuds and rushing water of the ruined frozen river, as he watched two tunnels off to his right give way and cascade down, he fought the urge to flee.

Was John down here? Had he survived these conditions? Doubt ate at him, but reason pushed him. He had to know.

He calmed himself with deep, cleansing breaths. He needed to lessen the risks. There wasn't much he could do to avoid a sudden crushing death, but he could lessen the risk of being washed away. He climbed back up the wall, retrieved his rope and tossed it down. Then, using his axe and hammer, he descended once again. Hanging his pack on an ice screw high above his head, he affixed a rope to another ice screw and tied it into a harness. Now he was ready to explore.

For an hour and a half, he searched the frozen nether world, not once rising to the surface. Once he moved his pack, four times his anchor, as he made his traverses and gradually moved up mountain. As he was moving his pack once more, he stumbled across John's pack high on a ledge above him.

Stashing his pack in a protected area out of sight and tossing the coiled rope over his shoulder, he fingered the 9mm hanging heavy in his parka pocket, reprising an old anger at Amy's unloading it. He awaited John's return.

A few minutes later, noticing a bright beam of light flashing across the crystal-like walls of blue ice, he smiled. Moments later, he heard the confirming footfalls of someone approaching.

When he finally saw John, Boyd began walking forward, his footsteps crunching audibly. John stopped and turned, and the flickering light of his headlamp fell across Boyd's face. "What are you doing here?" he growled.

"Hi, John. Just thought I'd help you look. You know, a buddy-system; it's kinda scary down here."

Boyd smiled and continued moving forward.

By 2:00, Amy was feeling better. She and Sherry had decided that Amy would visit Sherry in Portland for a while. Amy would return to Seattle tonight and visit her mother. She'd called her yesterday afternoon and given her a heads-up about the oncoming media blitz. She knew her mother was worrying; a visit might help calm her. Then tomorrow, Amy would drive to Portland.

They were in the dining room when Mo Knauer found them. If Mo had seen today's paper, he gave no clue. "Did John come back with you?" he said, his face bearing a welcoming smile.

Sherry and Amy looked at each other. "I haven't seen John," Amy said.

Knauer looked puzzled.

"John's climbing," Sherry said. "I saw him yesterday morning. He was all loaded up."

Knauer's eyes widened, and he dropped into a chair. He looked worried. "Are you certain?"

"Yes," Sherry said.

Knauer groaned, picked up a napkin, fingered it, then tossed it down.

"What's the matter?" Amy asked. "Can't you radio him?"

His fingers drummed an agitated beat. "No."

"Well, can't you radio somebody and have them find him?"

"Damn!" Mo said, preoccupied. He got up hurriedly from the table and turned to leave. "I know where John's gone. He shouldn't be there; it's too dangerous."

"What are you talking about?" Amy demanded.

He told them.

"I think I found something, John. I thought you'd want to know."

"What?" John's tone was guarded. "Where?"

"Well, maybe you'd better see yourself. It's a little farther up. We'll have to climb out."

John stared at Boyd, not wanting to trust, but unsure whether to challenge. "What are you doing here, Emery? How did you find me?"

Boyd laughed. "Mo. He called me, told me about the beeper. Said he suspected you'd do something stupid and come up here. He was worried about you, this glacier's so damn unstable."

As if on cue, they heard a deep rumbling, followed by a cascade of water down a passage a few hundred feet away.

"Did he tell you about the batteries?"

"Yes," Boyd said, his expression blank. "Curious, eh?"

"How do you explain it, Emery?"

Boyd shrugged. "I can't, John. That's one of the reasons I'm here. Donnie was my friend too."

"Really? Even after that deception with the extra pair of boots? Almost cost you the race, Emery. Must have been upsetting."

"Not really, John. I fell and got banged up. I couldn't have caught Donnie. He had too big a lead."

"Still, it couldn't have made you very happy."

"No. But I would have done the same thing if I'd thought of

it. Donnie just outsmarted me."

John watched him, framed against ice and cold.

"Look, John, I don't really want to stand here in the middle of this hell-hole debating events of thirty years ago. I told you I found something higher up. Now, I'm gonna climb out of here and pursue it. If you don't want to come, fine. But if this pile of ice cubes collapses on you, we'll just say a few prayers and see you in two hundred years when your mush comes floating out."

"What'd you find?"

"Maybe Donnie's axe. Higher up. I figure the beeper, being smaller, more like a bullet"—how he loved that metaphor—"moved down faster. The axe got stuck, probably close to where Donnie went in."

John wasn't moving. "How'd you find it so fast, Emery? I thought you were looking for me. Why were you up higher?"

Boyd feigned impatience. "Because, you dumb fuck, I figure Donnie is higher up. Like I said, the beeper slid down quickly, like swallowing a pill with water. I didn't think you'd be this far down." He turned and began chopping his way topside.

"What about our packs?"

"Mine's already there." He didn't want to waste time with packs. He'd return for his later, after the job was done. "One's all we need for now. Let's see if what I found strikes you as significant. One of us can always return for your pack."

John followed him up. Reaching the surface, he saw Boyd piling ice blocks into a make-shift marker to be topped with several feet of orange rope. While John finished wrapping the rope, Boyd turned and started off, moving at a steady pace.

"Where are we going?" John asked when he caught up.

"Just below the Cleaver."

As they climbed higher, Boyd in front, John several feet behind, John called out, "Say, Emery, how do you suppose those batteries came out? Any ideas?"

Boyd kept moving. "How the hell do I know?" he said over

his shoulder. "For all I know, one of the survey crew took them out."

"Max found it. He wouldn't have taken them out. Are you saying someone else did? That doesn't make any sense."

Boyd stopped and turned around. "Maybe it does, John, if Mo or someone made a fuss about it. Other than Max, they were tourists, John, groupies really. They were playing out their fantasies, and can't wait to go home and tell everybody what heroes they were. How would it be to be the guy everybody yelled at for fucking up an important find? In those circumstances, wouldn't somebody lie?" He turned and renewed his hurried pace.

Some several hundred feet further, John called out again. "How do you explain Donnie being in the Ingraham, by the Cleaver? You took that route, yet you didn't see him?"

"Damn it, John!" Boyd stopped, turned, and tossed his axe down in disgust. "I'm sick and tired of this crap. Cut it out." He fixed John with a hard, angry stare. But John didn't flinch. Seeing skepticism on John's face, he cursed and reached for his axe before moving forward again.

For several minutes, they climbed in silence, their pace rapid as they moved past the collapse site and further up the Ingraham.

Boyd angled to the right, toward the far end of a chasm just below the Cleaver. Just beyond the crevasse was a low, rocky ridge that marked the boundary between the right edge of the Ingraham and the left edge of the Emmons. As they approached the crevasse, some two hundred yards away, John yelled, "So how do you explain not seeing Donnie? I mean, you were right there. Surely you saw *something!*"

Boyd kept walking. Over his shoulder, he shouted, "I don't have to explain a damn thing. There *is* nothing to explain. But if you don't knock this shit off, and right now, I'm gonna say, 'Fuck you,' and leave you up here alone." He stopped again, turned and faced Whitney. "Now, do you want me to show you or not?" He pointed a short distance away to a flat area pocked with small, covered crevasses above a yawning mouth. "It's just over there."

John looked up and saw Boyd staring down at him. "Why'd you go so far over? This isn't under the Cleaver."

Boyd continued forward again, moving further to the right. His steps were determined, Whitney's questions ignored. As he walked, he removed his glove and slipped his hand inside his parka pocket. He thumbed off the safety.

John hurried to catch up. "Is it because that's where you put him, Emery? Is that where you put my brother?"

Almost there.

The heavy breathing told Boyd John was closing. Boyd picked up his pace. The crevasses were looming larger.

"Hey, Emery?" John was twenty feet away. "Where's your pack? What's going on? You planning to put me where you put Donnie?"

Boyd whirled, threw down his axe and pulled out the gun. He cocked it and adopted a shooter's stance, pointing the weapon at John's chest. John stopped in his tracks, and Boyd grinned at him. "Maybe I should say, 'Bingo!' John. Or, as the Brits say, 'By Jove, I think you've got it!'"

John stood quite still, stunned by the sight of the gun and by the impact of Boyd's words.

"You know, John"—Boyd relaxed in his stance but didn't lower the gun—"you were the only threat all along. I'd hoped it wouldn't come to this. But this stuff about your brother—the discovery of his beeper—was unfortunate. As soon as I heard about it, I knew I'd have to deal with you. Then, when you were seen going up the mountain, I knew it was now."

"So how's it going to end, Emery?"

Boyd laughed. "Don't be so fucking naïve!" He laughed again. "But don't worry; you'll have company. See, this *is* about where I put your dear brother so many years ago. Think of it, John. You'll be buried together, just like family are supposed to be."

John looked at him, sadness in his eyes. "Why, Emery? Why'd

you do it?"

Boyd chuckled. "You mean Donnie? Simple. You already guessed it.*"

"You're sick, Emery."

"Yeah?" His face went slack in madness, eyes empty. "I prefer to think of myself as an opportunist. I don't let anything—or anyone—get in my way. That's why I'm so successful. I win, John," he said. "Winning is everything. Sort of a romantic image, don't you think? You get to fuck the girls."

John stayed motionless. Ice cracked, water gushed far below.

Boyd laughed. "Well, don't spend your last moments thinking about that, John. Perhaps you'd be better off making peace with your maker. You've always believed in one, right?"

John looked around him. "You did it all, didn't you? Your partner... Jim Carlton... Who else, Emery?"

"Oh, several. The most recent ones began with a little blackmail on a federal judge. See, I was part of a team investigating his fitness. Well, I stumbled on an old acquaintance of his who let something slip, which led me to believe that the judge might not be up to snuff. Turns out, he'd used cocaine in college and lied about it to the FBI. So I tucked the information away and used it to fix a big case. But the judge couldn't live with what I made him do. He started drinking and badmouthing me, and I worried he was gonna talk out of turn. So one night, I found him at a restaurant up in the Cascades. I waited for him to leave, poured some booze down him and drove him off a cliff.

"Then, wouldn't you know it, my partner, Herman Klein, was asked to handle the judge's estate. Well, Herman finds a confession the judge wrote out. Christ Almighty! So I had to put him away too. I planted a snowmobile, carried Herman's body up to it, and was just getting ready to cruise on up to a crevasse, when Jim stumbled onto me."

Boyd waggled the pistol at him. "He would have blown my alibi, John. I hated to do it; I really liked Jim."

"You mad, sick fuck. How'd I miss it all these years?"

"C'mon, John, just think about it. It was just business. I had no choice. One just led to more." He laughed.

"So Amy was right about you." John took a breath. He would use an ice hammer, his only chance. "Oh sure, I thought there was something fishy about that poacher story; I just didn't think you could commit murder. Jesus! I was protecting you."

"And I thank you, John."

"Surely, you don't think you're going to get away with all this?"

"I do and I have," Boyd said, grinning. "I always get away with it, John. I got away with disposing of Donnie, didn't I? And Aimsley Castle too." Boyd saw John react to Castle's name. "Oh, yeah, him too. Again, I had to. Castle was going to expose a little securities fraud, actually the same matter where I blackmailed the judge. Ironic, huh?"

"You've had it. Amy's on your tail. She'll trip you up."

The gun barrel waggled again. "Afraid not, John. The police dropped the investigation, the newspaper too, although they don't know I bumped off their star reporter. Don't worry, they'll never find him either.

"Incidentally, your girlfriend got her wings clipped. She's been suspended for getting personally involved and for trying to influence an obviously baseless investigation. You see, John, there are no bodies. And I've got an alibi. That's far beyond reasonable doubt. They can't even indict me."

John moved his right hand to one of the two ice hammers clipped to his belt. He looked over his right shoulder, as if looking for help, using the turn to shield his hand. Boyd noticed the turn.

"No use, John. This glacier's off limits. Besides, no one can see in the fog."

The hammer came free smoothly in John's fingers. He threw, all in one desperate motion, as he dove toward a covered crevasse.

Boyd fired.

The hammer missed Boyd, as John disappeared in a white

cloud.

Boyd scrambled to the opening and saw John on a ledge some twenty feet below. He was rolling, leaving a trail of blood. He looked up with dazed eyes.

"Nice try, John. But one more for good measure." Boyd fired again as John lunged off the ledge, disappearing again into the white.

Swearing, Boyd walked around the edge of the crevasse, but the ice began to crumble under his feet. Jumping backward, he was sent sprawling but landed on hard ice. The crevasse opening collapsed, and the hole sealed over John Whitney's white cloud.

Boyd stood for a moment, staring at the sinkhole, then he brushed himself off, turned and retraced his steps to John's hammer. Picking it up, he walked some distance before tossing the hammer and gun into an open crevasse.

His job done, he began the trek back to where he'd left the packs. "So many girls left to fuck, John. I give it to them rough. You didn't know that about me, did you? I'm two-faced, John. I live in twin worlds, and now you're in my mountain." He kept muttering, his words lost against pale light and ice.

An hour later, he was just securing his pack to his rope when a search party, consisting of Mo Knauer, Max Brittain, Frank Maselli, Jim Grogan, Norm Reiter, Noah Seirig and Diane Edwards, appeared above him. They called to him, and he motioned them down. As they dropped, each person marveled at the eerie spectacle of the collapsed glacier.

Claiming he'd just found John's pack, Boyd said he hadn't searched here yet. The crew organized, anchored and spread out, searching in parties of two, coordinating by radio.

They searched for two days, up and down the collapsed glacier, sleeping in tents off the glacier because of concern for its stability. Finally, at the end of the second day, worried about safety after several close calls, Mo Knauer brought the search to an end. Several people protested, Emery Boyd the loudest, but Knauer was adamant. It was obvious, he said, that John had either been buried by a collapse or swept away. He wouldn't risk losing anybody else.

FORTY-EIGHT

Monday, August 12

Broken from a sweet reverie between himself and his mountain, Emery Boyd swung back from the window to answer the phone. "Mr. Boyd..." It was Jenny's office voice, the one she used when somebody was present. Boyd adjusted a cufflink.

"Yes, Jen?"

"Mr. Boyd..." Jenny repeated, an edge to her tone. "There's a Miss Brannigan here. She... uh... doesn't have an appointment, but she insists you'll see her."

"I'll be right there." There would be consequences to pay later, he knew. But what the hell: a little insecurity—jealousy—was good for a relationship, wasn't it?

He opened the door and welcomed Sherry into his office. As Sherry walked by Jenny, he saw hurt on Jenny's face. He shut the door.

Sherry walked over to the office window as Boyd approached her from behind. Placing his hands on her shoulders, he bit her ear. "Well, this is a pleasant surprise. Beautiful, isn't it. I spend a lot of my time at this window."

Sherry continued staring out. Boyd walked to his desk and stood behind his chair. "Can I get you anything?"

She didn't respond.

"Is something wrong?"

Sherry turned around, and Boyd saw tears. He moved to embrace her, but she waved him off, pointing instead to his chair. He sat down, waiting. Sherry took a seat opposite him, her eyes red. She pulled her large fabric bag onto her lap.

"The last three days," she said, raising her eyes, while at the same time groping inside her bag, "I've been waiting for clearance..."

"Clearance?"

"Clearance to buy this," she said, pulling out a Bulldog .44 revolver.

Boyd's eyes fixed on the cannon. He leaned forward, sliding his right hand toward the buzzer.

"Just sit back. I practiced all morning. About three hundred rounds, hollowpoint."

Boyd flattened his hands on his desk. He looked toward the door.

"You've been causing a lot of pain. It's time the score was settled."

"I'm sorry, Sherry. I don't understand. What are you talking about?"

"I suspected you from my first day on the mountain... when I read Amy's investigation notes. Then to try and learn something more, I slept with you, disgusting as that was."

"What?"

"Remember that night... when I asked you all those questions about storms?"

He sat, coiled, thinking.

"I was seeking confirmation."

"Of what?" *Roll down behind the desk, throw a shoe, distract her, break her leg.* "Tell me what's going on, Sherry."

"You weren't following any poacher. You couldn't track anybody in that storm. That was your error."

"Error? I *was* following him. Everybody knows that."

"You were the poacher."

"You've been listening to Amy. She's sick, you know that? Look, Sherry, I'm sorry if I've done something to upset you..." *A shoe to the head, pull her off her feet...*

"Let me tell you who I am. Amy wasn't the only one under-cover. I was Jim Carlton's lover. We met hiking at Crater Lake, then we returned to my place in Portland. We were going to get married. I found out he'd been killed, so I came to find out what happened to him, learn who'd destroyed my dreams."

A fine sheen of sweat formed on Boyd's brow.

"That night at the bar... I was going to go home with you... wait till you fell asleep... then take my knife and stab you in the heart... like you did to me."

She sucked in a deep breath. "But I wasn't sure I could actually do it. Then, after you ruined Amy and killed John, I knew I had to do it. You are evil. You can't be allowed to go on."

"Look, Sherry. You've got it all wrong. You know who really killed—" He hit the floor sideways, grabbing his shoe, hurling it, then he was scrambling, grabbing.

Sherry was very careful with her shot, placing it between his empty eyes. Boyd's skull disintegrated. The windows behind him were a mosaic of red, hair, and globs of gray.

Sherry reached into her purse and laid a handwritten note on the desk. Her last vision, as the door flew open and before she turned the gun on herself and pulled the trigger, was of blood running down the flanks of Mount Rainier.

EPILOGUE

Monday, August 12

Max Brittain was moonlighting on his own time and against Mo Knauer's express orders, continuing his own personal search for John Whitney. He'd managed to keep his schedule by basing at Muir, only a short distance away from the Middle Ingraham, taking charge of camp activities. His worsening facial condition prevented him from climbing during the day, so he searched at night and slept during daylight hours. If anyone suspected what he was doing, no one let on, and no one had reported him.

Tonight, he was focusing on the area below and to the right of Disappointment Cleaver, where he'd noticed a group of crevasses the night before. He was safe, since he was above the collapse point, but it was still forbidden ground.

Dropping down into the crevasse he'd chosen, he thought it a good prospect. It was old enough to have tunnels beneath it, and a series of ledges permitted descent by stages.

He wasn't expecting to find John alive; it had been almost a week, and John had no supplies. But if there was the slimmest of possibilities, Brittain wanted to give him a chance. If somehow

John had survived while looking for his brother, this was a good place to look. It was near Disappointment Cleaver, from which Donnie might have fallen.

It took him three stages and twenty minutes to reach the bottom of the glacier. Pulling a large flashlight out of his pack to enhance the illumination of his headlamp, he flipped it on and began to look around, calling John's name every few steps.

For two hours, he searched. Then, just as he was about to turn back, he spotted something strange about five feet up on the wall to his left. Peering closer, he thought it was blood. Taking off his glove, he ran his finger across the stain. Parts of it were wet. Excited now, he began calling John's name more urgently and searched for similar spots.

Some twenty yards further down the passage, he found another dark splotch; in fact there were several, all at about the same height, as if someone wounded had bounced or leaned against these walls.

Now he was running down the passage, following the splotches and calling out. Another twenty yards and he stopped.

Had he heard something?

He called out again, and thought once more he heard something, weak but definite. Looking to his left, he saw another tunnel leading past a mound some forty yards away, the mound apparently made up of collapsed cornice underneath another multi-leveled crevasse opening. Moving toward the mound, he noticed a red tinge at its base and a hacked-out area of the ice wall in front of it. Flashing his beam up, he saw an old pack partially embedded in the ice. The pack had been torn apart—no, *ripped apart*. Below the pack was more red ice.

"John!" Brittain yelled, his senses crackling. "Can you hear me?"

He heard something over by the mound, a soft tapping. Turning toward the sound, he saw more blood and a hole in the mound.

An igloo in a crevasse?

Why not? For someone as resourceful as John, an igloo made sense. Flashing his light inside the hole, Brittain gasped. Inside an old sleeping bag on top of a ground cloth, huddled in a fetal position, was a bloodied John Whitney, clutching an ice hammer in his gloved hand.

"You know, Max," John said, in a rasping whisper, "you really should do something about your face."

At 1:00 A.M., a restless Amy Galler was awakened from another fitful night's sleep by her mother, who was shaking her urgently. "Amy! Get up! You've got an urgent phone call!"

Amy turned over and covered her head with her pillow, only to have the pillow yanked off her head and the blankets yanked off her body.

"Amy! Damn it! Get up! It's Morris Knauer. He says he has to talk to you."

Amy flew out of the bed and raced to the phone. "Mo? Is that you? What's happened? Is it John?"

"Amy! Yes, it's me. Listen, I don't have long but I had to call. I got your mother's number from Charlie Scott. I've been trying to reach you for an hour."

"Yes, Mo! Tell me! What's happened?"

"John's been found, Amy! He's alive!"

Amy shrieked with a joy beyond words as her mother watched.

"Where is he, Mo? I must see him."

"He wants to see you too. He's being airlifted to the UW Medical Center as we speak. He's in pretty bad shape; he's been shot in the shoulder and has lost some blood, but he'll make it. He's conscious. Max Brittain found him below Disappointment Cleaver. Believe it or not, John found a lost climber's pack—lots of people fall off the Cleaver. And he made himself an igloo. I tell you, Amy, only one mountaineer in a thousand could've survived like that."

"Oh my God!" Tears cascaded down Amy's face. "I'll be right there, Mo. Will you tell him I'm coming?"

"I sure will." Knauer laughed. "But there's more: John found Donnie too. Maybe that helped keep him alive, the thought of doing right by his brother."

Check out these other fine titles by Durban House at your local bookstore or online bookseller.

EXCEPTIONAL BOOKS

BY

EXCEPTIONAL WRITERS

FICTION

A COMMON GLORY
Robert Middlemiss
A DREAM ACROSS TIME
Annie Rogers
AFTER LIFE LIFE
Don Goldman
an-eye-for-an-eye.com
Dennis Powell
A MEETING OF MINDS
Elizabeth Turner Calloway
BASHA
John Hamilton Lewis
BLUEWATER DOWN
Rick O'Reilly
BY ROYAL DESIGN
Norbert Reich
THE BEIRUT CONSPIRACY
John R. Childress
CRISIS PENDING
Stephen Cornell

CRY HAVOC
John Hamilton Lewis
DEADLY ILLUSIONS
Chester D. Campbell
DANGER WITHIN
Mark Danielson
DEADLY ILLUMINATION
Serena Stier
DEATH OF A HEALER
Paul Henry Young
DESIGNED TO KILL
Chester D. Campbell
EXTREME CUISINE
Kit Sloane
THE GARDEN OF EVIL
Chris Holmes
HANDS OF VENGEANCE
Richard Sand
HORIZON'S END
Andrew Lazarus
HOUR OF THE WOLVES
Stephane Daimlen-Völs
THE INNOCENT NEVER KNEW
Mark W. Danielson
JOHNNIE RAY & MISS KILGALLEN
Bonnie Hearn Hill & Larry Hill
KIRA'S DIARY
Edward T. Gushee
THE LAST COWBOYS
Robert E. Hollmann
THE LATERAL LINE
Robert Middlemiss
LETHAL CURE

Kurt Popke
THE LUKARILLA AFFAIR
Jerry Banks
THE MEDUSA STRAIN
Chris Holmes
MR. IRRELEVANT
Jerry Marshall
MURDER ON THE TRAP
J. Preston Smith
NO ORDINARY TERROR
J. Brooks Van Dyke
OPAL EYE DEVIL
John Hamilton Lewis
PRIVATE JUSTICE
Richard Sand
PHARAOH'S FRIEND
Nancy Yawitz Linkous
ROADHOUSE BLUES
Baron Birtcher
RUBY TUESDAY
Baron Birtcher
SAMSARA
John Hamilton Lewis
SECRET OF THE SCROLL
Chester D. Campbell
SECRETS ARE ANONYMOUS
Fredrick L. Cullen
THE SEESAW SYNDROME
Michael Madden
THE SERIAL KILLER'S DIET BOOK
Kevin Mark Postupack
THE STREET OF FOUR WINDS
Andrew Lazarus

SPORES, PLAGUES, AND HISTORY: THE STORY
OF ANTHRAX
Chris Holmes
WHAT MAKES A MARRIAGE WORK
Malcolm D. Mahr
WHITE WITCH DOCTOR
John A. Hunt

SPRING 2005

FICTION

A COMMON GLORY
Robert Middlemiss

What happens when a Southern news reporter falls in love with a WWII jazz loving English pilot and wants to take him home to her segregationist parents? It is in the crucible of war that pilot and reporter draw close across their vulnerabilities and fears. War, segregation, and the fear of death in lonely skies confront them as they clutch at the first exquisite promptings of a passionate love.

BLUEWATER DOWN
Rick O'Reilly

Retired L.A. police lieutenant Jack Douglas wanted only one thing after years on the bomb squad—the peace and serenity of sailing his yacht, Tally Ho. But Lisa enters his carefully planned world, and even as he falls in love with her she draws him into a violent matrix of murderers and terrorists bent on their destruction.

BY ROYAL DESIGN
Norbert Reich

Hitler's Third Reich was to last a thousand years but it

collapsed in twelve. In Berlin, in the belly of the dying Reich, seeds were sown for a new regime, one based on aristocratic ruling classes whose time had come. Berlin's Charitee Hospital brought several children into the world that night in 1944, setting into motion forces that would ultimately bring two venerable Germanic families, the Hohenzollerns and the Habsburgs to power.

THE COROT DECEPTION
J. Brooks Van Dyke

London artists are getting murdered. The killer leaves behind an odd signature. And when Richard Watson, an artist, discovers the corpse of his gallery owner, he investigates, pitting himself and his twin sister, Dr. Emma Watson against the ruthless killer. Steeped in the principles of criminal detection they learned from Sherlock Holmes, the twins search for clues in the Edwardian art world and posh estates of 1910 London.

CRY HAVOC
John Hamilton Lewis

The worst winter in over a hundred years grips the United States and most of the western world. America's first lady president, Abigail Stewart, must deal with harsh realities as crop failures, power blackouts, shortages of gasoline and heating oil push the nation toward panic. But the extreme weather conditions are only a precursor of problems to come as Prince Nasser, a wealthy Saudi prince, and a cleric plot to destroy western economies.

DEADLY ILLUSIONS
Chester D. Campbell

A young woman, Molly Saint, hires Greg and Jill McKenzie to check her husband's background, then disappears. It starts them on a tangled trail of deceit, with Jill soon turning up a close family connection. The deeper the McKenzie's dig, the more deadly illusions they face. Nothing appears to be what it seemed at first as the fear for Molly's life grows.

EXTREME CUISINE
Kit Sloane

Film editor Margot O'Banion and director Max Skull find a recipe for disaster behind the kitchen doors of a trendy Hollywood restaurant. Readers of discriminating taste are cordially invited to witness the preparation and presentation of fine fare as deadly drama. As Max points out, dinner at these places "provides an evening of theater and you get to eat it!" Betrayal, revenge, and perhaps something even more unsavory, are on the menu tonight.

THE GARDEN OF EVIL
Chris Holmes

A brilliant but bitter sociopath has attacked the city's food supply; five people are dead, twenty-six remain ill from the assault. Family physician, Gil Martin and his wife Tara, the county's Public Health Officer, discover the terrorist has found a way to incorporate the poison directly into the raw vegetables themselves. How is that possible? As the Martins get close to cracking the case, the terrorist focuses all his venom on getting them and their family. It's now a personal conflict—mano-a-mano—between him and them.

KIRA'S DIARY
Edward T. Gushee

A beautiful, talented violinist, seventeen-year-old Kira Klein was destined to be assigned to Barracks 24. From the first day she is imprisoned in the Auschwitz brothel, Kira becomes the unwilling mistress of Raulf Becker, an SS lieutenant whose responsibility is overseeing the annihilation of the Jewish prisoners. Through the stench of death and despair emerges a love story, richly told with utter sensitivity, warmth and even humor.

THE LUKARILLA AFFAIR
Jerry Banks

Right from the start it was a legal slugfest. Three prominent men, a state senator, a corporate president, and the manager of a Los Angeles professional football team are charged with rape and sodomy by three minimum wage employees of a catering firm, Ginny, Peg and Tina. A courtroom gripper by Jerry Banks who had over forty years in the trade, and who tells it like it happens—fast and quick.

MURDER ON THE TRAP
J. Preston Smith

Life has been pretty good to Bon Sandifer. After his tour in Vietnam he marries his childhood sweetheart, is a successful private investigator, and rides his Harley-Davidson motorcycle. Then the murders begin on Curly Trap Road. His wife Shelly dies first. A fellow biker is crushed under a Caddie. And his brother is killed riding a Harley. When Sandifer remarries and finds happiness with his deaf biker bride, the murderous web tightens and he grapples with skeptical detectives and old Vietnam memories.

PHARAOH'S FRIEND
Nancy Yawitz Linkous

When Egyptian myth permeates the present, beliefs are tested and lives are changed. My Worth vacations in Egypt to soothe the pain over her daughter's death. She dreams of a cat whose duty is to transport souls to the afterlife. And then a real cat, four hundred and twenty pounds of strength and sinew, appears at an archeological dig. Those that cross its path are drawn into intrigue and murder that is all too real.

SPRING 2005

NONFICTION

I ACCUSE: JIMMY CARTER AND THE RISE OF MILITANT ISLAM

Philip Pilevsky

Philip Pilevsky makes a compelling argument that President Jimmy Carter's failure to support the Shah of Iran led to the 1979 revolution led by Ayatollah Ruhollah Komeini. That revolution legitimized and provided a base of operations for militant Islamists across the Middle East. By allowing the Khomeini revolution to succeed, Carter traded an aging, accommodating shah for a militant theocrat who attacked the American Embassy and held the staff workers hostage. In the twenty-four years since the Khomenini revolution, radical Islamists, indoctrinated in Iran have grown ever bolder in attacking the West and more sophisticated in their tactics of destruction.

MOTHERS SPEAK: FOR LOVE OF FAMILY

Rosalie Fuscaldo Gaziano

In a world of turbulent change, the need to connect, to love and be loved is greater and more poignant than ever. Women cry out for simple, direct answers to the question, "How can I make family life work in these challenging times?" This book offers hope to all who are struggling to balance the demands of work and family and to cope with ambiguity, isolation, or abandonment. The author gives strong evidence that the family unit is still the best way to connect and bear enduring fruit.

THE PASSION OF AYN RAND'S CRITICS

James S. Valliant

For years, best-selling novelist and controversial philosopher Ayn Rand has been the victim of posthumous portrayals of her life and character taken from the pages of the biographies by

Nathaniel Branden and Barbara Branden. Now, for the first time, Rand's own never-before-seen-journal entries on the Brandens, and the first in-depth analysis of the Brandens' works, reveal the profoundly inaccurate and unjust depiction of their former mentor.

SEX, LIES & PI's
Ali Wirsche & Marnie Milot

The ultimate guide to find out if your lover, husband, or wife is having an affair. Follow Ali and Marnie, two seasoned private investigators, as they spy on brazen cheaters and find out what sweet revenge awaits. Learn 110 ways to be your own detective. Laced with startling stories, Sex, Lies & PI's is riveting and often hilarious.

WHAT MAKES A MARRIAGE WORK
Malcolm D. Mahr

You hear the phrase "marry and settle down," which implies life becomes more serene and peaceful after marriage. This simply isn't so. Living together is one long series of experiments in accommodation. What Makes A Marriage Work? is a hilarious yet perceptive collection of fifty insights reflecting one couple's searching, experimenting, screaming, pouting, nagging, whining, moping, blaming, and other dysfunctional behaviors that helped them successfully navigate the turbulent sea of matrimony for over fifty years. (Featuring 34 New Yorker cartoons of wit and wisdom.)